In the End Is Our Beginning

The
Appearing

In the End Is Our Beginning

The Appearing

kristen wisen

credo
house publishers

The Appearing: In the End Is Our Beginning

Copyright © 2007 by Kristen Wisen

Published in the United States by Credo House Publishers,
a division of Credo Communications, LLC, Grand Rapids, Michigan.
www.credohousepublishers.net

ISBN-10: 0-9787620-7-X
ISBN-13: 978-0-9787620-8-7

Scripture is taken from the NEW AMERICAN STANDARD BIBLE®.
Copyright © The Lockman Foundation 1960, 1962, 1963, 1968, 1971,
1972, 1973, 1975, 1977, 1995. Used by permission.

Lyrics for "You are the Lord" on page 81, copyright © 2006 by Steve Busch.
Used by permission of Burningbusch Productions.

Lyrics for "Restore My Soul" on pages 364-65, copyright © 2002 by Andi Rozier.
Used by permission of Harvestsongs.

Editor: Diane Noble
Cover design: Grey Matter Group
Interior design: Sharon VanLoozenoord
Author image: margaret visser photography

10 9 8 7 6 5 4 3 2 1

Printed in the United States of America

To David

Your patience, input,
and love are priceless.
Thank you.

In loving memory of my father,
Robert VanKampen,
whose passion for the Word
continues to touch lives today.

"Because you have kept
the word of My perseverance,
I also will keep you
from the hour of testing,
that hour which is about to come
upon the whole world,
to test those
who dwell in the earth."

REVELATION 3:10

Coffee. Again. As usual. Every morning around 6:30 a.m. the smell of coffee drifts into the bunkroom and stirs us from our sleep. I can remember when the sun used to shine through my bedroom window and wake me up. But not anymore. It hasn't been the sun for a couple of weeks. Now it is the smell of coffee. I don't really like the taste of coffee, but the smell is definitely comforting. It means Mom is awake and we all survived another night.

Survived. Funny word. It implies a life-threatening scenario. I never imagined that survival would be such a big part of my life. Survival was for dying children in third world countries. Or for people in countries ruled by Islamic terrorists. Or for the selected sixteen who were on a TV show and didn't want to be voted off. It's not that life has gotten difficult in America or even here yet. I guess technically most Americans aren't worried about survival. Just the ones I live with. We talk about survival all the time. Sometimes I wonder if we can just survive the living conditions.

Emma closed her journal and tucked it under her mattress along with her pen. Pens were scarce these days and the thought of losing her journal pen sent a chill down her spine. She had given up a lot, but her writing was one thing she would never lose. Emma sat on the edge of her bed and reached to the dresser on her right. She opened the bottom drawer and lifted her folded jeans. Lying on the bottom of the drawer was the package of twelve blue pens she had bought from Wal-Mart before they left. No one but Emma knew they were there and they had to last her a couple of years. Or so.

She shut the drawer as quietly as possible and glanced at her travel clock. For a fleeting moment she wondered if her dad had brought enough batteries, but then it occurred to her that time really didn't matter anymore. Except when it came to sharing a bathroom with eleven other kids. The clock said 6:54 a.m. Thirty minutes from now there would be a waiting line.

She stood and grabbed her towel that was draped over the end of her bunk bed. Her sister, Sarah, was still asleep on the top. Emma could see Sarah's curls falling lightly on her cheek and she reached up and touched her own hair. Though they were both blonde-haired and blue-eyed, Sarah's hair had natural curl and Emma's had natural frizz. Emma was glad her hair was long enough to pull into a sloppy bun, but she envied Sarah's controlled curls. Emma gently brushed back an errant curl from her little sister's cheek.

Sarah half opened an eye and squinted at her. "What time is it?"

"It's not yet seven. Go back to sleep."

"Get me when you get out of the shower. It would be nice to get a hot one today."

"I will," Emma promised and kissed her sister on the cheek. At sixteen, Emma loved her sister and considered her one of her best friends.

Emma hurried down the hall to the bathroom. As she passed through the outer area with its row of sinks, she whispered a prayer of thanks that the shower door was open. She quickly grabbed the reversible sign on the door and flipped it to read "Girls Only," entered, and slid the door closed behind her. Hot water was a precious commodity so, as usual, she stayed in the shower for only a few minutes.

Then she dressed, pulled her hair back, and returned to her room to wake Sarah.

As she padded down the hall, she passed Leighsa and gave her a quick smile. There was another blessing—getting to share her room with Leighsa. For as far back as she could remember Leighsa's family and hers were close. It really wasn't a surprise that they would all be together in the end.

As Emma quietly opened her door, she saw her brother emerge from the door down the hall.

She grinned at him. "Hey, Ben."

He squinted at her, rubbed an eye, and then captured a yawn with his free hand. "Are there girls in the bathroom already?"

"Yeah, sorry about that."

He yawned again, then headed back to his room.

When Emma opened her bedroom door, Sarah was sitting on her top bunk, her head almost hitting the ceiling, still in a sleepy fog.

Emma often missed her own room, but her new bedroom would have to do. Six girls in one room would never be ideal, but the key to keeping the peace was everyone keeping their stuff organized. And unlike the hopeless condition of the boys' identical predicament, the girls could pull this off. Of this, she was certain. She knew her friends well.

She glanced around the room at the other still-sleeping girls, proud of what they had accomplished. Then she noticed the top drawer in her dresser hadn't been closed all the way.

Leighsa had obviously borrowed a shirt again. She smiled. Better her than someone else.

As Sarah left for the bathroom, Emma hung her towel at the end of her bed, slipped on her tennis shoes, and headed to the kitchen. The cool, damp hallway was decorated with family portraits and favorite pictures from their past. Emma stopped and looked at a large frame that held a dozen pictures from a vacation her family took with Leighsa's last summer. They had gone to a small lake for a week of fishing, tubing, and playing wiffle ball in the yard. One of the pictures showed Emma with a large mouth bass, and Leighsa with a baby version of the same fish. Mr. Torey always teased Leighsa that she had been given his fishing genetics, rather than her mother's. Two pictures to the left showed Mrs. Torey with a massive northern pike.

Another picture was of Sarah, Ben, and their dad, holding their wiffle bats with victorious smiles on their faces. Emma remembered losing that final game and watching her siblings crowned "Wiffle Ball Champs," a title they would hold until the next vacation. Little did she know nine months ago that she would never swim in a lake again.

As Emma continued down the hall the scent of coffee grew stronger. She could hear the moms talking in the kitchen and the ham radio squawking in the living room. She rounded the corner and saw Mrs. Torey, Mrs. Phillips, and Mrs. Mason sitting at a table with their coffee and muffins. Her mom was in the doorway of the kitchen with a handful of napkins.

"Good morning, sweetie," Lily Hamilton said, smiling at her daughter. "Is anyone else awake back there?"

Leighsa and Sarah are in the showers." Emma reached up, loosened the elastic around her bun, fluffed her hair, then said, "And Ben was too late for his turn—so he headed back to his room. So, what's on the docket for today?"

"Now that Shiloh is finished, we're having devotions there at nine. Then back here for schoolwork—you know the drill."

Emma loved Shiloh. Even though it was just a bunch of logs and campfires, it was a much-needed gathering place.

"Mom, is it always going to be like this?"

"It's only been a month." Her mother's voice was soft but the look in her eyes told Emma she wasn't about to be pushed in front of the other mothers. "We're in a waiting game here. Your guess is as good as mine, but we need to settle into some kind of routine."

Emma sighed. Living with three other families was going to take some time to get used to. She knew better than to embarrass her mom but she also longed for some one-on-one time. It seemed as though she never was alone anymore, let alone with her mom or dad.

"Where's Dad?" Emma asked.

"He's with Mack finishing the plans for the Tabernacle."

"Why do we need the Tabernacle when we have Shiloh?"

"Honey, Shiloh is our temporary meeting place until we find something more permanent and protected."

"And warm!" added Mrs. Phillips.

Emma pulled out a chair and sat down at the table with Mrs. Torey, Mrs. Phillips, and Mrs. Mason. Her mother joined them with her coffee.

"Over the next several weeks," her mother said, "as the rest of the families join us, we'll continue to gather at Shiloh where we can worship and share information . . . just be together, until the Tabernacle is built out. Dad doesn't think it will take too long. Then we won't have to worry about bad weather or someone seeing smoke from a campfire."

Mrs. Torey put her coffee cup down and leaned forward, putting her elbows on the table. "I love the name Shiloh. It means 'the One who brings peace' and let me tell you, peace is what we are all going to need! Did you see the Potters and Westlakes trying to manage all those young children as they moved in? We are very fortunate to have our youngest already ten years old!"

"Yeah, and Ben's such a good boy—he'll never give us any trouble!" added Mrs. Mason.

"Just wait until the excitement of living here dies down," Emma said. "He's not always so accommodating."

Mrs. Torey sipped her coffee, then thoughtfully placed the cup back in its saucer. "Well, I can't help but feel a bit guilty that we have such a good setup here—wonderful lifelong friends, kids that get along. So the rooms are a bit cramped, who's complaining? It's like church camp and everyone loves camp, don't they?"

Camp? Emma tried to smile. Camp was usually a week long and in a cabin with outdoor activities. Here, the families of Grace Church of Shelton were living in makeshift homes in the middle of nowhere— and rarely could they leave. *And we're going to be here until we die. Or get raptured. Anyways, who ever heard of a camp inside of a cave? No matter how you look at it, it's nothing like camp.*

Rory Appleton hung up the phone.

"Donna!"

He waited ten seconds. *Three. Two. One.*

"Donna!" *Why it takes three times, I'll never understand.* "Donna!"

"Yes, dear," Donna answered from the kitchen.

"Call the phone company and tell them I want caller ID."

Frowning, Donna came into the family room from the kitchen. "But don't you remember? We decided not to spend the money for something so frivolous."

"I've changed my mind. Just order it," Rory growled.

Donna put one hand on her hip and held her position.

"Give me a good reason and I will."

"Dan Dougherty. There. One good reason."

"Did he call again?" she asked.

"Yes, he called again. I wish he'd just head out of town like the rest of them and leave us alone."

"Rory, why don't you just go tonight? That's why he's calling, isn't it?"

"Yeah, tonight's another meeting. I just think he's off his rocker. He and the rest of the wackos from church."

"Look at it this way. The people at that meeting need to hear the other side. If you're ever going to become an elder at Grace, you need to show some leadership. Now is as good a time as any."

Rory thought for a moment. She had a point.

"Dan said there are going to be about twenty-five men there. I suppose you're right. I could really establish myself. I probably shouldn't miss this opportunity."

"But don't go in there guns ablazin'! You have to act sincere in your questions, but show you're a man to follow once the rest are gone."

"You really do think I'm an idiot, don't you? Of course I'll handle it right!"

"I don't think you're an idiot, dear. I just don't want you to blow it."

"It's not going to be that hard, Donna. Ever since the elders announced a couple of months ago that it was time to make the move, half of the church changed their minds and chose to stay. It's a great thing to build a church on a dynamic and unusual view of the second coming, but when it means giving up your home, your job, and your life, that's more like a cult than a church."

"I'll never forget you saying five years ago that buying that land in North Carolina was a waste of the congregation's money. They were so secretive. Only the elders knew where the land actually was."

"You mean the mountains. They bought two, remember?"

Donna smiled. "Yes, I remember. I think you should one day remind the congregation that you never bought into their extremist viewpoint."

"When the time is right, I will." Rory paused. "Do you think you should come tonight? I'm not sure I will remember everything you want me to say."

Donna threw up her hands and headed back into the kitchen. Over her shoulder she yelled, "Every good man has a strong woman behind him who helped him get where he is."

Rory rolled his eyes. With a good woman, he thought, I could probably be somewhere other than living in Shelton, Michigan. With a good woman, I could probably have a better job than a struggling landscaping business. With a good woman, I could probably get a good cup of coffee now and then. And a good woman would answer the first time I call.

"Humph!" he grunted, knowing Donna would never hear him.

Nate Reed checked his watch.

7:22 p.m.

He didn't want to be late to the meeting at Dan Dougherty's house, but he should have left five minutes ago. He had stalled long enough and needed to make a decision. He saved the file on his screen and shut down his laptop. He slid it into its carrier and put it under his desk.

Sherrie peeked through the doorway.

"Are you going?"

"Yeah, I'm leaving now."

Nate stood and headed towards the door. As he passed Sherrie, she put her arms around his waist and stopped him. She looked into his eyes and smiled.

"Please have an open mind. I've been praying all day for this, Nate. I'm not going to lie to you. I know you don't fully understand this, but I know . . . deep down I know they're right. We need to go. We need to walk by faith. Ask questions, but I am praying God will open your eyes tonight."

Nate hugged her and wanted to kick himself. He thought he was past feeling this way, but sometimes it hit him out of the blue.

"I'll listen, Sherrie. And we'll talk when I get home. Fair enough?"

"More than fair enough." Sherrie's eyes twinkled. "I love you!"

And with a quick kiss, Nate was sent out the door. He climbed in his car and checked his watch again.

7:28.

Nate knew tonight would be life changing, and though he had planned for this moment, making the decision was a lot harder than he had ever dreamed. This not only affected him, but it affected his family. And putting them in danger was a high price to pay.

7:29.

I hate being late, he thought as he backed out of the drive.

two

Nate parked in front of Dan's house and was relieved to see a couple of men walking up the sidewalk, clearly unconcerned about being late. Though Nate was driven by punctuality, he put on his casual face and got out of his car. Betsy Dougherty was standing in the door and waved to him.

"Oh, Nate. I'm so glad you made it. I whipped up a batch of my chocolate chip cookies in the hope that you would come tonight."

Nate smiled and extended his hand, which she readily took.

"Thanks, Betsy. You're the best."

"Go ahead and find a seat and I'll bring you one."

"Make it two and you have a deal."

Betsy winked and turned towards the kitchen. Nate watched the sixty-seven-year-old matriarch of the church leave the room and he remembered the first time he and Sherrie had met Betsy and Dan. They had been in the foyer of Grace when the couple approached them. Their warm handshakes and engaging conversation was one of the reasons Sherrie had wanted to visit the church a second time. Betsy laughed easily and Dan's fatherly mannerisms were magnetic. Sherrie took immediately to Betsy. It turned out half the church came to Grace because of the Doughertys. They just had a way of turning a casual conversation into a spiritual discussion, and though doing that sort of thing in public was illegal, it didn't stop Betsy and Dan. They loved the Lord and had a heart for the church, which is why they were opening their house for this meeting.

Nate took a seat in the crowded living room and soon found two warm cookies on a napkin in his hand. Betsy gave a quick squeeze on his shoulder and then was off to feed another poor soul. The room began to quiet down and Dan took center stage.

"I appreciate you all coming tonight. Some of you are close to making a decision that will save your life and others aren't. Either way, God has brought you here and I want to invite His presence and guidance before we get too far."

He bowed his head and the rest of the room followed suit.

"Father, we are humbled as we enter Your presence. We desire Your help in the decisions before us and I personally ask, Lord, that You soften the hearts of the men in this room and give them understanding of Your Word and Your will. Bless our time and may our conversation be pleasing to You. In Your precious Son's name we come to You, amen."

In the corner, Nate saw Rory Appleton sitting with his cronies, already huffing and puffing. Nate laughed to himself. Rory was a puffed-up loser whose sole role in the church was to disagree with every decision the leadership ever made. Nate had been at Grace only eighteen months but that fact was painfully clear. Everyone in the room knew why he was there, and yet it seemed that Dan had graciously invited Rory, just as he had invited every other man in the room.

"Some of you are relatively new to Grace," Dan continued. He leaned forward in his chair, one elbow resting on the Bible that lay on his knee. "I want to field questions tonight, because by now you all know what Grace believes about the return of Christ. Most of the community knows by now."

Nate chuckled with the rest of the room, knowing how outspoken the congregation at Grace had been the few months before the move.

"But let me begin with a warning to you. I don't take this lightly. My wife and I have buried our only son and have no grandchildren. We have no family, but the church family, which depends on us. So we have chosen to stay in Shelton to try to be a source of help to believers when the great tribulation comes upon them. We understand that by staying, we are willingly giving ourselves up for death. If God so desires, we will see His return, but for now, our decision to be a help stands. You don't have to make that choice. You can decide tonight to act in faith and take your family to safety."

He sat quietly for a moment. Then Rory broke the tension.

"Dan, how do you justify asking this room full of men, most with families whom they are responsible for, to leave their jobs, sell their homes, pack up, and hide in a cave in North Carolina and wait for Jesus to return?"

Nate stifled another smirk at Rory's rudeness disguised as sincerity.

"Rory, you know how I justify it. With Scripture. Since its inception twenty years ago, Grace has stood on the truth that the Word warns of persecution before the return of Christ."

The man sitting to Nate's right interrupted. "Like the anti-intolerance laws? They limit us but they are hardly persecution."

Dan continued. "Those laws have simply been put in place to promote tolerance towards everything but the truth. The church in America has had its hands tied for years. We are not allowed to evangelize because it is considered proselytizing. America has removed any standards concerning morality and ethics, and replaced them with religious bondage. Don't fool yourselves—though we can meet as a congregation, we are not allowed to preach outside the church. We are not allowed to invite people in to church. We are hardly allowed to preach the Word freely because the law protects everyone's right to live without convictions. Homeland Security has even created a special division—the Domestic Investigations Unit—to infiltrate churches and shut them down for preaching anything outside the walls of their church. They even monitor what is being preached."

Dan had Nate's full attention now, but Rory was grumbling again in the corner. "So you're saying that limits on the church by the DIU are great persecution. How can you seriously compare that to martyrs in China and the persecution of believers all over the world? That's nothing!" Rory added disgust to his voice for emphasis.

"Just hold on, Rory. Let me finish. These limits here in America are simply precursors or preparations for a greater tribulation that is coming. No, the anti-intolerance laws aren't a great persecution. But they are spreading distrust and hatred towards Christianity that will only increase until Jesus returns."

Nate politely raised his hand to get Dan's attention. Dan turned to him, pointed, and nodded.

"I still don't understand why the time to move is now. I'm not even sure why we just can't stay here in Shelton. If Jesus is coming soon, can't He take us as easily from Michigan as He can from North Carolina?"

He didn't mean to be funny, but several chuckled at his question. Dan took it seriously, however.

"Nate, America has bought into a system that says we have nothing to do but wait to be raptured. Nothing to look for. Nothing to prepare for. Just watch things get bad in the world and keep our eyes on the sky. Unfortunately, this is not what Christ told the disciples to do. He told them to watch for the signs and at a certain point, to hide and wait for Him because things were really going to get bad. It's all found in Matthew 24."

"So what signs are you looking at that signal this hiding?" Nate thought that was a fair question.

"The first sign was Israel becoming a nation. The prophecies concerning the second coming deal with Israel back in the land and that happened in 1948. Secondly, they had to have control of their holy city, Jerusalem. That happened in 1967. Next, there needed to be a temple in Jerusalem for the Antichrist to desecrate. That happened two years ago, when Alexander Magorum of Russia negotiated the shared temple mount with the Arabs. Today, they are worshipping and sacrificing at the temple again. In addition to those specifics, the increase in war, famine, pestilence, and persecution of believers worldwide cannot be denied."

"But why now?" Rory called from his corner. "Come on, Dan, those are just generalizations. It's bothered me for years that Grace thinks it has the corner on truth. There is not one single other church in all of Shelton that is packing up and hiding. Most Christians sincerely believe Scripture teaches we'll be gone before the real trouble starts. Why in the world should we give up everything and hide when consensus says that's crazy?"

"Christ also says that as the church enters this time in confusion, its heart will grow cold to the things of God, and that family and friends will turn on each other. I think this happens because when the church finds out it is in the midst of the great tribulation, which Daniel prophesied, the church will panic and lose faith in God because they had a faulty understanding of the Scripture. Christ Himself predicts it."

"That's still not enough, Dan!" Rory exclaimed. Nate noticed the top of Rory's balding head was getting red and he was sitting on the edge of his chair now. "You are asking too much with too little evidence that we are in the last days."

Dan took off his glasses and rubbed his eyes. "Alexander Magorum is the final reason I believe it's time to hide. He is too powerful, too charismatic, and has accomplished too much. He has put together a stronger base than the European Union and created a new world order—yes, that's exactly what it is—with China, Russia, and Germany at its core. The Federation of World Powers has more influence than the

United Nations, which bows to its will. He is the only man I have ever seen who can hold hands with the Arabs and the Jews at the same time. He is a powerful man who I believe is the Antichrist, and he is creating his beast nation."

Nate knew that Grace church taught this. He wasn't sure how they could believe Alexander Magorum would become such an evil leader, the way Scripture described the Antichrist. To date, he had proven himself to be a philanthropist. He was a peacemaker. He brought in help to dying nations in Africa, negotiated peace among warring neighbors in the Middle East, and had improved trade markets around the world through relationships and communication. The guy was really a hero.

A man to Nate's left leaned forward, his expression intent. Nate recognized him from church. Tom Plance was the usher who greeted Nate and Sherrie every Sunday morning at the door of Grace Church. "Dan, this just all sounds so unreal. The cost is great if you're wrong. So, let's say we all quit our jobs, sell our homes, move to some mountain in North Carolina—which to date, is the best kept secret in all of Michigan—and then we wait. Let's say six months pass or a year and nothing really changes in the world. What is the plan then? At what point do the elders have the guts to say, 'We were wrong'?"

"Good question, Tom. Five years ago we purchased this land, because of the general decline in our society and the external worldwide factors—wars, famine, etc. We bought the land for insurance—a place to go if things got bad. We figured over the next decade or so, cabins could be built and a safe location would be there for the members of Grace. Two years after the purchase we discovered the mountains were filled with a cave system which could be renovated into individual housing units—about four families can live in each one. We realized that our plan of cabins on a mountain was less than what God had planned. When He says hide, He means it."

Dan shifted in his chair and continued. "Over the next two years the caves were built out by unit leaders—men who faithfully studied the Scripture and held to the belief that a hiding place was going to be necessary. Now we have these units finished and it seems as though it is just in time. All along, our leaders have immersed themselves in the Word and have desired to follow God's lead in this. Alexander Magorum has been a man of interest for a few years now. By the way, did you know religion is all but outlawed in Russia? He tolerates everyone and everything except Christians. So, what happens next?"

It seemed that Dan knew he had every ear. He inclined his head slightly, then paused. Nate glanced around the room. Some faces were passive; others were focused on Dan with unblinking interest. He guessed about half were leaning toward leaving.

"It's been almost three and a half years since Alexander Magorum made his peace treaty with Israel. By the middle of March, if we're right, he'll stop the worship at the temple in Jerusalem and demand the worship of the world. If this happens, we're right where we should be. The elders all feel confident we have the right man. There are too many pieces falling into place. There is talk about a one-world government and even unified global currency. However if we're wrong, we are praying for God's grace to restore us back into society."

Rory exploded. "That answer stinks! How lame can you be? Do you really want us to give up everything because the 'elders'"—he made quotations marks with his fingers—"believe it's time to go. Well, I study my Bible and I am not getting the same message."

"Rory, the elders are in complete agreement here. You are called to trust them and follow them. They have been given the responsibility to lead."

"Well, that doesn't mean diddly-squat to me. There are plenty of men in this room who love the Lord and study His Word. We could put a new elder board together right here, right now, and we'd probably be better off."

With that, Nate watched the momentum in the room start to shift. A few "Here, here's" rang out as if they were ready to vote. He was stunned at how quickly they changed their allegiance. He glanced at Dan, who looked tired, but not out of the game.

"Rory," Dan began, "you're going to do whatever you see fit. I could give you twenty references but you need to start with the basics. All I am asking you to do is read through Matthew 24 and see if it is possible that Jesus is describing the time we are living in."

Tom Plance stood, his six-foot-five frame towering over those sitting. "Many generations have seen war and famine. We are heading into a time of peace."

Dan held his ground. "I agree, Tom, but not with someone who had the ability to get a Temple built in Jerusalem alongside the Al-Aqsa Mosque. Not with someone who has unified the other side of the world into one government. And not with someone who only hates one thing in this world—organized religion!"

"It's just not enough for me," Tom said, heading for the door.

"Tom!" Dan called out to him. "He has no history! Look it up—he has no traceable past. He was orphaned, grew up in a boarding school where the teachers have all died, has no extended family whatsoever—he just appears on the scene and effortlessly moves his way from a PR assistant to an ambassador to the president of Russia over a twenty-year span."

Tom stopped at the door, then turned again towards Dan.

"I love you, Dan. You and Betsy have always been kind to me and my family. But I just can't walk away from life because someone in Russia seems powerful. Worse case scenario, what can he possibly do that would effect life here in Shelton? I think you're being an alarmist and an extremist. And I'm just not going to jump on that bandwagon. I can't."

Tom turned and walked out the door. A dozen other men took this as their cue to leave too. Rory Appleton followed that group outside. Through the window, Nate watched as he talked with the group on the sidewalk. No doubt he was petitioning again for eldership among the remaining church members. Or maybe he's just rounding up more landscaping business.

For another thirty minutes Dan talked about the urgency of the decision. He told the remaining men that by the time March fifteen rolled around, it would become increasingly difficult to get supplies, but he felt they could still make their way to the mountains of North Carolina. Again scrutinizing their expressions, Nate took mental notes of the men he thought might be willing to go.

The night wound down and as Nate was walking to the door, Dan called out to him. He stopped and turned as Dan walked over to him.

"What are you thinking, Nate?"

He shook his head slowly. "Sherrie really wants to go, but I'm just not as confident as she is about the timing."

For a moment, Dan didn't speak, seeming to study Nate's face. Then he said, "There are too many indicators that this is it. I can't emphasize enough how bad things are going to get after March fifteen. Scripture tells us we won't be able to buy or sell anything." He paused. "Think for a minute what this will do to families . . . it will make buying food almost impossible."

"So should I stock up now?"

"At the bare minimum." He paused again, his eyes boring in on Nate's. "Make the move and walk by faith, my friend."

Nate shook Dan's hand and headed out to his car. He knew the move was an extreme attempt to protect believers, but Sherrie really wanted to go and it couldn't hurt Nate to continue with this church on down to North Carolina. At the very least he would finally know where their land is located. And at the very best . . . well, only time will tell.

Nate headed home to tell Sherrie the good news.

three

One would think by now he would be used to it. Twelve moves in his seventeen years on this earth and Adam had packing down to a science. He zipped opened the large black suitcase which his mom had put in his room and started putting his clothes from the dresser into the case.

As he packed, Adam remembered the all-church meeting that started it all. He pictured Garrett Hamilton standing in the pulpit, laying out the vision of the elder board. In his mind's eye, he saw the reaction of the woman across the aisle from him when Garrett asked the church to prepare to move. She broke down in tears, which made Adam wonder if she was frightened or just overwhelmed at the thought of this being the beginning of the end days. He remembered the group of men who heckled the pastor as he tried to field questions with Mr. Hamilton. And he also remembered his dad choosing not to stand when those committed to leaving were asked to.

When that night was over Adam was pretty sure about two things. He was not moving to North Carolina. And the most beautiful girl he had ever seen was.

Her name was Emma Hamilton, and she was the daughter of Garrett Hamilton, the chairman of the elder board.

Emma.

Adam's heart skipped a beat when he said her name.

He had first spotted her at a youth event, which he rarely attended. She was playing the synthesizer with the makeshift praise band, made up of a pretty good guitarist and a drummer from the youth group. She also sang with a mike while she played and though he should have been worshipping, Adam just watched her.

Emma.

Staring at his open closet, lost deep in thought, Adam's excitement was beginning to build. Emma had been gone from church for almost two months now and he missed her smile and her laugh. They had never spoken, but there was something so gentle and kind about her, who wouldn't be attracted? And now, in a couple of days, his family would be heading down to the mountains.

"How's it going in here?" his mom asked, standing in the doorway.

He blinked, snapping out of his trance. "No problem, Mom, I think I can handle it." He grinned a bit sheepishly, Emma Hamilton still on his mind.

"Don't forget there is not a lot of space down there. Limit yourself. Bring the clothes that are in the best condition because they have to last us a while. I bought you a couple of new pairs of jeans." She pointed to a bag lying in the corner of the room. "Be sure to pack them."

"Fine, Mom, I got it."

"And don't forget to leave space for extra toiletries."

"Mom! Good grief! I got it already!"

"Adam, I just want to be sure we've covered everything."

"I know, Mom. I'll be fine."

Adam paused and other thoughts he'd been pondering since his parents' announcement came to his mind.

His mother turned to leave, and stopped. His face must have revealed his thoughts. "What?" she asked. "What is it, Adam?"

"What if we're wrong? I mean, what if Alexander Magorum is just another world leader like Putin or Gorbachev?"

"Adam, we need to trust our elders. They are discerning men. This Magorum is too good to be true. I know that sounds crazy, but he has set himself perfectly to take over. When we wouldn't step in and fight alongside Israel against Syria four years ago, he did. He single-handedly brought peace to Israel. His peace treaty with Israel and the PLO was unprecedented. Then he gave Prime Minister Rabin the temple mount back—how did he do it?"

Adam sat on his bed, and his mom crossed the room and sat beside him. She reached up and tucked one of his dark curls behind his ear. His hair was getting long, and Adam knew she would want to cut it before they left. "Christ gave the disciples a list of things to look for," she continued. "He said to watch for the signs just like you would on a fig tree to tell what season is coming. The signs are all there. Israel is a nation. They have peace like never before. Yet the wars and disease in the world are at an all time high. The Islamic terrorists have crippled some of the greatest nations, including us, forcing us to remove our protection overseas and focus on our own borders. We no longer can defend democracy in the world because we can't even protect our own land. The bombings in New York, L.A., and Dallas have crippled our economy." She paused, searching his face. "So, Alexander Magorum steps up and has become the hero of the world by offering protection where we once stood."

"Why did it take so long for you and Dad to decide to go? Is Dad unsure about the move?"

"No, your dad believes in it too. He just wanted time to talk to his brother and Aunt Jill before making the decision. They think we've fallen off our rockers and want nothing to do with it. I pleaded with them to just come and trust us on the details, but they wouldn't. And our story isn't unique. Most families are finding the same thing."

"So what will happen to Uncle Steve and Aunt Jill?"

"Well, I have never doubted their love for the Lord, but they're in for a wake-up call. Their church has told them there is nothing to prepare for, and I am afraid they will find themselves in a real bind. My prayer is that when the Antichrist is revealed we can get ahold of them and convince them to come down."

"Do you think they'll do it?"

"I don't know."

Adam's mom sat on the bed, deep in thought for a moment. Then, as if her batteries had just recharged, she snapped back to reality and stood up.

"Don't forget—if you are bringing your i-Pod you'll have to use a battery pack, so be sure to grab some batteries at the store before we go."

"All right, Mom. And hey," Adam added with another grin, "don't forget to stock up on chocolate chips. It may be a couple of years before Jesus comes to get us, and I don't want to give up everything good in my life."

Adam's mom smiled and headed back to her room to continue packing. Adam walked over to his desk and picked up a photo. It had been taken at the Christmas youth group party at church. Adam was on the far left, standing by a couple of guys he had met that night. On the opposite side was a group of girls. In the center was Emma. She was laughing when the picture was taken, and when he looked at the picture Adam swore he could hear the sound of her laughter.

He sat at his desk and thought about how messed up this whole situation was. Here he was, a junior in high school, soccer player, good student, relatively popular at school, and he's packing to go and live in a cave. He wasn't a troublemaker, but he was definitely a free spirit, and Adam wasn't sure how living in a cave was going to meld with his adventurous soul. Then again, being closer to Emma could be just the motivation he needed to behave and have a good attitude.

Emma.

"Snap out of it, buddy," he said aloud. "You're not moving to start a new life and date the girl of your dreams. You're moving to wait to die."

Faith is believing the Word of God and acting on it, no matter how I feel because God promises a good result. I learned this definition last year in my youth group and I am amazed at how the Lord is making me put it into practice today. I understand that just knowing what the Bible says is not enough. I know that it has to affect my life to really make a difference and that I need to trust that God's way is the best for me. But lately I have wondered if God was thinking about me in a cave, sharing a bathroom with eleven other kids when He said, love is patient, love is kind, doesn't act unbecomingly, is not easily provoked, and doesn't take into account a wrong suffered.

This morning was absolutely disastrous. A pipe beneath one of the sinks in our bathroom came loose in the night and by the time I got up, water was flowing down the hallway like a river through the cave. The flow was pooling at the end of the hall. I guess the ground is uneven and leans towards our bedrooms rather than the kitchen. I yelled down the hall to my dad, who I could hear in the kitchen and soon bedlam broke out. The boys heard the commotion and soon they were splishing and splashing down the hall, kicking water all over each other, as if they were at a swimming party. The girls then came out of their rooms and started screaming as the boys splashed them. Then the parents started yelling. They got the water turned off, but there was so much water in the hall that it took all morning to bucket it out the front door. I found myself standing in a line passing buckets of water for what seemed like an eternity. And all I really wanted to do was brush my teeth.

I had no patience. I wasn't kind. I acted like a child because I set my jaw and couldn't laugh at the situation. I was ticked before the first kick of water doused me. And I still remember who did it—stinking Seth Mason. He's the oldest kid here and he acts like an imbecile!

And here I go again. Just thinking about the morning gets my blood boiling. It's 3:30 p.m. and I just finished my schoolwork. The day is lost and though everything is fixed and dry, I'm still irritable. And I know that God's Word is true. If I had been patient and kind, I think I could have laughed with everyone else today, and my day wouldn't still be in the gutter.

I think the key to the faith definition is the phrase, "no matter how I feel." I used to think that my feelings are an indicator of right and wrong, but now I know that if I wait to obey the Lord until my feelings tell me to do so, it may never happen. I must choose to be obedient and let the feelings follow. Part of my irritableness is the fact that I know I have to apologize to a few people for the way I behaved this morning and if I had just sucked it up, I wouldn't have to humble myself now.

Well, buck up, little Emma. Life is not all about you and it is no longer the cut and dried predictable life of Shelton, Michigan. There may be many tests before this adventure is over and you had better handle the next one with grace, or you'll continue to pay a price.

Emma tucked her journal back under her mattress and headed back to the family room. She could hear her father talking and followed the sound of his voice down the hall to the front door. He was standing just outside the door with a cell phone in his hand and she knew he must be talking to Mr. Dougherty. Communication with the real world was limited now and would be even more so after the Antichrist would be revealed. There were ham radios set up in each cave unit, so that the families could keep in touch within the caves and mostly for emergencies. But there were only two cell phones allowed on the mountain. Pastor Gentings had one and her dad had the other. They were only to be used for communication with Mr. Dougherty, since he was still trying to send people to the mountain. Reception was sketchy at best,—sometimes on a rare clear day would her dad could get a signal right outside of the cave, but normally he had to go out to a clearing. Today must be one of those clear ones.

"Well, you answered all their questions and now it's really a waiting game. When do you think the next group will arrive?" Garrett Hamilton asked.

Emma watched her dad as he listened to Mr. Dougherty's answer.

"Nope, there's still plenty of room. Keep sending them. Changing subject here a moment, what is the news out there? Anything interesting going on?"

After a couple of minutes of uh-huh's and mmm's, Garrett finished up the conversation with a prayer for Dan's safety.

When he hung up, Emma walked back into the family room with her dad and asked, "How's Mr. Dougherty?"

"Oh, he's doing fine. He's not really making any more headway with the church members at Grace. He thinks he has three more families coming and he sounded a bit discouraged. However, he was happy to hear that the last four that joined us were settled in safely. On the news front, things are stirring in Europe—there have been multiple meetings with the leaders of the Federation of World Powers and it looks like they are getting ready for some kind of announcement in the next couple of weeks."

Lily Hamilton walked over to Emma and offered her a cookie, which she readily took.

"Are you heading back to the Tabernacle?" her mom asked.

"Yeah," replied Garrett. "Things are really flying over there. The generators for the electric have been working for about a week now and we're finishing the plumbing in the restroom area. Mack's working on installing the sound system and one of the new arrivals has some furniture making in his background. I haven't met the guy yet, but they're starting to make benches by the dozens!"

"What about taking Seth and Josh with you?" Lily asked. "They're going a bit stir-crazy and after the scene this morning, I think they need to work off some of that pent-up energy."

Emma glanced at her father, hoping he would take the boys away. As a matter of fact, she wouldn't mind helping just to get out of the cave for a while.

"It's three thirty already. There's really not much time left to work today."

"We'll have dinner at seven thirty. Put a broom in their hands and let them sweep. They have to do something."

"All right. There is a meeting tonight at Shiloh. Bring us a sandwich and I'll go get the boys."

"Oh, you're right! Tonight is a gathering. I'll bring you a great sandwich and I'll top it off with a kiss!"

"How about an appetizer to go?"

Garrett drew Lily into his arms and dipped her low. Emma knew it was because he had an audience and she gave him the response he was looking for.

"Do you have to make such a big deal out of a kiss?"

"Yeah, all right. I'm out of here." Garrett glanced back at Lily and Emma as he headed to get the boys. "What a blessing that we've had so little snow and the temperatures have been so mild this winter. Who'd have thought that in March we could have outdoor meetings and not freeze to death?"

"It's really great to be with everyone at one time," Emma said. "And with families still arriving, I'm not even sure who all is here from the youth group. I've got to admit, I am a little sick of just the kids in our cave, so Shiloh is a real treat."

Lily frowned at her daughter. "Emma, I thought you were coming out of your funk."

"I'm sorry, Mom. They're fine. I guess I am just a bit stir-crazy."

"You need to adjust to this waiting game, Emma. We're going to be here a long time." Her dad gave her a hug before heading out to check on things at Shiloh.

"Well, at least I have something to look forward to," Emma said.

"Come on and help get dinner going for the rest of us," her mom said as she turned to the kitchen.

"What's on the menu tonight?"

"We're having yummy meatloaf, mashed potatoes, and peas!"

"What happens when we run out of supplies?"

Her mom shot her a stern look. "As long as we can continue to get supplies from Mount Olive, we will eat like kings, but that time is soon coming to an end. Mack Silver tries to send different men each week to gather the mail, pick up newspapers, and buy supplies. The storage units are practically full, but I think we all have to be frugal with what we have."

"Could I go to Mount Olive with Dad?"

"I don't know, Emma. It's better to let the men handle it. We don't want anyone in the town to suspect we're all living up here, in case things get bad. Remember, Christ said to hide, and I think hiding means being somewhere you can't be found."

"I really doubt me running to Wal-Mart is going to give up our location."

Her mom walked over to Emma and gave her a squeeze. "I don't know. A pretty girl like you might attract a following."

Emma managed a smile. "Come on, Mom. I'll peel potatoes."

"No need. We make them out of a box now."

She tried not to wrinkle her nose. "Yum."

Emma began setting out the dishes and silverware for the dinner, buffet style. She glanced at her watch. Only three more hours until she would be with the youth group. Hopefully her parents would let her go early. Anything to get out of this cave.

Anything.

Rory found Donna sitting with a cup of coffee watching *Oprah* at the kitchen table. She jumped when he walked in the room.

"I hate when you do that!" she snorted at him.

"What? When I walk into my kitchen?"

"No, when you sneak into the house just to scare me."

"Like that is my greatest joy in life. I've got too much on my mind to devise ways to scare you."

"Why are you home?" Donna asked.

"It's nice to see you, too, dear," Rory answered. "I'm home because I just ran into John Folkema and we decided to call an emergency meeting at church. It's time to oust Dan Dougherty and his buddy Kevin Portman, and get a new elder board. The old board is all down in North Carolina and they left these two guys to babysit the rest of us. Well, we want to make this our church and tonight we're going to vote in a new elder board. I have Ray Bower coming to meet the members of the church. He's still a student at Central Seminary, but he is willing to step into the pulpit for the time being."

"What's his view on end times?"

"He says there're enough other things to study in Scripture that we don't need to pour over something we're not meant to understand anyway."

"What a breath of fresh air. If I hear one more message on the return of Christ, I am going to scream."

That's my girl, Rory thought to himself. Never lukewarm, always hot or cold.

"What time is the meeting?"

"Seven thirty tonight. I have from now until then to rewrite the doctrinal statement."

"What are you changing?"

"I'm going to use the one from Freedom Fellowship. I picked it up the other day and I'll tell you what—compared to Freedom's, we sound like a bunch of Pharisees. No women elders, no women teachers, no alcohol, no choosing God, no believing the earth could be billions of years old, no leaving earth before the tribulation. Ours is such a downer. If someone wants to believe in evolution, what do I care? If a gay couple wants to worship at Grace, more power to them. I'm tired of all the rules and regulations at church. We could all use a dose of tolerance."

"And now that the elders are gone, I think we'll have a whole new dynamic at church. It's time to make a change."

"Sure glad I have your support," Rory said sarcastically.

Donna looked at him, and he gave her the blank stare back. He was sure she got the point. He didn't need her approval to do anything. They were pretty independent in their marriage. Oh, he loved her and all that, he just didn't enjoy being around her that much anymore. That's what happened after forty years of marriage.

Rory laid his copy of the church doctrinal statement out in front of him and took the cap off the red sharpie he held in his hand. Then he opened Freedom's statement and started to compare. It took twenty minutes to cross out all the unnecessary, narrow-minded theology from Grace's doctrinal statement and another thirty minutes to type up the new one. He decided he would need to leave for church by six, so that he could make copies before the meeting.

Rory took a deep breath. What a blessing that the Lord got rid of the dead weight in one fell swoop. He said a quick prayer of thanks and by six headed off to church, with the new statement in hand and his Bible on the coffee table.

four

Nate Reed waited until the cave was empty to make his phone call. Phones were on the Do Not Bring list, so he had to keep it a secret from everyone, even Sherrie. He quickly dialed the familiar number and then realized he had no signal. Why would he? He must have been underneath forty feet of rock. Glancing around to make certain he wasn't seen, he slipped from the cave and found a less dense patch of forest. A couple of bars showed on the face of the cell phone. He punched in the number again, and this time the call went through.

Sean's voice mail picked up immediately.

"Hi, Sean. It's me. We're all settled in. Just checking to see if you received the last file I sent you. You can't reach me, but I will check my text messages as often as possible. I'll be in touch in a couple of weeks."

He flipped his phone shut just as footsteps came up behind him. He quickly dropped the phone into his front shirt pocket and put his hands up to his eyes, as if he was wiping tears away. He turned around and found Sherrie standing about ten feet from him. She seemed confused, and from her expression he couldn't sense whether or not she had seen or heard him. His mind raced with excuses when she broke the silence.

"Nate, what are you doing? Are you okay?"

"I'm just overwhelmed, Sherrie. There are times when the whole move overtakes me and I wonder what I have done."

"I know this is scary, but it was the right decision. And you've got a fallback with Smith and Brumbsy. They would be happy to take you back. You're their best auditor."

"I don't know if that makes me feel better or not." He feigned wiping another tear from his eye as he walked towards Sherrie, then he took her hand. "I'm sorry. I didn't want you to see me like this. I'm trying so hard to be strong. We'd better get over to the gathering."

"This is our first week down here and we're both going through a lot of adjustments. It's hard on everyone down here. But you don't need to suffer alone. I'm here."

They walked in silence to Shiloh. As they neared, Nate could hear music and faint singing. He squeezed Sherrie's hand and tried to ignore a vague sense of guilt, pleased that it was quickly replaced with a sense of duty. That night, he would plug the phone back into the battery-operated charger, just small enough to fit in his second pair of work boots at the back of the closet. No one would find it there. He shook off the lingering guilt and focused on the task at hand. He had a job to do, and in the end he might actually save some lives.

Adam spotted her as soon as he got to Shiloh. He had been so busy settling into the cave with his family and meeting the others who would share their new home that he had only wandered out of the cave once to get the lay of the land. He found Shiloh—that was easy. And he found the openings to about seven other caves, but he had no clue which door she was living behind. He had been tempted to knock and ask, but then he remembered that they technically had never even been introduced, so that might have been awkward. Finally, worship at Shiloh gave him his chance.

It was her laughter he heard first. Turning to the sound, he spotted Emma with a group of friends just a few rows ahead of where he sat with his parents. He found it difficult to keep from staring, especially when she combed her hair back with her fingers and adjusted the clip that held the curly mane in place at the back of her neck.

Once the meeting started he tried to keep his attention on Pastor Gentings. The meeting lasted about an hour. Half the time was spent singing and the rest of the time Pastor Gentings went over the rules and how to get necessary items from the supply units for the new arrival families. He reported that the storage units were now completely filled and introduced to the newcomers, Mack Silver's wife, Tara, who was in charge of withdrawals.

Adam smiled at the mention of Tara Silver because he had found the nearest supply unit to his cave on his trek out of his new homestead. There he met Tara who graciously gave him a quick tour. Adam was amazed at how much food had been stored in that unit and that was one of the smaller ones. There were four others filled to the brim. The cool, moist temperature was good for the dry goods and vegetable storage. Large freezers were filled with meat—mostly hamburger and chicken and when that ran out, there was freeze-dried meat, which Adam hoped he would never have to experience. Apparently one of the members of Grace was also a survival buff and knew exactly where to get MREs in bulk. Tara was kind and even a bit funny. Adam enjoyed the tour.

Pastor Gentings also mentioned the vehicle storage site, which was on the opposite side of the mountain from the caves. It took about two and a half hours of riding on a quad, an off-road four track vehicle, to get there and it held about a dozen vans. These vans were used to bring people to the mountain, as well as make runs into towns. It was located in a well-covered indent in the side of the mountain, to which the church added trees and shrubs to conceal the opening.

These twelve vans had made hundreds of trips up and down the mountain and back and forth to Shelton. Even Adam's family, though they came late, sold their car for about half of what it was worth and was driven to the mountains in a church van. Though trips to town were not as big a necessity now that the storage units were filled, Pastor Gentings said they were still necessary to get mail and receive news. The church had a post office box at the local post office and someone checked it weekly. When he mentioned a sign-up to take turns to town, Adam nudged his dad who gave him a wink.

As the meeting came to a close, Adam noticed that Emma had paid little attention to the announcements. She seemed so happy to be with her girlfriends that she barely even noticed the pastor was speaking. About halfway through the service Adam saw Emma's mom give her the evil eye from across the clearing, but that only quieted her for a few minutes.

"And finally, as usual, stay as late as you want here at Shiloh. We can keep some of these campfires lit for light, but just be sure, whoever is the last to leave, that all the fires are put out. I believe our youth pastor, Mike Torey, wants to see the high schoolers in the west corner for a quick get together—I think I even saw marshmallows!"

Adam heard a few hoots with that announcement. When the meeting was over, most everyone stayed to talk. There was a lot of hugging and laughing among the families, and then things quieted down as the new arrivals shared their stories of how they made the move and the price they paid with family and friends who wouldn't listen. Adam left his parents and wandered over to the youth area, keeping an eye on Emma the whole way.

She was still talking and laughing with her friends as she headed to the youth gathering. The last thing on her mind, it seemed to Adam, was the uneven path, or the rocky obstacles on it.

He saw the log—and pictured what was about to happen—before she did. Her toe caught. Her arms did a bit of a windmill dance, but just before she hit the ground, Adam, with great speed and agility, came up from behind and grabbed her elbow to steady her.

She turned to see who was helping her. Adam stood there with a big grin on his face. His mind suddenly went blank, and all the things he imagined he would say to her disappeared into thin air. "Hi," he finally said.

"Bet that looked kind of funny." Emma blinked at him, obviously surprised at his helping hand.

"Are you hurt?"

"Not really—it probably looked worse than it was. I guess I don't step high enough over these logs sometimes."

"Has this happened before?"

"Yeah, and I am sure I'll do it again. I'm not sure we've met before—my name is . . . "

"Emma." Adam finished. "I, uh, went to youth group once or twice and you were the girl on stage, right?"

Adam could feel his heart pounding.

"Yeah, that was me." Emma's smile didn't help the heart condition.

"I just got here last week with my parents. My name is Adam."

Adam extended his hand and she returned the gesture with a firm handshake.

"Hi, Adam. Thanks for helping me."

"No problem," he stammered. "I was heading over to the youth group, but I don't really know anyone. Can I go with you?"

"Sure, umm . . . I'm a sophomore—where are you in school?"

"I'm a junior. This is really weird not to be in school right now."

"Yeah, a lot of things are different here."

A few minutes later Emma introduced him to more kids than he would remember. He was far more focused on the one doing the introducing. As the evening came to a close the youth pastor said he was trying to set up regular meetings for the youth so that they could hang and just be together.

Emma leaned over to Adam and said in a low voice, "I might lose my mind if I don't get out of that cave every once in a while. How about you?"

"I haven't been here as long as you, but I sure do have a lot of little kids in my cave. I can see needing a break. Have you done much exploring?"

"No, my cave parents have limited our time outside, though I don't think it's really a big deal right now."

"Cave parents? That actually could have a double meaning!"

"I do like to play with words a bit," Emma replied. "I love to write, as a matter of fact."

"Really? What do you write?"

"Lately I am just journaling my experience—you know, in case we die in these caves someone can find my journal and I will become famous posthumously!"

"Kind of like an Anne Frank sort of thing?"

"Yeah, I guess so, except her story was far more devastating. I will probably just die of boredom."

"I can maybe help with that. Not the dying part but to stop you from dying. I, uh, I mean, nobody's ever died of boredom whose hung around me for any length of time. So, how about an hour or two of exploring the area tomorrow afternoon? What do you say?"

She was smiling but Adam regretted his boldness as soon as he said it. He was still hoping she would agree, when they were interrupted by a brunette, about the same age as Emma.

"Emma—are you ready to head back? Oops, sorry—who are you?"

She looked at Adam.

Emma jumped in.

"This is Adam and he's only been here a week. He's just offered to head up a mountain exploration team—are you interested?"

"Groovy! Count me in!"

Emma turned to Adam and explained, "This is Leighsa, my very best friend. And yes, she does talk like she's from the seventies sometimes, but you'll get used to it. What time do you want to go tomorrow?"

"Well, I have to help over at the Tabernacle until lunch, but after that I'm pretty much free. I haven't started studying yet and personally, I don't mind waiting another day. Let's go at half past one. We can meet here at Shiloh."

"I might bring Seth and Josh too. Josh is Leighsa's brother and Seth lives in my unit too. I think you'll like them."

"Then it's agreed. We'll meet here at one thirty."

"We'll see you tomorrow," Emma said. "Oh, wait! What if we can't get permission to go?"

Adam smiled at her. "You'll figure out a way. I have a feeling when you want something, few people get in your way!"

Emma grabbed Leighsa by the arm and the two of them wandered back towards the group, where Adam saw them meet up with a couple of older boys and then leave the clearing. They must be Josh and Seth, Adam thought to himself. He lifted his hand to tuck a curl behind his ear and then remembered his mom had gotten rid of the curls before they left.

Tomorrow will be a great day, Adam thought. He turned and headed back to his unit, barely noticing the jagged flashes of lightning in the distance, heralding a good spring storm's arrival.

five

After the meeting at Shiloh, Nate Reed headed back to his unit. The families were gathering for brownies and hot chocolate and Nate feigned a headache. When Sherrie asked if he needed her to go with him, he told her to stay and have fun. He was just going to bed.

In truth, he didn't want her there at all. He wanted to record some information while it was still fresh in his mind. Nate got back to his room and shut the door. He reached to lock it, planning a response when Sherrie would come to the door and ask why it was locked. But there was no lock.

I don't know who this Mack Silver guy thinks he is, but he's not that handy if he can't put a simple lock on a door.

He walked over to the dresser. His laptop was leaning against it on the floor, and he reached down to pick it up. Laptops were allowed, but there were no satellite hookups and of course, no wireless connections in the caves. Some used their computers to hold books and others played games on them. Sherrie didn't think twice about him bringing his laptop because most of the men had done the same.

He sat down on his bed and powered it up. Then he opened his Grace Word file and put in the password. Knowing he didn't have much time, he quickly jotted an entry:

- 3/11—Gentings is still the leader
- the food storage units are full and have enough food for a couple of years—perhaps food contamination would force them out of hiding
- total number counted a E t Shiloh tonight—284
- No substantive discussion, basically fellowship
- Large, indoor meeting facility almost completed
- I get the feeling Hamilton and Gentings make all the decisions around here and the people blindly follow

Nate heard commotion in the hallway and he quickly saved his memo and shut down the computer. He laid down on the bed and put his forearm over his face. Two minutes later Sherrie entered the room. She quietly walked over to Nate and pulled his shoes off. Then she unbuttoned his shirt and gently whispered in his ear, "Honey, let's get you out of your clothes."

Nate, acting as if he had been in a deep sleep, stammered a bit and sat up. Sherrie helped him take off his shirt and jeans and then tucked him back in bed. Three minutes later she was beside him with the lights off. Nate opened his eyes and stared into the darkness. Why is it getting harder to lie to her? He'd done it for so long that it was becoming second nature to him now. But lately, for some reason he couldn't fathom, he struggled to shake the guilt.

When he signed on seventeen years ago, he never dreamed that being a DIU agent would be so complicated.

"Oh my goodness, Emma! He's really cute and I think he likes you."

"Good grief, Leighsa, we just met. The poor guy's just looking for some friends." Emma couldn't help but smile. "Hey, Josh! Seth!"

The boys turned when they heard Emma call.

"I just met a new guy—he's a junior—and he wants to look around the mountain tomorrow after lunch. Wants all of us to go. What do you say?"

"Works for me," Seth said with a shrug. "Anything to get us out of the cave for a few hours."

Emma and the others started back to the cave.

Josh fell into step with Emma. "So when did this guy get here?"

"Last week some time."

"And," Leighsa said, "what Emma is not telling you is that he's really *hot*!"

"Leighsa!" Emma shoved her friend.

"Uh, oh! Does our little bookworm have a boyfriend?" Seth raised an eyebrow and gave Emma a knowing look.

"Come on, guys! I just met him!"

Seth and Josh proceeded to chant, "Emma's got a boyfriend, Emma's got a boyfriend!" until Emma couldn't take it anymore.

"Enough! You're not coming with us if you are going to act like third graders! You two are driving me crazy!"

The entrance to the cave came into view, and Emma picked up the pace to get away from Josh and Seth.

"Emma!" Seth called after her. "We're sorry! Please, can we go on your date tomorrow?"

Emma could still hear them laughing as she slammed the door shut behind her. When she came out of the entrance hall, she saw all four sets of parents sitting around one of the kitchen tables. She heard the others come in behind her and waited for them, whispering a quick prayer that they had gotten over their laughter.

"Did you guys have fun tonight?" Garrett Hamilton asked the group.

"Yeah," answered Emma.

Leighsa plopped down next to her parents, Seth and Josh sank into chairs across from theirs, then all three shot Emma an expectant look. Funny how they could give her such a bad time one minute then look to her for leadership the next.

"Um, Dad? There was a new guy at the service tonight. His name is Adam, and he really doesn't know anyone. He seems nice." Seth cleared his throat and Emma ignored him. "He asked if the four of us could show him around the mountain tomorrow. Do you think we could do that?"

Lily spoke first. "After schoolwork?"

"Of course," Leighsa said.

Mrs. Torey frowned. "Where are you going to go?"

Emma let out a breath she'd been holding. "He wants to explore, but I thought we could show him where the supply units are and point out which caves are occupied."

Seth leaned forward, his elbows on the table. "I thought we could check out the progress at the Tabernacle."

Garrett looked thoughtful, and for a moment didn't speak. Emma knew he was weighing the danger. A chill traveled up her spine—though she wasn't sure if it was the sense of danger, or the sense of adventure leaving the caves might bring—that caused it. Finally, her father said, "I don't want you gone too long. I don't think I have to remind you how careful you must be." He paused, still looking uncertain. "Finish your schoolwork first. The day may be coming when you won't be able to wander freely, but for now—if you're careful, I don't think there is any harm in it."

"Don't worry, Mr. Hamilton. We won't let Emma be alone with this guy." Josh smiled at Emma. She returned it with a cold hard stare.

"Emma, is there something else we should know?"

"No." Emma could feel her cheeks flush. "Josh is just jealous that I met a new kid before he did."

"And, the new kid's HOT!" laughed Leighsa.

"Good grief! You guys have to behave tomorrow!" Emma regretted she ever agreed to go on the walk.

"Oh, we'll be fine," answered Seth. "We promise."

Her father finally stepped in to save the day. "Emma, I am proud of you for reaching out to a new arrival. This is hard enough without friends and I am sure the fact that he is 'hot' has nothing to do with it." He winked at her and her anxiety melted away. Emma loved her dad and he was the only one who could tease her without consequence.

Emma stood, gave her dad a hug, and headed to bed. The rest of the group followed soon after. A few minutes later as she climbed into bed, she thought about the coming day and couldn't help smiling to herself. She decided to get up early so she would get her journaling and schoolwork done with plenty of time to spare. That one thing could keep her from going, and she wasn't about to let that happen. Her mom was such a stickler about staying on top of her schoolwork.

She had to admit it did seem a bit nonsensical to continue studies with the end of the world coming soon, but the parents of Grace had agreed that education was still important. Emma believed it was just to fill the waiting time, but there was a niggling concern deep down inside her that made her wonder if it could be because the parents weren't sure it was really the right time to go into hiding.

"So?"

Sarah's sweet whisper from above sounded a bit inquisitive.

"So what?" answered Emma.

"Who is he? And don't act like you don't know what I am talking about!"

"Not you too . . . "

"Come on—you only spent all evening talking to him!"

"He's a new arrival. Adam."

"And . . . ?"

"And what?"

"Is he nice? Is he smart? Usually those big, strong jocks are dumb as doornails!"

"I'll tell you after tomorrow."

"What's tomorrow?"

Emma heard Sarah sit up with that last question.

"Leighsa, Seth, Josh, and I are going to hang out tomorrow afternoon with him."

"Can I come?"

"Sorry. I don't want to overwhelm him with my beautiful little sister hanging on his every word."

"Not fair! I'll behave."

"I'll let you know how it goes."

"Good night, Emma."

"Good night, Sarah."

Emma scrunched her pillow and settled into it with a smile on her face. Tomorrow will be a great day. Then she heard a faint rumble, like a metal cart with wheels being pushed down a distant hall. She listened for another moment and then she heard it again.

"Thunder," she said out loud.

"What?" asked Sarah.

"Nothing." She whispered a prayer, thanking God for the meeting at Shiloh and asking Him to clear the weather. Then she drifted off, the soft and even sounds of breathing from five other girls lulling her to sleep.

The next morning, Adam was sitting at his dining table, books spread out, studying fiendishly when his father came in from outside. The outside door was down a hall a bit, but Adam could hear the rainfall before he saw his wet father emerge from the hallway.

"Don't tell me . . . " he started.

"Good morning, Adam," his dad said.

"It's raining?" Adam asked the obvious, with disappointment in his voice.

"From the looks of it, it has been raining since last night. Things are pretty soaked out there."

He shut his book with a little too much force. "I had plans this afternoon."

"Plans? What are you talking about?"

"I was going to hang out with some kids I met last night. "

"Bring them here."

"Oh, right! So they can watch more Dora cartoons or the Teletubbies with my roommates?"

"There's a whole shelf of DVDs over there," Adam's dad pointed to a cabinet by the television. "I'm sure there's something more exciting than the Teletubbies in there."

"It's just that we wanted to look around outside . . ."

"Maybe it will be clear by lunch."

"Whatever."

"Well, finish your breakfast and let's get over to the Tab. I get you until lunch, right?"

"Yeah. I'll be right over."

As Adam finished his breakfast, he looked around the room. The caves had been hooked up to a generator and natural gas lines, which ran their electricity and heat. He walked over to the cabinet by the TV, opened the door, and scanned the movie titles. He'd seen most of them. He took a deep breath and let reality sink in. Cave life meant limits.

By noon, the sun was out and though things were soaked, Adam's plans were definitely back on. After lunch, he headed over to Shiloh and waited for Emma to arrive.

When he saw her coming, he stood and waved.

Stop being such a dork, he reprimanded himself. Just be cool. Be yourself.

He took another deep breath and could feel his heart pounding again. He knew it was hopeless. He really was a dork and he wasn't very cool, but Emma would find that out sooner or later so there was no point in hiding it.

"Hi, Adam!" Emma waved back. He thought he heard some snickers from the three friends behind her.

Adam walked over to the four and Emma made quick introductions.

Seth began, "We thought we would show you the storage units and the Tabernacle, but Emma tells us you've been over there already. Is your dad the one who is making the benches?"

"Uh-huh. It's actually a pretty simple process. You guys should come and help—it would go faster with more hands."

"That would be great! Staying in the cave all day is putting me to sleep." Seth said.

"I'd like to head over there to see what we find." Adam pointed in a direction that led the kids away from the living and meeting areas. "Have you been over there?"

"Well, no," started Seth. "But we shouldn't go too far . . . "

"It'll be fine. I'm great with directions and I found some tire tracks, so someone has been this way. We'll just follow the tire tracks and see where they take us."

"It sounds like a plan to me. Let's go!" Emma put aside her fears for their safety in her excitement to look around.

For the next hour, the young people shared about life in Shelton. Emma, Leighsa, and Josh all had gone to the same high school, Shelton East, while Adam found out that Seth actually had gone to his school, Shelton North.

"I thought I recognized you," Seth said. "Do you play basketball?"

"Actually, I played on the soccer team. I just shoot around but not for the school."

"Yeah, that's it! I saw you play soccer."

Adam nodded. "That's all in the past now, isn't it?"

"How are you doing with all of this?" Emma asked Adam.

"You mean the move?"

"Yeah, I mean, we've all grown up at Grace and we've been taught since we were little what to look for and prepare for during this time.

I remember my dad used to say he thought it would be in either his or my lifetime, and here we are. But, you've only been at Grace for a year and a half. Is this hard for you?"

"You know, initially, my mom and I were blown away by Grace's view on end times. We talked our dad into taking the end-times class at church. We studied the Scriptures together. I always thought prophecy was unclear and too hard to understand, but that class really opened my eyes."

"Who taught that class, do you remember?" asked Seth.

"It was an elder—Mr. Mason, I think."

"That's my dad—he taught that class like three times a year. He's got it down by now." From the look on his face, Seth was obviously proud of his father.

"So, am I struggling? I won't say this has been fun, but it's definitely an adventure."

They had been walking for over an hour when Emma looked at her watch. She was about to mention the time when Leighsa broke the silence.

"My dad thinks any day now, we should know."

"Know what?" Adam asked.

"We will know if Alexander Magorum is the Antichrist."

"What does he think will happen?" Adam asked again.

"Daniel gives us a timeline for the last seven years and in the middle of it the Antichrist stops the worship in the temple and demands the world to worship him. That's what my dad thinks is going to happen."

"Mine too," added Emma.

"Then there won't be any more lingering doubts whether we did the right thing or not." Leighsa grabbed a dead branch from the ground and used it as a walking stick.

"So, assuming this event happens," Adam said, "what happens next? Things will really get bad for Christians and Jews in the world, but do you think things will stay quiet here and then one day we wake up and are caught up to the heavens with Christ?"

"I know that's what everyone is hoping for," Emma said. "But I don't know. My mom says that we no longer need to make food supply runs because we have enough for about three years stored already. If we don't get supplies, I don't know how we will get news. Whenever a newspaper is brought in, I read it after the dads in my cave are done with it. Things in America sound normal in the paper. So maybe life will just be quiet here and then it's over."

Josh threw in his two cents. "Well, I think it's going to get crazy here. I bet we'll have soldier's combing the mountain trying to find us and helicopters shining spot lights on us at night."

"Nice imagination, Josh." Leighsa whacked him on the back with her stick.

"Ouch! Come on!" Josh tried to rub his back but couldn't quite reach it. "You know, Jesus said that He will cut this time of persecution short for the sake of the elect. It's going to be really bad and if He wants to have someone to return to, He'll come early for us."

"I just can't believe this is all really happening," Adam said. "It just seems too bizarre to think we might actually be living and watching prophecy being fulfilled. Boy, a year ago I never thought I would be here. My family has been in a lot of churches and we have never been taught the Scripture about Christ's return quite like this!"

"What were you taught?" asked Emma.

"Most churches didn't even mention the return of Christ. The few that did said we didn't have to worry about it because we would be gone before anything bad happened. So why study it if we aren't even going to be around? My mom tried to talk to some of her friends, but they think we've been brainwashed. One woman literally laughed in her face."

"I'm sorry to hear that, but I'm really glad your parents came to Grace. And just in time, it seems."

Adam thought he saw Emma blush when she said that, and he added, "Well, time will tell, won't it? Whoa!"

Adam stopped in his tracks and the rest followed suit. Ahead lay a clearing with water sparkling in the sun. With a shout, he ran towards the clearing and again, the rest followed.

"Wow! Look at this!"

"We must be near the base of our mountain," Seth said. "I heard there was a lake at the base of the two mountains."

Two hundred yards of open field led to a huge lake, which the five explorers ran toward. There was a large, flat rock that rested at the edge of the lake and the kids, following Adam's lead, climbed on top and surveyed the land. Since it was still cold, the meadow surrounding the lake was mostly yellow grass with a scattering of trees here and there. The water was crystal clear and though it was March, they thought they could see minnows near the shoreline. Josh jumped off the rock and felt the water.

"Whoa! Really cold!"

"What did you think, stupid?" his sister said. "That it was a hot water spring?"

"They have those in North Carolina," he retorted. "Hey, look at that tree!"

Josh pointed to a weeping willow whose branches hung out over the water. Adam knew exactly what Josh had in mind.

"Great for swinging!"

"What a great find, Adam!" Emma said, and then, looking at her watch, her voice dropped. "Guys, I think we have a problem It's a quarter to four and we're supposed to be home at four."

Leighsa's face turned pale. "It'll take us a good hour and a half walk to get home. Oh, boy, are we going to get it!"

"It's going to take us longer that that," Seth added. "We were walking downhill the whole way here."

Adam stepped back into his leadership role. "Don't panic," he said. "Nothing's going on back at the caves and we'll be back in time for dinner. I don't think we should mention the lake, because they'll know how far we wandered, but if we tell them we just lost track of time, it should be all right."

"I don't want to lie," insisted Emma.

"We're not lying and we did lose track of time," Adam said. "It's just that we wandered a bit too far and they may not be too happy with us. We're not lying, we're just omitting."

"Omitting sounds like lying to me."

"It'll be fine, Emma. I'll tell you what. Blame it on me. Tell your parents I was leading and you guys couldn't get me to turn back. I don't really care because my parents aren't concerned about when I get back. Come on, let's get going."

Much of the time getting home was spent in silence. They reached the cave at ten after five, and Emma stopped to say good-bye to Adam. She had seemed cool with him on the jog back and he wanted to try to straighten things out.

"I'm sorry for getting you in trouble," he said. "I won't put you in this position again. I promise."

"That's okay. We're only an hour late. I guess it's not a big deal. It's not like we were out drinking and driving, right?" She laughed and his heart skipped a beat again.

"Emma, before you go, I wanted to tell you something."

"Yes?"

"You mentioned that you like to write." He looked away from her gaze for a moment, feeling his face flush. "It's really a coincidence," he finally said, "but I do too. I was wondering if you would want to read one of my short stories." He lifted his eyes to hers, then smiled as her face lit up.

"That would be great!"

"Assuming I'm not in trouble, I'll run it over tomorrow."

"I'll introduce you to my parents too . . . assuming they're not fuming or anything."

"You'd better get inside."

Adam watched her enter her cave and then he sprinted back to his own. He knew he would get an earful from his mom. He'd never been good at being on time and living in a cave hadn't changed that bad habit. What a great day, he thought as he swung open the door and slammed it shut behind him, letting everyone at the dinner table know the missing child had returned.

six

"True greatness is found in leadership. History has proven this theorem. From Caesars to Kings to Presidents of States, no nation will ever be great without a great leader. Tomorrow, as we stand before not only our own countries but the world, we will present them with true, great leadership. I assure you, my friends and comrades, the announcement of the Federation of World Powers Currency Act will be not be challenged but will be embraced as sheer genius. Even America will be attracted to its perimeters, for greatness has a magnetic effect which is undeniable."

The nine heads of the FWP applauded and Alexander Magorum accepted their appropriate response. He had created a flawless system.

One step closer to his ultimate goal.

One by one, the leaders signed his Currency Act, committing to unify their currency into the One World Denomination system. It was a very simple decision. Changing one's currency would ensure financial stability.

Alexander Magorum was the mind and the power behind this new gift to the world. His banking system which was set up to handle the new currency was the most technologically advanced ever designed, and yet remarkably simple. All banks would be required to change over into the One World Denomination software and all customers would have a computer chip embedded in the top of their hand, as simple as a prick on the finger. When a member scanned their hand, immediately a picture of the customer would come onto the screen along with their personal ID number. If the picture matched, then the charge would be made on the customer's account. You could choose to debit the amount or charge it to your monthly statement. Easy as that.

Alexander Magorum took in the room. He had planned every detail of this day. He had chosen this ballroom because of the sheer size. The twenty-five-foot-tall ceilings sparkled with the reflection of the lights from the multiple crystal chandeliers. The deep red carpet had an elegant allure and the one round linen-covered table in the center of the large ballroom signified equality among the leaders, as well as the fact that they alone were leading the world into a new era. The fact that he himself wasn't an equal with these men was inconsequential at this moment. Today was a day of historical significance, but the future would prove his higher role.

He had planned and dreamed of this day. This day and the next. But first things first.

There will be no tomorrow if today doesn't succeed.

He looked around the table. China to his left, then Turkey, Iran, Iraq, Greece, Hungary, Libya, Ukraine. Germany to his right. And he represented Russia. That was a struggle at first, but he understood the need to distance himself from a stereotype. Plus Moscow had great ballrooms.

Behind each FWP leader stood his interpreter. Whenever Alexander Magorum or Ferco Szabo spoke, the interpreter would lean over and speak in the ear of his leader. It was manageable and relatively organized, however he didn't like the extras in the room. He would have to address this issue at a future meeting.

This was just the beginning of the Federation. By summer the room would be filled with tables, but these ten would always sit on his right and left. Though they weren't leaders on the same plane as himself, they were still leading the way for the rest of the world. The sheep at the head of the herd, following the good shepherd.

Alexander Magorum had explained to these men ad nauseam for the past six months that the Federation of World Powers would guarantee this banking system, offering countries financial benefits for using their system. They would be given favorable trading percentages on their imports and exports with these nations, as well as offered government contracts that would typically be farmed out to other nations. Preferential treatment in the loan department was a given. There would no longer be any need for traveler's checks—one could bank in any country using this system.

The list went on and on. What was not stated in the legal documentation was the cost of not joining. He would make his system so appealing that rejection came with a cost. There was an underlying agreement between the members of the FWP that nonmembers would be cut off. No trading, no contracts, no favors—even existing fiscal relationships would be dissolved. There were enough third world countries willing to sign up that factories and labor agreements could be moved to those countries so that their citizens would benefit from their membership. While those facilities were being built, existing contracts would stand, but eighteen months from now, there would be quite a price to pay for not joining.

This was just the beginning of the pressure.

But today was the day to begin putting legs to his system. After six months they were all ready and willing to sign.

Look at them, so eager to follow. They want to be called leaders and yet all they do is follow. Not a single one of them offered a word of input or even a punctuation change. They just agreed to the document as is. Leadership flows from within and they will learn from the best.

As the signing was completed, Alexander Magorum nodded to Szabo.

"Well, gentlemen, our work here is done for today," declared Prime Minister Szabo of Hungary. "Thank you for coming. This is a day that will go down in history as one of the most significant acts of peace. Perhaps there will be a Nobel Prize in it for us."

At that, the men rose to their feet and cheered. Szabo raised his hands to quiet the room as the men remained standing.

"Tomorrow we will stand behind President Magorum as he announces our agreement to the world. It will be a glorious day for all of us! Prime Minister Avi Rabin has graciously offered the steps of his glorious temple for our press conference. Since there would be no temple without Magorum's help, how could we refuse? Please arrive at the airport no later than 11 a.m. For security purposes we will be taking several planes.

"We will have a late lunch on the way to Jerusalem and then the press conference is scheduled for 7 p.m. There will most likely be individual interviews following the conference, so speak with your personal secretaries as to what has been arranged for you. Your limousines are waiting at the entrance. Sleep well and we'll see you in the morning."

Magorum glanced around the room as the men walked to the door. Because many of the men had to speak through translators the chatter in the room became deafening, but one thing was clear. They were pleased with their decision to join the FWP. They truly believed that history would remember them as great leaders because of this decision.

They have no idea what tomorrow will hold.

seven

When Emma entered the cave, her mother didn't seem to have noticed she was late.

"Hi, Mom," Emma said tentatively, as her mom busily set the tables for dinner. She could hear the other mothers were in the kitchen.

"Oh, Emma, you're just in time. Will you help me get the tables set?" Her mother handed her a stack of napkins to fold and place.

"Sure," Emma said, a bit confused. "What's going on?"

"I just got word that the men heard some disturbing news. They're meeting over at the Tabernacle site. Apparently, Mack Silver got a radio system up and working and they're getting an all news station pretty clearly. They've been playing it all day while the guys work over there."

"So, what's the problem?"

"No problem, it's just that we wanted to feed the kids and get a movie going before the men get home so that we can talk."

Emma picked up the utensils and looked behind her. Leighsa and the boys had disappeared, apparently to clean up. "Um, sorry about being late, Mom."

"Oh dear, I forgot you were out today." She stopped and turned to Emma with a puzzled look. "Why are you so late?"

"We just lost track of time. But we made it home for dinner, so I don't think there is any harm done?"

"It's fine, honey. I'm just glad you didn't get lost or anything. Where did you go? Did you see any fairies or ogres?" Her mom laughed and headed into the kitchen to get the salt and pepper shakers. When she came back out, Emma was still trying to decide how to answer her question, but her mother had already moved on.

"Run down the hall and get the kids, Emma. It's time to eat."

Emma obeyed, breathing a sigh of relief. She didn't think it was a big deal to tell her mom they had gone to the lake, but that would have let out the big secret and she didn't want to be the one to do it. Anyway, it wasn't like they would ever go back there.

Dinner was over by six, which was rather early by cave standards. Emma heard the mothers decide to let the kids play some games and start the movie at eight. Lily had a feeling that the men were going to be pretty late, so she suggested making up plates for them which could be warmed when they got home.

And her mother was right. The men were really late for dinner. Garrett was the last to arrive home. When he walked into the family room, the kids had settled in for another viewing of *Big Fish*. Emma saw her dad's eyes meet her mom's and she could clearly see exhaustion and concern on his face. She knew he was hungry and tired. She also knew when a conversation was to be held at a later time. Emma saw her mom look around the room, acknowledging all the bodies and then back to her husband.

"Want some dinner?" she asked.

"That sounds good," Garrett said as he collapsed into one of the recliners.

He kept his eyes on his wife. She smiled at him and pulled her ear. Emma loved when she would catch her mom doing that to her dad. It was a wordless way of saying, I love you, and Emma had hoped someday she would have a husband to pull her ear at too. She was pretty sure that dream was dead, but she still enjoyed watching the exchange between her parents. Emma saw a small half grin appear on her father's lips and she turned back to the movie.

Her mother heated up a plate with a generous serving of meat-loaf and mashed potatoes with gravy on it for Garrett. Comfort food. There was not a lot of conversation between any of the wives and the husbands, but Emma could tell something had happened. She figured they would talk in their bedrooms, which was just about the only place they could ever be alone.

Emma could hardly keep her eyes open, she was so tired from her adventurous day. She wanted to write in her journal so she headed to bed before the movie was half done. She noticed Seth and Josh were gone too, and when she got to her room, Leighsa was sound asleep on her bunk. Maybe going to bed early wasn't such a bad idea, she thought as she slipped into her pajama bottoms and climbed under the covers.

She reached for her journal, but then, once again chose to wait until morning to write. She was just too tired. The smell of coffee wafted down the hallway and slid under the girl's bunkroom door. Though she had been sleeping only an hour, Emma opened an eye as the aroma of coffee swirled around her head. Because there were no windows, she had no idea if it was already morning or not and she reached for her travel alarm clock. Hitting the snooze button illuminated the LCD display.

11:09 p.m.

Coffee at night?

Emma sat up and swung her legs off the edge of her bunk. She reached for her robe and slipped her arms into it without getting up. When she stood, she tied the belt around her waist and crept to the door. Without making a sound, she exited the room and made her way down the cool, damp hallway.

I wish I had grabbed my socks, Emma thought as she passed the bathroom. She could hear talking and as she approached the entrance to the great room, she could see the parents sitting at a table. *This must be the meeting time of the parents after all the kids are asleep.* Careful not to be seen, she edged her way as close to the entrance as possible and then slid into a crouch. She wrapped her robe around her knees and tucked the edges under her toes. Maybe this would keep them warm.

"Well, for starters, we got a call from Dan and Betsy today," she heard her father say. "We already knew that rumors were flying about the so-called disappearance of Grace Church. There were enough of us who explained to family and friends what we were doing, but the church remnant is really struggling. Apparently, Rory Appleton has set himself up as the new chairman of the elder board and has surrounded himself with his cronies."

Emma strained to see their reactions, but couldn't move without being seen.

"What happened to Dan and Kevin? I thought the church had agreed to let them step in and build an elder board?" Emma recognized her mom's voice.

"Well, apparently last night there was an emergency meeting, Rory showed up with about twenty men and additional signatures dismissing the current elder board. Since the church is down to eighty-five people, they had a majority and Dan felt it was better to step away than cause a scene."

"We've never been a congregational rule church, Garrett!" Mrs. Torey said. "How could this happen?"

"Like I said, they're really struggling. Rory has thrown out the doctrinal statement because our end-times position is too narrow and controversial. Those who stayed behind to witness have decided to meet at Dan and Betsy's house and have their own service. In the mean time, Rory has brought in a seminary student to fill as pastor and apparently he has pretty liberal views."

Mr. Torey continued. "Dan also said that the anti-Christian sentiment has continued to grow in Shelton. He said that there was a rally at the mall a few days ago for a growing clan of skinheads. He's seen them here and there, but the rally was only for local skinheads and it was packed. Swastikas and anti-Jew graffiti were painted on the glass windows of the stores to set the mood of the rally. The newspaper reported that the rally speaker spewed hatred for the government as well as Christians, Jews, and any other non-Caucasian race. After the rally, the skinheads went on a rampage in town and vandalized some churches and schools. They didn't hit Grace, but they did spray paint "Jew Lover" on Dan's front porch. It seems Dan's testimony is getting around town."

"Will someone please explain to me how churches have been gagged, so as not to break any tolerance law, but skinheads can openly attack others and get away with it?" Lily's voice shook with emotion and disgust.

Mike Torey answered, "Lily, does this really surprise you? There is no such thing as equal rights and freedom of speech in America any more, at least not when it's concerning Christians."

The four couples sat in silence for a moment. Emma could hear sniffling and she guessed it was from her mother. She knew why her mom would be so upset. Dan and Betsy Dougherty were like surrogate grandparents to the Hamilton family. Lily had pleaded for them to come with them, even offering her own bedroom, saying she would sleep in the great room on a couch if she had to. They refused though, and Emma's mom understood why but it was still hard to accept. They were responsible for leading so many people in the church to Christ that if anyone could have an impact in the coming months, it would be them. The news of the vandalism on their house was probably too much for Lily to accept. She hadn't expected the persecution to start so soon.

Mr. Mason broke the silence. "We also heard some news on the radio today. It said there was a huge summit meeting of the Federation of World Powers leaders. Something big is going on and tomorrow, March fifteenth, there is going to be a big announcement in Jerusalem."

Again, silence.

Emma caught her breath, knowing the significance of the date.

"You have got to be kidding—this cannot be a coincidence, Garrett, can it?" Lily still sniffled, but clearly the conversation had taken a turn.

"When's the last time you believed in a coincidence? Was it a coincidence we all decided to move into caves we didn't even know were here? You know there is no such thing as a coincidence. You also know that we expected this. It shouldn't be a shock, but it still feels like one."

"So, what do you think the announcement will be? Do we know for sure it will be in Jerusalem? How will we find out what is . . . " At the same time it dawned on Emma, it seemed to hit her mother that the men were sober because someone was going to be sent to watch the announcement personally. That meant leaving the mountain. It also meant going into the town.

And it would be one of these men. Maybe all of them.

"We have to do this," Stan Phillips said. "With the limited radio stations we get, we have to go. It's the only way we'll know for sure. This press conference is the whole reason we are here. We'll know right away whether or not we made a mistake, but we have to see it ourselves."

Garrett jumped in. "It's not dangerous right now. We won't be recognized and we'll hardly be seen. We know there are TV screens at O'Mally's in Mount Olive. We'll swing in around 11:30 a.m. for an early lunch. The press conference is set for 7 p.m. Jerusalem time, which is noon for us, so we should be able to catch it."

"But we quit going into town a month ago when the people started asking questions about our mail deliveries and our large supply purchases. Why not send a couple of men who haven't been seen in town yet, that no one will recognize. How many of you are going, anyways?" Lily asked.

"Pete Johnson, myself, and Pastor are going, that's all," Garrett said. "Please don't worry. I am going to carry a tape recorder in my pocket so that everyone can listen to it later, but honey, I have really stuck my neck out on this one—I need to be the one to witness it."

Emma wished she could see her mom's body language. She was sure she would not be happy with this decision.

Her mother then said, "If Magorum is the Antichrist, then tomorrow he will reveal himself to the world as a man risen from the dead. We have no idea how people will respond, even in a restaurant in little Mount Olive."

Garrett's voice was gentle and calming. "But I am expecting it and will not have to worry about driving while in shock. We'll be fine and with the blanket of prayer you and the others will be weaving while I am gone, we won't have to worry about a thing."

Emma's feet were like ice by now and she had to get moving because it looked like the meeting was almost over. Quietly she stood and crept back down the hall and slid into her bed. Tomorrow really was a big day. The church had pointed to this day back at the meeting when the elders announced the move. Life had gotten busy and everyone was so caught up with cave dwelling that it was hard to believe that it was already March fifteenth.

March fifteen. One month before tax day.

March fifteen. The start of March madness.

March fifteen. The beginning of the end of the world.

Emma heard the murmuring of voices down the hallway, with snatches of conversation laced with both wonder and concern as her parents discussed the dangers of leaving the mountain, then prayed for their own safety and for that of their brothers and sisters in Shelton. Emma finally dozed off talking to the Lord about what March fifteen would actually hold in store.

———✦———

At three in the morning, Nate quietly climbed out of bed, put on his robe and slippers. He retrieved the phone from its charger and quietly opened the door. It didn't make a noise and Nate gave credit to Mack Silver for at least knowing how to WD-40 a hinge.

He carefully walked in the dark hall towards the front door and unbolted the deadlock. He left the cave and worked his way to Shiloh. He had the best reception there because of the cleared trees. There he was able to text a quick message to Sean:

> 3 snt 2 twn 2 vu anncmnt
>
> O'Mally's in Mt Olv
>
> 11:30
>
> Brng pic of Harrison 2 id
>
> Plz photo 4 file
>
> TX—NR

The message only took a minute to type and a minute to send. Nate was back in bed by 3:32 a.m. Sherrie stirred as he climbed back into bed.

"Everything all right?" She rolled over and laid her head on Nate's chest.

"Just used the restroom. Sorry I woke you."

She bent her knee and laid her leg over top of his. When she slid her foot down his shin she was surprised to find his icy toes.

"Wow! Have you ever got cold feet!" she exclaimed.

"Better today than on the day we got married! I must be getting old—you know, poor circulation …"

Sherrie's slow rhythmic breathing convinced him that she was back asleep. He lay in bed thinking about how he got where he was. He went to college and graduated near the top of his class with CPA added to his name. Three years after college, he was married and had a baby on the way. He was approached by a man in his firm who asked to go to dinner with him. He would never forget sitting across from Bill Watterson, one of the partners of the firm, and having him explain that he worked part-time for Homeland Security and one of his responsibilities was to recruit trainees. One month later, Nate was in training for a new department called the Domestic Investigations Unit. The job was conditional on anonymity and secrecy, so when he took the job, Nate had to agree to keep it from his wife.

Nate reached over and put his hand on Sherrie's shoulder. He really did love her. She was organized, efficient, and a lot of fun to be around. And she was religious. That helped his decision to take the position, because his job was to infiltrate churches and to make sure they were following the new anti-intolerance laws. For the past seventeen years Nate had reported on countless churches, staying a few months at any given location. Sherrie thought he was just a great auditor who was constantly moving from one project to another. *It's been hard on her. Some day I'll have to tell her the truth.*

Nate glanced at the clock. It was almost four. He asked himself why he had been willing to lie to her for so many years. He knew the answer. Because his work was part of a service to protect his country and he was a patriotic guy. He didn't mind moving around a lot because he felt like he was contributing to the well-being of the country.

And the job wasn't that hard. Most of the churches were pretty generic in their teaching so there wasn't any reason to stick around very long. He would write up a gen-back file, short for generic background, on each of the staff and leadership in a church. If there was any suspicious activity, like subversive teaching or purposeful evangelism, then he would stay longer to detail the violations. Only four times in nineteen years did Nate have a church closed. Other than that, some churches were fined but most were pretty compliant towards the anti-intolerance laws.

Unfortunately, an unavoidable side effect of his occupation was the fact that Sherrie had bought into the whole religion thing, hook, line, and sinker. And what could he expect? She didn't know he was working at all those Bible studies and get-togethers. She was apparently "growing in her faith" and so was he, as far as anyone could see. When Sherrie and Nate visited Grace, Nate knew there was something different there than at the other churches he had attended. He immediately recognized the intolerant verbal signals: "Jesus is the ONLY way," "pray for the lost," "witness to those who need Christ," "inerrant Word of God." All the stereotypical signals were there.

Yet there was something different that he hadn't heard at any church in fifteen years—their end-times teaching. It was everywhere. In most sermons it was at least alluded to if not harped on. All the other churches either didn't even address current events or dismissed the coming of Christ as an event for which no one could prepare. They believed He would return at any moment, remove the church, and then God would start judging the world for a final seven-year period. But not Grace.

It was Grace's end-times theology that kept him lying awake in a cave. It was so radically different that he told his superior that there may be a suicide cult brewing among this group. They were willing to sell everything and "hide" while waiting for Christ to return. At one meeting, Nate expected trial-sized cups of Kool-Aid to be handed out. Though technically they weren't breaking the laws, Nate thought they were a potential danger to themselves.

So he contacted his superior, Sean Aumonti. He explained about the church's exit strategy. He wanted to move with the church members rather than stay in Shelton. Sean allowed Nate to continue his investigation, sensing that this might be a bigger fish than the others they had hooked.

Now, as he lay in the dark, the anticipation for tomorrow's announcement weighed heavily on Nate's mind. Here these people had talked about something big on March fifteen and now there is actually some kind of announcement? Can that possibly be a coincidence? Nate, who rarely prayed because he wasn't convinced anyone was on the receiving end, carelessly whispered a prayer.

"If You're really out there, could You arrange it for me to go and hear the announcement for myself? Maybe that would help me believe. Amen."

Worst case scenario, nothing happens down here and eventually these people disband and go home. Best case scenario, Nate stops a mass suicide and gets a book deal. Then he could come clean with the truth to his wife and retire on the royalties and paid speaking engagements. I mean, how many DIU agents actually saved the lives of helpless, brainwashed cult members?

He closed his eyes, imagining the title of his future book—*Cult Uncovered: the Infiltration and Salvation of Grace. No, too long. How about, Saving Grace: a DIU Agent's Memoirs. Yeah, I like that. Saving Grace. Now, if I could only convince myself that these people down here are actually helpless and brainwashed, maybe I could get some sleep.*

Morning came sooner than Nate ever expected. At 5:00 a.m. there was a knock on his door.

"Yes?" Nate answered groggily.

"Nate, it's me, Pam."

Nate recognized Pete Johnson's wife's voice.

"Anything wrong?" he asked as he sat up.

"Yeah, kind of. You know how Pete was supposed to go with Garrett and Pastor this morning to Mount Olive for the announcement?"

"Yeah." Nate's heart began to race.

"Well, Pete got hit with the flu early this morning around four and he still is throwing up. Pete didn't think the other two should go alone, so he asked me to see if you wanted to go. The guys are meeting at the quad shed at five thirty. What do you think?"

"Are you kidding? I'll be there! Thanks, Pam, and oh, tell Pete I'm sorry he's sick, but I appreciate him asking me to go."

"He said he could tell by the look on your face last night that you wanted to be there. Be safe and hurry back."

The door shut and Nate sat there for a moment.

"Well, you'd better throw your jeans on, dear. It's 5:07."

Nate leaned over and kissed Sherrie on the forehead. He threw on his clothes and ran down to the bathroom to wash his face and brush his teeth. He grabbed a muffin from the kitchen and headed out to the shed where the quads were stored, then he stopped a minute. He could hardly believe that it was truly a god who answered his prayer, but just in case he had better thank him.

"Um, thanks for hearing me last night. I feel a bit guilty about getting Pete sick, but there's not much I can do about that now. Uh, and thanks for the muffin. Coffee would have been nice too, but beggars can't be choosers. Amen."

"Who are you talking to?"

Nate turned and saw Garrett walking towards him with a flashlight in one hand and two travel mugs of coffee in his other.

"Uh, Pete got the flu and asked if I would go in his place. Any problem with that?"

"Not for me. It's this way." He handed Nate a cup of coffee and added, "Pete always has cream and sugar, so you're stuck with his order."

Nate took the coffee and in his head added another thank you to his prayer. He let Garrett lead the way, though he knew full well where the shed was located. He hadn't spent much time with the pastor or Garrett, though he knew just about everything they had ever done. He knew how much they made since they were in high school, how many speeding tickets they were given, whether or not they had debt and even where their favorite restaurant was. He was definitely thorough in his research, plus he had government records at his fingertips. He wondered what he would talk with them about on the two hour drive into town.

As they walked, Garrett turned to him. "How are you guys doing in your cave? You've only been here a week, right?"

"We're doing all right. Sherrie really likes Pam Johnson—she knew her before the move—and that has really helped."

"So you're settling in too?"

"Yeah, I've been helping at the Tabernacle. My father used to be a furniture maker and I picked up a few pointers from him back in the day. Mack was talking about benches or pews and I have some ideas for those."

Up ahead, Pastor Gentings stood in the doorway of the shed, three machines already pulled out and ready to go.

"Great! I've heard about that. And how're your kids doing?"

"I've only got one son and apparently he's been hanging out with some kids he met. I think that will help overall."

Garrett finished the conversation with one final question.

"What's your boy's name?"

"Oh, sorry about that. His name is Adam."

eight

15 *March, 7:00 a.m.*

Moscow, Russia.

Magorum took one last look in his mirror. Everything had to be perfect today. After fifty-three years of hiding his face, he only had nine hours left. Then never again. The whole world would know who he is and they would bow. One way or another, they would bow.

He crossed the hall from his bedroom and entered his study. The candles were still lit on the table. He shut the door behind him.

"I'm here for final instructions."

He sat and waited. Minutes ticked by with no movement or noise. The second hand on his watch became annoyingly loud. Yet he sat. He didn't move. He knew the drill. He would come when he was good and ready. It was kind of a test—if Magorum showed impatience, he would wait longer. If he sat quietly, he would come more quickly.

A warm breeze passed through the room and Magorum stood. It swirled around Magorum's feet a couple of times then shot up and around his head. It whisked through the chandelier in the center of the room, rustling the curtains and bending the candlelight. When it calmed down, he spoke.

"I saved you from the pit for this day. Do you remember your last home?"

"That was my past. I choose to remember it no more. I look only to my future and the opportunity to serve my savior."

"Remembering isn't all bad, you know. Like remembering who gave you a second chance and remembering the Enemy, the One who put you in torment. Today, what you will reveal to the world will drop all men to their knees. It is something no one has ever seen before and may cause you to forget your past. Don't ever forget. I can give life and I will certainly take it away if necessary."

Magorum didn't even wince at those words. He was sold out to the plan. Nothing would make him deviate.

"Master, you have my undying devotion."

"It is time for passion, my friend. Like the old days. Get the crowd stirred with your words. I have made promises to you that you have seen fulfilled. Today you will not be alone. I will be with you, more than I ever have been before. I will empower you and I will give you signs that men will never be able to explain! I have also prepared Szabo for his role in your administration. He will be of great support to you. He will perform wonders that will assure the world of your ability to reign. After today this world will never be the same!"

Magorum took a deep breath and closed his eyes. He could hear the wind stirring in the far corner of the room. It flew with great speed directly at him, like a great eagle diving at its prey, and then stopped inches in front of his face.

"Open your eyes, my child. I want you to see this."

Magorum slowly opened his eyes. Before him floated the most beautiful and yet terrifying image he had ever beheld. The Morning Star, created more beautiful than all, hovered in front of his face. He had flowing golden locks that glowed like embers at the ends. His hair seemed to fill the room and waved gently in the air. His eyes were endless black holes, casting a look of determination, rebellion, and evil all at one time. For a brief instant Magorum feared falling into the vast blackness, but the fear was fleeting and he refocused on the angel's face. His jaw line was massive, as if he could swallow a man whole if necessary and his lips seemed to be on fire. His body disappeared in a misty cloud as he hovered in front of Magorum.

Magorum tilted his head back, afraid to blink, eyes fixed on the creature. The being lowered himself, as if taunting Magorum, and then in an instant, he vaporized into two streams of mist. He entered into Magorum's nostrils and filled every vacant space with his being, literally from head to toe. Magorum took a deep breath, as if he could help him get the job done quicker, but Lucifer had already taken up residence before the breath was completed.

Now he was ready. Magorum glanced at his watch. It was time to go. Not that they would leave without him. He chuckled to himself. In his head, the laughter was deeper and more commanding than ever.

nine

Nate, Garrett, and Pastor Gentings climbed on the quads and headed to the vehicle storage site. Since no one had gone down the mountain in a month, the paths to the unit were completely covered in snow, but the men knew where they were going. Garrett told Nate they all had to be careful not to travel on the same path, so as not to create a permanent route to the caves.

The vehicle storage site was on the opposite side of the mountain as the cave openings and it took about two and a half hours of riding to get to it. By 8:30 a.m. the men were heading down the dirt road towards Mount Olive.

"Do you mind cranking the heat?" Pastor Gentings asked Garrett from the backseat.

Nate had offered to sit in the back, but Pastor insisted on giving Nate the joy of sitting in front.

"I've ridden up front with Garrett all too often and my doctor said my heart can't take the excitement anymore!"

Soon the heat was blasting and they thawed out their hands from the cold ride.

"It's going to take a couple of hours," Garrett said to Nate.

"Yeah, I remember," Nate said.

"I wanted to give us some extra time, in case a tree is down on the road or something. You never know what you'll find out here."

The warmth in the car was making Nate drowsy and he took off his coat.

The sun was rising and the woods had an eerie glow to them. Pastor broke the silence.

"So, Nate, tell us about your past."

Nate took a deep breath and began to tell his prefabricated history. He'd done it so often it was second nature to him now. Lately, it was harder to lie, but if he focused on his wife and son, it was mostly truth and that was easier to stomach.

Rory Appleton aimed for the snooze button on his alarm clock with his right hand. Squinting, he picked up the clock and brought it close to his face. 8:45 a.m. He had allowed himself to sleep in because of the late elders' meeting two nights ago followed by dinner with the interim pastor last night. But it was the elders' meeting that filled his thoughts. With a satisfied sigh, he lay back on his pillow and recalled the closing prayer of his dear friend, Bill Baker.

"And finally, Father, we pray for our friends who have left us. Open their eyes to the lies of their leadership. We are so grateful for Your raising up of Rory and the direction he has given Grace in light of the disastrous decisions of our past leadership. Thank You for purging the church and protect those who blindly followed as sheep."

"Those poor sheep in North Carolina," Rory murmured to himself. "Technically they are still members of Grace Church of Shelton. Perhaps I should drive down there and see if . . . "

"Who are you talking to in there?" called Donna from the bathroom.

"Just thinking out loud, dear," he replied.

"You got home so late last night—did dinner go well with the new pastor?"

"Interim pastor. Ray is great. It's such a breath of fresh air not to have to battle Gentings anymore! We were having such a good time last night that we didn't realize how late it was. You're really going to like him."

"Why do you say that?"

"Because he's very practical and funny. You won't struggle to stay awake each week like you usually do."

Donna just grunted, obviously choosing to let his comment go. "What were you just saying about North Carolina?"

"Since I am the chairman of the elder board now, I believe I have a spiritual responsibility to check on those misguided members."

Donna stepped from the bathroom into the doorway of the bedroom, half her head still covered in curlers.

"They're going to know soon enough they made a big mistake. Rather than visit them, you elders should come up with a plan of what you are going to do when they all come crawling back into town, looking for jobs and homes. You know they are going to expect us to bail them out. You should tell them, 'tough luck—you made your bed so sleep in it.' It's not our job to clean up their mess."

She disappeared back into the bathroom and, with a yawn, Rory sat up and stretched. "Well, if you aren't the voice of compassion today. Here's what I was thinking. If I can find out exactly where they are and do go down there, the people will know they have the opportunity to return and that we care about them. It's really not their fault they followed Gentings and his posse of arrogant men. I think it would really eat away at him if people came back home now."

He swung his feet over the edge of the bed and stood.

"Did you remember that today is their big day? This is supposed to be the Antichrist-reveals-himself-to-the-world day. March fifteen. I haven't turned on the news yet, but I did notice the moon hasn't turned to blood and the sun is still in the sky."

Donna chuckled. It annoyed him that she always laughed at her own jokes.

Rory walked into the bathroom, and stood in front of his sink. Donna was finishing her hair at the far sink. He looked in the mirror.

Yeah, I remember this is their big day. It's a big day for me too. It's the day everybody will have to admit I was right.

Adam was sitting at the kitchen table eating his bowl of Frosted Flakes when his mother came in the room.

"Devotions are at Shiloh again this morning. We need to get over there by nine."

"What time is it now?" Nate scooped another large spoonful in his mouth.

"8:37. Will you be ready?"

"Yeah. I'll hurry," he said, shoving in another spoonful. "So, what's going on?"

"First of all, your dad was awakened this morning and they asked him to go with Garrett Hamilton and Pastor Gentings to hear the announcement. Dad was thrilled. Imagine all that time in the car with those men, and to hear the announcement. It's a double blessing."

"Mom, those guys put their pants on one leg at a time, just like you and Dad."

"Yeah, but they are true men of God. They could be a great influence on your father. Anyways, because of their trip to town, the church wanted to have a prayer time for them."

"Sounds great."

Adam finished his cereal and headed to the bathroom. Luckily it was empty. He turned on the shower, stuck his head under the spray, and quickly washed his hair. Then he trotted to his room, pulled on a clean T-shirt and some jeans. By the time he got over to Shiloh, the devotions had already begun. He spotted Emma sitting with her mother and forced himself to wait until later to say hi.

After a few songs, Mike Torey got up and called for a time of prayer.

"We don't know what the outcome will be today, but we do know it is in God's hands. If Magorum doesn't reveal his true identity and intentions, we may be on the wrong track here. I spoke with Pastor Gentings before he left and he said, even if it's not what we think it is, we aren't going to make any quick decisions. Our timing could be off." He paused, his gaze sweeping across the upturned faces before him. "If we're right, we are entering a time of great tribulation like the world has never seen. Like the church has never before experienced. We need to pray for the church, our family members who wouldn't come, and for those we love in Shelton, who continue to offer help to the body."

A few *amens* arose from here and there. After about fifteen minutes of prayer in small groups, the music began again. Several of the men had brought their guitars and before long, the songs of the saints seemed to rise and fill the woods with a sweet melody of salvation and praise:

> *You're not only Savior*
> *You're not only Father*
> *You're not only Ruler of the heavens and the earth*
> *You're not only Faithful*
> *You're not only Wonderful*
> *You're not only Giver of the grace that will restore*
> *You are all of these things and so much more*
> *You are the Lord! You are the Lord!*

When the last note faded, Mike continued. "'And he will make a firm covenant with the many for one week, but in the middle of the week he will put a stop to sacrifice and grain offering; and on the wing of abominations will come one who makes desolate, even until a complete destruction, one that is decreed, is poured out on the one who makes desolate.' That's Daniel's prophecy in chapter nine where he speaks about what we believe is going to happen today."

Mike paused and looked around. He had everyone's attention, even the little ones on their mother's laps. Adam felt a chill run through his body and he wasn't sure if it was the significance of those words or just the cool chill of the air.

"We know that a 'week' is a seven-year period. The halfway point is when the Antichrist reveals his true identity and begins his plan to kill every Jew and Christian on the face of the earth. Satan believes that if he can wipe out all of God's children before Christ returns, then he can keep the title to the earth, but we know the ending."

A hallelujah was called out from Adam's far left.

"From the covenant that Magorum signed with Israel up to today, exactly three and a half years have passed. It is not a coincidence that he has a press conference on the steps of the temple in Jerusalem today. What happens after this will be the church's greatest nightmare."

Mike paused and Adam watched the youth pastor fight back tears. Adam felt ashamed that the consequences of the tribulation didn't seem to arouse any emotion in him. He was safe. He had friends here. The food was good. What happened off the mountain really wasn't his problem. But seeing Mike moved to tears gave Adam reason to pause.

"Is there a chance we're wrong? We'll know after today, but we're exactly where we need to be if we're right. Jesus said, 'When you see the ABOMINATION OF DESOLATION which was spoken of through Daniel the prophet, standing in the holy place . . . , then those who are in Judea must flee to the mountains. Whoever is on the housetop must not go down to get the things out that are in his house . . . For then there will be a great tribulation, such as has not occurred since the beginning of the world until now, nor ever will.'

"Jesus gave ample warning and we have taken heed. By one o'clock this afternoon, Garrett, Nate, and Pastor should know what we're all anxiously waiting to find out. We need to be together today. We need to be praying for their safety, as well as those we left in Shelton. We need to pray for the church and we need to pray for Israel."

Another round of *amens* surrounded Adam.

"On a lighter note—I have some good news. It seems that we are just about ready to use the Tabernacle. If the men and high school boys give me a couple of hours today, I think we can meet there tonight!"

Spontaneous applause broke out and Adam noticed people were smiling again.

"Let's plan on an early dinner tonight and meet at the Tabernacle at six to hear from the men. The sound system is working, so hopefully we can listen to their tape and hear the announcement ourselves. Or maybe we will decide we need to pack up. I highly doubt that, but we do need to hear from them and rather than let the news spread like wildfire, let's do it together."

As the families wandered away from Shiloh, Adam caught Emma's eye. She had smiled at him when he came in and now she gave him an even bigger smile. Emma worked her way over to him and he could tell she was being careful not to trip on any logs.

She tucked an errant strand behind her ear. "So, did you bring one of your stories for me?"

He couldn't help smiling at her. "I didn't even think about it. Got up too late," he explained. "I was going to head over to the Tabernacle, but we could go by my place get the story first—if you'd like."

"Sure, let me tell my mom."

As she turned to find her mother, Adam touched her arm. She looked back at him. "Was there any fallout from your being late last night?"

"No, everyone was so preoccupied with today's announcement, I didn't even have to lie. Which, by the way, I don't enjoy doing." There was a playful tone in her voice, but her eyes said she wasn't joking.

"I feel pretty awful about that. I told you I wasn't going to put you in that position, and I mean it." He grinned. "Honest."

"Yeah, you did." She smiled into his eyes, which caused that heart problem to start up again. "Wait here and I'll tell my mom where I'm going." Emma ran over to her mother, chatted for a minute, then her mother looked at her watch.

"All set?" Adam asked when Emma returned.

"Yeah, no problem."

As the two made their way to Adam's cave, Adam asked, "Have you named your cave yet?"

"Named?"

"Yeah, named. I mean, if we're going to be here for a couple of years, we might as well name the cave. It's much nicer to say, 'I'm going back to Tara,' rather than 'I'm going back to the cave!'"

"You named your cave 'Tara,' from *Gone with the Wind*?"

"That was what my mom suggested but she was overruled. There were actually a lot of good suggestions: Grand Central Station, The Money Pit, South Fork—another of Mom's suggestions after some lame TV show nobody has ever even seen—Wuthering Heights, Bedlam, and oh, my personal favorite, Disney World, submitted by one of the little ones in the cave." He halted mid step and pointed to a log. "Careful here."

She smiled. "So . . . what name did you pick?"

"Petra."

"Petra?"

"It means 'rock.' Clever, huh?"

Emma nodded but her quizzical look remained.

"The real Petra is a city carved out of a mountainside in Jordan. It was occupied by nomadic Arabs, and Rome tried several times to take it over but was unsuccessful. To get there you have to literally travel through mountain crevasses—it's really a spectacular city. But being in a mountain and all, I thought it fit my cave perfectly. I have a book with a picture in it, if you want to see it."

"So, you were actually reading a book and learned this?"

"Yeah, I used to do my homework back in my old life."

"And you came up with the name?"

"Yeah, and I stuffed the ballot box so it would win."

Emma laughed and Adam reached for her hand to help her over another large log. After she was safely over, Adam held on to her hand a bit longer.

"Do you mind . . . ?"

Emma blushed and pulled her hand away. "I'll make you a deal. You can hold my hand when you come up with a name for my house which is just as good as Petra!"

Adam's eyes twinkled. "Deal. That'll be easy."

When they arrived at Petra, Emma waited in the family room as Adam poked his head in the kitchen to tell his mother that she was there. As Sherrie Reed walked out of the kitchen, she told Adam he needed to run a quick errand for her.

"Mr. Johnson headed over to the Tabernacle, even though he isn't feeling well. He asked if he could borrow Dad's boots—his were still wet from yesterday and he doesn't want to walk around with damp feet all day. I don't know what Dad was wearing when he left this morning, but he has an extra pair. Would you go see if you can find them, then take them to Mr. Johnson?" She turned to Emma. "Hi, Emma. You haven't been here yet. Would you like a tour?"

Adam interrupted. "Mom, I think I am going to stay and help too. So I'll walk Emma home and then run to the Tabernacle."

His mother agreed, and while she showed Emma around the cave, Adam ran down the hallway to his bedroom. He changed into his work jeans and grabbed his latest story for Emma. Then he went down the hall to his parents' room.

He went to the closet, stooped, and rummaged through his father's shoes. Toward the back were two sets of work boots. He picked up the first, then noticed the other pair was cleaner. As he reached for them he saw something that looked like a cord sticking out of one of the boots. He pulled on it, surprised to find that it was connected to something heavy.

Adam sat down on the floor and placed the boot onto his lap, then reached into the boot and pulled out a battery charger.

He sat back, stunned. He knew exactly what it connected to. And he knew his father had no business having one. Cell phones were forbidden.

ten

After the first hour of small talk in the car, Pastor Gentings turned the conversation to the topic at hand.

"Garrett, it's time to put your vote in."

"What are you talking about?" Garrett glanced in his rearview mirror at Pastor in the backseat.

"Who's it going to be?"

"Uh . . . still lost."

"Come on, don't play dumb! It's been a major topic of conversation between my wife and me, and I am sure you and Lily have a theory."

Nate was starting to figure out the relationship between this pastor and this elder. They were apparently close friends who enjoyed a camaraderie that came from a longtime relationship. Plus they teased each other easily.

Garrett didn't flinch. "I don't know where you're going with this one."

"Who's the Antichrist going to be?"

Nate jumped in. "Magorum, right?"

Nate saw a look flash between the pastor and Garrett in the rearview mirror, and he knew he had answered wrong.

Pastor said, "Sorry, Nate. Of course you're right, but I'm talking about Magorum revealing who he really is."

"Now, I'm the one who's lost. What do you mean?"

"Scripture tells us that when the Antichrist desecrates the temple, he also reveals that he is a man who is raised from the dead."

"What? Where does it say that?"

"It's in Revelation thirteen and seventeen," said Garrett. "One says he is a man who used to rule over a nation which persecuted Israel in the past and the other says he died of a head wound. When he reveals who he is, he'll show the scar from that wound and the whole world will recognize and believe."

"So," Pastor Gentings said, "looking at the past nations who persecuted Israel, you get a list of six for sure and a possible seventh. Egypt, Babylon, the Medes and Persians, Assyria, Greece, and Rome." He counted the nations on his fingers. "The seventh could be Germany because they killed more Jews than any of the other nations, even though Israel was out of the land."

"So, who are your options? Only leaders who died with head wounds, right?" asked Nate.

"It really boils down to two—Nero and Hitler," answered Garrett. "My wife and I lean towards Hitler, just for the world recognition factor."

"We do too," added Pastor.

"So, let me get this straight. You both think that today at the press conference, Magorum is going to say that he's really Hitler?"

"Crazy, huh?" Garrett's face held a strange smile as he spoke.

"Well, we'll know shortly," Nate said, "but I've got to tell you, there's no way the world will embrace Hitler. If it has to happen literally, I think Nero is a better choice, because following someone who says he was once dead and thinks they were Nero in a past life, is more plausible." He shook his head at the mere thought of it.

"I agree it will be an unbelievable turn of events," said Pastor. "But you're assuming that Hitler is hated all over the world. Hitler is a hero to some. I saw a YouTube video of Iran's army marching in the form of a swastika. There are whole nations who deny the Holocaust ever happened. Hitler was a masterful speaker and he convinced a whole nation to follow him."

Garrett continued. "And you're missing a big piece of the puzzle. This guy is going to be driven and controlled by Satan and his demons. A third of the angelic realm fell with Satan and that's a huge force supporting the Antichrist. When all of Satan's efforts are focused on the success of this one man, you won't believe what he can accomplish. Don't let anything surprise you."

Garrett nodded towards the coming sign. It read Mount Olive 22 MILES. Nate glanced at his watch. "We're making good time."

"Yeah," said Garrett. "We'll be there in less than half an hour. If we're early, we can run over to Wal-Mart and get a gift for the women. Maybe then Lily won't be so mad that I came."

Pastor laughed and reached over the front seat and patted Nate on the shoulder.

"I know this sounds unbelievable, maybe even ridiculous. But it's not my plan, and it's not my prophecy. God is in control of this and He knows the hearts of men. Why is this happening now? Maybe it's because the hearts of men are now prepared to accept a risen Hitler or Nero. Maybe it's a risen Pharaoh, but I doubt it. I can't say stranger things have happened, but I won't let this surprise me. I believe it because God's Word says it."

"I heard once that the Antichrist was not a person, but that it was more of a sentiment against Christians and Jews. Doesn't that make more sense?" Nate was no longer keeping up a front, but was truly into the conversation.

"No, because Scripture gives too much physical description for it to be a mindset or a nation. *He* will take his seat in the temple. *He* will reveal his head wound." Pastor Gentings stopped and cleared his throat. "The first time Christ came, he fulfilled every prophecy literally. Why wouldn't He do that with His second coming?"

The men rode the last fifteen minutes in silence. Occasionally Garrett would make a comment to Pastor, but Nate wasn't paying attention. What in the world was he going to see today? How can these two guys seriously expect Magorum to be someone other than the Russian leader he's already proven to be? Are they really so warped that they expect to see him pull off a mask, like on Mission Impossible, and reveal he's Nero? Or heaven forbid, Hitler?

They drove into town forty minutes early and, not wanting to arrive at the restaurant right away, filled the car with gas and, as Garrett suggested, stopped by the store for a few gifts for their wives and families. Nate picked up some DVDs that he knew Adam would appreciate, and he bought every box of Ziplock bags he could find. He had heard the women say that they hadn't brought a big enough supply of them and were starting to reuse the ones they had. It was a considerate gift and made it look like he was planning on staying a while. He always had to play the game. He also bought Sherrie a bottle of perfume.

The men walked into O'Mally's at 11:41 a.m. and were seated in a booth on the far right side of the room. The televisions were already on. Three large projector screens showed three separate stations, one European soccer game, one ESPN highlights, and thankfully, the third was on CNN. Garrett switched the channel control dial to the third screen and the men could clearly hear the newscast.

Nate sat in the booth next to the pastor. Images of the bronze altar in front of the temple in Jerusalem were already flashing across the screen. Various news stations had gathered at the base of the steps of the altar, roped off at least twenty feet from the large podium set up for the press conference. There was a lot of activity and movement among the reporters, and a crowd that seemed to number in the hundreds had gathered to hear Magorum speak.

Nate glanced around the near empty restaurant and noticed a man sitting alone in the corner on the opposite side of the room. Their eyes met briefly before the man looked away. He lifted his cup of coffee and took a sip.

That must be him.

The waitress blocked Garrett's view as she took the man's order. Then she made her way over to their table.

"You three know what you're ordering yet?" She looked tired already and it was only 11:30 a.m.

Garrett grinned. "We'll all have cheeseburgers and fries. With Cokes all around. It's been a while since I've had a big, half-pound, greasy burger and fries, and I'm going to make the most of it."

Nate nodded and shot another look at the man in the corner booth. He hoped the booth was tapped and the man would get it all.

Thinking what a great scene this would make in his book, Nate sat back and sipped his water.

Rory Appleton rushed into his kitchen and grabbed the remote off the counter.

"Hon, can you fix a quick sandwich?"

"Yeah, what's"—

"There's a news conference at noon. Ray Bower just called and told me about it. I don't think it's anything but, well, you know, I'm a little jumpy today. Get me a diet too."

Rory flipped on MSNBC just as they were breaking for a commercial. It was 11:56 a.m.

"So, where're you guys from? I don't recognize you."

The waitress had returned with the Cokes and was making small talk. Nate could tell that Garrett and Pastor were not in the mood to talk. The commercial would be over any second and they didn't want to miss any of the announcement.

"Um, just passing through. Thanks." Garrett reached for his drink.

"You got Michigan plates?"

"Yeah."

"So you're from Michigan?"

"Yeah."

"Well, what're you doing down this"—

"Melanie, your order's up!" The waitress turned to leave and Nate saw Garrett flash a look at Pastor.

"Just in time," Garrett said under his breath.

Nate glanced over at the table in the corner. Melanie was now making small talk with the man in the corner. I hope she doesn't distract him too.

The commercial ended and the reporter's voice was heard with the picture of a well-miked podium in the middle of the screen.

"If you are just joining us, we are all awaiting the arrival of the members of the Federation of World Powers. At seven o'clock here in Jerusalem, President Alexander Magorum of Russia will be addressing the world with a joint statement from the FWP members. We know their planes arrived just about three hours ago in Tel Aviv and—um, excuse me, just a moment . . . "

The picture scanned over to the reporter as he put his hand to his ear, apparently receiving a message in his earpiece.

"Um, this is quite unusual. There has been a last minute change. Apparently, the announcement will be held inside the temple with only a few of us reporters being invited to video it. Thankfully, CNN is on the list. Uh, we're going to break to a commercial, so we have time to set up, and then we'll be right back. This is Austin Stone reporting for CNN."

The screen showed a dancing lizard selling insurance, and Nate looked at Garrett and Pastor.

"Not really a surprise, would you say?" Garrett asked.

"I was wondering how he would desecrate the holy place from outside, but I wasn't going to be the one to say it!" Pastor Gentings said.

"What a day." A low whistle escaped Garrett's lips.

"Yeah," Nate said. He was a bit confused, but he was going with the flow.

Alexander Magorum had given Ferco Szabo a list of handpicked reporters who would be given the privilege of covering the announcement. He was standing at the far end of the temple, in front of a small incense altar and a heavy, large curtain. Prime Minister Rabin was bounding down the center of the temple, obviously fuming about the change of venue.

"President Magorum! What is the meaning of this! You cannot be in here—this is a holy site for my people and you are desecrating the temple! Even I am desecrating the temple by being in here!"

"Calm down, my friend." Magorum put a hand on Rabin's shoulder. "Since we're already in here and the temple will have to be cleansed, we might as well have our press conference in here."

Behind them the door opened and the privileged reporters and their cameramen began to enter. Rabin turned.

"No! No! Out! Out!" he yelled, but it soon became clear events had moved beyond his control.

Magorum spoke again. "What I am about to announce to the world will change the world forever."

"Yes, I know that a one world currency is just one step away from a one-world government. That still doesn't give you the right to desecrate our temple! How will I explain this to my people?"

"Your weakness is revealed in a crisis. My strength is increased in a crisis. That is the difference between you and me. Now we must prepare for the conference. I gave you this land. The least you can do is give me thirty minutes inside the temple."

Magorum turned his back on a still fuming Rabin and tried to clear his mind. He would deal with Rabin sooner than Rabin expected. He glanced around the room and took in the sight. The main room of the temple was completely overlaid with gold. There were gold plated braids and vines running the length of the room on the ceiling and burning candelabras lining the room on both sides. In front of the candles were tables with baskets of unleavened bread. There was no other light source in the room and the cameramen were grateful they didn't need additional power. A large spotlight and microphone system was being set up for Magorum so he would be seen and heard clearly.

Magorum took his place at the microphone. The reporters were ushered to their places within fifteen feet of him. Rabin had quieted and was now standing to his left, looking pale. Szabo moved into his place on Magorum's right and the eight other FWP leaders stood behind the three men. Along each side of the room, the priests of the temple in full costume lined the walls, murmuring with obvious concern.

Magorum nodded to the guards at the doors. They opened the temple doors and in an orderly manner, the public filled the room. Reporters who were not invited to film then entered, madly writing all they saw on paper tablets, cameras left outside. In addition to the public, reporters, and priests, a heavy security presence, organized by the FWP military, was also in place. Within five minutes the room was full and an uneasy quiet reigned.

The cameraman directly in front of Magorum held up his hand and counted down on his fingers from five. At the number one, a red light flashed and the cameraman pointed to Magorum. He waited a beat, took a deep breath, and spoke.

"I want to thank you for your patience tonight. A last minute change caused quite a commotion, but when we are done I am sure you will understand everything."

Alexander Magorum paused a beat and continued.

"Today I stand before you as a world leader who has earned the trust of his comrades. Six years ago I took office in Russia and I set out to draw the world together for the sake of peace. Today my leadership and programs have spoken loudly and clearly. I am a man of my word. Now I have the support of the men standing behind me and their respective nations."

He turned and nodded to the leaders behind him. They nodded in return, smug and secure looks on all of their faces. He turned back to the mike.

"My accomplishments have brought peace where none could be found. Third world nations, such as Somalia and Nigeria no longer fear civil war. Their governments have stabilized and have received financial and physical help from the Federation of World Powers. China and North Korea no longer threaten the world with nuclear development. I have persuaded them to turn their focus from aggression towards peace. I have shown them the benefits of contributing to a cause, rather than threatening the cause. Israel enjoys freedom like it never has before. The children no longer carry gas masks to school in their lunch boxes. They live without threat of Arab aggression. Why is that? Because I have protected them."

Another pause for effect. They were hanging on his every word.

"True leadership starts with people following. The Arab nations who have chosen to follow are in and of themselves leaders. They have shown the world that peace can be attained. I respect the Arab people. They are a culture with vision. They will be great allies to me in the days ahead. Since peace has arrived in the Middle East, what is stopping the world from uniting? Tonight I promise, the world WILL live in peace."

With that statement, a cheer burst forth from the crowd. They loved him. He was a great leader. He had done everything he claimed, so why wouldn't they love him?

"Today, my fellow members of the Federation of World Powers have joined me in making a financial alliance. We will distribute to each government leader as well as the news agencies our formal agreement to consolidate our monetary system. This alliance is for the benefit of the economic growth and security of our respective nations. I have always believed that great are the tasks of the national government in the sphere of economic life. As of yesterday, our ten nations have begun the process of unifying our currency, and we invite the rest of the world to follow suit."

Magorum turned and looked at his fellow leaders. They inclined their heads toward him with confidence, having no idea what he was going to say next.

"My dear friends believe this is what I called this meeting for. However, there is more."

Garrett flashed a look at Nate and Pastor sitting across the table from him. No one had even noticed that the burgers had arrived.

So, does he pull his mask off now? Nate wondered to himself.

"I was once a man who failed his people. I made promises that I could not keep. In the end it cost me my life. I have not made those mistakes this time around. I have not turned the world against me. I have systematically proven that my vision is pure and my motives are true.

"There is power in the masses, power in vision, and power in aggression. Today I come before you with the support of the masses, applied vision, and the aggression to accomplish my goals. But I also have a power source that before today has never fully been realized."

A small drop of sweat appeared on Magorum's forehead. His eyes pierced the camera lenses with undaunted nerve. His breath remained controlled, yet his voice rose in strength and volume.

"Today, I will hide no longer. What I am about to reveal is not meant to turn you away but to explain why my efforts to unify the world have been successful. I am not the man you think I am. I am greater than Alexander Magorum could ever be, for I have a power that soars beyond human capacity. I once dreamed of a superhuman race that could defeat death itself. Today, I will prove to the world once again that I am a man of my word."

Magorum stepped back from the microphone and stood perfectly still before the audience. He slowly raised his hands out from his sides until they were parallel with the ground, palms up, forming the shape of a cross. He dropped his head backwards and began to tremble. A gasp spread through the crowd.

Suddenly the doors to the temple swung open and then slammed shut, as if a draft had quickly pulled them closed. The crowd turned their heads just as a wind blew through the room and swirled around them like a warm whirlpool of air. It extinguished the candles, so that the whole room went dark, except for the spotlight on Magorum. Women put their hands to their heads as their hair blew wildly in the wind and the cameramen fought to keep the cameras still.

The wind circled several times through the crowd and then worked its way to the front of the room. It wasn't a blowing force, but a specific channel of air, like a river, purposefully winding its way through the room. Once it reached the front of the room it swirled around the leaders, who struggled to remain calm. Then it pulled away from them and began to twirl around the feet of Magorum. He did not move. He reveled in the chill of the moving air. The wind slowly worked its way up his body, like a twister swallowing its prey, until his whole body was a twirling, swirling blur of color.

Magorum let out a cry, not in pain but victory. It echoed through the golden room and the onlookers froze in anticipation. Then the wind lowered itself until it only wrapped around his feet. Then, as quickly as it entered the room, it flew through the crowd towards the door, knocking over two unprepared women in its path. The doors opened just in time, the wind made a roaring exit and the doors slammed shut again. The room was completely quiet and the air was heavy and still.

All heads returned their gaze to Magorum, but he was gone. In his place stood a man of similar build but completely different face. A face that seemed familiar, yet out of place . . .

Nate stared at the television. He could hear Garrett pray under his breath, "Oh God, please . . . "

" . . . have mercy on us all!" The blood drained from Rory Appleton's face as the man on the stage began to speak again.

"Yes, that's right. No need to adjust your televisions. It is truly as you see!"

The crowd gasped again when they clearly heard his accent. Clear. Harsh. German.

"I told the world I could defeat death and today I am living proof of that very fact. Please do not be afraid—I have come to bring true and lasting peace on earth."

Adolph Hitler turned and faced his comrades in arms. He could have warned them, but chose to share their response with the whole world. Szabo glowed in pride and respect, but in actuality he was prepared. Hitler watched the rest struggle to remain composed. Most kept a pleasant look on their faces, but Hitler was sure their minds were racing with the consequences of their alliance. Only one turned green and raised a hand to his stomach. Hitler would have to remember that the Ukraine was a country of weak leaders.

Hitler's eyes settled on Rabin. Rabin was not in the alliance as yet, but he did have a covenant with him. Rabin's face was blank but Hitler could see the vein in Rabin's temple pulsing heavily.

"Quite a surprise, wouldn't you say?" he said to Rabin. He turned back to the microphone. "By now, many of you are wondering if this is a trick, a staged drama to produce a response. I assure you, it is nothing of the sort—death has been swallowed up in my victory."

He turned his head sideways and lifted the hair behind his right ear, revealing a scar about the size of a quarter, from the bullet that took his life years ago. He heard the cameramen shuffle to zoom in on the spot, though he was sure most had no idea what they were focusing on. He counted on the network reporters later using their resources to figure out the significance of the scar.

Adolph Hitler turned again to the crowd and gave them time to quiet down. The dull murmur, a mixture of disbelief and horror, died down and he continued with an explanation only he truly understood.

"In this world there are obstacles to face and overcome. Politics alone pit man against man. But what if man could unite? Set aside their differences for a purpose greater than any individual? The Enemy is no longer a man or a nation, or even a group of dissidents. I have discovered the true Enemy of mankind, and I am here today to call mankind to unite! As one we can defeat the ultimate Enemy!"

Hitler took a handkerchief out of his pocket and wiped his brow.

"Who is this enemy? you ask. I have been to the depths of hell and I know Who put me there. He is my enemy and He is yours too. He intends to send all of you there. He alone stands in the way of peace and prosperity.

"Now is the time to unite!" Hitler raised his voice and his fist in unison. "We must if we are to defeat this Hebrew God! I have proven to you that I can lead the world to peace. You cannot deny this! I disguised myself so that you would readily follow and now that you trust me, it is time for you to know who you are truly following.

"Today I stand before you, in this Hebrew God's place of worship, to give you a choice. Follow me and live. Or follow Him and die!" Another fist in the air. "I am your only chance for salvation. I alone have the power to save you! I have power beyond your wildest imagination!" He clasped his hands to his chest and lowered his voice. "And I will join with you to use this power against a God Who thinks He has the final word. He wants man to worship Him but He only offers an eternity of torment and pain. I have been there. I have not only seen it but I have felt it. I have lived through it and was saved from it. I was pulled from the depths and offered a plan to save mankind. The very power which raised me from the dead is available to you. My lord and master is Lucifer, and through me he is offering you salvation from this destiny."

From the back of the room a daring voice rose above the gasps.

"Prove who you are! Why should we believe you?"

Hitler was completely calm. "You do not believe me? Then I will show you. Prime Minister Szabo, please join me in a demonstration!"

Szabo stepped forward and saluted Hitler.

"Heil, mein Fuhrer!"

He raised his right hand and saluted with the straight-arm made famous during Hitler's first reign. Szabo turned his attention to the large curtain that hung behind the small altar at the back of the room. It was beautifully woven velvet, twelve inches thick, embroidered with golden thread. Angels were suspended in the purple fabric, as if they were protecting what was placed behind.

Szabo opened his arms and in a loud voice called, "Oh, father, now is the time to show your strength. Send fire from above and reveal to us your might!"

A column of fire ripped through the ceiling. Chunks of the roof were consumed by the flames before they reached the floor. The fire hit the ground in front of the veil and lapped at its fringe. Then, in the blink of an eye, the curtain caught on fire and was consumed in front of the stunned crowd. The priests lurched forward, as the Holy of Holies was exposed to the whole room of people, but were restrained by the security forces. Once the veil was completely gone, the column of fire retreated back up through the roof, leaving a black, gaping hole of the night sky in its wake. A few women screamed as the crowd shifted to look through the damaged roof, and several of the priests began to rip their robes and wail.

"Welcome to the Holy of Holies." Szabo's voice rose above the crowd. "This is the supposed dwelling place of the Hebrew's God Most High."

In the center of the back room sat the Ark of the Covenant, a beautifully decorated golden box with two large kneeling angels on the top, faces bent downward towards the center, wings outspread.

"Do you see the seat between the golden angels? That is where He sits. A throne of sorts, yet it seems empty to me. Doesn't it look empty to you, Herr Adolph?"

"There is no king on that throne." Hitler's eyes flashed with desire as he looked at the Mercy Seat. Soon it would be his.

Hitler looked at Szabo and simultaneously they thrust their hands forward, fingers extended towards the Ark of the Covenant. Immediately streams of fire flew from their hands. The FWP leaders fell to their knees to avoid being burned as the fire sped past them and hit the golden angels with a force that bent them back. The gold began to melt with the heat of the flames until the shape of angels was no longer distinguishable.

They dropped their hands and the fire stopped. The melted golden lump that was previously the Ark of the Covenant started gathering together into a new shape and form. Initially, the molten gold simply grew into a column but then a form appeared. A nose and chin, arms, and legs soon revealed a new idol in the temple. When the shaping stopped, it was clear who the object of worship would now be.

A twelve-foot likeness of Hitler now replaced the Mercy Seat of God. Screams were heard along with gasps and the wailing of the priests. Several people fainted, but thankfully the cameramen held their composure.

Adolph Hitler turned and faced the cameras.

"Thank you for your help, my friend. Make no mistake"—he pointed two fingers toward the ceiling—"my power comes from Lucifer himself; the Morning Star that fell from heaven will now save us from the Hebrew God's plan to destroy us all.

"Today I call on the world to take a stand. If you are with me, you will join forces with the greatest alliance in the history of the world. Together we will defeat this God. But if you stand with Him, we will be forced to remove you from our midst. There is no room on this earth for intolerant, insolent enemies of the FWP. If we rid the world of our enemy's people, then He will lose His foothold and His presence here. When we do that, we will have complete reign and His plan to destroy us will be defeated. Our only hope is to kill them all."

Hitler was completely aware of the power within him, driving his speech, driving his mind. It was time to push mankind into action. He knew belief alone was not enough.

"So decide. If you stand with me, you will do two simple things. First"—he again raised one finger—"you will place my number on your forehead, so there will be no mistake who you side with. Six hundred sixty-six—the number of months I spent in torment before Lucifer rescued me. Six hundred and sixty-six reasons I will fight this battle to my death. I will never go back there.

"Second"—he now raised two fingers—"you will build an idol for your home and your town squares to remind you of whom you worship. This idol can be constructed with whatever you have in your homes, but it must bear my image, my face. That is how everyone will know you are aligned with a new leader.

"These two simple things will show your alliance. If you are found without a mark or an idol, all will know that you are an enemy of the Federation of World Powers and there is only one fate for you."

He paused for effect.

"Death."

Complete silence.

Hardly a breath could be heard. Hitler, aware of Rabin's weak and trembling figure behind him, decided to end his misery.

"How will I enforce this, you ask? Let me give you a demonstration. Prime Minister Rabin, come join me for a moment."

Rabin reluctantly walked over to Hitler's side.

"Are you a member of the FWP?"

"No, my country is not."

"Will you take my mark?"

Hitler noticed that Rabin struggled to slow his breathing. Rabin leaned in toward Hitler and their eyes locked. In a voice barely audible he answered: "Take the mark of a man who tried to exterminate my people? You failed before and you will fail again. No one will follow you, a crazy man. Of course I will not wear your mark!"

Hitler's eyes narrowed and he leaned closer to Rabin. "Say it again for the entire world to hear."

Hitler put his hand on Rabin's shaking back and pushed him toward the mike.

"I . . . will . . . not . . . take your mark."

A high-pitched screech came from the hole in the ceiling. Hitler stepped away from Rabin as all heads turned upwards to see an impish gray creature with glowing orange eyes looking down on them. The screech was not one of pain, but of mocking laughter. There was almost a delight in it. He jumped into the hole and as he fell, wings unfolded and he glided to a stop, hovering in front of Rabin's face.

The creature was hideous. It had a twisted face with no hair, except a few gray whiskers hanging from its chin. Its naked body was proportionally human, but definitely not from this world. Its arms hung almost to the floor and it folded beneath its body hind legs, which were elongated and gangly. Hairless wings attached to its back, reminding Hitler of a gargoyle he had once seen. But the eyes were the most terrifying of all its features. They were inhuman. Dead. Yet they glowed with a fire only found in hell. Hitler hated those eyes. They reminded him of a past so horrific, his stomach would turn at the mere thought. Yet today, the demons were at his beck and call. This was quite a shift from the past.

The demon began to stretch out and the creature's shape morphed into a long stake. It looked like a branding iron with a sharpened tip that glowed red with heat. The stake thrust itself into Rabin's heart. Rabin grabbed hold of the stake and opened his mouth, but no sound came out. He fell to his knees as the stake exited his body. He fell forward, face down, motionless. Dead.

The creature reshaped and flew back up to the opening in the ceiling. He stopped and hovered there. As people looked up again, they saw not one but thousands of sets of orange eyes looking down upon them. The demon beckoned to his legion to follow and one by one they jumped through the hole and flew around the room.

Hitler stood and watched approvingly as they flew in a straight line, like the wind that had pierced the crowd earlier. Then they broke ranks and flew with abandon. Their screeching was terrifying, as well as deafening, as they whirled past the helpless crowd. This threatening display of strength lasted only a few minutes, but Hitler was positive that for those in the room it felt like an eternity. Finally, in one motion they all flew straight at the opening and out into the night sky.

By now complete mayhem had broken out in the room. Women who weren't screaming were crying. Hysteria was on the verge of consuming the crowd, but the security force stood motionless.

His face dripping with sweat, Hitler looked down at the body of Avi Rabin. He wiped it again with his handkerchief. It was time to finish his speech.

He set his face with a rigid, steely expression, then pointing a finger at Rabin's body, he said, "He belongs to a nation which is not part of the FWP. My power still reaches him. I am speaking now to all world leaders. Sign on with me in the next seven days, or I will ask my aides to persuade you. No mark means alliance with the enemy. I will give the rest of the world two months from today to comply."

He took a breath and forced a smile back on his face.

"If you join me, you will have a life of freedom and supply. Everything you've ever wanted. There will be food for all, jobs for all, and true peace on earth. Man must no longer raise his hand against man. He must raise his fist against God. As soon as we rid the world of our enemy, we will live in peace. The mark identifies association. In sixty days, we will know exactly who we are fighting with and who we are fighting against."

With that, Hitler looked at Szabo, who then walked over to him. Together they headed through the crowd toward the temple doors. As they entered the crowd, the security force formed a wall of protection around them. The crowd backed away and made a corridor for him to pass through. They had quieted to hear his final instructions and now the audience was overcome with fear.

As they walked through the crowd, someone in the back yelled, "Hail to Hitler! Long live Hitler!" Hitler stopped walking and stood still in the midst of the crowd, staring straight ahead. His ears strained for the slightest sound. His heart pounded but his face showed no emotion.

Whether out of sincerity or out of fear, he did not know, or really care, but one by one the people in the temple fell to their knees. Then there was another call in the back corner of the room.

"Hail to Hitler!"

The chant was soft at first, but soon everyone in the room wanted him to hear.

"Hail to Hitler! Hail Hitler! Heil Hitler! Heil Hitler! Heil Hitler!"

Hitler began walking again, past the kneeling crowd. He looked at Szabo and said, "They have chosen wisely."

eleven

Garrett was quick to start the car and get on the road. They had about five hours of travel time before they reached the Tabernacle for the six o'clock meeting and it was already one-thirty. They were going to be late.

The first ten minutes of the ride was spent in silence. Nate struggled to process the images he had just seen. In the last ninety minutes he saw a living Adolph Hitler, an army of demons, the desecration of the temple, the murder of Avi Rabin, and fire fall from, well, not from heaven but from who-knew-where. And none of this seemed to surprise either of the other men. They knew what God's Word said and they believed it would happen. Relief seemed to have flooded over them as they believed that God had led them to an understanding of the Scriptures and the end times.

It was Pastor who broke the silence.

"I don't know what to say. I guess it doesn't matter how much you prepare for the worst, when it happens it still makes you sick."

"That, my dear pastor, is definitely an understatement," Garrett said. "I am relieved we didn't move three hundred people into a cave to turn around and send them back home again. But I've got to tell you, I'm frightened right now."

"Frightened?" Nate asked. That hardly seemed to be the word he thought Garrett would use. He was prepared. He was in hiding. What was he afraid of?

"Because Christ said this time was going to be so bad that He himself is going to end it early for the sake of His children. If He didn't, if He let the Antichrist rule his final three and a half years, I honestly believe every believer will be wiped off the face of the earth."

Nate was sitting in the front seat again by Garrett. He glanced in the side view mirror and watched the image of Mount Olive shrink in the distance. His head was so full of questions he almost didn't know where to begin.

"So what will happen to those who stayed behind in Shelton?" he finally said.

As if still deep in thought, Pastor Gentings didn't answer right away. Then he said, "I don't think it will be as difficult now to convince some of the other families to join us. We've still got empty caves, don't we, Garrett?"

"Yeah, we have room for more, but we're going to have to be very careful. We've entered a new phase. It's now a matter of life and death. We can't just open our doors to just anybody. We'll have to be sure they are legit."

Nate turned to look at Garrett. "What do you mean?"

"True believers who want to hide. Not infiltrators who will give up our location for a reward." His forehead furrowed, Garrett rubbed his temples as if he had a headache.

"Do you really think people would do that?" There was that guilt again.

Pastor jumped in from the backseat. "Matthew tells us that families will turn against each other—brothers against brothers, husbands against wives."

"I'll be honest with you," Garrett started, "I was thinking that this was going to take a while for the world to accept, but when those demons flew through the ceiling and around the room . . . how can anyone deny that?"

"I admit, that was pretty convincing." Nate tried to hide the tremor in his voice. He was pretty worn out by now and was struggling to come up with an explanation for what he had just witnessed.

"Can you even imagine being in that room?" Pastor Gentings said. "Oh brother! What a show of force. All those witnesses—I wish we could hear what the news is saying about it."

"I'll see what I can find on the radio," started Garrett, "but first, I have a question for you. What do you think we should do about Dan and Betsy?" Garrett glanced into his rearview mirror at Pastor when he asked that question, so Nate kept quiet. "They're really the only ones left in Shelton who know where we are. And I know they'd die before revealing our location, but I am rethinking letting them stay. Those demons were terrifying and the thought of Betsy being killed like Rabin or tortured . . ." Garrett, his voice shaking with emotion, obviously couldn't finish the thought.

An uneasy silence filled the car for a few minutes, as each of the men seemed lost in their own thoughts.

"Maybe we give them a few weeks to work things out and then tell them to get down here." Pastor Gentings leaned forward, resting his forearms on the back of the front seat. "But I really doubt they'll leave. Why don't you give them a call later tonight. Or better yet, tomorrow, and get a feel for what is going on out there."

"I'll call them. Lily's going to have a hard time with this."

"Because she and Betsy are close friends?" Nate asked, trying to rejoin the conversation.

"No, because she knows what the Bible says about how the martyrs die during this time," Garrett said.

"How do they die?"

Pastor Gentings voice was subdued when he said, "They will be beheaded."

Again, silence followed the dire pronouncement.

"We need to stop for gas," Garrett said after a few minutes. "There's a station coming up, just before the mountain." He reached for the radio and switched it to AM. He rolled the knob until he found a news station.

Nate could feel his phone resting in his coat pocket. When they stop, he would look for an opportunity to contact Sean Aumonti, his handler.

Beheading. Hitler. Demons. He shuddered as he put his hand on the back of his neck and rubbed for a moment, deep in thought.

Rory Appleton sat staring at the television long after the announcement was finished. His phone was ringing off the hook, but he didn't move to answer it. His sandwich sat on the table half eaten, and he didn't even want it anymore. His wife sat next to him, rubbing his back and telling him everything would be fine.

"We'll figure this one out, dear. It's going to be okay."

That was Donna's response to everything, Dan thought, staying in his trance. It was going to be okay when he lost his job at the post office. It was going to be okay when his brother put a gun in his mouth and blew his brains out unexpectedly. It was going to be okay when their swimming pool foundation cracked. It's always going to be okay.

"Stop saying that."

"What, dear?"

"Stop saying it's going to be okay. We're in a real jam here. I mean, were you even paying attention to what just happened?"

"I was sitting right here beside you, Rory."

"Just stop talking, Donna. I need to think. And take the phone off the hook. Fight the temptation to answer it."

"So the elders were right?"

"No, they weren't right!" Rory exploded. "Nothing is going to happen here in Shelton, Michigan. We will go to work, do our laundry, buy our groceries like usual, and we'll watch what happens on TV every night. Nothing is going to change here. This does not affect our lives one bit. And if I hear you say the elders were right one more time, so help me Donna, I'll"—

The phone rang again.

"Take the phone OFF THE HOOK!" Rory roared and stood. He bounded out of the kitchen and locked himself in the bathroom. He stood at the sink and turned on the faucet. His cupped hands, caught the water, and splashed it on his face, trying to clear his mind and possibly wake himself up from this nightmare. He raised his head and looked at his dripping reflection in the mirror.

"Nothing will change here," he said to himself in the mirror. "Things may get bad in Europe but we're too far away. You need to pull yourself together and call Ray."

"Who are you talking to, honey? Are you all right in there?" Donna's voice came from behind the locked door.

"Adolph Hitler?" Rory asked himself, ignoring Donna's questions. "That's who Satan picked? He's going to have a fight on his hands. Who in this world would ever follow a madman? Yeah, that's the answer! No one is going to follow him. This is all going to blow over." He started to laugh. "And they'll be sitting in a cave somewhere eating power bars while I'm up here, feasting on steak and potatoes!"

"Rory? Rory! What's going on in there? You're scaring me! Open the door!"

He continued to laugh, because it made him feel better and because it was bothering Donna. Both were the two fundamental driving forces behind almost every decision he made.

The day on the mountain had slowly passed, excruciatingly slow for Adam. He had gone to the Tabernacle to help prepare for that evening's gathering, but his mind was with his father. Adam was thrilled when he heard his dad got to go with Mr. Hamilton and Pastor Gentings. But as the day wore on, Adam fought his imagination.

What if the Antichrist demanded that all Christians be arrested immediately and some police happened to be eating in the diner and saw them pray for their lunch and arrested them on the spot?

He also was confused about the phone charger he found in his father's closet. He knew that there were only two phones on the mountain and no one else was supposed to have one. So why would his father break the rules? Or maybe he was asked to keep one?

"Hey, that broom works better if you push it!"

Adam snapped back to reality at the sound of Seth's voice.

"Sorry about that. I've got a lot on my mind."

"Don't we all? Have you noticed how quiet it is in here?"

Adam looked around and save the sound of sweeping brooms, pounding hammers, and the occasional feedback from the sound system, there wasn't a whole lot of conversation going on, especially considering there were about forty people helping with the cleanup.

"Where's your dad?" Seth asked. "Isn't he finishing up the benches?"

"No, he was asked to go with Pastor and Mr. Hamilton because Mr. Johnson got the flu."

"Oh, man, he's really lucky. I would have loved to go. I'm dying to know what happened today!"

"Yeah, I'm right there with you. What's up with the radio? I thought they played it in here while the men worked."

"It's only getting static. Mack thinks a wire is loose or a connection is bad. He's working on it now and said he might get it fixed by tonight."

Over the sound system, Mack Silver interrupted everyone.

"Hey, everybody. It's four o'clock now, and we're to be back here by six. Why don't we all go clean up and have dinner? Things are in good shape here. Thanks for all your help."

The mike went dead. Adam saw the men taking their brooms and tools over to one corner of the room.

"Here, I'll take your broom," he said to Seth.

"Thanks. I'm going to catch up with my dad. I'll see you tonight."

Adam leaned their brooms on the back wall and took one last look at the Tabernacle. The benches were lined up, like a sanctuary, with a wide center aisle, and room on the edges to come in from the sides. At the front of the room was a small stage of sorts, a platform lifted about eighteen inches off the ground. A microphone stood in a stand and there was a music stand for a pulpit. In the back of the room, near the hall that led to the outside of the cave was a small sound booth, where the controls for the sound system lived, as well as a radio system. Adam turned and headed back to Petra, mind still spinning.

As he entered the cave, he could tell something was wrong. There was a lot of yelling and running and it seemed to be coming from the kitchen area. He rounded a corner to find water on the floor and Adam knew immediately what was wrong.

His mother called to him from the kitchen, where water was flowing.

"One of the pipes broke and Pete is turning off the valve. We need buckets and mops to clean this up."

"Where are they?" Adam called back to her.

"We have the ones from the kid's bathroom, but will you go to the parents' bathroom and see if there is anything in there?"

"Sure!"

As Adam ran down the hall to his mother's bathroom, he met Mrs. Johnson who was holding a mop and two buckets.

"I've got these from back there, Adam."

She rushed past him and he stood in the hall, alone, facing his parents' bedroom door. All he could think of was the charger. He wanted to see it again. Everyone was at the flood site, so he reached for the knob. He turned the knob and entered the room. He quietly shut the door behind him and ran to the closet. He grabbed the older work boots and reached down inside. He pulled out the charger and looked at it.

It was definitely a phone charger. The port was too small for a computer, and why would he hide a computer charger in his boot anyway? But why does he have one and where is it? His dad must have taken it with him to town. Why would he need a phone? To call the Doughertys? Why wouldn't Mr. Hamilton do that?

There had to be a logical explanation and, in Adam's mind, he settled that the phone must be something he was asked to bring for some reason. He would ask his dad about it and then everything would be explained.

He left his parents' room and headed for the kitchen to help bail water. Then as soon as the water was turned back on he was going to hit the showers. Maybe if he bailed water for a bit, his mind would stop racing.

Then again, maybe not.

Nate used the restroom while Pastor Gentings and Garrett filled the car. When he came out, both men were walking into the gas station. He got in the front seat and positioned himself so that he could see the men returning to the car. He powered up his phone and called Sean. It took a few precious minutes to connect, minutes Nate didn't have to spare.

"Aumonti."

"Hi, it's me—Nate."

"Nate? I'm surprised to"—

"I can't talk long. I went with two of the men from the church to Mount Olive to hear the press conference. It's a long story why, but needless to say I saw it all. What in the world is going on?"

"What do you mean?"

"You saw it, didn't you?"

"The press conference? Yeah, I did. Homeland Security hasn't come out with a formal statement yet, but we're looking in to the validity of the whole thing."

"You mean, whether or not it was really Hitler? Whether or not those were real demons terrorizing that room of reporters? Whether or not Rabin was killed on live television?" Nate didn't know why panic was welling up in his chest, but the events of the day were starting to take its toll.

"More or less. By the way, I just talked with Melanie Westering, an agent in Mount Olive and she's sending me the audio."

"She?"

"Yeah. Posed as a waitress, I think."

"Sean, this whole thing is freaking me out! Numbers on foreheads, idols in homes—this can't be serious!"

"Listen, everything's going to settle down and we'll figure out what our response will be. I'm not really into the whole 'follow Hitler or die' concept, but I've always liked Alexander Magorum. So just sit tight and do your job down there and the next time you call, I'll have more information for you. How much longer do you think you'll be?"

"In light of this press conference, I think I should just be patient and see where this thing plays out. At least another month or two. The men here are already talking about more coming down—I've got to run. They're coming back."

Garrett and Pastor Gentings were returning to the car, coffee and doughnuts in tow and a newspaper under Garrett's arm.

"Okay, well, I'll wait to hear from you and then"—

Nate quickly shut the phone and reopened it. He held down the power button. They were just about to the car when the phone powered down. He dropped it in his coat pocket. He could feel his heart racing and a drop of sweat roll down the side of his face. He swiped at it with his sleeve and opened his door for some air. Garrett climbed in the driver's seat and handed a cup of coffee to Nate.

"Cream and sugar. You didn't complain this morning, so I figured it was safe."

"Great, thanks."

"Kind of hot in here?" Garrett asked. "You look a bit sweaty."

"Oh, I think I dozed off. This coffee will be just what I need."

From the backseat, Pastor Gentings handed a box of doughnuts to Nate.

"Here, you're going to need one of these too!"

"Perfect."

Garrett started up the car and they headed back onto the highway. Nate sat quietly while Pastor relayed NBA scores and standings to Garrett.

The agent is sending the audio, Nate thought as he replayed his conversation with Sean in his mind. His casual tone, considering the supernatural event that just occurred, seemed so strange to Nate. Why wasn't he alarmed? Or confused? It was almost like Sean was completely blind to the significance of the event. How could two like-minded men see the same thing and not respond the same way? Maybe he and Sean weren't as like-minded as they used to be.

And not because Sean had changed.

Sean Aumonti sat at his desk in Lansing, Michigan. He clicked on his calendar on his computer and the page for March fifteen came on the screen. He scrolled down to 1:15 p.m. and clicked on the space beside the time. The bar turned blue and he began to type.

Contact with Nate Reed in North Carolina. Slow progress with cult. Requested a couple of months, unless activity increases. Should hear from him in four to eight weeks.

Sean hit enter and then clicked on 1:00 p.m., highlighting the space beside the time again. Once again, he typed.

Contact with Melanie Westering. Sending me audio on the Reed case in North Carolina. Also was able to place tracer on vehicle. Available in the future if needed.

Sean saved his notes and closed his calendar. He sat back in his chair and thought through the events of the day. The phones in his office were starting to ring off the hook, but Sean wouldn't answer any until he had logged his data. That's how an efficient office was run and with forty-seven DIU agents under his authority, he was nothing if he was not organized.

He hit the speaker button on his phone and a young woman's voice responded.

"Yes, Agent Aumonti?"

"I will take calls now and when you get an official statement from Homeland Security, be sure to bring it right in."

"Yes, sir. Will that be all?"

"Yes."

Sean hit the speaker button again and immediately the phone rang.

It was going to be a long day. The sooner he received a statement, the sooner he'd have answers for the good people of Michigan.

twelve

Emma sat with Leighsa and Sarah. It had been a long day for everyone. She was actually tired of talking about the possible options of what had happened at the press conference. Everyone was speculating and she was weary of wondering. It wouldn't be long before her dad was back and they'd all know. She was also curious about what her dad thought of Mr. Reed.

By six o'clock, almost everyone had arrived and the noise level was rising. Emma saw her brother wrestling with some friends and she shook her head. He has no idea how important this news is to all of us, she thought to herself.

"Emma?" Leighsa elbowed her best friend.

"What?"

"You're kind of lost in thought there and I just wanted to point out that someone just arrived."

"My dad?" Emma was ready to hear the news.

"No, better than that. Adam." She gestured to the entrance of the Tabernacle and there, standing in the doorway, was Adam.

Emma waved and he had started to make his way toward her when radio static was suddenly heard over the microphone system. But then it silenced again.

Sarah said, "It sounds like they are getting something. I think Mr. Silver has been working on the radio all afternoon."

"Hi," said Adam, as he neared the girls. Emma noticed that his blue long-sleeved T-shirt made his matching eyes almost glow.

Emma stood and put a hand up to her hair, to tuck any strays back into place.

"Hi, Adam," she said with a smile.

"Things look good in here, don't you think?" he asked.

"Hi, Adam! I agree. This place is totally funky!"

"Hi, Leighsa," he said, then turned back to Emma. "How are you doing?"

"I'm just anxious for my dad to get back. The time is really dragging."

Static was heard above the chatter and everyone quieted down again. Intermittent voices alternated with the static. Suddenly a voice from the back of the Tabernacle yelled, "They're here! I can see their lights! Three quads heading this way!"

It was 6:45 p.m. and Emma drew a deep breath. She wasn't going to relax until her dad walked through the door, but she felt better already. She met eyes with her mother across the room and they both smiled. It had been a long day for everyone.

Pastor Gentings was the first to enter and was greeted by Mack. Garrett was close behind and was nearly tackled by Emma. She threw her arms around his neck and said, "I'm so glad you're back, Dad!"

"Thanks, hon. How did things go here today?"

Emma pulled back and saw her father's eyes meet her mother's. Lily touched her ear, and he did the same. Emma knew now was not the time for small talk.

"We'll talk at the cave. You have work to do now."

"Thanks." He made his way up to the front, where Pastor Gentings was already standing, talking to his wife. Emma thought her dad looked worn out and his mouth was very narrow. He always seemed to purse his lips when he was deep in thought or else really mad. Emma couldn't tell what had happened at the press conference by the look on his face. It could go either way.

She made her way over to her mother and Sarah, and quickly sat down. The benches in the Tabernacle were made with back boards and Emma was surprised they were actually comfortable.

"Do you mind if I sit with you?" Adam said, suddenly appearing beside her.

"Sure, have a seat." Emma could feel heat rising in her face and hoped Adam didn't notice her cheeks reddening. Why did he make her feel like this? She tried to concentrate on what was happening up front. The congregation quieted as the pastor leaned over to see if the mike was on.

"Does this thing work yet?"

"Loud and clear, Pastor!" someone hollered from the back.

"Well, we're not surprised to see you all waiting for us. Sorry it took so long to get back. It's been quite an eventful day and we're going to get right to it. I'm going to let Garrett tell you what's up."

Her father walked to the mike, stood for a moment, and then shrugged his shoulders. Emma wondered if he was struggling with how to start. But she knew her dad and didn't think he would pull any punches.

"Rather than set the stage, we decided to come right out with it."

Emma smiled.

"We were right. Magorum is the Antichrist. But it's not really that simple. We knew he would be a historical leader, raised from the dead, and though it sounds crazy, he's actually Adolph Hitler."

A collective moan spread across the room. Emma felt a chill run through her body and she folded her arms across her stomach. Tears came to her eyes, not because she was afraid, but because she was so grateful to be in a safe place. She focused her eyes, ears, and thoughts on her father's words, not wanting to miss a detail as he continued to talk.

"In about sixty minutes time he transformed his body from Magorum into his original form, revealed his army of demons, destroyed the Holy of Holies, and murdered the Prime Minister of Israel."

Gasps were heard around the room.

"He has demanded the worship of the world. He claims he has seen the other side of death and what awaits the world, and the only way to stop that destiny is to rid the world of God's followers. We know that means believers and, of course, he has added Jews to the list. He has offered the mark as protection and demands that everyone erect a statue of himself in their homes. It's been an unbelievable day."

Everyone sat in silence for a moment, obviously processing the information. Emma jumped when a cry came from the back of the room.

"Hallelujah! Jesus is coming!"

Her heart began to soar with the simplicity of the call.

"Praise the Lord—He is our Provider!"

"He shall reign forever and ever!"

"He is our Shield!"

"Come quickly, Lord Jesus!"

One by one the congregants of Grace Church stood and raised their voices in praise and adoration of the One True God. Emma stood also, tears streaming down her face. There was no fear, only anticipation and worship.

Pastor returned to the microphone, open Bible in hand.

"Revelation 3:10–12 tell us: *'Because you have kept the word of My perseverance, I also will keep you from the hour of testing, that hour which is about to come upon the whole world, to test those who dwell on the earth. I am coming quickly; hold fast to what you have, so that no one will take your crown. He who overcomes, I will make him a pillar in the temple of My God, and he will not go out from it anymore; and I will write on him the name of My God and the name of the city of My God, the new Jerusalem, which comes down out of heaven from My God, and My new name.'*

"We have been faithful to the Word of God, and He has promised to protect us. We will not stand His wrath, for who can face the wrath of God? No, we will be taken before then, but He says He will *keep* us from the hour of testing. This word *keep* in the Greek means to protect within a sphere of danger. It's our mountain in the middle of America. Things are going to get bad out there, but we will overcome. He who overcomes—the word there is NIKE—everyone say that, NEE-KAY."

The congregation repeated after him. "Nee-kay."

"We are overcomers—we will persevere through this time of Satan's final attempt, and we will overcome."

"Ni-ke!" Emma cried with the rest of the room.

Pastor Gentings's voice continued to raise. "Through the power of the One Who raised our precious Jesus from the dead, we will overcome!"

"Ni-ke!"

"Come quickly for Your overcomers, Jesus!"

"NI-KE! NI-KE! NI-KE!"

The battle cry of the faithful rang through the Tabernacle. Emma noticed Adam and Sarah were crying too. She turned to Adam and grasped his hand, not because of affection for him, but for the bond they had in Christ. She took Sarah's hand too and the three of them sang with the congregation the great hymn of old, "How Great Thou Art." When they got to the last verse, completely overwhelmed, Emma could only listen.

> *When Christ shall come with shout of acclamation*
> *And take me home what joy shall fill my heart.*
> *Then I shall bow in humble adoration*
> *And there proclaim, My God, how great Thou art!*

When the singing stopped, one by one the people settled onto the benches again, wiping tears and hugging those around them. Emma tried to pull her hand from Adam. He squeezed it as if he didn't want to let go. She looked at him, and he smiled as if waiting for a response from her. She smiled into his eyes and apparently that was all he needed. He gently held her hand in both of his as the men continued to describe the press conference in great detail to the people. At one point, Emma felt a sharp elbow in her side but chose not to give Sarah the satisfaction of a response.

As the men talked, whenever there was an especially shocking detail, like the death of Rabin, the people cried, *Ni-ke!* The congregation had a focus now. They would survive. They would overcome.

As the questions from the congregation began to slow, there was some commotion in the back of the room and Emma turned to see Mack Silver, who had been fiddling with the radio during the meeting, waving his arms.

"What's up, Mack?" asked Garrett from the front.

"I got the radio working again. Do you want to listen to the news station for a minute? It's all they're talking about!"

"Go ahead and turn it up."

The radio was switched on to the sound system in the room. Garrett joined his family to listen for a while. Emma thought he looked even more weary, now that the meeting was almost done.

"*. . . waiting to hear from Congress as to what the American response will be. Word from Washington is that they are meeting with the President and Vice President behind closed doors even at this moment. Press Secretary James Crevelle read a statement fifteen minutes ago confirming the authenticity of the press conference in Jerusalem.*

"*In Tel Aviv, the Knesset has appointed Daniel Abramoff of the Israeli Liberal Party as their new Prime Minister. Mass rioting has erupted in the streets in response to the appointment, as well as to the murder of Rabin. The Knesset has made no formal statement as to how*

*they will respond to the death of Rabin, except to announce funeral
arrangements for Monday and a national period of grieving between
now and then. There is no indication of how they will respond to Hit,
ahem, . . . ahem . . . , excuse me, Hitler's ultimatum for a response by
noon on Saturday, the Sabbath day for most Jews."*

Simply speaking the name of Hitler was sticking in the reporter's
throat.

As the adults and teenagers listened intently to the news which
verified the men's account of the announcement, Emma saw a young
man walk in through the back hallway of the Tabernacle. He was
wearing hiking boots, jeans, a long-sleeved T-shirt and a plain navy
hooded sweatshirt. He wasn't anybody's husband, brother or son
from the room, as far as Emma could tell. As he got closer to her row,
Emma nudged her dad and pointed at the man. Garrett stood and the
man raised his hand to him to stop. Then he folded down his fingers,
leaving one still raised, as if to ask for one moment.

The young man walked up on stage and tapped the microphone.
It was off. Garrett looked from the man to the sound control area
where Mack was playing the radio. Mack had seen the man and with
a nod from Garrett, he turned off the radio and flipped the mike
power switch to on. Emma wondered why her dad let him speak, but
the peace on his face assured her it was all right. By now the whole
congregation was watching the man.

"Excuse me, if I could have your attention, please."

The young man had a gentle yet commanding voice.

"I have been sent from Elohim," he began.

Emma caught her breath and leaned forward. "He knows why
you are here. He has sent me to give you a message."

He spoke slowly and deliberately, as if to let the room process
every word.

"I work with a team of messengers and our message will be given
to the whole world. There is only One True God and it is the God you

serve. The time of the great tribulation is at hand. There are no gray areas any longer. If you take the mark of the beast, you will make your alliance with Satan and you will not spend eternity with God. Period. It's as simple as that. If you refuse the mark, your life may be required of you by Satan, but your eternity will be secure. I can't put it any plainer. This world is turning upside down, but be confident that you can still stand on the Word of God. Stay in it, know it, act on it, and rest in it. And for those of you who are still wavering in this room, whatever you do, don't take the mark. It will seal your eternity, because there is no turning back if you do."

The young man definitely had everyone's attention. He stood still, facing the crowd. He smiled warmly at the congregation and it appeared that he had tears in his eyes.

"I'm going to show you something because I think you can handle it."

Then he unfurled his wings, which had been concealed until now. Emma gasped at their brightness—they were whiter than freshly fallen snow. And they were huge! Each wing was double the height of the angel and together, fully stretched, spanned almost fifteen feet across. The angel was no longer dressed in jeans but had a flowing white robe with a golden trim that almost looked liquid when he moved. It shimmered and sparkled more than the purest diamond.

Emma felt light-headed and dizzy. It was as if her eyes had gone out of focus, like she was looking through water. She reached up and rubbed them to try to clear them. But they weren't blurry. The room was. All around the exterior of the room images began to appear. They were light in color and hazy initially, almost like a fog was filling the room, but as time passed the images became clearer.

Angels surrounded the whole room. Each wore a white, shimmering robe like the one who made the announcement. There were hundreds of them, suspended in the air, their wings gently moving to keep them in place. Light filled the room and for a moment it looked like it was snowing. Tiny specks of shimmering light fell from the ceiling and faded before they touched the floor. Emma reached out to touch the light, but flickering specks disappeared before they touched her skin. The angels gazed down on the people with peaceful and pleasant expressions, so as not to frighten anyone. Emma was not alarmed or frightened, but felt completely safe and even joyful.

The angel's wings began to gently move and he lifted himself above the congregation. In a very quiet voice, yet one heard by all, he said to them, "Elohim is very pleased with you. Do not fear the wrath of man. God is with you. Wait for the appearing."

When he said that, Emma thought he had looked straight at her.

"You have been faithful, dear Philadelphia. Overcome to the end."

Three strong pumps from his wings and the angel vanished into thin air. The rest of the angels followed suit, one by one. When the last angel disappeared the shimmering lights faded and the people sat in silence.

Emma heard her father say to her mother, "A sign from heaven. Why is He so good to us?"

She looked over and saw her mom smile back at him and reach her arm around his waist, laying her head on his shoulder. He returned the embrace and looked past her to Emma and Sarah.

"Let's go girls. Sarah, go get Ben."

"But Dad, don't you think"— Sarah began.

"There's nothing more to say tonight," Garrett said with a smile on his face. He turned and headed toward the door with Lily.

Emma looked at Adam.

"Can I walk you back to your cave?" he asked.

She nodded, and the two teenagers headed out the door with the rest of the congregation. She noticed the group walked along in silence. It was as if they didn't want to taint the event with words.

As they headed back to the cave, Emma noticed that Adam was struggling.

"Are you all right?" she asked.

He stopped walking and turned to her. In the moonlight, Emma could tell he was choked up.

"I guess I didn't really believe what we were seeing was truly prophecy being fulfilled. When the angel talked about those who were still wavering, do you think he was talking about me?"

"I don't know, Adam. I thought it was a strange comment. I mean, even though we all moved down here, there was a little doubt in all our minds that we might be wrong. I am not sure who he was talking about."

"I just can't believe what we just saw. I mean, I don't even know what to say ..." Adam reached up and swiped at his cheeks, which were damp from tears.

"I heard your dad say that God was good to us. Oh, Emma, what would have happened to my family if we hadn't come to Grace?"

"I know a lot of believers who are in a very bad position right now, Adam. And things are only going to get worse."

"That's an understatement. They're going to get killed. Slaughtered, Emma! I have an aunt in Minnesota and grandparents who are still alive. What will happen to them? You don't think they'll take the mark, do you?"

"I don't know, Adam. Did you talk to them before you left?"

"I didn't but my mom did, and they wanted nothing to do with it. They wouldn't even listen to her. My grandparents wanted Mom and me to come live with them—they were sure my dad had gotten us involved in some wacked-out cult!"

"Are they Christians?"

"Yes, but they don't know anything about end times. My mom wrote them a letter and told them to open it if anything would happen, like what happened today. In the letter, she told them to get out of their town and hide. She made it pretty simple."

"Then you just have to pray for them. It's all you can do, now, Adam. I know it's hard. We have family out there too."

The two walked a bit in silence. Emma saw the entrance to her cave. She didn't want to end the night on such a sad note, so she stopped and turned to Adam.

"Don't lose sight of what happened tonight. I know that there are circumstances outside of our control that we can worry about, but we can't forget what a great gift God has given us. Adam, we saw angels tonight. Angels!" Emma's heart filled with joy as the word fell from her lips.

"You're right, Emma. It was awesome. My head is just spinning."

"This is my stop. I'll see you tomorrow sometime?"

"I'll try to come by in the afternoon. See you later."

Emma watched Adam walk away, clearly distracted by his conflicting emotions. She entered her cave and went straight to her room. The other girls were getting ready for bed, and she flopped onto her bunk. As the others chattered about the angels and the evening, she closed her eyes and pictured the angel. She did not want to forget one single detail.

After all, it's not every day you get a visit from an angel. Then again, who knows what tomorrow holds.

thirteen

Rory had instructed Donna to tell people he was not home. Originally, he had instructed her to not answer the phone, but she couldn't help herself. It was second nature for her to pick up the phone when it rang. Like Pavlov's dog. So he changed his instructions and now she was to lie for him.

Rory sat in his Barcalounger with the remote in his hand, thinking about his meeting last night with Ray Bower after the press conference. They had agreed that time was going to be their friend. They prayed about how they should handle the congregation's questions and felt that God would have them wait to see the true extent of Hitler's power, if indeed it really was Hitler. Rory struggled to concentrate at work the following morning, so he headed home for lunch.

As he turned on the television, he heard a knock at the front door.

"I'm not home, Donna! I don't care who it is!" Rory muted the TV to hear the conversation. But all he heard was a muffled voice and then Donna's footsteps through the kitchen.

"There's a young man at the door and he wants to talk with both of us."

"You told him I was home?"

"No, he said he knew you were watching TV and asked to speak to the both of us. He said he won't leave until we both come to the door."

"What is he selling?"

"Nothing is in his hand and he has no backpack or briefcase."

"Fine." Rory hoisted himself out of his recliner and headed to the front door. He saw the man in the doorway and didn't recognize him.

"I don't know what you're selling," Rory started, "but we're not interested!"

"I'm not selling anything, sir. I have a message for you."

"Are you a delivery man?" Rory glanced at the driveway, expecting to see a vehicle with some identification on it but the driveway was empty.

"I am delivering a message from God."

"God." Rory looked at the dark eyes of the messenger and he was keeping a straight face. "Fine. I'll bite. What does God want you to tell me?"

"Taking the mark of the Antichrist will eternally separate you from the presence of God."

"And who would the Antichrist be?"

"Adolph Hitler. You know who he is, Rory. Don't be so bullheaded. And don't take his mark."

"Who sent you? How do you know my name? Is Gentings behind this?" Rory was frustrated at this prank. It wasn't funny.

"God has sent me to all men. If you take the mark of the beast, you will align yourself with Satan, and God will not forgive this offense. You will be separated from God for eternity."

Rory had enough. He stepped back and slammed the door. He could feel his chest pounding and tried to calm himself. Donna stood back with a shocked look on her face.

"Why did you do that?" she asked.

"He's not from God, he's from Hamilton and Gentings. I am sure they sent him to make me feel bad! He's probably one of Dan's 'witnessers.' Well, I don't have time for this! Make me a sandwich. I need to get back to the office."

Rory stormed out of the room, leaving Donna and her objections still standing by the front door. He wanted to look and see if the man was still standing on his porch, but didn't want to give the sender the impression that he really cared.

Seven minutes later, at a quarter after twelve, there was another knock at the front door. Donna ran to the door. Rory saw his sandwich was ready and he walked into the bathroom to wash his hands.

"Oh, hi, Dan," she said loudly, standing in the doorway, but not inviting him in. Rory stood in the bathroom drying his hands and listened to their conversation, hoping that Donna would act out of character and not reveal that he was home.

"Hi, Donna. Is Rory home for lunch today? I have been trying to get ahold of him but couldn't get an answer, so I thought I'd stop by."

"Oh, we've been here. You must have been dialing the wrong number. The phone hasn't rang at all lately," Donna lied. "Rory is here. Rory?"

Once again, Donna's brilliance shines through. Rory came out of the bathroom and walked to the door.

"Hi, Dan. What do you need?" Rory didn't want to appear overly friendly.

"I was wondering if we could talk for a minute. I'm sure you saw the press conference yesterday."

"Of course I did." Rory put a hand up across the doorway, as if to imply entrance was going to be impossible.

"Well, I think it raises some interesting questions and thought we could talk for a moment. If you're not too busy . . . "

"Of course I'm busy! I do work for a living!" Rory humphed and did his best to seem put out, but Dan still waited for a response. "I have a limited amount of time for lunch, but come on in and make it quick."

Rory turned from the door and led Dan into the kitchen where his lunch sat on the table waiting for him. Rory had no intention of asking Dan to eat, so he sat down and started right in on his sandwich. Dan sat across from him and folded his hands on top of the table.

"I'll just cut to the chase, Rory. The past couple of months have not been overly warm between the two of us, but I think in light of yesterday, it's time we set our differences aside and work together."

"In light of yesterday? What is this about? Do you want to come back to the church or something?" Rory looked at Donna. "You see, Donna, didn't I say they would come crawling back?"

Dan shifted in his seat and leaned forward, clearly not amused.

"Rory, you're missing the point. Yesterday the Antichrist desecrated the temple and threatened the whole world with a choice. He demands that we all take his mark."

Dan paused and Rory didn't flinch.

"Are you trying to scare me, Dan? Did you send that kid over to warn me about taking the mark too? He was here just before you arrived. Is he sitting in your car waiting for you to finish threatening me?"

"I don't know who you are talking about, Rory. I came alone. Listen, the church cannot take this mark. It will mean certain eternal death for all. I think it's time to get the remaining church members down to North Carolina. They'll be safe there. They will welcome all of you, readily putting our past differences aside."

Rory started to laugh. He looked over at Donna, who joined him nervously, and at that moment, Rory had a strange affection for the woman who was trying to support her husband but was relatively clueless.

"Have you lost your mind?" Rory leaned in, so as not to be threatened by Dan's physical position. "I agree with you to a point. This leader turned Hitler is possibly the Antichrist, but let's not jump to conclusions. I'm still waiting for CNN to declare this whole thing a smoke and mirrors trick. You know this guy has offered DNA to prove he's Hitler. When it comes back negative, this should all go away. He'll be charged with Rabin's death and life will go on."

"What about the demons? The orange eyes? The demon-to-a-spear-to-a-demon transformation?"

"Like I said, smoke and mirrors." He had him on the run, so Rory leaned back casually in his chair and reached for his sandwich again. "Technology what it is, who knows what really happened. But let's say it is the Antichrist. Life's going to stink in Israel, but nothing is really going to change here. We're too far away. We'll do just fine on our own, but thanks for the offer."

Rory took a large bite of the sandwich.

"Rory, let's set our pride aside. You know what God's Word says about this guy. It says he demands the worship of the whole world. Scriptures say that you will not be able to buy or sell without the mark. What will you do then?"

"When the Scriptures were written there wasn't even an America! When John wrote Revelation he didn't even know about this side of the world! It's not for us. It's for Israel. I'll bet a lot of Jews come to America for protection."

"John didn't write Revelation. He copied it down. It was Jesus' revelation given to John. You know what faith is, Rory. It's believing the Word of God and"—

"Yeah, yeah, I know, 'acting on it, no matter how I feel because God promises a good result.'" He leaned back in, and pointed a finger for emphasis. "Don't preach at me. I do believe the Word of God and my actions are kicking false teachers like you out of the church. My phone has been ringing off the hook all day with people wanting to know what our church believes. I'm not going to encourage a panic. Nothing's going to change here." Rory stood. "I think we're finished."

Dan stood also. "We have a month to get people down there. After that the window of opportunity will close. I spoke with Garrett Hamilton this morning and that's what they have all decided."

"Well, I don't see you running to safety."

"Betsy and I are committed to staying to help as many people as we can. We are stocking up on supplies right now, filling our basement with food and water. I would suggest that you do the same. Those calls are only going to increase as things get worse, and you had better re-think your answer."

"Or what?"

"Leadership is always held doubly accountable. You are now in leadership, Rory. You will answer to God."

"Is that your pat answer to everything? We'll all answer to God and I have nothing to be ashamed of."

Dan looked at Donna and that infuriated Rory.

"Why are you looking at her? She is staying because she knows I'm right!"

"This is not a game, Rory. It's going to get bad. You have to think about Donna. How's this going to affect her? You know where to find me when the time comes. There's still a month to change your mind. I hope for your sake you do."

As Dan walked out of the kitchen, he looked back at Rory and nodded his goodbye. Then he walked to the front door alone and let himself out. Rory paused a moment then walked to the door. Dan was not going to have the last word.

He opened the door and saw Dan driving away. He also saw someone walking down the sidewalk, away from his house. He rec-ognized the young man who had just stopped by. He watched him for a couple of minutes, go from house to house, talking only a few minutes at each door.

"What a waste of time," Dan muttered, then turned to Donna. She was quite pale and looked rather frail at the moment.

"What's wrong with you?"

"What if Dan's right?"

"Listen to me, Donna. Nothing's going to change here. Trust me. Would you rather be living in some dark, damp cave right now, with bats flying at you and people catching pneumonia from the cold?"

"Well . . . no. But"—

"No 'buts,' Donna. We're going to be fine. I know I can be harsh with you at times," Rory put his arm around his wife's shoulder, "but I would never let anything happen to you. You believe that, don't you?"

"Yes, I do."

"Now, I've got to get back to work. You probably shouldn't answer the phone still, unless you want to field the questions. Ray and I are going to have a question and answer time at church on Sunday to try to calm everyone's fears. If you do talk to anyone, just tell them that."

Rory uncharacteristically kissed Donna on the forehead. He was rewarded with a smile on her upturned face. He supposed it was worth it just for the goodwill it caused. He turned and headed out the door to his car.

As Rory Appleton pulled out of his driveway, in the back of his mind there was a nagging fragment of a sermon Gentings had preached. He couldn't remember much of the message, but he remembered the title. It was called "The Gospel Angel" and for some reason, as Rory passed the young man walking on the sidewalk, he had a fleeting thought that maybe that man was a gospel angel.

I didn't know angels wore jeans. God must be more liberal than I thought. I wonder if He likes drums too.

Rory laughed, nervously at first, then full belly the rest of the way to the office.

At twenty-two, Evan Stillman was a well-seasoned Shel-head. He sat in his car and looked into the mirror. Shel-heads usually didn't smile, but since the press conference, he couldn't wipe the smile off his face.

This was the moment he had dreamed of.

This was the moment they all had dreamed of.

He got out of his car, his bald head gleaming in the sun from a fresh shaving. He stood with pride, looking at the meeting place where it had all begun. He was only fourteen when he first had walked through the doors of the Shelton Chapter of the National Skinhead Association. He had gone with a boy he had met at the mall, whom he only knew as Steel. Steel had shown him the ropes. Explained what was wrong in America. And Evan would forever be grateful for Steel's guidance.

Too bad Steel's in jail right now.

Evan carried with him an old VCR tape. He was early, so he could get everything ready. Tonight he would show his brothers the interview that gave them their reason for meeting. Their reason for living too. The first time Evan saw this documentary, Steel was inducting him into the association. At the end of the documentary, Hitler's valet, Heintz Linge, was interviewed saying that before Hitler died, he instructed him to tell the army to fight for the coming man. These were supposedly his last words.

Evan knew one day Hitler would rise again and he was prepared to fight for him. Evan's heart raced as he entered the abandoned strip mall which would now be considered Hitler's headquarters in Shelton, should he ever visit. As he looked around at the meeting place, Evan wondered if Hitler had any idea how strong his following was in America, and especially there in Shelton. Anything he asked of him, Evan would do. The Shel-heads had long been indoctrinated in the return of Hitler and now they had the awesome task of assembling his army to carry out his requests. The Shel-heads were sure to rule the world with Hitler as their leader. They were ready and willing to do whatever it takes, and Evan really meant "whatever."

Evan put his hand to his forehead and gingerly touched its swollen skin. Evan was the first person in Shelton to have 666 tattooed on his forehead. Evan wanted the most ornate tattoo he could afford, which wasn't much at the moment, but it was the intention that counted. Three hundred and twenty-seven dollars later, Evan had his mark. It was two inches high and the numbering was done in black.

A red cloud of dust surrounded it, with demonic eyes, bloodshot and glowing orange in the bottoms all three of the sixes. It was rather impressive. If Evan ever did have the honor of meeting him in person, he was sure Hitler would never forget his loyalty engraved on his head.

He also had completed his idol, though he could still improve it. He had spent hours printing pictures and symbols off Google. He then carefully laminated each image and superglued them all around the border rim of his computer screen. Then he downloaded multiple pictures of Hitler that would scroll through a set sequence as a screen saver. His wallpaper was a picture of himself superimposed onto an old picture of Hitler saluting one of his soldiers. He carefully placed candles of different heights all over his desk, and bought a special red one for the center of his display. It was a cinnamon-scented one. He hoped Hitler liked cinnamon. Thus his place of worship was ready to go.

Tonight it was important that Evan lead by example. One look at his forehead and they would follow. Evan picked up the old pizza boxes and beer cans and threw them in the corner. Maybe he was meant for greater things. But first he would have to serve in Shelton.

Evan carried the television over to a table at the far end of the room. He connected the VCR player to the television and turned on the TV. He popped in the tape and fast-forwarded to Linge's speech. Evan stood in front of the television, volume full up and mouthed the interview. He knew every word.

He was that serious.

He was that committed.

He was that devoted.

And Evan was pretty sure that with devotion like his, he would meet him one day.

What a difference a day makes! Yesterday the temple in Jerusalem was a place to worship God. Now it is a place to worship Satan. Yesterday I had never seen an angel before. Now I have. Yesterday I had never had my hand held by a boy. Now it's been held and wants to be held again!

Emma smiled with that last comparison.

I wonder what the average American is thinking today. I wonder if they slept well last night. Survival is now a question on the mind of every American, not just Christians. Will Americans take the mark or will the demons come and wipe them all out? So many questions with very little answers. We have thought about survival for years and now many are thrust into survival mode with no warning. It is amazing how accurate the Scriptures are. Then again, the Author is divine— what do you expect?

I wonder what the president is going to do. Does he realize the seriousness of this event? I remember seeing him on the steps of a church in Washington with his wife—as if he was a regular attendee. If he is a believer, what will he do? Will he die for Christ? Will he disappear without a trace? Will he take the mark? I wonder if an angel has talked with him yet.

Pastor Gentings has taught about the message angels during the end times. That's who came to talk with the congregation last night. He was the most beautiful being I have ever seen! His eyes were so gentle and compassionate—I wonder if that's what Jesus looks like. Someday soon I will no longer live by faith alone, but I will live by sight. All these questions will be answered and I won't be sitting in a cave, wondering what is happening in the real world.

Emma closed her journal and sighed. The other children were in the living room area, diligently working on their schoolwork, but Emma had already finished and was journaling.

"What's that for?" asked Lily, who was sitting across the table from her, reading a book.

"I just feel so conflicted!"

"Conflicted? What do you mean?"

"Now that we know we are in the last days, and we know we have been faithful and obedient, and we know Jesus is coming soon, you would think all my questions would be answered. But they're not. I have a million more."

"Like what?"

"Like, what is going on in Shelton? How quickly will people take the mark or do they think it's a joke? What will our president do? You know, he acts like a Christian."

"Well, this will be a real test for him."

"What's going to happen to Grandma Kane?"

Lily sat quietly and Emma knew she shouldn't have asked. She got up from her seat and walked behind her mother and wrapped her arms around her neck, placing her chin on her mom's shoulder.

"I'm sorry, Mom. I know you must be worried."

"Aunt Kelly will have to take care of her. I don't question their love for the Lord and I know they would never take the mark. I just pray that they will contact us in the next month, or else they'll miss their window of opportunity. I have to leave them in God's hands."

"Maybe it won't get too bad and they'll be all right."

"I think that's wishful thinking, Emma. Jesus said it would be a tribulation like the world has never seen before. It's going to be horrible. I'm not sure how Satan is going to do it, but he doesn't have much time left and he's going to have to work quickly."

"How can they contact us?"

"They have the post office box address in Mount Olive and they can write us. I think Dad will try to call them too. Several have asked to call family and I think the elders are going to let them do it."

Emma hugged her mother tighter. She knew she got her imagination from her mother, and she also knew it was causing her to worry.

"I'm sorry, Mom. I shouldn't have said it."

"It's not like I wasn't already thinking of it. Will you pray for them?"

"Every day and every night."

"Thanks, Emma." Her mother touched Emma's cheek. "Now, how about lunch? It's my turn to make it today."

"I'll help you." Emma kissed her mom and went to get some napkins. She grabbed her journal, ran it to her room, then went to the storage room and found the napkins. She glanced at her watch and it read 11:07.

Emma was sorry she made her mom sad and she whispered a quick prayer for her as she set the tables for lunch. She loved her parents dearly and hated when she caused them pain.

"Please give me sensitivity with my words, Lord. May I use them to lift people up and not to hurt them. And, though I know You are coming soon, please don't let me hurt my parents between now and then. They have enough on their mind. In Jesus' name I pray, amen. Oh, and thanks for that beautiful angel. I wouldn't mind if You sent him to gather me up to heaven in the near future!"

Emma quickly set the table and headed to the kitchen. Lily was already boiling water for mac and cheese and had started on the sandwiches. Emma squinted at the peanut butter and wondered how many sandwiches could be made from one of those bulk jars.

"I know what you're thinking," her mother said, raising an eyebrow. "But the good news is, the food is going to be much better in heaven, so buck up, and start spreading!"

Emma picked up a knife and turned her thoughts to the future wedding feast.

Sometime during the night, Adam came up with a plan. The details came to him just after the men left the caves for their meetings, and the moms began their days of housework and cooking. He was still mulling over how to pull it off when the young people trailed out of the cave and headed for the Tabernacle for devotions. They would soon be home for their schoolwork, so time was of the essence.

He took a deep breath as he padded down the hallway to look for his mother.

"Mom? Do I feel warm to you?"

Sherrie Reed put her hand on her son's forehead and shook her head.

"You feel fine to me. Why, don't you feel well?"

"I didn't sleep well. I have a stomachache."

"Did you have breakfast?"

He shook his head weakly. "Thought it might make it worse. His mother looked worried. "Maybe you should go back to bed."

"I don't want to cause any trouble." He was beginning to sound like Ferris Bueller so he backed off a bit and gave her a wan smile.

"No, it's not a problem. I'll check on you after devotions are done."

"Thanks, Mom."

Adam felt a little guilty for lying but that quickly faded when the voices in the living room died away and the front door slammed shut. He quickly made his way down to the parents' hallway. He could hear Mrs. Cowlings rummaging around in her bedroom farther down the hall. She must have stayed behind. He held his breath, opened the door to his parents' room, and quickly entered.

Adam went straight to the closet. Kneeling down, he reached for his father's boots. The first one was empty. So was the second. The second pair of boots was farther back and slightly out of reach. He leaned forward and pulled on the toe of the boot to slide the whole thing out to where he could have a better look.

Nothing.

He sighed. Maybe this was his reward for playing Ferris Bueller. Then he pulled out the fourth boot. Something dragged with it.

The cord. Same as before. He reached into the boot and pulled it out. It wasn't attached to anything. He sat back with another disappointed sigh, then he reached inside and checked the toe of the boot.

His fingers wrapped around the cell phone. He pulled it out and for a moment just stared at it, briefly wondering if he really wanted to know who his father had called.

Then curiosity got the best of him. He powered it up. Waited until he got a menu, then scrolled down and stopped at the "recent calls" option and hit enter. A ten-digit number appeared.

He blinked then looked again. The same number had been called multiple times. It was the only number his father had called. And it wasn't his grandparents' number as he had hoped.

His heart sank as he again stared at the number. He paused before pressing the "contacts" button. The address book appeared on the screen. Attached to this number was a name Adam had never heard: *Sean Aumonti*. There was no business name or address typed in, only the name and number. He went back to the "recent calls" option and looked at the dates and times of the calls—a couple of times the first week they were on the mountain, several calls before they came and then this past week there were four calls to this Aumonti.

Adam turned the phone off and put it back in the toe of the boot. He felt around in the back of the closet to see if there was anything else but shoes back there. Nothing. He walked over to his parents' dresser and pulled open a drawer. He felt strange doing this, but that feeling didn't stop him. He looked through all the drawers, careful not to mess anything up and found nothing unusual.

Adam walked over to the bed. He felt under the pillows. Then he got down on his knees and looked under the bed. Still nothing. He felt a bit ridiculous. What was he expecting to find anyway? Was his dad a spy? Was he working undercover? Yeah, right, he thought to himself as he got off his knees and sat down on the bed. He heard a crackle when he sat on the mattress. His heart skipped a beat.

"You have got to be kidding me," he said out loud this time. Was there really something stuffed in between the mattress and box springs? If his dad was a spy, he wasn't a very clever one.

Adam reached under the mattress and felt a file folder. He pulled it out and flipped it open. The top page had a small picture of Pastor Gentings on it. The page was some kind of a form which had been filled in on a computer. It recorded his height, approximate weight, hair color, family descriptions, address, employment information— basic facts about the pastor. The second page, which was stapled to the first, contained three typed paragraphs describing Pastor Gentings in detail—his friendships, his sermon contents, and his personal hobbies and habits.

The next dossier contained two pages describing Garrett Hamilton. Then another two describing Mike Torey. And Pete Johnson. And Mack Silver. All the elders and deacons were covered as well as ten additional families from the church. Near the bottom of the pile was a copy of Grace Church's doctrinal statement, highlighted and marked up in multiple colors, with notes written in the margins.

That's when Adam recognized his father's handwriting, and realized he had been clinging to the hope that these reports had been given to his dad. But it was obvious his dad had written them all.

Adam sat on his parents' bed, trying to sort this all out. Why would his dad be keeping a file on the church leaders? Why did he have a phone, when they were not allowed? Did his mom know about this? Could this somehow be something he was asked to do by the church?

He knew the answer to his last question was a resounding no.

He took out the last several pages of the file. They were letters written on official letterhead stationery with the "Homeland Security/ Domestic Investigations Unit." They were written by his father to Sean Aumonti, an apparent department head and contained detailed notes about meetings Adam's dad had attended. One of the letters included two maps church members had been given of the mountain, cave locations marked, as well as driving directions from Shelton.

Every bit of secret information given to church members who were moving was in this file.

Adam's hands started to shake. There really was no explanation except the obvious one. His father worked for the government and was reporting on the church's activities. From the looks of it, he'd been doing this for a while. Adam had heard of churches under investigation and every once in a while a church was shut down for breaking the anti-intolerance laws. Was his dad responsible for any of those closings?

Adam quickly shut the file and stuffed it underneath the mattress again. He heard footsteps in the hall and quickly prayed they belonged to Mrs. Cowlings. There was nowhere to hide, so he chose to just stand in the room and face whomever would enter. But the footsteps passed the door and continued down the hall until Adam couldn't hear them anymore.

Adam's mind was racing with questions. Could his dad be a double agent, protecting the church rather than an informant? Unfortunately nothing in the files indicated false information. Maybe his dad had gathered information, but hadn't given his file yet to anyone. That theory died quickly, because there were too many phone calls to this Aumonti to think that no one knew where they were.

He struggled to breathe. The implications were almost too much to bear. He had to get out of that room. He needed fresh air. But he didn't think he could fill his lungs with enough air to make it to the front door of the cave. He sat back down on the bed, put his head between his knees and took slow, labored breaths until he calmed down.

Then it hit him. He had no idea what to do with this information. His father was a spy for the government, and all their lives were in danger.

He looked up, toward the closet again, as his breathing eased. The phone had to be disabled. And he was the only one who could do it. He went to the closet again, pulled out the phone, and holding it in the palm of his hand, stared at it again.

It couldn't look like sabotage. His father would suspect someone had found out, and before that happened, Adam needed to buy some time.

The battery already showed only partial life left and would soon need charging. So the charger needed to malfunction. Holding the plug, he yanked on the wire that attached the phone to the charger. He pulled harder until he could felt the wire give. He then tested the connection, smiling at the result. When his father plugged in the charger, it would look normal but the connection would be dead.

He stuffed the phone back into the boot toe, positioned the two pairs of boots near the back of the closet just as he had found them, and went to the door.

It was quiet in the hall. Catching his breath, he stepped out and made his way back to his bedroom. Everyone would be back in about fifteen minutes and lunch would be served about two hours after that. He would go about his normal routine, study, eat lunch, and then come up with a reason to see Emma. That would give him some time to decide if he should tell her about his discovery.

Unfortunately, now he really did have a stomachache.

fifteen

"**I**'ve invited the Reeds over for dinner tonight."

Lily was in the kitchen talking with Garrett and at the mention of the name "Reeds," Emma's ears perked up. Anything having to do with Adam was an easy distraction, especially from her homework. It had been six weeks since Hitler's announcement and the angel's visit to the church, and Emma was definitely taken with him. Every morning at devotions, Adam sat with her and usually by midafternoon he would show up at her door. They found they both enjoyed playing cards and almost every evening they played Hearts and Oh Heck with Emma's parents.

"The Toreys and Phillips are having dinner at the Gentings's and the Masons are over with Mack and Tara tonight. I thought it would be the perfect time to invite the Reeds to join us, especially since we are getting to know Adam so well."

"Great idea," Garret said. Emma heard the kiss that followed.

"Good grief, you two—I can hear you."

Laughter flowed from the kitchen, then her parents walked to the table, coffee in hand. A moment later Ben came from the bedroom hallway, carrying his math book.

"Mom, can you help me with this?"

"Sure, honey. Sit down."

As Lily helped Ben at one end of the table, Garrett sat down next to Emma at the opposite end.

"It was good getting to know Nate Reed a little better when we went to town, but I really haven't talked much with him since then," her dad said. "He was quiet but seemed nice. What's your take on him?"

"I haven't really been around him much, but I like Mrs. Reed a lot. She makes great brownies." She grinned.

They spoke for a few minutes about the day's plans, then her father said, "I need to head over to the Tabernacle. I'm monitoring the news stations from noon until four today."

Lily looked up from Ben's math homework. "Do you have just one shift?"

"Fortunately, there're enough of us to cover the shifts just once a week each. For now, we're only listening from eight in the morning until eight at night. There's no need to make it twenty-four hours—at least, not yet. If you need me, you can call me on the radio."

"I'll be listening for your update—will you make sure our radio is on before you leave? It seems someone keeps turning the volume down." Lily raised a brow and then squinted knowingly at Ben.

"I haven't touched it—I promise!"

Garrett rubbed Ben on the head as he went into the living room where the ham radio sat on a small table. He adjusted the volume then headed toward the front hallway.

"What time is dinner?" he called over his shoulder.

"I told Sherrie six o'clock."

"I'll be home before that."

Emma returned to her own schoolwork, stacked neatly in front of her on the table

"Mom, shouldn't we be studying Hebrew or something like that?"

"What do you mean?"

"Well, don't you think we'll speak Hebrew in heaven? It makes sense to learn it now, rather than waste time on chemistry and world literature."

Her mom seemed to be swallowing her smile. "Hebrew is difficult to learn. Besides, you can take the class in heaven, if you need it. Now, back to work."

Emma glanced at her watch. Seven hours until she would see Adam. It was going to be another long day in the cave.

Emma was in the kitchen baking cookies for dessert when she heard her father's voice over the video that was blaring in the living room. The young people were strewn on the couches and floor, watching Mission Impossible for the fourth time. Emma peeked out of the kitchen and saw her father struggling with an armload of magazines and newspapers.

Josh and Seth hurried across the room to help. "Wow, Mr. Hamilton, where'd you get all of these?"

"Mack did another run into town to check the mail. He bought every magazine and newspaper he could find."

"Is there a *Sports Illustrated* in there?" asked Seth, wildly flipping through the magazine pile.

"I doubt it. Mostly just news—wait! Here it is."

Seth grabbed up the *SI* and held the magazine over his head in victory, just then Josh grabbed it and made a run for the bedroom. With a loud wail, Seth took off after him. Emma laughed as her dad grumbled good-naturedly. Then he yelled, "Hey guys, bring that back when you're done."

Mr. Torey and Mr. Phillips heard the commotion and entered the living room from the parents' bedroom hallway. When they saw the table of newspapers and magazines, they headed straight to the table and hurriedly sorted through the contents.

"*Time* magazine has Hitler on its cover," said Mike Torey.

"So does *Newsweek* and *Business Week*," added Stan Phillips.

"He's everywhere," Garrett said quietly, shaking his head.

Emma walked over to the table. Leighsa, who had been watching the movie, joined her. It didn't take long to register that Hitler and the FWP was the main topic of every periodical and news headline.

"Here's an article about the banking system change over in America," Stan said. "It looks like the FWP has made changing to the One World Denomination system pretty flawless. This article says that by May tenth, the dollar will no longer be accepted and the magog will take its place. Most banks and businesses have already put the magog into use."

Garrett added, "This article says that all but two senators and four representatives in the house have taken the mark and"—

"Here are pictures!" Leighsa interrupted. "Sorry, Mr. Hamilton, but this magazine has pictures of senators and, oh, look! Here's the president—with a mark."

Emma gasped and quickly moved in beside Leighsa. She almost grabbed the magazine out of her friend's hands to see the photograph. There was the President of the United States and his wife, shaking the hands of the Premiere of France, all of them with the numbers 666 on their foreheads. Not huge marks, but high on their hairline.

Tears welled in her eyes. "I thought he was a Christian. How could he do this?"

"Emma," her father said, "there's a lot going on out there we don't know about. We can try to read the papers and listen to the radio, but we're really in the dark."

"But, how can people be jumping on board so quickly? This is Hitler. In school, he was considered the villain. Now, he's a hero. I just don't understand." Tears were streaming now and Emma swiped at her cheeks, trying to keep them under control.

Mike jumped in. "This article says that within the first week, much of the free world agreed to join the FWP. The issue of Hitler aside, the financial and economic benefits were just too good to pass on. Each country wanted a seat on the FWP council. Four nations that refused to join found their presidents dead on March twenty-third, when the seven day grace period was up."

"What about Israel?" asked Lily, who had now joined from the kitchen.

"Prime Minister Abramoff has taken the mark, along with his cabinet. It's right here in *Newsweek*," Stan said, as he thumbed through the pages.

"They've made a deal with the devil" Lily walked over to Emma and hugged her.

Stan picked up another paper. "Look at this photo—Israel has given Hitler a beautiful penthouse apartment and office, overlooking the temple mount in Jerusalem as a show of support. It says he plans on living there part-time."

"It's like the world has lost its mind—or its memory," Mike said, shaking his head. "Unbelievable."

Garrett looked up from his copy of the *New York Times*. "Look at it this way," he said. "The world has been offered a new system of government and a currency which makes business and travel easier than ever. The benefits are overwhelming and the costs of not joining are staggering." He pulled out a chair at the table and sat. "In addition, there's the threat of demons hanging over their heads if they don't join. So the world leaders lead by example, take the mark, benefit their country and do their best to change their opinion of Hitler. And all of this is accomplished through a demonic delusion, which only those with the Holy Spirit are not susceptible to."

"I don't even know if it's demonic—it could just be outright sin and rebellion to God," Stan added.

"It just doesn't make any sense," Emma said. "Can't the world see what is going on? Hasn't anyone ever heard of 666 before?"

"When does sin ever make sense, Emma?" her father said. "Man has replaced God's truth with lies and here we are—marriage is a temporary state, not a permanent commitment. Pornography is rampant and has seeped into television and music. Foul language is commonplace, along with lying and cheating to climb the financial ladder. So why is it so difficult to accept a dead tyrant, raised back to life, defeating death, and offering peace to the world? Why not? Plus he brings a spiritual element into it by his show of demonic power. Who would question it when he is providing everything he said he would, with power to boot?"

Mike looked up from his article. "It says here the president has assured the people that the American way of life will not change. If anything, it will prosper with this decision. He explains the convenience of using the One World Denomination system and the benefits it brings American investors. And down here it says the only cost to the individual citizen was the investment of having 666 tattooed to their forehead after the ID chip was inserted in their hand. Both procedures are being offered together for a standard fee of $19.95. One of the nonnegotiable rules of the FWP was no number, no chip. For those on welfare or government programs, the fee would be waived." He glanced around the room at the others. "It's absolutely incredible to me that people are jumping on this bandwagon."

"We're not out there to see the delusion, Mike," Garrett said. "I know it doesn't make sense, but we're secluded and protected from the whole thing here on the mountain."

"Thank goodness for that!" Eva Torey said from the doorway. "Now, enough of this talk. Mike, you and the kids need to get ready to go. The Phillips too."

"The whip has cracked, folks," Mike said with a playful grimace. As he turned to go to his room he glanced at Garrett and held up the magazine. "Okay to keep this a while?"

Garrett nodded.

"Let's go, kids," Mike said, looking at his watch. "We don't want to be late."

Thirty minutes later, there was a knock at the front door and the Reeds arrived. Emma ran to the door and let them in. They followed her down the front hallway to the living room area. She tried to keep from looking at Adam while their families chatted about life in the caves. But every now and then, their eyes met and she felt her cheeks flush. Then she noticed he was quieter than usual, as if something was bothering him.

When they sat down to dinner, Adam at her side, he seemed to grow even quieter. As their parents laughed and talked, she figured he was just nervous and left it at that.

"Mack Silver came back from town today with a load of newspapers and magazines," Garrett said. "We've been reading all afternoon and it's a bit shocking to see the general acceptance of Hitler and his one-world government plan."

"Really?" Nate said, cutting into a piece of ham. "I'd love to see some of those magazines. I feel so isolated from what's going on out there. Does Mack still send various men each week to town?"

"At this point, two men go each week to check the post office box and get supplies. In another couple of weeks, our money will no longer be accepted and without the mark, we won't even be able to buy gas, so the trips will be over."

"I'd be willing to take a trip, if Mack needs it," Mr. Reed said.

Emma noticed Adam throw a quick look at his dad and then stared at his plate. She looked at his plate too, and realized he had just moved his food around, but hadn't really eaten a bite.

As the parents continued to talk, Emma nudged Adam.

"Everything okay?"

"We need to talk."

The look on Adam's face frightened her. It was one of those "I-need-to-break-up-with-you-but-I'm-not-sure-how-to-do-it" looks. Emma's heart sank and she lost her appetite too. That was obviously why he'd been so quiet.

The rest of dinner was a blur. She was keenly aware of every movement Adam made, but practically oblivious to any conversation at the table.

"Emma? . . . Emma!" Lily raised her voice, drawing Emma out of her daze. "Clear the table and put out coffee cups, please?"

Feeling a flush heat her face, she stood and helped Sarah clear the table. She went into the kitchen where her mother was rinsing the dishes.

"Mom, is it all right if Adam and I go for a walk during dessert?"

"Sure, but don't wander far. Help me get this out and then you can go."

With her right hand, Emma took the plate of cookies her mother handed her, and with her left, she took a little oblong plate with bowls of powdered cream and sugar on it.

She carried them to the table, then paused as she heard her dad's words.

"One of the articles focused on the idols people are making. Apparently, the president isn't mandating the idols, but in the true American tradition, each family is to follow their own conscience and do what they want for their own home. However, all cities and towns will have a government subsidized idol put in its center."

"Amazing," Sherrie said. "And people are taking the mark too?"

"One of the articles said it's become Hollywood chic to add a precious stone to your tattoo. Even placement of the mark has taken on a life of its own. Whether above the right or left eyebrow, high in either corner, dead center or off center, your placement tells your sexual preference, social status, and religious beliefs." Garrett paused. "If I remember correctly, left eyebrow rumors homosexuality. The color purple means upper crust. Dead center are loyal centrists and those who hide their number at the edge of their hairline were heralded as Christians or Jews who are covering their bases. It seems that the mark has become a fashionable way to express oneself."

"But the deadline is fast approaching," said Sherrie. "Doesn't everyone have to mark up by May fifteen?"

"Yeah, and then it will get interesting. No mark, no currency. No mark, no food, gas ,or bank account. The mark really gives you the freedom to live, but I'm not sure what the idol in the home is going to do. That is still yet to be seen."

Adam finally spoke up. "Have there been any more supernatural displays from Hitler or that sidekick guy?"

"Szabo?" asked Garrett. "Well, I haven't read everything, but it sounds like he does demonstrations here and there. I don't think Hitler has had a formal speech since the press conference in March."

Lily entered from the kitchen with a pot of hot coffee in her hands. "Coffee anyone?"

Garrett, Sherrie, and Nate all nodded and Lily poured four cups.

Emma touched Adam's hand. When he looked up, she said, "Want to go for a walk?"

"Sure." He grabbed a cookie and stood. Then he leaned over and grabbed another one. "They look good." He raised his eyebrows as if he couldn't help himself.

The parents laughed and continued on in their conversation as Emma and Adam headed for the door. Emma felt a knot forming in her throat when she reached for the doorknob. She turned to Adam before opening the door.

"Am I going to cry?"

"What?"

"Should I get some Kleenex?"

"Just go, Emma. We need to get out of here."

Adam followed her outside and shut the door behind them. The darkness of the woods seemed to envelope them and Emma's despair continued to grow.

Well, it was fun while it lasted. Buck up, Emma. It's not the end of the world. Well, actually, it is almost the end of the world . . .

This one was going to be hard to document in her journal.

sixteen

Rory Appleton sat in the second pew from the front. He wore a new crisp white button-down shirt with freshly pressed khakis. On his head was a plain, navy blue baseball cap. He knew this was unusual, but there was a reason for it. Ray Bower, also in a navy cap, was doing a splendid job of calming the congregation and soon it was going to be his turn to talk. He looked at Donna beside him, and marveled at how long it took for her to grasp the concept of binding and loosing. But if she could get it, then the rest of them could.

"And now," Ray said as he finished his message, "I am asking one of our elders, Rory Appleton to address some of the social matters at hand. There will be a time for questions at the end. Rory?"

Rory stood and made his way to the front. When he turned to face the congregation, he was pleased to see the sanctuary was almost filled. Since the migration of half of the church, Rory had been concerned about being able to pay the bills, as well as support a staff at Grace, but with the move to a more liberal pastor, the pews quickly filled and his fears were put to rest.

He waited until the people quieted. Rory was born for moments like this. Being a natural leader and all, he was also the king of the dramatic pause.

"I tell you the truth, whatever you bind on earth will be bound in heaven, and whatever you loose on earth will be loosed in heaven."

Again a pause.

"That verse in found in Matthew eighteen. This verse is important because it gives the church the authority to come together and make decisions that God will bind and loose on behalf of the church. Today, we are binding a truth concerning our church and we have the confidence that God will bind it in heaven. Our elders are in complete agreement and we know that when even just a few elders, as our case may be, are gathered in His name, He is there in the midst of them."

An "amen" was thrown from the back of the room and Rory was energized to continue. This time he raised his voice and spoke even more forcefully.

"These are difficult times, however we still maintain that life in Shelton, Michigan, and in the rest of America, is going to remain constant. The decision that faces us today is an economic one. We have prayed and studied the matter and have come to a decision."

The room quietly awaited the decision.

"Before the foundation of the world, believer's names were written in the book of Life. That is a fact. No one can pluck these dear one's from the Father's hand. Another fact. God knows our devotion and our love and He also expects us to provide for our families. Today we are declaring that taking the mark is solely a means of provision in an economy which is changing its currency, not aligning with the Antichrist. Therefore, we are recommending as an elder board that the men of the house or the women, if they are single, should take the mark of this new economy to provide for their families. Yes, I know that the coincidence of the number 666 is disturbing. However, it is merely a coincidence and nothing more. To show our unity in this decision, I am asking Ray and Bill Baker, our other two elders to join me on the stage."

The audience stirred as the three men joined each other on stage, all wearing the plain navy baseball caps.

"We would never ask you to do something which we were not willing to do ourselves. Therefore, today we declare here on earth that taking the mark of the FWP is acceptable in God's sight."

As if on cue, the three men reached up and removed their caps, revealing marked foreheads. All three were done in black ink and were inconspicuously placed high at the hairline. The numbers were no bigger than a half of an inch, but were clearly visible. A few women in the crowd gasped and Rory responded.

"This is our obligation to provide for our families. As for idols in your homes, we believe that this crosses the line and becomes worship of the FWP and we will not condone this action. All you need to do to exist in the world is wear the mark so that you can receive your chip. Your bank account will be accessible, and life will go on as usual. Obviously, we need to pray for Israel and for the Christians who will be persecuted overseas. Perhaps we can contact churches in Israel and offer to bring some believers here to America. What do you think, gentlemen?"

Rory liked this whim, and the other marked men on stage nodded in agreement.

"Now, are there any questions?"

A man in the back stood.

"Yes?"

"I had a man visit my house, claiming to be an angel, telling me if I took the mark, I would spend eternity in hell. Could he be telling the truth?"

"I am sure many of you had similar visits," Rory said, as most in the congregation nodded in agreement. "But if you study Scripture, angels never have to tell anyone they're angels—it's obvious to the recipient of the message that an angel is talking to them. So the fact these men had to tell us they were angels makes me think it was a hoax. Also, we as elders are binding this truth and Matthew tells us that whatever we bind, God will stand behind. You have to take the mark for financial accessibility, not for worship of Hitler. It's as simple as that and God knows your heart. He knows you want to be responsible. Remember, God is the One who will judge the hearts of men."

Another man stood and Rory nodded to him.

"Is it a problem for our wives and children if they don't take the mark? I thought everyone was supposed to do it."

"Technically, that's what Hitler wants, but in America, we just need access to our bank accounts. If your wife wants to buy the groceries and gas, she may need to get the mark too. I understand there are some logistics that will have to be worked out, but ultimately, you only really need one person to be marked in your home."

Rory stood waiting for more questions, but his flock was relatively satisfied with his explanation. The fact that he was already marked was brilliant, and he took full credit. He told Ray and Bill that if they were marked together, the people would follow and he was right.

When the meeting was over, Rory made his way to Donna. She forced a smile and said under her breath, "Why didn't you tell me you had been marked?"

He returned the forced smile and answered, "It's really not a big deal. Be grateful and greet the people. We'll talk later."

"But"—

Rory took her by the elbow and propelled her through the sanctuary to the back door.

"Rory—*ouch!* You're hurting me."

"Just get to the door and be pleasant."

As they exited the church, Rory let go of her elbow.

"Don't question me in church. The people are looking for me to be their leader and my wife can't be a problem."

Donna didn't say a word but got in the car and continued her usual cold-shoulder treatment.

"When you're through with your hissy fit, I'll graciously accept your gratitude and we'll move on with life. I took the mark to provide for you. The least you can do is say 'thank you'."

Donna turned her back to him and looked out the window and Rory fumed. As he drove, he forced himself to think about the meeting and before he knew it, he was patting himself on the back once more for a job well done. It was a good night, even for a man with an ungrateful wife.

Emma and Adam sat on two logs facing each other, about fifty feet from the entrance to Emma's cave. They had sat here often, talking about life, sharing stories and laughing but the tone was completely different tonight. Adam was tired of carrying this burden alone and it was time to ask for help. He met Emma's teary gaze, and wondered why she looked so scared.

"I've got a problem and I need your help."

"Are you breaking up with me?"

"What?"

"Just say it and don't sugarcoat it."

In a heartbeat Adam realized why she had been looking so scared. He tried to stifle his laugh but couldn't hold it in.

"You're laughing at me?" Now she was frowning at him.

"No, no! I'm sorry." Adam fought to control his laughter. "I'm not laughing at you, and I am definitely not breaking up with you—you're my best friend and I need you more than ever right now."

Emma wiped her tears with her fingertips and she smiled at him through watery eyes.

"What's wrong? You hardly said a word at dinner."

"I found something in my parents' room . . . " Adam leaned forward with his elbows on his knees and he grasped Emma's hands in his own.

"About a month ago I found a phone charger in my dad's work boots—in his closet. Mom had sent me to grab them and take them to Mr. Johnson the day my dad went to town with yours to hear the announcement."

"A phone? Why would he have a phone?"

"I wondered that myself, so I skipped devotions one day to check it out. I thought maybe he had a phone to call my grandparents, but there was only one number. And it was called repeatedly. I checked the number in Dad's contacts address book. It belongs to a man named Sean Aumonti."

"Aumonti? Is he a relative?"

"No, I've never heard of this guy. So I started looking around the room and I found a secret file hidden under the mattress."

"You're kidding. A secret file? What was in it?"

Adam sighed and looked away from her. "A report on all the elders and deacons of the church. It had pictures and the doctrinal statement and it even had the maps of the mountain, with all the cave entrances marked."

Adam sat for a moment without speaking and let Emma process what she was hearing.

"There was a report on your dad too," he said finally.

"What was in it?"

"Just a basic description. It did say that he was one of the main leaders—he and Pastor Gentings, and that the people tend to blindly follow them."

"Where did your dad get these reports?"

"That's the real problem. He wrote them."

"What? Why?"

"At the end of the report were a couple of letters, describing the church and referring to us as a cultlike group. The stationery said Homeland Security." He paused, dropping his head. "I think my dad works for them."

"You didn't know this?"

"I thought he was an accountant."

"So what did you do? Have you talked to him?"

"No, I pulled out the wire on his charger so he can't charge the phone. He won't be able to make calls until he gets a new charger. When I heard him offer to go to town for Mack Silver, I knew why."

"Are you sure the phone doesn't work?"

"I've checked it and it's still dead."

Adam looked at Emma. Her eyes were soft in the moonlight. "I'm sorry I dumped this on you, but I didn't know what to do. I still don't."

"Well, let's think this through logically. If your dad really does work for the government and the government knows where we're hiding, then none of us are safe here, unless your dad hasn't given his file over to anyone yet. If he doesn't work for the government, then why would he have a file? He has to work for them, doesn't he?"

"I can't think of any other explanation."

Silence again, both deep in thought. Adam looked down at Emma's thin fingers as she played with the ring on her right hand.

"If he's reporting to the government, does that mean he's not a believer? That this has just been a job for him?"

Emma's question was fair but it also hurt.

"I think so, except he hasn't built an idol, at least not that I've seen. There's no number on his head either. That's a good sign, right?"

"But why would he spy on us if he was a believer? Could he be helping us somehow? Do you think my dad knows about this by any chance?"

"I don't know."

They sat in silence for a couple more minutes, each trying to come up with a reason to believe Adam's dad wasn't a villain. It was Adam who broke the silence this time.

"Engedi."

"What?"

"Engedi," Adam repeated.

"What are you talking about?"

"That's the name I came up with for your cave. Engedi. It's where David used to hide from Saul up in the mountains. There was a spring of fresh water in the mountains and he would go there to rest. When I need to get out of the craziness of Petra, the only place I want to be is at Engedi."

Adam thought he could tell Emma was blushing but he wasn't sure because of the shadows from the moonlight. He thought he should clarify.

"Being at Engedi is so different than being at Petra. Everyone's nice and all, but your parents are really deep. I love to talk about stuff with them that I could never talk about at home."

"Like what?" Emma asked.

"Doctrine, prophecy. My mom loves to study but my dad isn't really interested. And now I think I know why."

"Well, maybe you should try to witness to your dad."

"What do you mean?"

"I mean, try to find out if he really is saved. Before you march in and accuse him of something, I think you should try to witness to him. And I think you and I should commit to praying for him. It's not like he can contact anyone right now, so he is really a captive audience."

"But what if he's told someone where we are?" Adam looked at Emma, fearing the consequences.

"Well, right now, we're not really in danger and hopefully we'll figure out what's going on with your dad before it gets bad."

"I don't know that we're supposed to keep a secret like this, Emma. Maybe we should tell your dad."

"Let's give it some time—a week—and you feel him out."

"All right. I've sat on this for over a month now, I guess another week won't hurt."

Emma looked at Adam and smiled.

"Why are you smiling?" he asked.

"Engedi. I like that! I thought you had forgotten our deal."

"No way! Are you kidding? Now I'm wondering what I have to come up with to get a kiss . . . "

"And a kiss would help our friendship because . . . "

" . . . because if I kissed you now, I could return my concentration back on the problem we were discussing instead of sitting here thinking about kissing you."

"As long as it is for a good cause!"

Adam gently took her face in his hands and leaned in. The kiss was short but very sweet, and it was everything Adam had hoped it to be. He felt his heart jump and he pulled back to look at her.

"Now, back to the matter at hand," said Emma.

Adam smiled at her and stood.

"Come on, let's walk while we talk."

"I do think that no mark is a good sign. He couldn't really hide one, could he?" asked Emma.

"With that hairline? Nothing's a secret on that forehead!"

That made Emma laugh.

"So, we could wait until the fifteenth and see if he puts a mark on, right? In the next week, if he gets a mark then everyone will know what's up and if he doesn't, then maybe he is on our side."

"Or maybe I should just ask my dad? Just come out and say it. 'Dad, are you a spy?' After all, he is my dad."

"Good grief!" Emma exclaimed. "Why does life have to be so complicated? Let's stick with our first plan and pray about it. Could we pray now?"

Right there, just outside of Engedi, Emma and Adam knelt to pray.

"Father, Emma and I are in a bind here. We are asking that You would give us wisdom to know what to do here. There's a big part of me that thinks I don't even know my dad, but another part of me that wants to trust him. Please give me an opportunity to share Jesus with him And Lord, if he is here on false pretenses, open his eyes and save him."

"And Lord," Emma added, "Protect Your faithful children here on the mountain. This problem may be out of our hands already, but I know it's still in Yours. We love You and thank You for Your gracious and merciful protection of us. In Jesus' name we pray, amen."

"Amen."

Emma and Adam reentered Engedi, hand in hand, wondering what their parents had talked about for the past hour. When they came around the corner, they found them deeply engrossed in a game of cards. Adam looked at Emma and shrugged his shoulders. The burden already seemed lighter.

But when he awoke the next morning the weight was back again.

seventeen

One week before the deadline he had imposed on humanity, Adolph Hitler chose to make a public statement. Until now, he had allowed Ferco Szabo to travel the globe, proclaiming the benefits of a one-world government and showering the airwaves with miraculous wonders. Hitler had been seen, either shaking hands of various leaders who were presenting their marked foreheads for approval or standing with a smug smile, watching his right-hand man produce wonders. But after seven weeks, Hitler wanted the world to know he was not a patient man.

Adolph Hitler and Ferco Szabo sat in wingback chairs in his office. Only one cameraman and one tech-support had been allowed in the room. When the red light turned on, he knew it was time to speak. Knowing the effect of his old accent, he laid it on thick for the camera.

"Today I greet the world on behalf of the Federation of World Powers. Welcome to my headquarters in Jerusalem. Beside me sits a man many of you know by now, Ferco Szabo, the President of Hungary. We requested this honor of speaking with the world today to remove any doubt that you as members of a united world may have about taking the mark.

"By now, most of the world has transferred its banking system to the One World Denomination system and are using magogs. The ease at which this process was accomplished will go down in history, I am certain. I personally want to thank the members of the FWP for their foresight as well as their oversight in this matter."

He turned to Szabo, who sat with a half smile on his lips. It was a dignified look for a sober occasion.

"Ferco, my friend," he started, crossing his right leg over his left and leaning toward his accomplice, "one of the most asked questions of you in your travels this past month was the timing of our request. Many have asked you if you believed two months was sufficient time for the families of the world to make a decision to take our mark and follow us. I would like to know what you told them."

Szabo cleared his throat, straightened his tie and looked into the camera.

"What most people do not understand is that we are at war. The Enemy is preparing for battle even as we speak, and we need to know now exactly who and what we are dealing with."

Hitler was careful to keep an interested look on his face and display the occasional nod in agreement.

"Yes," Szabo continued. "I accept that our timetable is extremely rapid. Still, we do not know when our enemy will strike and every day is one day less to prepare. Once we know our alignments, we will go hard and fast against those who have stiff-armed our cause. There simply is no place in this world for those people. Trust me—we will compensate every person who will help us rid the world of these dissidents. Our goal is lasting peace. We must realize our very existence depends on our success in ridding the world of the Enemy's people."

"Perhaps a demonstration will help them understand what you are talking about." Hitler offered his line exactly on cue.

Szabo rolled up his sleeve and held his hand out before the camera.

"Our cause is like my hand. It is healthy and strong and in this form it is rather useful. I can feed myself with it. I can surf the net with it. I can even hold a baby with it. But if it were to become diseased . . . "

He removed his tie and unbuttoned two of the buttons on his white dress shirt. He reached his hand into his shirt and pulled it out again. It was no longer a smooth tan hand, but a decaying, peeling, stench-ridden piece of dying flesh. Leprosy had left his hand completely useless, except to be dinner for the maggots that dripped from the open sores. As the cameraman suppressed a gasp, the disease literally inched its way up Szabo's arm.

"If left unattended, this will kill my whole body."

He stood and walked to Hitler's desk. The camera followed. He set his arm on the desk and pulled out a machete. With one swift motion he lowered the machete onto his forearm, severing the diseased arm from his body. Blood spewed forth from the amputated arm, splattering the desk and covering Szabo. He winced but still didn't cry out in pain.

Holding up his bleeding stub he said, "Now I have saved my body because I got rid of the disease. It may be painful, but in the end I have saved my life."

He stuck his stub back into his shirt and miraculously pulled out his hand. The blood was gone and the hand was fully healthy again. The cameraman and the tech looked at each other in disbelief.

"Please forgive the graphic nature of my illustration. It is an old trick I saw years ago and was impressed at its effectiveness even then. Make no mistake. Those who align with the Enemy are a disease to the body as a whole. We must amputate them from our midst. Then we will heal and lead wonderful lives."

Hitler walked over to Szabo and, standing tall, shoulders back, spine ramrod straight, gave him a classic Hitleresque arrogant nod. It had worked well for him decades ago. He knew it would again. "Well said, my friend. Well said." Then he turned again to the camera.

"One week from today, the world will know who is—and who is not—the disease in society. Together we can unite and bring prosperity to the world that can only come through peace. So today, if you do not have a mark, go now and do not be labeled a disease in your community. There is only one way to deal with disease."

He paused as the cameraman zoomed in for a close-up. Staring into the camera lens, he said, "Isolate it and wipe it out."

The red light turned off and Hitler took a deep breath.

The tech turned to his cameraman and asked, "Did you get that?"

"The whole world did," he said, to Hitler's satisfaction.

eighteen

Three new families from Shelton made their way to the caves and were warmly welcomed and embraced by the church members when they arrived. On their second night, the congregation gathered at the Tabernacle to meet them and hear what was happening in Shelton. Nate and Sherrie headed over without Adam, assuming he was already there with Emma. They sat down next to Pete and Pam Johnson just as Pastor Gentings stood to introduce the first of the three new families.

"Gary Prince spent his whole life in Shelton. He was a banker and is a father of three. His wife was a schoolteacher at the local elementary school. When Hitler first revealed his identity, they were in shock. Gary, why don't you come up and tell us how you ended up down here?"

Pastor shook the fifty-one-year-old man's hand and gave him the mike.

"We both grew up in the church. We were taught that one day someone would demand the worship of the world, just like Hitler did, but we assumed we were not going to be around to see it. We couldn't believe our eyes when it happened. My wife still has nightmares because of Rabin's murder."

Nate watched the response of the congregation. They soaked up every word, nodding and agreeing with every word he spoke.

"The day after the press conference, there was a knock on the front door and a young man told us not to take Hitler's mark. He said that we would be separated from God for eternity if we did. At first, I thought he was a Jehovah's Witness or some other cult freak, jumping on the opportunity to make life more confusing, but he didn't give us any pamphlets or even ask to come in. He just said, 'You need to be an overcomer. Go to the Word for your answers.' Then he left."

Gary Prince shifted from one foot to the other.

"Later that day I was filling my gas tank at the Marathon on Jackson, and the guy at the pump next to me said, 'You're not going to take the mark, are you?' I looked at him and told him he was the second person that morning to say that. He introduced himself and invited me over to his house for coffee. He was actually kind of pushy and wouldn't take no for an answer.

"The next thing I know, my family is sitting at Dan Dougherty's kitchen table, eating a slice of Betsy's apple pie."

Nate chuckled at that one, for he and Sherrie had found themselves at that same table, doing the same thing.

"He showed us Scriptures and spoke with such authority—we were completely blown away. All our questions, all our objections, all our preconceived beliefs—he answered with God's Word. Every single one. We sat there and wept. We repented of our ignorance and thanked God for giving us another chance. When I think of what my family was going to go through . . ."

Tears filled his eyes and the words caught in his throat. Pastor Gentings, standing next to him on the stage, put his hand on his shoulder.

"We cannot praise Him enough for His provision. I know we're coming late to this place, but whatever you ask of my family or me we will do."

"I know many of us can relate to how you feel right now," Pastor Gentings said. "Even your story about the Doughertys. Out of curiosity, how are they doing? We have not been able to contact them for a week or two now, and are wondering if they're all right."

"Dan and Betsy have been forced out of the church and meet with a small group who are committed to helping as many people as they can. Dan told me that at Grace, from the pulpit, the congregation was instructed not to accept phone calls from any of that group. Grace has also instructed the men to take the mark to provide for their families, claiming God knows their heart and would want them to be responsible."

There were several audible gasps and Nate heard Sherrie sniffling. He glanced over at her and when he saw the tears streaming down her face, he put his arm around her and pulled her close.

When Pastor Gentings spoke again, he seemed to reflect what was on the minds of the people. "The consequences of that decision are overwhelming."

He stood quietly for a moment and then thanked Gary for his testimony. Two more men were called up and gave similar testimonies. They added stories about Hitler's prophet and miracle man, Ferco Szabo, listing the miracles he had displayed and the response of the world. Nate listened intently to the testimonies of the new men. He had listened to countless testimonies through the years, but he had paid little attention to their content. He reported the testimonies, but never tried to understand the hearts of those who gave them.

Now, as he listened to the new families' stories, he paid attention. These were intelligent, reasonable men who were speaking. As he thought about it, he realized all the men down here were impressive. They were bankers, lawyers, carpenters, and teachers. Real people who were sold out to the message of the Bible. He had always thought Christianity was for the weak, but living with these people put a new spin on it.

As the third man finished his testimony, Nate thought back over the past month. He had spent a week trying to fix his battery charger, but gave up after that. Soon he was going to have to get to town to make contact with Sean and get a new charger for his phone. Five days ago he had offered to run to town for Mack Silver to get the newspaper and check in with the Doughertys, but so far, no one had taken him up on his offer. For him to leave was nearly impossible without breaking his cover, so he would have to just wait on Mack or see if another opportunity would arise for him to get away.

Glancing around the assembly, Nate made a decision. Without contact with the DIU, he couldn't take any action on his own. In light of the latest current events, he wasn't so sure he was in a bad place with his family. Now, with the newest arrivals giving testimony to the truth of God's Word and the signs of the times, Nate was more confused than ever.

Then a new thought hit him. What if he changed the direction of his investigation?

What if he investigated Christianity? Really investigated it for the first time in his life?

He sat forward, intrigued by the thought. Could he prove it false? What if he couldn't?

His breath caught in his throat at the implication. Either he had to prove it false . . . or he had to start believing it with his whole heart.

Until now, he had assumed that religion was for the weak and uneducated, but living with these people he found that they were neither weak nor uneducated. They were bright, intelligent, concerned, loving people who put complete trust and faith in God. More specific than that—they trusted Jesus.

His investigation would not just involve Christianity. No, he needed to investigate Jesus. He would do it quickly and with finality. Whatever the evidence proved would determine his future actions. He would either prove Jesus a liar and turn these people over to the Homeland Security, ending this little adventure.

Or he would prove Jesus was exactly who He said He was: God.

"Honey, are you ready to go?"

Sherrie was standing, gazing down at Nate, who was still sitting on the bench. He stood and looked around, somewhat bewildered. Most of the congregation had already gone.

"Sorry," he said to Sherrie. "I've just got a lot on my mind."

"Don't we all. I feel so isolated here and though part of me wants to know what is going on out there, another part wants to cling to ignorance."

"I know what you mean."

He took her by the hand and exited the Tabernacle. They walked in silence, Nate still deep in thought.

If Jesus really is God, then I have a whole new problem to deal with.

Nate knew the DIU had enough information to find these people on their own, without any more of his help. He would have to tell the elders what he had done and figure out how to undo it. Unfortunately, it was probably too late at this point to stop anything. Nate's big decision would be a costly one, no matter what his conclusion.

Mack Silver had been to Petra once in the past month. They had some issues with their water heater and he fixed it in about an hour's time. When Adam walked into his living room and saw Mack sitting at the table with his dad, his heart jumped into his throat. Somehow, he knew what Mack Silver was about to ask his father.

"Nate, Garrett Hamilton told me you've offered to make a run into town for me."

"Sure did." Nate handed Mack a cup of coffee.

Adam tried not to look concerned as he flopped down on a nearby couch, but he had no intention of leaving.

"Tomorrow I've got to meet the gas tanker to fill the storage tanks. It would be a big help if you'd run into town for me."

Adam's heart kicked into a double-time beat and he felt sick inside. His dad had to get into town to fix his phone. He wouldn't turn down an opportunity like this.

"Sure thing, Mack. If I remember right, I'll just take a quad over to the vehicle storage unit and get a van there."

"If you want, I can send someone with you."

"Oh, I don't think I'll need that . . . "

"I'll go with you, Dad," Nate jumped up from the couch and headed to the table to take a seat by his father. "I know how to ride the quads and it would be fun for a change of scenery."

Nate frowned. "You have your studies, Adam . . . "

"Come on, Dad, it's not going to hurt anything."

Mack sipped his coffee. "It's probably safer to send two. If a quad breaks down, then you're not stuck somewhere. I'll leave two sitting right outside of the Tabernacle in the morning." He tossed Nate a set of keys. "You should leave around 6:30. You'll need to run by the post office and check our box. Here is the key for that." He slid that one across too. "Then you can give the Doughertys a call from a pay phone. We've been having trouble with our cells up on the mountain and we just want to check in with them. Here's our phone card—prepaid, of course, and their number. Nothing will be traceable."

There, thought Adam, the decision was made.

Nate took the keys and phone card and put them in his wallet. Mack thanked him and told him to leave the quads back at the Tabernacle when they got back.

"Don't hang around too long; they seem to notice everything down there."

"Don't worry about a thing," Nate said, then he walked Mack to the door.

When his father returned, he didn't look too happy that Adam was going with him. Still sitting at the table, he buried his head in his studies and pretended not to notice his dad's irritation. He wasn't sure why he had volunteered to go, but thought it may bring things to a head with his father.

"We'll leave at six," Nate said stiffly, and then left the room.

I'll be ready at five thirty then.

The next morning, Adam was up and dressed by five. He'd spent a restless night, punching his pillow and flipping from side to side. He dreamed about waking up and finding his dad already gone. He was relieved when his father wandered out of his room at 5:15 to start the coffee.

"What are you doing up so early?"

"Just thought I'd do some reading. That . . . and I'm anxious to go."

Didn't someone once say a half truth is a whole lie? Adam felt bad for lying but kept a straight face.

"I'll be out in fifteen."

Fifteen minutes later, with travel mugs of coffee in their hands, the two headed for the quads. It was a cool ride, but now that it was May the trees were budding and there was less of a bite in the air. By eight they were in the van heading to Mount Olive.

His dad glanced across the seat at Adam and raised an eyebrow. "So, how're things going with you and Emma?" Before Adam could answer, he added, "You're over at her place a lot lately."

"Her family is really nice, Dad. We play cards and watch movies. Mr. Hamilton loves to talk about Scripture. We lose a lot of time to that."

"Do you like that, or are you just being polite?"

"Oh, it's great! I love spending time with someone who knows the Word backwards and forwards. It doesn't matter what I ask, he knows where to find the answer in the Bible. I've never been around somebody like that before."

With a burst of clarity, Adam realized his answer sounded like a comparison and he quickly stammered, "Not that, well, I mean . . . "

"Don't apologize. I know I can't compete with an elder. I do the best I can, but I know my knowledge is pretty limited. Adam, do you understand why we are at the caves? I mean, do you believe it? I didn't really give you an option of coming or not."

"Of course I believe it, Dad. Too much has happened not to believe. It amazes me that everything that was written thousands of years ago is coming true right before our eyes. Like the angels—that was awesome!"

"Well, why do you think Jesus is coming back now? Why didn't he just become king the first time he came?"

It occurred to Adam that his father was asking questions that an unbeliever would ask. Emma had told him to try to figure out where his dad was spiritually and here was his chance. If he would lay out the gospel in a simple, easy way, maybe his dad would understand.

"We were studying this in youth group. The way Mr. Torey put it, when Jesus came the first time it was to save us from our sins, not to save Israel from Rome."

"I heard it said once that Judas's problem was that he wanted Jesus to overthrow the Roman rule in Israel and just didn't get the big picture."

"A lot of people missed that. Mr. Torey said they thought the Messiah was going to free them from the Roman rule, but physically freeing them wouldn't solve the spiritual problem that every man has—our sin separates us from a holy God."

"So the first time He came," Nate said, "He paid our price for sin on the cross."

"Right. Sin deserves death. Jesus took our place, being perfect, and died for us. Now that the price has been paid, we can spend eternity with Him."

"So why come a second time? To become king?"

"Yeah, kind of. The second time He comes, He can deal with the rebellion of man against His Father and Himself. He will come to reclaim the world and get rid of those who have rejected Him. Then in the end, He will set up His kingdom, but not until after He recreates the world."

Adam reached into his coat pocket and pulled out a bag of pretzels and offered them to his dad.

"No thanks," Nate said. "I'm impressed with how much you know about this. But I still don't understand why Satan thinks he can win. And why does he think someone like Hitler would help his cause?"

"Maybe it's because Hitler is spectacular enough to get everyone's attention. He hates anyone who worships Jesus. His master is Satan. And throughout history Satan has tried to get rid of God's people. If he can do that, he gets to keep control of the earth. He tried to accomplish this through Egyptian Pharaohs, Haman, Herod, and even Hitler. He even tried to have Jesus killed before it was His time. Now Hitler shows up on the scene, offering world peace. The only cost is ridding the world of believers. Jesus has to come to put a stop to this rebellion."

They were now entering Mount Olive, passing other cars. Traffic seemed normal, and even the sidewalks were being used for pedestrian traffic. Then Adam sat forward with a frown. There was not one person without a black mark on their forehead.

"Look at how the people are falling for it," he breathed.

"And you're telling me that the Bible tells about all of this," said Nate.

"It predicts the mark and the idols. It even predicted the rising of a dead world leader! What I don't get is why people aren't falling on their knees and repenting of their sin and pleading to God for mercy. But that's what sin does, Dad. It turns us from our Creator and before we know it, we are worshipping the creature instead."

"None of these people have a second chance with God?"

"What did the angel say? 'Take the mark and be separated from God for eternity.'"

They sat in silence for a couple of minutes. Adam worried that he had poured it on too thick, but this might be his only opportunity to share his faith with his father. In the silence, Adam cried out to God to open his father's eyes.

They pulled into the post office parking lot. Nate told Adam to wait while he picked up the mail. His dad was gone for just a few minutes. There were about five letters in his hand when he returned. All of them were addressed to "Hank Johnson", an alias Mack had made up and told the Doughertys to use if they were sending mail.

Next they found a pay phone outside a convenience store and while Nate called Dan, Adam quickly ran and bought a couple of newspapers inside. He watched his father the whole time and was positive he had only dialed one number.

So far so good. Adam watched his dad closely on the phone. *We've done our errands and there's no reason to make any more stops! With me here, there's no way he'll get his charger fixed.*

Adam headed back to the car and relaxed for the first time.

"Hi, this is Nate. I only have a few minutes and if I start talking nonsense, you'll know I have to run."

"Nate? Where have you been?"

Sean sounded surprised to hear from Nate again.

"My cell charger isn't working. I think a wire came loose or something."

"You haven't been able to get away?"

"No way—I was lucky to get away today! Listen, things are stable here. I think I need more time to finish my investigation. Are we in a hurry?"

"How long do you need?"

"A couple more months at least."

"A couple of months? You've got to be kidding me!"

"Listen, I can see someone coming now, so I've got to be quick. Everything's stable. No one's talking about suicide, but no one's taking the mark or making an idol either, which is suicide in itself, right?

There's enough going on up by you, don't worry about us. When my report is complete I will make contact with you and we'll set up the sting. Sound good?"

"It's just taking longer than I had expected."

"Good to talk with you, Dan. And be sure to give our love to Betsy. You know how everyone loves the Doughertys down here! We arel praying for all of you up in Shelton."

"Got it, Dan and Betsy Dougherty in Shelton. I'll look into it."

"Bye."

Nate felt kind of sick to his stomach. He had to give Sean something to show he was still working, and Dan and Betsy were the first names that came to his mind. The Doughertys were in his file anyway, so it's not like he gave him anything new. Yet he still felt like he just led a couple of lambs to the slaughter. At least he bought himself a little more time. Himself and everyone else, for that matter.

Adam strolled up with four newspapers in his hand.

"Ready to head out of here?"

"I thought we could run over to the Wal-Mart and pick up a gift for mom. What do you think?"

"Well, we should really be getting back."

"I'll tell you what, I'll drop you off and you run in and get her some lotion or something. I'll fill the van and we'll kill two birds with one stone. Hey—and as long as our money still is good, we should grab some fast food too!"

"I could die for a Big Mac and a chocolate shake," Adam said, grinning.

"McDonald's it is then."

Nate dropped Adam off at Wal Mart and headed back to the gas station he'd seen earlier. While the van was filling, he had just enough time to run around the corner to a Radio Shack he had earlier spotted behind the gas station. He was waiting on the sidewalk with a full tank when Adam came out.

After feasting at McDonald's, the drive home was relatively quiet. Adam dozed for the first hour and fiddled with the radio for the second. The quad ride through the woods seemed to last forever for Nate, who was already hungry again and exhausted from the emotion of the day.

Sherrie looked relieved when Nate and Adam walked into the kitchen.

"Oh, good! You're back!" Sherrie kissed Adam on the cheek and then threw her arms around Nate. "How'd it go?"

"No problem."

With a wide smile Adam handed the bag to her. "We got these for you."

His mother smiled as she pulled out the bottle of lavender lotion he'd picked out and three boxes of Ziplock bags.

"What's with the bags? Your dad got me some last time he was in town."

"I heard Emma's mom say they were like gold on the mountain."

"Such a thoughtful boy." Sherrie pinched his cheek.

"I'm going to run this over to Emma." Adam a held up a small bottle of perfume.

"Don't forget—we're eating soon!" Sherrie called after him as he ran out of the room.

Nate dropped into a chair in the family room. He had accomplished a lot today. He knew exactly what he had to do. No matter what the cost to himself or his family, it was time to take action. He would find Garrett in the morning, which just happened to be May fifteen.

The next morning came after a fitful night of sleep and Nate found himself completely distracted during the Sunday morning message. It wasn't until he heard his name that he snapped out of it.

"Nate Reed made the run into Mount Olive yesterday and brought back a letter from Dan and Betsy. We've had some problems with our cell phone and haven't talked with them for the past couple of weeks, so it was good to hear from them."

Pastor Gentings was wrapping up the Worship service with a greeting from the Doughertys.

"They are encouraged by the number of Shelton residents who still have not taken the mark. They have a challenge for us. Initially we set a closing date of, well, today, May fifteen. As of today, we were not going to take any new families. Dan has requested that we rethink our position on that. He feels that they still have an influential voice in the community, but if we remove the option of people joining us here for safety, it greatly reduces their ability to minister."

Nate still struggled to pay attention. He knew that after the service he needed to grab Garrett, and the actuality of that conversation was making his stomach do somersaults.

"Last night the elders met with Mack Silver and discussed the possibility of expanding our community to our second mountain. As you all know, we haven't used that land yet and it has larger caves rather than the small units we discovered on this mountain. Mack feels the larger caves could house families with a bit of remodeling. We could add restrooms and makeshift kitchens. Furnishing them will be tougher—but it's our hope that if more people come they will bring some furniture with them. We feel that the Lord provided these mountains for protection and we should do what we can to use them for that purpose. So, starting tomorrow morning we are going to go over and scope out the situation and come up with a plan. Anyone who would like to come with us is welcome. We'll be leaving from here at seven thirty."

After I talk with them, that plan may be moot.

Pastor Gentings closed with prayer and dismissed the congregation. Because there would be another press conference at noon, today being the mark deadline, most cave units left one person behind to listen while the rest served lunch. The congregation would meet together again at seven for a time of singing and prayer. As Garrett and Lily were leaving the Tabernacle, Nate worked his way through the crowd and caught up to them.

He grabbed Garrett by the arm.

Garrett turned and smiled when he saw Nate. He extended his hand and Nate shook it.

"Good morning, Nate. What's up?"

"Could I talk to you a minute?"

Garrett turned back to Lily who was waiting for him.

"Go on ahead, Lily, I'll be right there."

Nate's heart was pounding out of his chest, but he was done playing games.

"I won't take up too much of your time, Garrett. I was just wondering if I could come over this afternoon and speak with you. Maybe Pastor or Pete should be there too."

"Is there a problem?"

"Well, it's kind of complicated and it does affect everyone here. I'd rather wait until this afternoon. Around three?"

That comment obviously caught Garrett's interest and he agreed.

"Sure, I'll get a hold of Pete and Pastor. See you then."

Garrett shook Nate's hand and tried to make eye contact with him, but Nate averted his eyes. There was no reason to wreck his next three hours, since they would probably be the last few carefree ones he would have.

nineteen

Adolph Hitler assumed his position in front of the Holy of Holies and waited for the red light. This press conference was much different than the one two months ago. This one did not have an audience and only one feed was necessary to reach the world. Life would be far more efficient with him in charge.

The light on the camera turned red.

"Today is May fifteen. The Federation of World Powers is now complete. We are a united force, intent on peace and prosperity for all. Our tentacles reach around the world and there is not one single country who stands opposed to us. Today, the world is united."

He glanced down at the floor of the temple. This was now his house of worship. He was on hallowed ground. He looked back at the camera.

"There is not one single country . . . but there are single individuals. For two months you have been allowed to choose. Today free will ends. A leader who allows free will to reign has no power at all. True freedom comes in conformity and today a line has been drawn. There are only two sides."

Adolph Hitler raised his left hand and smoothed his hair from the right side of his head down to the left. His right hand hung straight to his side.

"The Hebrew God has chosen for Himself a people—a race, if you would—who have set themselves above humanity as a whole. They are a deterrent to our cause and we will not tolerate their insolence. They proclaim they serve a God of peace, and instead they await the coming of One who will bring peace. Rather than bind themselves to humanity, they separate themselves."

Hitler's energy was steady and his voice was low and calm. He did not want to reveal anxiousness or anger, but he wanted to portray a controlled focus.

"Though the Prime Minister of Israel has chosen to align with the Federation, many of his countrymen have shunned his example. Throughout the world there are others who also desire to live outside of our system, placing themselves on what they consider a higher moral platform. They look down on you," he pointed with two fingers at the camera, "and sneer at your choice to join the New Federation. They believe they are too good for us and that they are above us."

He stopped to refocus.

"Today, for those of you who bear my mark, freedom is yours. You have education opportunities and employment options that have never existed before. Travel and banking are now secure and limitless. You are part of a solution, part of a global initiative that provides and cares for all. You will not be forgotten or overlooked. You are valuable.

"If you do not bear my mark, your future is destitute. You cannot purchase. You cannot travel. You cannot work. Today is the last day of tolerance for you. Tomorrow everything changes.

"Today every government will receive a directive from the Federation of World Powers to begin to take into custody those who are our enemies. In a peaceful and prosperous world, there is no room for dissidents. Thus the mark system has separated those who desire peace and those who don't. This directive provides financial incentives to citizens who aid the government in collecting the enemy. They will be gathered, given the opportunity to join us, tried if they refuse, and disposed of."

Hitler paused for a moment to let those words settle in. He was no longer trying to win a popularity contest, but a battle for humanity.

"Hell is a very real place. Most religions agree on this point. I am not here to promote religion but reality. I desire to live in flesh and blood, but there is a spiritual realm that cannot be ignored. If we do not remove the enemy we will cease to exist. Our time is short to handle this matter, therefore the FWP will provide whatever incentive it takes to accomplish our goal.

"Together we will overcome the Enemy and usher in the greatest race of all," he purposefully raised his voice and his right fist. "One that is free from intolerance and judgment. We shall rule ourselves and be of one mind. We shall free ourselves from the merciless wrath of a loveless, empty God."

Hitler held his arms out, as to embrace the viewer.

"Therefore, I declare today, May fifteen, World Independence Day, for on this day battle lines have been drawn and on this day we begin our fight for independence!"

His arms dropped to his side and he nodded a curt farewell. As planned, the red light turned off. He took a deep breath and swiped his hair again.

The room cleared, except Szabo stayed.

"Well, done, Adolph."

No reply.

"Do you think the people will respond?"

Hitler sensed doubt and his eyes flashed. "We have to start somewhere, so we start with trials. When that doesn't work, we will use more force to try to take out large groups at a time. In the end, my idols will convince people to take matters into their own hands and it will be every man for himself. But we can't start there. We will end up there. We don't have much time."

There was stirring behind the golden image of Hitler.

"Are your forces ready?" Szabo called to the figure behind the idol.

"We don't receive our instruction from you, we only take orders from Lucifer."

The hunched figure peeked around the image and growled at Szabo, but he stood his ground.

"Lucifer comes and goes as he pleases. Surely he has given you your instructions for tonight."

"Of course he did. Why do you think I came here? It is only out of respect to my master that I check in with you. You are just his human tool."

Hitler, not appreciating the disrespect of this demon, spoke up. "As I am sure you recall, I've seen angels and you really have deteriorated from your original glory."

The demon growled again, baring fangs to underscore his distaste for Hitler.

"Get used to taking orders from me," said Szabo. "Lucifer has given me authority and you will obey. You don't want to anger your master, do you? There are plenty of demons who would kill for your position."

"Are you threatening me?" Another sneer.

"I'll ask you again, are your forces ready?"

"Ready and waiting."

"Then get going and be thorough."

"Your wish is unfortunately my command."

The demon disappeared and Hitler looked at Szabo.

"The demons struggle with the power given to us. In and of themselves, they are magnificent creatures with abilities beyond our imagination. But demons cannot rule this world without man, so they have to work with us. Tonight, the world will receive a gift to aid our cause."

Szabo grinned and added, "It's going to get interesting, don't you think?"

"I don't have time to think. I can only obey. I've been there, Ferco, and I cannot ever go back. My motivation is greater than sheer power. I know what's at stake."

"I can't even imagine what you went through." Szabo put a hand on Hitler's shoulder.

He pulled away. "If we don't succeed, you won't have to imagine it. You'll know because you'll be there next to me."

The door of the temple opened and an aide stuck his head into the room.

"Sir?" he called.

"Yes?" Hitler answered.

"There's been a massive earthquake in Iran. They are estimating two hundred to three hundred thousand dead."

"I'll be right out."

"And sir?" The aide's voice faltered, as if he feared delivering more bad news.

"Yes?"

"Fourteen cargo planes headed to Zimbabwe with relief supplies have been lost over the Indian Ocean. A rare tropical storm has taken down the radar. We think the planes might have gone down in the storm."

"All fourteen?"

"Yes, sir. The limousine is out front."

"Thank you. I'll be right out."

The aide disappeared and the door shut quietly. Hitler stared at the statue of himself. His eyes glazed over and he could hear the statue talking to him.

You knew He would play dirty, so don't get rattled. A little earthquake and a tropical storm can't thwart your plan. Get in the limousine and get back to work. There's much to be done.

Hitler could hear the dull roar of the reporters who had gathered outside the temple, in the hopes of getting a comment or a picture.

He glanced at the door, stroked down his hair one last time and said to Szabo, "The demons had better work quickly."

He glanced at his watch and headed toward the door. He would wait a while and then turn the heat higher. That would give the demons time to settle in before things got really hot.

twenty

Evan Stillman reached up and rubbed his freshly shaven head. He pushed back from the table and stood. Looking down at the table, the plastic container that once held his frozen dinner no longer held its appeal and he picked it up and threw it in the garbage can. Once again, his mother was too engrossed in some TV show to make dinner, so he had heated up dinner in the microwave and ate alone.

Then he headed to his bedroom. As usual.

He walked over to his desk and pulled open the top drawer. He picked up the box of matches he had taken from Chester's Bar and Grill. He lit the candles on his desk and sat down in front of the computer screen. He watched the pictures of Hitler scroll through the sequence he had handpicked and he wondered if he had been thorough enough in his creation of his idol.

Today's press conference had been awesome. Hitler was the same as he was in the forties but he was definitely an updated version. Cooler clothes, hipper words, same mannerisms. It was surreal. Evan knew today was the first step in ridding the world of Jews. The only thing that bothered Evan was the fact that some Jews had taken the mark. With or without a mark, he would prefer a world without Jews and he was pretty sure Hitler would agree.

He pressed the space bar and the screen saver faded into his wall-paper—the picture of Evan and Hitler together.

"Nice mark."

Evan looked around to see who was in his room but his room was empty.

"I said, nice mark."

This time Evan recognized a German accent. He shook his head in disbelief but needed to see for himself. He looked back at his computer and saw that the background picture of himself saluting Hitler had changed. Hitler was no longer in a profile position, but he was facing the screen. He started walking closer to Evan, as Evan sat in front of the computer. He came closer until only his face covered the screen.

"How much did that set you back?" the screen inquired.

Heavy German, but definitely understandable.

Evan followed the eyes of the image on his screen and put a hand up to his forehead. The mark.

"Uh . . . a couple of hundred. Uh . . . what's going on here?"

"Did you see the announcement today?"

"Yeah."

"Well, I am a little gift sent from you-know-who to help you."

Evan stared at the screen for a few minutes without speaking. The Hitler on the screen stared back and blinked several times. Then he reached up with his left hand and swiped his hair into place.

"Are you . . . ?"

"No, I am not Hitler. I am just a helper he's sent to instruct you in the coming days. Nice gift, huh?"

Evan stared at his computer, hundreds of questions running through his mind. Under his breath he whispered, "You have got to be kidding me . . . "

"Trust me, Evan. This is no joke."

Evan sat back in his chair and watched his Hitler turn and walk back to his position on his wallpaper. He chuckled once to himself and then quickly quieted. This was going to be way cooler than he ever imagined.

Nate received word that the three o'clock meeting had to be postponed, due to another pipe burst, not at Petra but at Pastor Gentings's cave. When Garrett received the call on the radio that Pastor was up to his knees in water, he sent Josh over to Petra to tell Nate the meeting would have to be after church. That would work out better anyways because the youth would still be at the Tabernacle for dessert and the cave would be empty of children. Nate thanked Josh and told him to tell Garrett he and Sherrie would come over after the meeting.

Pete, Pastor, and Garrett were sitting at the table with a cup of coffee and a brownie when Nate and Sherrie arrived. They had not attended the evening worship and though she tried to hide it, Sherrie's eyes were swollen from crying. Nate brought the file with the information he had gathered and set it on the table.

"Come on in and have a seat." Garrett motioned to the table. "Can I get you a glass of water or coffee? Some dessert?"

"No, thanks, not for me. Is Lily here?" Nate didn't want Sherrie to have to face these men all alone.

"She's back in the bedroom. Want me to get her?" Garrett offered.

"Since I brought Sherrie, maybe she could be here too." Nate's voice faltered and he pulled out a chair for Sherrie to sit in and then sat beside her.

As Garrett ran down the hall and to find Lily, Nate sat nervously quiet at the table and Sherrie began to softly cry again. She opened her purse and pulled out a tissue. Soon, Garrett and Lily were back and seated themselves at the table with the others.

"Well," Garrett started, "since you called the meeting, Nate, I'm going to hand it over to you. Would you mind if I prayed before we began."

Nate nodded in agreement, grateful the few more seconds to compose himself. He reached over and grasped Sherrie's hands, which were folded in her lap. She wouldn't look in his eyes, but bowed her head for prayer.

"Father, we are so thankful for Your love and guidance in our lives. We ask that Your presence and work in our lives would be evident tonight. Please give Nate courage and strength as he shares his concern with us and may we be Your hands and feet to help him at this time. In Your precious Son's name we pray, amen."

Garrett picked up his coffee and took a sip, handing the conversation over to Nate. Nate released Sherrie's hands, cleared his throat and began.

"I don't really know where to start, so I'll start fifteen years ago. I was twenty-six years old and had been married for two years. Adam was an infant. I was working as an accountant for a large firm when I was approached by one of the senior partners in the company. He had a friend who recruited for Homeland Security, specifically the Domestic Investigations Unit."

Garrett furrowed his eyebrows and asked, "That's the department which investigates religious groups for intolerant behavior, right?"

Nate wasn't surprised that Garrett would be that quick to connect the dots. He leaned forward with his forearms on the table and continued.

"Right, along with a lot of other things. This friend had asked him if there were any bright, young accountants in his firm he could do without. The life of an auditor often requires travel, so it makes for a perfect occupation to move about the country with the excuse of the job requiring it. The firm got a nice finder's fee and I agreed to go undercover."

Nate looked at Sherrie. Tears were flowing again.

"Sherrie didn't even know until last night that for the past fifteen years I have been working for the government. We would move every couple of years and in that time I would investigate several churches in the area, file my reports, and move on. Sherrie knew we couldn't really set down roots anywhere, but she always attended church with me and got involved wherever we went. Through our time at these churches, Sherrie and Adam both gave their lives to Christ. I was too busy observing the people that I didn't listen to the message. Technically, I wasn't being paid to hear the message. Actually, I went into this job with the presupposition that the message was faulty."

Nate saw Lily reach over and take her husband's hand. Pete and Pastor Gentings were no longer touching their food. He had their undivided attention.

"Most churches we went to didn't break any laws and if they did, after I left they were penalized and only two were actually shut down. Grace was different than any other church I investigated. Your teaching on end times was radically different than anything mainstream. This caught my attention and I felt that this might be a larger investigation than usual, because of your land purchase down here and your plans to skip town."

Nate cleared his throat again. He knew he sounded like a self-righteous fool, but he didn't want to hide anymore.

"I thought I was onto some crazy cult. I envisioned myself saving the people from mass suicide down here and, in my mind, I already had the book written about my experience. This was going to out me as an undercover agent, but it was also going to make me rich."

Nate nervously wrung his hands as he spoke. This seemed to make the others nervous also, as they waited for what was coming next. Sherrie had quieted down again, but still wouldn't look at him.

"So we joined the church, moved down here, and Magorum turns into Hitler. I still can't believe that you got sick that night, Pete. And why you asked me to go with you, I still can't figure that one out, except for the fact God had a greater plan than I could see. Seeing Hitler's transformation with my own eyes . . . it was sickening, actually. Suddenly, rather than investigating all of you, I started to listen to you. Everything you taught was coming true. When those angels appeared in the Tabernacle, how could I ignore the truth anymore?"

With that question, Pastor nodded in agreement. Nate looked at Pete and Garrett, who were still quiet and very pale.

"The testimonies of the new families pushed me to the edge. God was really active and working in the lives of these people. I had to change my investigation and figure out if God was real or not . . . if Jesus was really God who died for the sins of man—maybe even my sin.

"The next week was incredible. I read the Word like I never had before. I doubt it was a coincidence, but at the same time Adam was asking me all these questions that forced me into the Word even more to find the answers. Then yesterday I did the town run with Adam. I turned the tables on him and asked him what he believes. Leave it to the simplicity of a kid, but he laid out God's plan so plainly I knew it was true."

Nate paused and shook his head.

"No, God opened my eyes and I believed for the first time."

The words stuck in his throat and Nate could feel his eyes welling with tears. His chest began to ache and he struggled to hold it together, but wanted to finish.

"I was so blind—blinded by my own arrogance and pride, and all the time God was drawing me to Himself. I got home and after dinner took Sherrie out for a walk and fell apart. Not only do I not deserve His forgiveness, but I have done a greater sin than I know how to fix!"

Nate knew he had to give the final blow and face the consequences. It broke his heart that everyone else was going to pay for his sin.

"I've blown it for all of us. I've deceived all of you and I've given the enemy a map to our front doors."

Nate pushed the file across the table to Garrett. Garrett pulled the file in front of him and opened the front cover. Pete and Pastor leaned closer to see what was inside. Lying on top was the dossier on Pastor Gentings. His picture, his background, everything. Garrett pushed it over to Pastor, then flipped to the next one. There was Garrett's picture. He looked up at Nate with an expression of shock, or maybe it was fear—Nate wasn't sure what he was thinking.

The next was on Pete. And it went on and on. Garrett saw the correspondence which was given to the members before the move in the file. A copy of the doctrinal statement, analysis of the plans of the church, timing, location—it was all in there. Nate was a very thorough agent. So thorough it may cost them all their lives.

Garrett, whose face had turned pasty and white, looked at Nate. He knew by now these three men were weighing the consequences. Tears streamed down his cheeks.

Nate felt a panic well up inside of him and he started to ramble.

"Asking your forgiveness just isn't sufficient. I've put all your families in danger—in certain danger. I'll do whatever it takes to help fix this and I have a few ideas but I can't keep this a secret anymore. I will submit to your leadership. The Lord has placed you in that position for a reason and I've worked outside of it long enough. One option"—

"Hold on there," interrupted Garrett. "Slow down. We need to chew on all of this for a bit. Just give me a second here."

All attention turned to Garrett, and Nate quietly waited for him to speak.

"First things first. Yes, the security of the flock is a high priority, but I want to back up to you, first. You're saying that when you came down here you weren't a believer but you are now."

Nate shook his head in agreement.

"I was so self-centered, I couldn't see beyond my own nose. I played the game so well my family didn't even know. And yes, I have confessed my sin to God and I want to repent and go the opposite direction. I'm just not sure He can forgive me for what I've done. It's not just my life I've messed up, I've hurt everyone here. Why would He give salvation to me?"

Garrett put his head in his hands and sat for another moment. Nate could see Garrett struggling with a response, knowing that all the years of planning and secrecy to protect the congregation was in vain. Pastor and Pete were quietly flipping through the file and Sherrie was crying again. Lily had placed her hand over Sherrie's and Nate appreciated her comfort at the moment.

"Nate, I have to be honest with you here," started Garrett. "It is taking every ounce of my strength not to reach across this table and pummel you. The only thing holding me back is my fear of God."

He stopped and shook his head.

"But what makes my sin forgivable and yours unforgivable?"

It wasn't a question to be answered, so Nate continued to sit quietly.

"Of course He forgives you—He's in the business of forgiving."

"I've cried out to Him and begged His forgiveness. I just can't imagine that He would do this in my case."

"Well, let me ask you this. Here and now, I can only think of one thing he won't forgive. Have you marked your head?"

When Garrett asked that, Sherrie raised her head and shook it no, responding for her husband.

"No, only by God's grace I held off on that," Nate said. "Originally I was going to have this investigation wrapped up before the deadline today, but my phone broke and I couldn't communicate with my superior officer. It was during this time that the Lord opened my eyes to the truth of His word. If my phone had been working, this would probably be over by now and I'd have my mark."

"You have a phone?" Garrett asked.

Nate nodded.

Pete jumped into the conversation. He directed his comments to Garrett.

"It's hard to overlook the hand of God in this one, Garrett. The Lord kept Nate from making an irreversible decision. He protected him; and I, for one, think He will protect us. Remember the angel's message? He said God was pleased with us and he called us 'Philadelphia.' That's a reference to a church who were overcomers. God promised a sphere of protection in the midst of tribulation—He says He'll keep them from the hour of testing. I don't think He overlooked Nate at the time. If our cover is blown, God will supernaturally intervene. We knew we couldn't pull this off without His help."

Though Nate wished he could be an optimist too, he was too much of a realist to believe what Pete said could be true.

"Nate, what you need to know, right off the bat, is that you are forgiven and you are welcome here," Pastor Gentings said. "Your guilt over your sin is evidence that you understand what a precious gift forgiveness is. First John 1:9 tells us that if we confess our sins, that God is faithful and just to forgive them and cleanse us from all unrighteousness. You are forgiven and you have been cleansed. Salvation is not for righteous men but for sinners and that includes each and every one of us here in the room."

Garrett returned to the conversation.

"He's right, Nate," Garrett nodded as he spoke. "You can be confident in your salvation. I don't mean to make you feel bad here but we need to talk some things out to find out what we need to do."

"I completely understand."

Lily spoke up. "What about you, Sherrie? How are you doing in all of this?"

The men turned their attention on the tearful wife, and she wiped her eyes and spoke.

"I'll be honest with you. I think I'm still in shock. It's hard to process all this information in just twenty-four hours, but basically my life has been a lie."

For a moment, Nate thought he could feel his heart breaking. He loved Sherrie and had always been a faithful husband, but his lies had been costly. Trust was gone.

"My mind is racing through the past fifteen years, replaying conversations and scenes that didn't make sense at the time, but do now. And worst of all, I feel responsible for being so ignorant and allowing this to happen!"

She began to weep again, and Lily put her arm around her shoulder to comfort her.

"No, Sherrie," Nate said. "None of this is your fault. I was the one who lied. I am responsible. The only thing you ever did was love and care for me and Adam."

"It's going to take some time for her to process all of this," Pastor Gentings said to Nate. "We'll help her through. Sherrie, you need to remember, though Nate is responsible for his sin, he wasn't under the influence of the Holy Spirit. He was lost and what he was doing made sense to him in his mind. He thought he was protecting you and serving his country."

Pastor reached for his coffee, and Nate felt a bit of relief with that action. The tension was great in the room and he spoke again.

"Sherrie, I know we don't have much time left on earth, and asking you to forgive what I've done to you seems so trite. But I love you and I'll do whatever you want me to do to make this right. I was thinking, I could go back to headquarters in DC and pay my superior a visit. If I can get my hands on the file, I could destroy it and that might keep you safe here."

"Would you come back?" Sherrie asked.

Nate couldn't tell whether she wanted him to or not.

"I wouldn't have to. I could just stay away, I guess. I know now that things are only going to get worse, but my boss doesn't know that. If I can get that file, even though he knows there's a group down here, he may never find you."

Sherrie turned to Pastor Gentings. "We can't send Nate out there—he'll never survive without a mark. Do we have to sacrifice him for the safety of the rest of us?"

"Sherrie, we wouldn't put him in that position," answered Pete. "We might need to keep him in contact with his superior to find out the plan."

He paused and thought for a minute. "Would it be possible for you to just tell him you misread the situation and ask him to close the file?"

"I don't think he'll fall for that. I can't just stop communicating either, because DIU protocol will leave us alone for about two months and then storm the mountain. I'm really at a loss right now."

"When's the last time you had contact?"

"Yesterday, instead of calling the Doughertys I called Sean, my handler. I thought it would buy us some time down here."

Garrett stood up.

"You did the right thing in coming to us. We need some time to process everything. We'll pray over it and let the Lord show us what to do."

Pete added, "I'm afraid we also need to let the others know what is going on so that they can be praying. I don't mean to put you in a bad spot, Nate, but they need to know."

Nate shook his head, wondering how he would ever face the congregation again.

"I'm going to keep your file here," said Garrett. "I want to see if anything would catch my eye that might help. And one more thing— would you mind giving me your phone?"

"I'll bring it over in the morning."

Nate stood and Sherrie followed suit. They started heading toward the door and Garrett put his hand on Nate's shoulder. Nate stopped and turned.

"God is faithful and He'll help us through this."

Garrett shook hands with Nate and walked them all to the door.

"It's going to take some time for us to figure out what to do, " he said as they were walking. "Maybe we do nothing. The world out there is going to have enough trouble of their own to worry about a few Christians hiding in the mountains."

Nate stopped just short of the door and turned to the men.

"Please forgive me for deceiving you. I am so sorry."

"Of course we forgive you," Pastor said, putting his hand on Nate's shoulder and giving it a squeeze. "It's time to get home. Nate, you're going to need to talk with your son before this all gets out. I will call a unit leader meeting in the morning. Does that give you enough time?"

"Yeah, I'll talk to Adam and the others at Petra. Pete, you'll be there with me, right?"

"Sure," said Pete. "Give me a few minutes here with these guys and then I'll be home."

The door shut behind them and Sherrie and Nate walked back to their cave. Sherrie had stopped crying but he was out of words. He felt as though a great weight had been taken from his shoulders and he reprimanded himself for feeling that relief. Then he felt Sherrie's hand slip into his and it surprised him. He stopped and looked at her in the darkness of the woods.

"I have gone back and forth a hundred times today, from being angry to being grateful."

"Grateful?" Nate asked.

She reached up and touched Nate on the cheek, sliding her free hand into his other one.

"Grateful that you know the Savior. No matter what you have done, I love you and don't want you separated from God for eternity, or from me for that matter. I am so thankful that God has saved you. But I am at a loss about our life together. What else was a lie? Why was it so easy for you to lie to me?"

"Sherrie, I just wasn't processing things right. I didn't see it as a violation of our marriage. And I have never been unfaithful to you—ever! I love you with my whole heart. I just separated what I had to do for work and justified it as part of my responsibilities."

"How can I be sure of what you say?" She let go of his hands and raised hers in frustration. "How do I know you're telling the truth now? How do I know there aren't other things you've lied about?"

"You can't know for sure. I've lost the right to ask you to trust me. But I can't lie anymore. Ask me anything and I'll tell you the truth. I just don't know what else to do or say. You have the right to question me, I know that."

"I can't believe how hard this is! I never dreamed of anything like this! Yesterday, my biggest worry was having you and Adam come home safely from town and today I am worried about …"

Sherrie stopped.

"Adam."

Nate's chest ached again. He took Sherrie's hand and began walking again.

"I know," he said. "This is only going to get harder. I don't know what Adam will say. But I had better get home and find him."

"He's probably not back from the youth meeting yet."

"Then it's going to be a late night."

Sherrie stopped again and looked at Nate.

"I'm here. We'll get through this together. Be patient with me, all right?"

Nate wrapped his arms around his wife and the two of them stood in the forest and cried. It was not sorrow this time, but a healing cry that came from his heart. He was feeling a peace that could only come from his Creator and he whispered a prayer of thanksgiving into his wife's ear as he confessed over and over his love for her.

twenty-one

Emma and Adam made their way back to Engedi, following Sarah and Ben, who were walking just in front of them. The sounds of laughter and conversation drifted toward her from the other kids who trailed a ways back down the path. During dessert time at the Tabernacle they hooked up an old karaoke machine that the Phillips had brought along and sang at the top of their lungs until they were almost too hoarse to speak.

Emma smiled as she remembered Adam and Josh's touching rendition of "A Whole New World" that had the room in stitches and Seth's "What a Wonderful World" impersonation of Louis Armstrong left the youth leaders speechless. Sarah and Emma sang "Sisters, Sisters" from White Christmas. When they finished Ben told them not to quit their day jobs, something he'd once heard their dad say.

The performance of the night came from Leighsa, who sang "Give Me Jesus" a cappella. The whole room sat in silence when she was finished until Adam called from the back of the room, "Ni-ke!" Soon all the kids were chanting. Emma was amazed that the kids got it—they understood that life was all about Jesus and nothing else. When Leighsa sang the last verse, "Oh, when I come to die . . . give me Jesus", it just seemed to touch all of them. Soon they would either die or be caught up to heaven—either way they would be seeing Jesus. Their hearts soared at the thought.

"What are you smiling about?" Adam asked as they walked. He caught her hand and held it.

"Tonight," she said, still smiling, "was so much fun!" She swung Adam's hand and ducked underneath it, finishing with a playful spin.

"Seth and I are going to get the music list so we're better prepared next time." After a moment's hesitation, he said, "Emma?"

"Yes?" She glanced over at him and noticed his sober expression.

Instinctively, she turned with him to see if anyone was listening. Then Adam said in a low voice, "I'm going to talk to my dad tonight. I don't know what will happen, but I can't hold onto this information any longer."

"You're doing the right thing, Adam. You've got to talk to him." A breeze caught her hair, and she reached up to tuck a loose strand of hair behind one ear.

Just then a rustling sound carried on the breeze toward them. Something about it was different—and Emma halted mid step, her heart pounding. Everyone else seemed to hear it at the same time and stood still. All conversation and laughter ceased.

Emma squinted into the dark night, trying to identify the sound. Not footsteps. Not a machine, but it was more than wind through the trees.

It was working its way across the mountainside. And heading straight for them.

By now the sun had long ago dipped below the horizon and the woods had taken on a dark and ominous look.

His voice trembling, Seth yelled for everyone to turn off their flashlights and try to hide.

Emma swallowed hard and glanced at Adam, who still held her hand. In a heartbeat, he pulled her toward a nearby tree. The others scattered through the woods, hiding behind logs or in some narrow stands of trees.

The sound drew closer now, seeming to ride on the wind. The temperature rose . . . from warm to hot.

Emma peered out from behind the tree. In the distance a pair of orange eyes came into focus.

She shivered, wanting to look away from the fearsome sight. But curiosity got the best of her, and she couldn't. The object was traveling on the wind, and as it drew closer, what had seemed to be a single set of eyes morphed into two, then three, then a dozen or more. More than a dozen. Hundreds!

It was too late to run.

Besides, where could they go to hide?

Her heart caught and she licked her dry lips. Adam tightened his grip on her hand, and she could hear his ragged breathing.

Then she remembered. The press conference. The orange-eyed demons.

The hot wind raged around them, now whirling, stinging, taunting. She stifled a cry.

Around her she heard the muffled cries of the other young people. Their fear matched hers.

The demons drew closer, so close the heat burned her skin. She wanted to cry out, but held tightly to Adam with one hand and hugged the tree trunk with the other. Adam was doing the same. The heat became even more intense and she closed her eyes. Behind her, she heard some of the younger children crying.

The eerie rustling seemed to die. Though not disappear. The hairs on the back of her neck stood up . . . as if something was watching her.

She opened her eyes and gasped. A demon circled the trees near them and seemed to focus in on Adam. She let out a cry and another demon was immediately eye level with her. Its gnarled, hairless face was inches from hers.

Emma's knees went weak. She wanted to scream, but no sound would come.

In her heart, she called to the Lord, knowing He alone would hear her cries.

The glittery orange eyes taunted her as if to say her prayer would do no good.

She called out to the Lord again, this time aloud.

The heat around her continued to rise and Emma could feel sweat beading on her brow. The demon's eyes were like orange flames, but they didn't dance. They seemed dead, like a dying ember in a campfire. It opened its mouth and a rancid smell came from its lips. It was blowing on Emma's face and she shut her eyes again.

As the demon blew its fetid breath from its lips, she could feel the wisps of hair that had fallen onto her face, lift and fall back down. The heat intensified, and she blinked back the sting of tears, calling out to the Lord once more.

Then without warning, the heat seemed to dissipate.

Emma opened her eyes. The demon's face still hovered over her, but the body seemed to be disappearing into a mist. She heard Sarah whimpering to her right, but other than that, there was utter silence in the woods.

Then she heard Adam's voice.

"We have no mark and we have no idols here. You are not welcome. So get off our mountain!"

The demon in front of Adam hissed. Emma's demon stirred and she resumed her prayers, this time for Adam. Hearing his voice had strengthened her courage.

In a spitting hiss, the demon answered, its voice reverberating through the woods. "You may not have invited us, but we know you are here. It won't be long until we visit again."

"We serve God Almighty! Visit us again and you'll have to answer to Him."

"Is that a threat?" A wicked, chilling laughter echoed over the mountaintop.

Emma pulled her eyes away from her own demon and turned her head to watch what was happening with Adam. He had let go of her hand and stepped away from the tree where they were hiding.

The demon circled, swirling around his legs, then waist, then chest, stopping again at his face, yet never touching him.

"Why do humans think they can threaten us?" the mocking voice said. "We do not take threats lightly." The creature laughed, the sound of it sending chills spidering up Emma's spine. "Oh, we will be back all right, and you will be sorry you did not invite us the first time, kid."

"You have no power over us and you have no right to be here. And my name is not 'kid.' You can call me . . . Ni-ke!" Emma heard Adam's voice waiver, but at the sound of the word "nike" Emma's courage began to seep once more into her whole being.

"What did you say?"

"I said, Ni-ke!" This time Adam's voice rose with force.

As the sound burst from her lips, Emma blinked. "Ni-ke!" she yelled. "Ni-ke!"

Adam joined her and the two of them cried their victory chant. Soon all the children were chanting and Emma's heart was practically beating out of her chest, not from fear but from courage. The woods were filled with the overcomer's battle cry!

The demon in front of Emma started to pull back. It's face, still gnarled, furrowed its brow, turned, and left. She glanced over to Adam again, and his demon had done the same. One by one the demons turned their backs on the children and continued their way through the forest. The temperature dropped back to normal and the chill gave her the shivers. She stepped away from the tree, just as Adam ran over to her, followed by Sarah and Ben. She wrapped her arms around her siblings and Adam hugged the whole bunch.

"Are you all right, Emma?" he whispered in her ear.

Emma nodded against his shoulder, her whole body shaking. Ben and Sarah had pulled away, but Adam kept his arms wrapped around Emma.

They embraced for just a moment, until the group from Engedi gathered around them. Josh and Seth were uncharacteristically quiet and Leighsa was crying.

"You guys did great!" Adam said to the younger children.

"I can't believe you spoke to a demon, Adam," Ben said. "That was so cool." He almost looked envious.

"How did you know what to say?" Emma asked Adam.

"I was trying to figure out what was happening and then it hit me—these demons were looking for a place to dwell. I knew there was no place for them and before I realized what I was doing, I was talking!"

"Mine blew on my face," Sarah said.

"Mine too," Emma said. "Could they have been looking for marks?"

"Could be," Adam said. He took Emma's hand as the group started back to Engedi.

After a few minutes, they reached the door to the cave and everyone but Emma and Adam went inside. Adam gave her a goodnight hug and whispered again in her ear, "Pray for me." Emma knew he was still troubled about the conversation he needed to have with his dad. She pulled back slightly, looking up into his face. She reached up to touch his cheek with her fingertips, and said, "I will." She kissed him and watched him walk into the darkness.

Inside, Emma could hear the young people telling the parents what had happened. Mike Torey was on the ham radio and sending out a warning to the rest of the families to get their kids inside if they weren't home yet. Emma pulled her father aside and asked if they could speak alone.

He nodded. "I need to talk to you about something too. It's about Mr. Reed."

Emma blinked in surprise. "Mr. Reed?"

"He was over here tonight and told us some things that are rather upsetting. But you go first. What did you need?"

"Can we go somewhere where we can be alone?"

"Mom's tucking Ben in bed. We can go to my room."

Emma and her dad walked down the hall to the parents' bedrooms. Pictures hung on those walls too. Each woman had hung wedding photos and Mrs. Phillips brought a painting of a Lake Michigan shoreline. She said it was there to remind them of home.

Emma followed her dad into his room. He sat on the bed, and she pulled the chair from the small desk in the corner over to where he was sitting and took a deep breath.

"You said Mr. Reed was by here tonight ... was it about the phone?"

Her father studied her for a moment then nodded. "How did you know?"

"Adam found the phone hidden in one of his dad's work boots. Later he looked around his dad's bedroom and found a file containing reports on all the elders and Pastor Gentings"—

Her father held up one hand to stop her. "I know all about it," he said quietly. "That's what Mr. Reed came over to tell us."

She sat back in surprise. "He told you?"

Her dad nodded. "Everything—about the phone, the file, his role with the government. Everything."

"Dad, I'm really sorry that I didn't say something sooner. We were trying to figure out what it could be, hoping for the best ... " She paused as it hit her what her father had just revealed. "His role in the government?"

"Yes, he is an agent. But he's not turning us in. He told us tonight how he came down here expecting to find a cult and instead, he found a Savior. It's a very convincing testimony of God's grace, using Adam and others here on the mountain to open his eyes."

"So . . . we're not in danger?"

"He has put all of us at risk, but we'll just have to deal with it. It's just another issue we'll have to leave in God's hands. Like the demons. They were searching for something, and who knows what will happen now that they know we're here. But I don't think we did something wrong. It's just one of those things out of our control that we have to trust the Lord with."

"I kept my eyes open most of the time, Dad. They were searching our faces. The demon in front of me blew in my face and lifted my hair with his stinking breath. I think they were looking for the mark."

"I'm sure they were. When they found no place to dwell here I don't think they had a choice but to move on. They know we're here, though, and so does Mr. Reed's superiors. We'll do the best to protect ourselves, but I think we'll have to put limitations on outside activity."

Emma didn't like the sound of that. The gatherings at the Tabernacle were a lifeline for the youth and the congregation as a whole. Then there was Adam. Would she be able to see him as often as before?

"Limitations?" She tried to keep the worry from her voice.

Her father nodded, and her heart fell.

Rory Appleton stared at the television in his bedroom. He was lying on his bed, remote in his hand, surfing the channels for something interesting to watch. He was bored with the offerings, and after a few minutes got out of bed and walked to the open door.

He looked out into the living room and saw Donna watching a made-for-TV-movie. He quietly shut the door, walked back to his dresser, and opened the top drawer. He pushed the neatly rolled socks to one side. There at the bottom of the drawer was a manila folder.

He glanced over his shoulder again to make sure the door was shut and then pulled the folder out of the drawer. He flipped it over. On the front cover was a taped picture of Adolph Hitler's face.

The image he had made was done in haste. Certainly not his best work. He had downloaded a picture of Hitler from the Internet and printed it. Though it was only about two inches square, he had taped it to the front of the folder. Ingenious, really. Easily hidden, but when he opened the folder a bit, the "idol" would stand on its own. Donna would have a fit if she knew. He had told the congregation not to make one, but he wasn't sure that would fly with the new system, so to cover himself he had this makeshift idol that technically would count if needed. He had no intentions of bowing to it or praying to it, or even displaying it. But, should anyone ask to see his idol, he and his wife were covered. He could pull this out of the drawer and save both of their lives.

Rory put the folder back in its place, pulled the socks over it, shut the drawer and grabbed his pajamas from the next drawer below. He went into the bathroom and changed out of his clothes. He brushed his teeth and washed his face. As he dried his face with the pink and white towels Donna had recently bought, he wondered why she never consulted him before changing things around the house. He looked at himself in the mirror and his eyes rested on the number. 666. It was like something from a horror movie. And the world was buying it.

"If you can't beat 'em, join 'em."

"Did you say something, dear?"

Rory heard Donna's voice from the living room. He walked out of the bathroom and mumbled, "I'm tired. I'm going to bed."

She didn't respond, but was obviously engrossed in a captivating, predictable story line that any menopausal woman would dream to live. Rory went back into the bedroom and closed the door. He threw off the decorative pillows, another recent purchase, climbed into bed and closed his eyes.

Doesn't it kind of bother you that you have the mark and she doesn't?

Rory was close to dozing off, causing his thoughts to drift.

I mean, you are the one risking everything. She just sits there and watches television, not a care in the world. You have to bear the fact that you have an image in your top drawer and a mark on your forehead. You're the one who has to answer for that, not her.

Rory opened his eyes. It was kind of frustrating that he was losing sleep over a decision that protected Donna, and Donna apparently didn't even think twice about it.

She had better be worth the price you might pay, buddy. You've made a lot of sacrifices for her over the years, but this one tops them all.

Rory's eyes flew open with a start. Was he thinking these things? Or was he actually hearing them?

He glanced around the room again and rolled over on his side, his gaze going to the dresser where the idol was tucked beneath his socks.

The sound of the television annoyed him even more than before, and he grabbed Donna's pillow and put it over his head.

twenty-two

Adam and Sherrie slept in late the next morning. Nate got up and went with Pete to meet with the eighteen unit leaders, made up of elders and deacons plus a few laymen. When Adam did finally walk into the dining area, his mom was sitting with the other moms and she was crying again. He walked over to her and put his hands on her shoulders.

"Good morning, Adam," she said as she wiped another falling tear from her cheek.

"Did you sleep, Mom?" he asked.

"Yes, I took some Tylenol PM and it knocked me out."

Adam heard the door open, and Nate and Pete walked in together. Nate looked whipped and Adam actually felt sorry for him. The men joined the women at the table and Pete spoke first.

"That went as well as could be expected, don't you think, Nate?"

"They were gracious. I don't think Mack Silver is going to come over for coffee any time soon, but I understand."

"So what happened?" Adam asked.

"Pastor Gentings explained the situation," Pete said. "At this point, we don't know of anything we can do but pray. The men agreed to organize prayer times in their caves, and ask for God's wisdom and protection. We know this was not a surprise to Him." Pete smiled and Adam realized it was the first smile he had seen all morning.

"We discussed a lot of scenarios, and for now I'm going to keep in contact with my handler—just to check in occasionally and continue to get a feel for what's going on out there."

"They're letting you keep the phone?" Sherrie asked.

"No, Garrett will keep it and will be with me whenever I use it." His dad looked embarrassed and Adam felt bad for him.

Pete continued. "We've also decided to put restrictions on outside movement."

"What do you mean?" Adam leaned forward. "Restrictions?"

"In light of the demonic visit last night, we don't want any attention drawn to the mountain. As far as most people around here know, we're not even here. We don't know if the demons will monitor us or tell others where we are. We're really not sure what that was all about, but we think it is much safer in the caves than outside of them."

"So we can't go outside at all?" Adam suddenly felt like a prisoner.

"We'll let there be some movement late in the day, like at dusk. And we'll limit the Tabernacle meetings to just once a week."

Nate had walked over to Sherrie and was whispering something in her ear. She stood and Adam wondered what was going on.

"You'll have to excuse us," Nate said to the women and Pete. "We're going to go talk for a bit."

Nate took Sherrie's hand and led her back to their bedroom. Adam watched them go, but at the moment he was more concerned about how he was going to get to Engedi on a regular basis.

Pete continued to talk with Pam and the other women.

"Mack Silver is also starting work on the second mountain. He and Tara are going to move over there, so that they can oversee the new build out."

"Why?" Pam put down her coffee mug and gestured to an empty chair beside her.

Pete walked over and sat, as Pam poured him a cup of coffee.

"The cell phones are no longer working. Our accounts were closed as of the fifteenth, so we know we won't be able to communicate with Dan unless someone heads to town. But in the last conversation Pastor had with Dan, he really felt that he was going to be able to send more people down here."

"But don't we still have space in some of the caves on this mountain?" Pam asked.

"One or two have some room, but we're mostly filled. The way we see it, we'll need the room if we have more families arrive. We also have some time on our hands and a project always gives a focus and keeps us busy."

"So, basically we can't go outside and we're building out more caves just to keep busy till this is over?" Adam was getting pretty good at stating the obvious.

Pete met Adam's gaze and once again, Adam saw a gentleness and kindness that made him ashamed of his tone.

"We don't know how long it'll be before Christ comes, but we do know that God created us to be like Him—creative. He instructed Adam in the garden to work. It's what man does. Building out another cave system allows us to plan together, work together, be together. We're setting up a system where women will come to handle the meals and the men will work on three day shifts—three days gone and two weeks back here. So, it's not going to be overwhelming to anyone, but gives an outlet to create and a goal to focus on."

Pete ran his fingers through his graying hair and seemed tired.

"How about the high schoolers? Do we get to help?" Adam asked.

"Absolutely—we couldn't do it without you." There was that smile again.

"When do we start?" Adam grinned. Things were looking up.

"Mack's working on a schedule and is taking a group over tomorrow to check out the job. He had the foresight, thank God, to bury and fill propane tanks and we have lots of extra supplies. Your dad's woodworking will come in handy because we'll be building out more of the space than we did here."

Adam's stomach turned at the mention of his dad. It was a dose of reality in the middle of a dream. They can play hide and seek here, but because of his dad, they were most likely going to be found and all the time-wasting projects in the world can't take that fact away.

As the women continued to chat with Pete, Adam headed back to his room. He had too much to think about, from his parents' marriage being on the edge to not seeing Emma much anymore to wondering how long he would live in a cave. His head started to ache and he flopped down on his bed and shut his eyes. The initial excitement had officially worn off and now reality had arrived.

He was living in a nightmare.

This is officially the longest summer of my life.

Emma set her pen on the bed beside her and flipped through past pages of journal entries. Each day was identical to the one before. Schoolwork. Eating. Watching DVDs. Playing cards. No new TV shows. No news. No fresh air. No escaping the crowds of children in the cave.

There were two things responsible for her maintaining her sanity. The first was the fact that her mom let her go to the other mountain and help cook when it was Lily's turn to serve. Emma loved that. Getting away, the ride through the woods, the excitement at the other cave system.

The second thing was Adam's friendship with Seth and Josh. Because he was buddies with them too, the parents all agreed to sleepovers and Adam was at her cave almost more than he was home. That made life bearable.

Mr. Silver made a mail run yesterday and Dad got another letter from Mr. Dougherty. He says that most people in Shelton have put a mark on their forehead, but there are still some who are holding out. Mr. and Mrs. Dougherty do not feel that their lives are in danger, though the Shel-heads have vandalized their house several times and shout obscenities at them when they go out.

Mr. Dougherty wrote that life in America is really pretty normal for those who have marked up. There have been some pretty bad droughts out west and the price for basic staples—bread, milk, meat—have skyrocketed, but those who have magogs can buy and sell with ease while those without marks can only get food if someone will exchange services for goods. And the government shuts down businesses if they are found helping non-markers. Mr. Dougherty says he gets most of his food, other than what he has stored in his basement, from a farmer who grows his own vegetables.

So why does the summer feel long? Well, it's almost July and I am as white as a ghost. Fresh air and sunshine are things from my past. Yes, I am continuing my education, reluctantly and Mom has graciously backed off a bit, but to fill one's day with schoolwork hardly makes the time fly.

Now, if I had my way, I would pack a picnic lunch, complete with ham and cheese sandwiches, homemade cookies, crackers and cheese, and large, fresh green grapes, and I would have a picnic at the lake. I would lay out a blanket on the large rock that rests beside the lake, and after lunch, I would lay for hours, watching the clouds drift by and name the different shapes and images I would see. Occasionally I would jump into the lake and cool down, then I would return to my rock and continue to bake myself until I was well done!

But, it is just a waste of time to daydream about something I'll have to wait for heaven to do, so back to reality, I guess. Heaven . . . now there's something to dream about . . .

A knock at the bedroom door made Emma jump. Sometimes she could find a quiet corner and write. When she did she was lost to the world. The knock was a wake-up call back to reality.

"Come in," she said.

It was Seth. "Adam just got here and your mom said she needs help in the kitchen."

"Well, why don't you help her and I'll sit with Adam?"

"Yeah, right."

Seth closed the door and Emma put her journal and pen back under her mattress. She stood and walked over to her dresser. Her father and Mr. Phillips had built the bunks in her room, but she was using her dresser from Shelton. She ran her finger across the front edge, remembering her bedroom in Michigan. It had been much larger and much emptier. Quiet moments like this were few and far between. Emma looked in the mirror above her dresser and considered putting on some makeup.

"Adam will just have to get used to you without makeup," she said to her reflection. *"I could put some on, but when it runs out . . . "*

Emma stopped talking and just stared at herself. She could faintly hear her mom calling her name down the hall and knew it was time to go. She reached up and pinched her cheeks.

Stop dreaming about the lake, Emma. It only makes you feel worse.

She left the room and her wishes behind, and put on a smile for Adam.

For a couple of weeks Nate continued to check in with Sean. Sean let him know how things were progressing in the real world and from his perspective life had never been better. Being in the Domestic Investigations Unit was the perfect place for someone who wanted job security. Special incentives were being offered for information leading to the arrest of nonmarked citizens, not that the absence of a mark was a crime yet, but they were quickly heading in that direction.

Sean had told him that finding a valid crime committed by a nonmarker, mostly involving the anti-intolerance law, was being well compensated. Three hundred, tax-free magogs, which were equivalent to three hundred US dollars in the One World Denomination system, were offered for each nonmarker whose arrest proved valid. Most nonmarkers, once they found themselves in jail and separated from their families, were willing to be marked to get out. If your arrest resulted in a nonmarker becoming marked, there was an additional one hundred twenty-five magogs in your paycheck.

Nate was in the perfect position to get information because Sean still thought Nate worked for him and Sean loved to talk. So, Nate just asked a lot of questions and got a lot of answers.

"The agents are having a field day!" Sean's voice resounded with pride. "We're taking in nonmarkers for anything and everything! The jails are filling up with offenders and since it takes about six months to get a court date, most of them are caving in and getting marked just to get out of jail. The quicker they get out, the faster we get our bonus in our paychecks!"

"So if they mark up, you're getting four and a quarter for each of them?"

"Yep. Last week alone, I had eight of my arrests released with marks. That was an extra thirty-four hundred in my paycheck!"

"So what's happening to the people who won't get marked?" Nate asked, angling the phone away from his ear so that Garrett could hear the answer.

"Right now we're shipping them to Ann Arbor. There is a camp there."

"A camp?"

"Yeah, a retraining camp. In theory, it deprograms nonmarkers and after four weeks, if they have marked up, they are sent home. If not they're sent to prison, but I think it's something worse than that."

"What are you talking about?"

"Well, Hitler did like to get rid of his enemies the first time around. Why wouldn't he do it again?"

"You mean exterminate them?"

"That's your word, not mine. I don't know what happens to them, but I don't think it's good."

"Hitler has that much power."

Sean laughed and Nate shook his head at Garrett as if he had no clue what was funny.

"I keep forgetting you're in the middle of nowhere. The FWP is a powerful union, Nate. Unlike anything history has ever seen. They have cash flow that no one can stop. The markets flow in their favor and then continue to spread the wealth. Yeah, Hitler's there, but what the FWP is accomplishing despite unusual weather disasters and famine in certain areas of the world, is incredible. So bottom line, it is only in our benefit to work with the FWP. And really, we're only weeding out odd ducks, anyway. You know, superfundamentalist Christians, obstinate Jews, and some UP rednecks who don't watch the news."

Aumonti laughed again and Nate was amazed at his callousness.

"Listen, Nate, at this rate our agency is going to quickly fill up with rich young men. It's just cash in our pockets and the FWP has made it easy on us. No mark? Off you go. So, it's been six weeks now, are you ready to cash in yet?"

"Uh . . . well," Nate was stammering and Garrett lightly elbowed him in his side. "I really don't have enough valid, um, offenses for you to barge in and arrest these people yet."

Nate looked at Garrett and Garrett nodded hopefully.

"How many people do you have up there right now?" Sean asked.

"Around seventy families or so."

"Let's say you bring in the men and their wives, which the women will be able to be charged too, most likely, that would make . . . ummm . . . around forty-five thousand in your pocket with a potential additional eighteen thousand if they all take the mark eventually—tax free. Come on, Nate, what are you waiting for? You can't tell me you like it down there?"

"Well, what's your hurry? Do you get commission on your agent's arrests?" Nate forced a chuckle, as if he was joking.

"Actually I do, and the sooner we act the better. Listen, the FWP really wants to weed out the enemy quickly so that we can all just move on and enjoy life. Every nonmarker still on the loose is just a reminder that the enemy still exists. They have kids and they are breeding rebellion in them by not taking the mark. We need to get this over with and get rid of them now!"

"How are the nonmarkers surviving without magogs?" Nate asked, trying to steer the conversation away from the church.

"Many of them stocked up or have gardens or something like that, and others turned in cash on the black market for magogs. They think this is a passing phase, but it's not."

"I guess I have been gone a couple of months but what has happened to the American way? What's happened to the freedom to choose for yourself what kind of life you lead? It's really scary what's happening out there, Sean, and what scares me the most is how quickly Americans have bought into this Hitler worship system."

"What're you talking about? Don't you realize who we're dealing with? Have you been hiding so long that you have no clue? This whole system is so much bigger than just Adolph Hitler. This is Satan! Hitler is just his human pawn. We are dealing with Satan ruling the world and you know what? Once our manhunt for nonmarkers is over, Satan is a pretty liberal dude. He's all for freedom. Free sex, free drugs, free addictions, free anything goes! He tolerates everything except God followers. So, if getting rid of a small percentage of the world's population brings us freedom and even immortality, I say let's get at it!"

"Immortality? What do you mean, immortality?"

"He raised Hitler from the dead. Common sense says he can keep us all from death. He wants to take our death threat away and he alone offers life!" Sean paused a moment. "Listen, you really need to get out of there. You've been with them so long you're starting to sound like them."

"I guess I have been here a long time."

"I'm giving you a week and then we're coming in."

"A week?" Nate tried to hide the shock from his voice. "You've got to be kidding me. I'm nowhere near ready"—

"You've had enough time. Have your ducks in a row by the time we get there. I want to know who we're taking in and what their charge is. I know none of them are marked yet, so we can start there. We can call them an underground organized rebellion cult, who threatens the American way of life. Whatever we need to call it, just do it. The more you accuse, the more money in both our pockets."

"But, Sean"—

"No more buts, and no more time. You're really starting to worry me. Someday you'll thank me for saving your life and lining your pocket. One week."

The phone went dead. Nate looked at Garrett who was standing beside him and listening to the whole conversation.

"This is bad." Nate didn't know what else to say.

Garrett and Nate were standing in the clearing at Shiloh. The neat rows of trees were now scattered and angled to look more natural, rather than like a meeting place. Garrett sat down on a log and put his face in his hands.

"Father," Garrett prayed aloud, "we've got a week to figure out what to do. There's nowhere to move these people. We're going to need some help here."

twenty-three

"Hello, Mrs. Stanley," Rory said with a smile. He had counted thirty-two women without marks, but with marked husbands. It was really starting to irritate him that all those women sat there smugly in their seats without a mark, while their husbands bore the weight of possibly upsetting God with their decision.

"Hi, Stacey." Nod, smile. *Thirty-three.*

As he scanned the room, he noticed a couple of women with numbers. He appreciated their willingness to stand with the men. Most were single mothers who had no other way of supporting their children. A couple of them were just single women, choosing not to become a burden on the church. There was one widow who took the mark too, but she claimed she was mad at God for taking her husband and she had her own issues.

"Can I get the door for you, Marilyn?" *Thirty-four.*

Rory thought back to the widow, while he held open the front door of the church. She did have a point. God wasn't being very loving by putting them all in such an awkward position. Why would He allow the church to enter this trial so unprepared?

He closed the door and headed to his car. The service had gone long this morning and Rory had reprimanded Ray afterwards, reminding him that there is no reason to force these people to sit in their seats longer than an hour. Donna had feigned illness and was probably at home in front of the television again.

"Have a nice afternoon, Mrs. Kingsley," Rory called across the parking lot. Smile. Turn the head. Sneer. *Thirty-five.*

I will probably ask Jesus personally why He wasn't clearer about His return. If He had just been clearer, then there wouldn't have been all this confusion. Of course, by the time I see Jesus, all of this will be but a vapor and I'll probably be too busy to even remember to ask Him, with all the responsibility the Lord will give me in heaven.

Rory was struggling to concentrate lately. His mind seemed to wander aimlessly these days. The only place where his thoughts were impeccably clear was in his bedroom. There he could reason and think through all of his concerns without being distracted by mundane details. He longed to be home. He longed to think clearly. He had some decisions to make about his own life. Why was he paying a price for a delinquent wife? He had decisions to make and needed someplace he could think without distraction.

He knew exactly where that place was.

By the time he got home, Donna was setting the table for Sunday lunch. He walked past her and went straight to the bedroom. His head was aching and thankfully, she didn't say a word. Or did she? He wasn't sure.

Rory sat on the bed.

"Why should I pay the price for her?" he muttered.

"So you have finally come to that realization?"

Rory jumped from the bed and swung around to see who was talking to him, but his room was empty.

"Who's there?" He ran to his closet and flung open the doors. Empty, but for the clothes.

"In here."

The heavy accented voice came from his dresser. A foul taste came to his mouth, and he immediately knew whose voice was speaking to him.

He opened his drawer and moved the socks off of his idol. He pulled it out and set it up on the dresser.

"So you really thought God would overlook your mark?"

Hitler was talking. Rory was speechless.

"You chose to provide for yourself and now He will punish you for it. Forever. And she sits in there, eating whenever she wants, has you fill up her car so she can go wherever she wants and there is no cost to her."

"Yes," Rory whispered. His legs felt like they were made of lead. He couldn't have moved if he had wanted to.

"I am here to help you. I understand what you are feeling. I have been talking to you for a few weeks now. You were just unaware that it was me."

"But . . . "

"I am your friend. I know it is difficult to carry the weight of the church on your shoulders and to carry on with your landscaping business."

"How did you know—?"

"It is a good thing you took the mark. You are providing for Donna. You are also providing for all your employees."

Rory breathed a little easier. "That's true."

"Donna does not know how good she has it, but soon she will understand. Just remember, I am here for you."

Donna called to him from the kitchen, telling him dinner was ready. Rory felt a stab of panic and quickly slapped the folder back into his drawer. He pushed the socks over top and slammed the drawer shut.

As he reached for the doorknob, a still, small voice drifted toward him from the dresser.

"Enjoy your lunch, Rory. We will talk later. We have a lot to cover."

Rory shut the bedroom door behind him and headed to the kitchen. But it wasn't lunch he was thinking about. No, the image he couldn't push from his mind was that of the idol. And how the lips moved on Hitler's mouth.

For the first time, Rory wondered if he had sold his soul to the devil.

"So I was thinking, if we could move everyone over to the second mountain, when they arrived they would find our homes evacuated and would figure we had moved to another location."

Nate looked across the table at the elders and deacons. His mind had been racing all night and he had hardly slept. Six days until the raid and counting.

"I could even call them and tell them you had found me out and forced me to talk. I could be convincing."

"Yeah, and you'd be lying," Pete said, sitting next to Nate. "We haven't had to lie to live here yet and we're not going to start now."

"I think we're all in agreement that you're done talking with Sean," said Garrett. "You're one of us now and you need to be done with the double agent thing. We know they're coming and that's all we need to know."

"I don't think we should move to the other mountain," Paul Cowlings said. He was a deacon, who lived in the same cave unit as the Reeds. "If we abandon these caves, they could ransack them or burn them and we'd have nothing to return to. The caves on the other mountain are not even livable yet—without running water or heat, we'd be in trouble over there too. I think we need to stay and protect our homes."

"With what?" Garrett said. "We chose not to stockpile weapons. Each unit leader has a handgun, but most of us don't know whether the safety is on or off."

Nate felt the tension rising and his heart sank. He just couldn't fix this, no matter how hard he tried.

"How did you live in Michigan and never hunt?"

Nate glanced over at Pastor Gentings, who was ribbing Garrett in an attempt to lighten the mood.

"Who wanted to hunt when you could golf?" came the answer. Still a bit gruff, but he was coming around.

"I've got a couple of automatic rifles in my cave too," Nate said. "I'm not sure if I mentioned that before or not."

Garrett looked over at Nate. If looks could kill, he would probably be dead.

"Do you know how to use them?"

"What does it matter, Garrett?" asked Pastor. "We're not going to lie in wait for the DIU to show up and then snipe them all to death. If we even shoot at one, they'll drop an arsenal on our mountains and that will be the end of us. We have to trust the Lord to cover us on this one. We also need to prepare the people for the possibility of arrest. Sean told Nate that the men and women alike would be charged—the kids would probably go into foster care. This could be the end of it, unless the Lord intervenes. But we aren't going to kill anyone. That's never been part of the plan."

Yeah, and it was never part of the plan to have an undercover agent give maps to the enemy either. Nate hung his head.

"So we're just going to sit and wait for them to come, is that what you're telling me?" asked Garrett, who was on the edge of his seat by now.

He looked up again when Pastor Gentings said, "We'll hide as best we can, but by faith we need to trust that Nate's being here was not a mistake but part of God's plan." His words soothed Nate's feelings of sorrow over what he'd done. "We also know He called us Philadelphia, and to that church He promised He would protect them within a sphere of danger. So, by faith we'll prepare the people and even the children for captivity and then we'll call upon the Lord to save us. I think this is our best option. Going on the offensive—even the defensive with these people is only going to cause more trouble than we already have."

As Nate headed home, he had a long conversation with the Lord. He had let Pete and Paul leave first so that he could walk alone.

"Father, I don't know how I could live with myself if this church gets separated because of me. I know You have forgiven me and I even know that Jesus has already paid the price for this sin of mine. I just don't know what to do with the guilt. I can't sleep and I can't concentrate, and I can't come up with what to do. I have no choice but to trust You. I know that sounds pretty lame, as if it is a last resort, but I'm not used to giving control of my life to someone else."

Nate stopped in the woods. He could see his cave entrance in the distance, but he wasn't finished talking with the Lord. He sat on a fallen tree and looked up at the stars.

"I see You everywhere, Lord. These woods, the stars, my son, and my wife—all of them are gifts from You. Forgive me for doubting. Forgive me for trying to help You out. I rest in Your control and Your love. One other request"— Nate heard a snap and saw a squirrel run into a hallow stump nearby. "Give Garrett the grace to forgive me. I could tell he was really struggling tonight and I sure can't blame him. But Lord, he's a good man. I've brought him pain and I am asking You to give him peace tonight. In Jesus' name I pray, amen."

The families of Engedi called a meeting for after dinner. It was Monday night and there were four days left until the DIU raid. As Emma waited for the meeting to begin, she sat on one of the couches in the living room and braided Sarah's long blonde curls as she sat on the floor in front of her. Ben jumped over the back of the couch and landed on the cushion next to Emma.

"How many times has Mom told you not to do that?" Emma reprimanded Ben for this act usually two or three times a day.

"So, what do you think we're going to talk about?" Ben asked.

Sarah turned her face to Ben in utter disgust.

"Where have you been for the past day, Ben? Are you totally clueless? We're talking about the raid, dummy!"

Emma yanked on Sarah's braid, producing an "ouch!" from her sister.

"Sarah, stop that. Leighsa, sit here with us."

Leighsa had just entered the room and slid in between Ben and Emma, pushing Ben over with her hip.

"Come on! I was here first," Ben whined.

Some of the other families had drifted into the room. Leighsa glanced around as if to make sure she wasn't overheard, then she leaned over to Emma and whispered in her ear.

"I heard Dad and Mom talking today. They think we're all in trouble."

Leighsa's face was white with fear. Leighsa, who rarely worried about anything, let alone paid attention to anything but her nail color. Emma took her hand. "It'll be all right. You'll see." Leighsa bit her lower lip and squeezed Emma's hand tightly.

Garrett and Lily were the last two to arrive and they grabbed two chairs from the dining table and pulled them into the living room. There were twenty of them all together and the three couches, four loungers plus extra dining chairs held them all. The young people were unusually quiet, except for Seth and Josh snickering in the corner about some joke one of them had made up.

Garrett cleared his voice. "You all know that we have received information about a raid that is going to happen in the next couple of days. We have decided how we are going to handle it and want to make sure you all understand what is going to happen."

He reached over and grabbed Lily's hand. Seth and Josh quickly quieted down, and Emma glanced around at all the parents. Without exception they had the same worried look.

"The raid is scheduled for Friday so starting on Wednesday, we are putting volunteers in the woods as lookouts, in case they arrive early. When the agents arrive, they will call on the radio and that's when we have to act. Each family will hide in the parents' bedroom. Mike and Stan will shut off all the lights at the breaker box and lock the front door. We know this won't keep them out, but it will force them to search with flash lights and possibly they could miss a hallway."

Seth raised his hand.

Garrett nodded to him. "Seth?"

"Don't we have a gun in the cave here? Aren't we going to defend ourselves?"

"Shooting DIU agents is not the answer. We know the Lord hasn't called us to murder and though this plan isn't overly clever, we are praying that the agents won't be very thorough." Seth's face gave away his distaste for Garrett's answer.

Seth's dad, Marty, jumped into the conversation.

"Kids, we are up against a wall here. When we made the plan to hide, we knew it wasn't foolproof, but we were trying to be obedient to what Christ instructed believers to do."

"Then God had better protect us if we are being obedient." Seth's voice revealed some bitterness.

"You're exactly right," Marty agreed. "We do believe that our obedience will be blessed, but we're not in a position to give God an ultimatum. If He allows this raid to be successful, then we have to be prepared for the consequences."

Marty looked over to Garrett who chose to explain those consequences.

"If the agents find us, most likely they will separate the men, the women, and the children. We will be prosecuted as adults, while you kids will probably be put into a foster care system."

"No!" cried Emma, tears starting to flow. "They can't separate us, can they?"

Fear welled up in her chest and she squeezed Leighsa's hand even tighter than before.

"I know this is frightening, Emma, but yes, they can and they will separate us. I don't know the process, but I do know if we refuse to take the mark, we will all be put to death."

Emma released Leighsa's hand and put her hands to her eyes, rubbing the tears away.

"And you must refuse the mark, each one of you."

Garrett looked around the room and all the kids sat wide-eyed.

"The angel that the Lord sent us said taking the mark meant separation from God for eternity. It doesn't matter what man does to us here, we have to be faithful to God. This is a serious choice and I want to be sure you all understand that no matter how they threaten you, you cannot take the mark."

Lily interjected. "Even if they say they will release your parents if you take the mark, don't believe them. Satan has only one objective and that is to rid the world of all believers. If you take the mark you will live until the wrath of God comes, but then you will die and spend forever in hell. You know the truth, and you are going to be called to act on it."

"Living by faith," Emma said, sniffling. "Believing the Word of God and acting on it, no matter how I feel because God promises a good result. This will be a true test of our faith."

"It's a test of faith for everyone, and many will pass, but it will cost them their lives," said Mr. Torey.

"So, we hide in the bedrooms and wait to be taken away," said Josh. Emma looked over at him and thought she saw anger.

"Hide and pray, Josh," said Garrett. "We're asking God for protection, and determining to be faithful whether or not we get it."

"Another thing you haven't mentioned, Garrett, is what we're planning to do outside," Mr. Mason added. "We're going to drag trees and shrubs and try to disguise the cave openings, in the hope that they won't be so obvious."

"At least that gives us something to do," said Seth, nudging Josh.

"We'll start on that today and you boys can help," said Garrett. "Listen, I know this sounds bleak. It's not what we had planned, but we can't change the facts. We just have to prepare for it. I talked with the men and we're going to split up and have family prayer time now, and your dads can answer any other questions you may have."

Garrett and Lily carried their chairs back to the table and told the kids to wait for them there. The Toreys and Masons went back to the parents' bedrooms and the Phillips headed back to the girls' bedroom. As Ben, Sarah, and Emma waited for their parents to join them, Emma could hear her dad in the kitchen talking to Lily. His tone of voice was stern and she heard him mention Mr. Reed's name.

"I'm telling you, I don't like it," Garrett was saying as he came from the kitchen, coffee cup in hand.

"Please, Garrett," said Lily. "You said you forgave him and you have no choice but to trust him."

"But I don't have to let him be one of the lookouts."

"He feels responsible and is willing to risk his own life by being outside of the caves for the raid. Can't you see that he is trying to make this right?"

Garrett pulled out a chair and sat down next to Ben. Though Ben and Sarah were quietly talking, Emma was still all ears.

"Risk his own life? He's risked all of ours and his being outside might be a ploy to help Homeland Security and not us. Have you thought about that?"

"His wife and son are a part of all of this. He's not going to put them in danger. You need to trust, Garrett."

Prayer time was short and the kids opted to let their parents pray for all of them. Emma didn't think Sarah and Ben understood the full weight of their predicament, but she sure did. Even more so. Emma had a loyalty to Adam that produced a protectiveness for Mr. Reed that she couldn't explain. She chose not to question her dad, but felt torn between wanting to forgive and wanting to stay loyal to her father.

Emma sat at the table after her family left. She put her head in her hands and rubbed her temples. There was definitely enough to worry about for the next couple of days, so she decided not to worry about Mr. Reed. If he was fooling them, time would tell, and if he wasn't, it probably wouldn't matter anyway. Emma determined to pull Sarah and Ben aside and make sure they understood what Dad was saying about the mark.

She looked around the cave. With the possibility that these may be her last couple of days there, the cave suddenly wasn't as oppressive as it had been a couple of days ago. She would miss the echoes and the coolness, the movies and the dinners all together.

"Stop it, Emma," she said out loud. "Don't plan for the worst. We may still be here a long time." But as she walked back to her room, the impending raid lay heavy on her mind.

Thursday evening Adam showed up for dinner at Engedi. He and Emma played cards with Garrett and Lily for a while, but he could see Garrett was struggling to concentrate so the game didn't last long. The others had started a movie, but Adam wanted to talk alone with Emma. They sat at one of the dining room tables and whispered back and forth until Lily came over and offered them popsicles.

"No, thanks, Mom," Emma said.

"Too late," Lily replied. "I've already opened them."

Emma looked up at her mom standing there with two popsicles in her hand, a blue one and a red one.

"What are you"—

"I hate when popsicles melt inside, so you had better go outside and eat these. Here, take them and get out before I change my mind . . . or before your dad comes back from the bedroom."

Lily winked at Adam and Emma and nodded her head toward the door.

"You've got forty-five minutes and then I want you back in here. Got it?"

"You're the best, Mom!"

Emma flung her arms around her mom, who almost dropped the popsicles. They each grabbed one and headed toward the door.

"Stay near the entrance."

"Yes, ma'am." Adam grinned at Emma's mom and thanked the Lord that he could have some time alone with Emma.

Once outside, he found Emma's hand and led her to their favorite log. It was a beautiful night and the lush scent of summer filled the forest. Because the trees were in full summer bloom, the moonlight was scattered through the leaves.

"What do you think will happen after tonight?" he asked Emma.

"I don't know, Adam. My heart says we'll be fine, but my head says we're in trouble. It's been a long week of worrying and I don't think my worrying helped one bit."

Emma straightened her back and cocked her head, as if she had arrived at a conclusion. "So, I've decided to stop worrying and expect the best. I think twenty-four hours from now we'll still be sick and tired of our caves and as safe as ever!"

Adam loved Emma's faith. Whether or not she really believed it, she would encourage until the very end. They sat quietly, both deep in thought until finally Adam got up the courage to ask Emma a question.

"Um, Emma, you know that my dad is going to be outside of the caves starting tonight. I was wondering, do you think my mom and I could stay here tonight? Dad has to be at his station all night and I'd rather be with you than anywhere else."

Emma looked confused and so he added, "I'm scared we'll be separated and I won't know what happens to you."

"You're really not making me feel better."

"I'm not saying this right. I just want to be here with you."

Emma smiled. "I think it's a great idea—let's check with Dad when we go back in."

They sat in silence as they finished their popsicles. The night was warm and humid, and Adam could hear an owl in the distance. He still had more on his mind and if he was going to say it, now was the time.

"I'm only going to say one more thing, and then I'm done trying to scare you."

"Go ahead," said Emma and she scooched closer to him on the log.

Adam stared at the ground and spoke. "If anything does happen tomorrow and we get separated, I want you to know I'll do whatever I have to, to find you. On earth or in heaven. I'll find you."

"When you say whatever, you don't mean you would take a mark, right?"

He quickly looked up at Emma, surprised by her response.

"Of course not. All I am saying is you don't have to worry about anything—I'll be there to take care of you." Adam looked away and shook his head. "This just isn't coming out the way I want it to. I guess I'm more nervous about tomorrow than I thought. I'm not worried about being found. I'm worried about losing you."

"You won't lose me. We're not going anywhere, remember?"

Emma stood up and took Adam's hand and pulled him to his feet. He stood and wrapped his arms around her. They embraced, and for just a moment Adam was able to believe that Emma was right—everything was going to be fine. As soon as she let go, however, the fears crept back in and insecurity replaced faith.

"Come on, we'd better find Dad and get the green light on tonight."

Emma led Adam back to the cave opening and they found Lily and Garrett wiping the counters in the kitchen.

"Dad? Do you think Adam and Mrs. Reed could stay with us tonight?"

"I think that's a great idea, Emma. Adam, you'd better go get her now, as long as it's all right with your dad."

Adam thanked him and headed out the door. He knew his mom would appreciate being with the Hamiltons. As he pulled the door closed behind him, he thought he heard Garrett say something about "a protection for us all," but he wasn't sure if he had heard correctly.

Sean had arrived in Mount Olive on Wednesday. It had been a busy two days. The Mount Olive Police Department had given him a desk in the back of the station with a phone and a printer. He had brought his own laptop, which held all the information he needed to wrap up this operation.

"Excuse me, Agent Aumonti?" A petite brunette with striking green eyes interrupted his thoughts.

"Yes, Officer O'Brien?" *I'll bet she wears colored contacts.*

"I have the bus order for you to sign."

She handed him a single sheet of paper and he noticed her neatly manicured fingernails.

Obviously a slow town, if the police officers have time to do their nails.

"Thank you," he said, looking at the order. "How many are they sending?"

"Ten. I think we could have managed with eight, but if you want to separate the leaders, you'll need at least one extra bus."

"Perfect. What time do they arrive?" Sean picked up a pen and signed the order.

"They'll be here at five tomorrow morning, ready to follow you to the base of the mountain."

Sean handed the paper back to Officer O'Brien and she walked away.

She has to know this raid is making me rich.

The congregants would have to be processed in Mount Olive but then would be transported back to Michigan to be charged, since they were all Michigan residents. Nate had told him they weren't armed, so he doubted there would be a big struggle to take them into custody. Still, the agents would be armed but they were instructed to only use their weapons if they felt physically threatened themselves.

Sean flipped open the case file in front of him. He pulled out a stack of papers and quickly flipped through them—pictures of the key leaders and their descriptions, as well as a map laying out the location of each occupied cave. Nate had been thorough and now Sean had to count on him to come through with the charges. Initially the men will be separated from the women and charged individually. The children would be put in foster care and the adults would go through the "take-the-mark-or-never-see-your-family-again" program. Hopefully most would take the mark and get their family back, but being radical fundamentalists, he couldn't predict their behavior. Either way, he was out to make a nice bonus.

He closed the file and stood. He picked up his wallet and keys and put them in his pocket and grabbed the file. On his way out of the station he stopped at Officer O'Brien's desk.

"Here's the file I need copied. I think fifty copies will suffice."

Officer O'Brien took the file from his hand and met eyes with him. She batted her beautiful, color-enhanced eyes and said, "No problem. I'll put them on your desk before I leave."

Sean, sensing a connection, tested the waters.

"So, what's there to do in Mount Olive on a Thursday night?"

"Things don't really heat up until Friday around here. And by tomorrow night, you should have reason to celebrate."

Her eyes danced and he got the message. *Tomorrow night it is.* He turned to leave as Officer O'Brien opened the file to be copied. Sean heard the air conditioner kick on as he walked out the front door, and was surprised how hot and muggy it was outside.

If it's hot like this tomorrow, that bulletproof jacket is going to get old real quick. Sean decided to turn in early and get a good night's sleep, considering the big day ahead. It would be nice to have this case closed and the cash in the bank.

Another day, another magog . . . With that thought, he climbed in his car and pulled away from the station.

twenty-four

Nate pushed the LCD button on his watch.

10:02 p.m.

His family was safely tucked away at Engedi and he had been sitting in the woods for about fifteen minutes. The sun had set and darkness covered the mountain.

He should try to sleep now, since the DIU raid would most likely begin before dawn, while everyone was asleep. A couple of hours would be great, but Nate couldn't turn off his brain, which continued to spin through the options and possible outcomes of the next day. He tried praying but the words wouldn't come.

Nate was sitting in a small crevasse, formed from a heavy rainfall. It was large enough to keep him well covered but from where he sat, he had a clear view of three cave openings. The doors were well covered with brush, but were not completely hidden. And then there was the problem of the well-worn entryways. Nate couldn't believe this was the best they could come up with.

He had asked Garrett for his gun but his request had been denied. It was probably for the best, since he wasn't really an outdoorsman anyway. The other lookouts were placed at various positions down the mountain, since no one knew which path would be taken up the mountain. Nate had never been on a raid before, because he was more due diligence, rather than field ops. But he had heard about them.

In his mind, he pictured quads and trailers, a Humvee or two, and lots of armed agents. They wouldn't bring buses up the mountain, since there was no road, but the people would be herded onto trailers or made to walk. Undoubtedly families would be separated and bused into town to be charged in Mount Olive.

Nate's ears perked when he heard a rustling in the woods.

Footsteps.

Then voices.

He leaned forward to try to look out of his hiding place, to see if it was a couple of the men who were to be in their lookout positions. He didn't hear any engines so he was pretty sure it wasn't the start of the raid, but he held his breath and tried not to make a sound.

The steps came closer but Nate couldn't see behind him to get a visual. Then he saw them. Two male figures in white. Well over seven feet tall. He recognized them immediately because he had seen them once before. In the Tabernacle. Floating over his head.

Angels.

Nate's heart raced, yet he stayed hidden and watched.

The angels, in their glowing, flowing white gowns, stopped at the cave nearest Nate. In the silence of the night, he could clearly hear their voices.

"At least they tried," said one.

"The openings are still visible," answered the other. "Only a blind man could miss them."

"We can fix that."

The angels separated and centered themselves in front of the cave. Each stretched out his arm, with their palms facing the opening. As they stood there, greenery started to form. Trees sprouted from acorns lying on the ground and grew into fully mature trees.

Vines stretched from other trees and connected the new ones to give the appearance of age. Shrubs appeared from nowhere and weeds filled in the gaps. The worn entrance became freshly grown grass, never touched by human feet. When the angels were finished, there was no evidence of a cave opening let alone human life anywhere. When they seemed satisfied that even the keenest human eye would be fooled, the angels dropped their arms and spoke again.

"This one looks good, do you not think?" said the first angel.

"Perfect, if I might say so myself," answered the second.

"Do you want to approach the man hiding in the rocky crevasse or shall I?"

Nate stiffened.

The angel turned and moved toward him, seeming to float across the distance between them. There was no sense hiding anymore, so he stood and stepped out from his hiding place. His eyes were fixed on the approaching angel and the sheer size of this being caused fear to seize his heart.

"Don't be frightened. We've taken care of those inside, but you're going to have to cover yourself if you really want to stay out here."

Even in the dark, Nate could feel the warmth of the angel's eyes. Every muscle in his body ached with anticipation of what he would say next, and Nate forced himself to steady his breathing.

"The search is going to take a couple of days because they are not going to give up easily. You and the other men should go back to your caves and stay with your families. Each of you can squeeze in and the foliage will cover over your tracks. By Monday morning it will be safe to come out. We will come on Sunday night and remove the trees."

The angel stopped and touched Nate's shoulder. His touch was warm and firm, and sent a jolt of energy through his body.

With that, he rose above Nate and disappeared. The other angel was gone also. Nate fell to his knees and then face down on the ground. Tears flowed from his eyes and he sobbed in the darkness.

"Thank You, Father. You are so good to me. How can I ever repay You?"

Nate laid on the ground for a few minutes and let the relief of God's provision wash over him. Joy burst from his heart when he realized he would get to share the good news with the congregation.

He grabbed his radio from his belt and held down the transmitter button. "Check-point one, three, four, five, and six. This is number two. Do you all read me?"

One by one the other lookouts answered.

"I'll explain later, but everyone must get back to their cave right now. You'll understand once you get there! Copy that?"

Each man confirmed the instruction and Nate ran through the woods back to Engedi where Sherrie and Adam were sleeping.

When Nate ran in the front door of Engedi, it was about 10:45. Sherrie was in her robe and Lily was pulling out two of the hide-a-beds in the family room. Several of the children had already gone to bed and the adults and a few of the youth still awake were gathered in the dining area. They all looked surprised when Nate ran in.

"What's wrong?" Garrett asked as he walked toward Nate. "I heard you over the radio send the others back."

"I'm here for the night," Nate said, wiping the sweat from his brow and trying to catch his breath. Nate met Sherrie's eyes, and she gave him a quizzical look in return.

"What do you mean, Dad?" Adam looked alarmed. His dad's eyes were red and Adam could see he had been crying.

"I could spend the next half hour trying to explain to you, but I think seeing is believing."

Nate turned and headed back down the hall towards the front door. Naturally, the room full of inquiring minds followed, Garrett in the lead. When he got to the front door, he turned and waited until the hall filled up. His heart started to pound again, knowing the joy the rest would feel when they saw for themselves. He pulled the door open and stepped aside. The woods were so thick just inches outside the door that it almost looked like a second door. Nate himself was surprised how much more growth filled in after he climbed through it and entered the cave. The group moved closer to get a better look and Garrett reached out and touched a vine.

"What . . . ?" Garrett couldn't even put words to his questions.

"More angels," Nate smiled.

"How . . . ?"

"Rather easily, if you can imagine."

"When . . . ?"

"Just a few minutes ago."

"For the love, Dad! Quit asking questions and let Mr. Reed tell us all about it!" Emma said what everyone was thinking.

As Nate explained what had happened, the families walked over to the newly sprouted thick foliage outside the front door and touched the branches and leaves, reverently. Nate's tears returned and he met Garrett's eyes. Garrett inclined his head in a slight nod, looking as relieved as Nate felt.

After he finished speaking, he overhead Emma tell Adam, "I told you so." Nate wasn't sure what she meant, but for now, he was with his family and the Lord was protecting all of them.

"We'd better get on the radio and let the people know there's nothing left to worry about," Mike Torey said, as he headed over to the ham radio in the corner of the room.

Sherrie hadn't left Nate's side since the moment he began speaking to the families. Now, she reached for his hand, and for the first time in weeks, he felt relief from the burden of his sins. Christ had paid the price for them and tonight, God had taken away the consequences too. It was more than he deserved and now his wife was at his side. His heart rejoiced!

After Nate answered everyone's questions, families drifted off to the various quarters. Nate pulled off his boots and jeans, and slipped into bed next to Sherrie. She slid over next to him and kissed him on the cheek.

As he closed his eyes, his mind wandered to the story of Noah. He pictured him closed up in the ark, not sure what was happening outside but completely safe and protected on the inside by God. Protected within a sphere of danger. A familiar feeling. As he dozed off, he wondered, with all those animals, if Noah slept well or not.

God gave Nate one final gift that night—sweet, deep, dreamless sleep.

Sean Aumonti, twenty DIU agents, three squads of area SWAT teams, and the local police officers met at the base of the mountain at 6 a.m. They brought with them twenty-five quads with attached trailers. Most had left Mount Olive an hour earlier and were finishing their third cup of coffee as the group gathered for instructions. Sean handed out information packets to all of them and gave final instructions.

"We need to locate the pastor and the elders as soon as possible and separate them from the congregation. It seems this church can't do anything without their approval, so the quicker we separate them the better."

It had been two years since Sean had been on an operation of this magnitude and the anticipation gave him a real rush. The adrenaline flowed and he spoke as one who did this weekly.

"You have pictures of these men in your packets. When you locate one, please let dispatch know who you have and take them to the first bus in the line of buses at the base of the mountain. The buses should be here in about twenty minutes. In addition to their leadership, you also have a picture of our undercover agent, Nate Reed. As soon as he is located, I want him sent down the mountain to me, so that he can go over the charges and make sure the people are separated appropriately. Stay in your groups and when you raid the caves, shut down the ham radio units immediately, so that no messages can be sent between caves. The map in your packet gives the approximate location of the cave openings, but from my understanding they are pretty much in the open. They have wooden doors installed and the ground will be well worn where they've gone in and out of the caves."

"Excuse me, Agent Aumonti?" A police officer in the back got Sean's attention.

"Yes, officer?"

"My map looks more like directions to the mountain. I don't think it has cave locations marked on it."

Several agreed and Sean flipped through his master file and couldn't find the cave map.

"Get Officer O'Brien on the radio and ask her where it is."

He looked through his file again and started to fume.

"Sir, she never saw a map."

Sean paused a moment and regrouped. He was sure there had been a map, but he remembered it well enough to continue without it.

"This isn't a setback. We all have enough expertise to find these caves. There are about twenty in all and their entrances should be well worn. I know we have the right mountain and we're on the right side, so before they wake up and see us first, let's get going. Stay with your teams and report on channel four when you find a cave. Secure the families, march them out and, we'll take it from down here."

As the men split into their respective search teams and headed out, Sean walked over to base operations and sat down by the radio. He wanted to listen to any and all radio activity. He reached for the phone sitting on the table next to the radio and dialed Nate's number. No connection. He tried again and again, but soon gave up, assuming Nate had to be in a clearing to get the signal.

Ten o'clock came and went and there had been nothing but radio silence. Sean picked up the radio and asked for a status report.

"Team Alpha reporting no evidence of human activity in quadrant seven."

"Team Gamma reporting the same in quadrant four."

One by one the squad leaders checked in with no sign of the church. The officer from Mount Olive who was manning the radio overstepped his bounds.

"Are you sure you have the right mountain, sir?"

"Of course it's the right mountain!" Sean growled and continued to wait for good news.

Hours passed with no results and now the men on the mountain were beginning to get frustrated. Finally, at eight o'clock they called off the search for the day.

That evening, Sean sat at his desk in Mount Olive going over the paper work. Officer O'Brien continued to claim there had not been a map with the file he had given her and Sean was starting to suspect a cover-up.

"Let's look at the facts here," he said to the empty room. "First, Agent Reed knows today is the day but makes no attempt to contact me or receive my calls. Second, the map of the mountain mysteriously disappears. Third, little green-eyes won't even make eye contact with me anymore."

Sean stood and paced a few seconds. He picked up the phone and quickly dialed a number. "What are the odds I can get my hands on a couple of helicopters?" he said when the call was picked up.

He listened for a moment, then said, "I owe you one. Can you get them here by eight? Thanks."

Sean disconnected the call and walked to the window. Beyond Mount Olive lay a flat wasteland, leading to a mountain range. How could three hundred people just disappear?

And where was Nate? He could only come up with two options. Either Nate gave him the wrong information or this group had swallowed their last glass of Kool-Aid. And why would Nate set him up?

Did he want the arrest all to himself? Did he think he could just walk three hundred people into the police station all alone? He was going to need his help, but after making him look like a fool, Sean was in no mood to help.

Sean suddenly had another revelation. He pulled his cell out of his pocket and quickly dialed the number for the DIU DC Surveillance Unit.

"Hi, this is Agent Aumonti. Who's this?"

"Agent Brown."

"Sorry to call so late, agent, but I need you to pull up a tracer that was placed back on March fifteen."

"That's what I'm here for, sir. No apologies necessary."

Fifteen minutes later, Agent Brown located the tracer and sent the link to Sean, who was waiting at the Mount Olive Police Department. Sean leaned back in his chair. He had the right mountain and tomorrow, he may not have the church, but he'd have their car.

The next morning, Sean himself took the portable tracker and with a team of agents headed toward the tracer's signal. By nine o'clock they had found the vehicle storage unit. From the outside it looked as if someone had put some thought into concealing the entrance. Inside they found twelve vans. Sean had an agent dust the vans for fingerprints, so that he could prove who used these vehicles. The area was thoroughly searched, but led to no other signs of life.

"This proves there is life on this mountain," said Sean. "I want tracers on all these vehicles and if one of these vans leaves the mountain, I want the driver arrested and brought straight to me."

Soon the tracers were in place and the storage unit was cleaned, so that no one would know they had been there. By the end of Saturday, there was no other indication that the church existed and the hunt was called off.

Sunday morning Sean drove himself back to the mountain and put his car in park. He climbed out of his car and leaned on the hood, staring at the mountain. Sean could be a patient man. This raid had been an embarrassment until he found the vehicle storage unit. But they didn't get the payoff they had expected and now Sean had suspicions that Nate was somehow responsible for this debacle. He must want a bigger cut. Why else would he let this fall through? Unless . . .

"Agent Aumonti? Are you there?"

Sean's radio cackled. It was dispatch from Mount Olive.

"Yeah?"

"I'm just letting you know the buses are leaving and the SWAT teams will be sending their reports in the next couple of days."

"Great. Thanks."

As Sean imagined the buses pulling away, he knew his head was on the block for this raid. The cost was heavy and someone had to pay.

I'm not giving this one up. Someone will leave the mountain eventually, and when they do, they'll get to meet me. All I want is one. Then we'll see how long it takes me to find the rest of them.

twenty-five

"**H**err Hitler? Herr Hitler? Sir, we need your vote."

"Vote on what?" Hitler didn't try to hide his disdain or his boredom.

"Your vote on the new worship centers."

"You want my vote on worship centers? I'll give you something better than worship centers."

Hitler stood and faced the room full of FWP leaders. One hundred and ninety-two in all. One representative from each country in the whole world, sitting at tables in the shape of a square so that all had equal voice. Each was plugged into a translator with an earpiece. Hitler removed his earpiece so that he could move about the room and still be heard.

"Thousands of years ago men all spoke the same language. Did you know that? This threatened God and so He confused their language so that they could not unite in strength. They were building a tower to honor their strength and God put a stop to it by taking their ability to communicate away from them. We are here today to discuss many improvements in our countries, one of which is the building of houses of worship, to bring glory to our savior, Lucifer."

"What a waste." He thrust his hands in the air. "Do you not realize that the greatest worship you can offer him is to rid your countries of the followers of God? Our enemy wanders freely in your countries while you discuss houses of worship. He will only save us when we obey. Do you really think he will help us while we do nothing? Nobody ever gets something for nothing. Yet you sit there, acting like you have done something wonderful by putting marks on your heads. What are you doing to please your master?"

Hitler motioned for the leaders to remove their earpieces. When they did not respond immediately he yanked the piece from the ear of the person nearest him and threw it on the table. The others stared at him, their fear almost palpable, and when he lunged at the second person, they quickly removed their earpieces.

"God may have confused our language years ago, but He no longer rules here. Today I give you back our language. If you understand me, stand!"

As if rehearsed, in unison the whole room of leaders took to their feet. Shock replaced fear as none could believe they no longer needed a translator. All eyes were on him as he began walking back to his chair.

He leaned forward, his hands on the edge of the table. One by one, he met the eyes of the leaders, his own gaze unblinking, all-knowing, cold. "Have you ever seen power such as this displayed? Well, believe it now. I have given you this gift, but it is not freely given. I want the followers of our Enemy dead! No more excuses. No more deadlines. I want them dead. Dead!" He pounded his fists on the table. "No mark? Then cut their heads off."

He walked around the table and stopped beside the Premiere of France. Laying his hand on his shoulder, he turned him so that he could look him in the face.

"Do you understand me, Monsieur Jeveaux?"

"Completely."

Hitler let go of Jeveaux's shoulder.

"Instead of discussing houses of worship, let's discuss acts of worship. I want numbers. I want to know your country is clean. Give your people incentives and get this done." He continued to walk around the tables making his demands. "If you're not sure what I am talking about, watch the news tonight. We are running out of time and this rebellion must end. So get to work and get this done. NOW!"

With that, Hitler left the room and slammed the door. Szabo slipped out the door, caught up with his leader, and walked with him to the limousine. "We are no longer planning a battle, we are at war," he said to Szabo once they were seated.

"Let's be reasonable, sir. You only revealed yourself four and a half months ago. I believe we are making good progress."

"Szabo, since you have such phenomenal assessing abilities, tell me this. When is Jesus coming back?"

Szabo sat quietly. He couldn't answer. How could he know? Hitler suspected Szabo wasn't even sure Jesus was coming back. Up until now, he was probably just taking Hitler's word for it.

"What did you think of hell?"

Another unanswerable question.

"Until you can answer those two questions I don't want your opinion. *Good progress?*" He practically spat the words. "There is no such thing as good progress. We don't know how much time we have." Hitler turned to the window as the limousine headed back to his penthouse apartment in Jerusalem. After a moment, he tore his gaze from the window and stared again at Szabo. "This is not a game— this is life or death. It is now time for me to become the commander I was meant to be from the beginning."

Szabo fell silent. Ignoring him, Hitler dialed his phone and put his plan in motion. After a few minutes, he flipped his phone closed and sat back with a satisfied chuckled. This evening's spectacle would put the fear of Satan in people's hearts. Of that, he had no doubt. He chuckled again, but the sound contained no mirth.

twenty-six

Evan Stillman's mother was busy in the kitchen when he walked into the house.

"Where did you go so early this morning, Evan?" she asked.

"None of your business."

"Do you want a snack? We won't be having dinner for a couple of hours still."

"Already ate."

Evan dropped onto the couch. His head was aching. He was sick and tired of working with idiots. He could tell when people were the real deal. He was so tired of the Shel-head wannabes, acting all angry at nonmarkers but unwilling to put their words into action. He was tired of the three-hour meetings where people just flapped their lips about the problem but had no solutions. He had solutions. Only a real leader would have solutions. So, he was going to have to lead. Lead by example.

He remembered a story told to him a long time ago about a leader who was constantly taunted by the actions of some religious schmo. Day after day he was annoyed until he finally built a tall gallows and ordered the guy hanged. Evan couldn't remember how the story ended but he remembered the leader's name. It was Haman, and the schmo's name was Morty-guy or something like that.

Evan had his own Morty. As he sat on the couch, he thought about old Morty. Every day this guy was on the street, warning people who haven't taken the mark to resist. The guy had to be eighty or ninety years old. He said Hitler is evil and true salvation comes from Jesus Christ alone. Man, this guy was getting on his nerves! He was going to make a spectacle out of this Morty. He was going to lead by example. He just had to wait for the right time. When that time came, the first on his list was old Morty. Or Dan. Whatever his name was, he was going to fall hard.

Evan's mom interrupted his daydreaming.

"Turn on the TV, Evan. You won't believe this."

Evan picked up the remote off the coffee table in front of him. He turned the television on and the news station came into view. He turned up the volume.

"Today, in Russia, Adolph Hitler's current home country, a law was passed giving incentives to turn in nonmarked citizens. If you turn an unmarked person into authorities, you will receive five hundred magogs. If you turn in a whole family, you could receive as much as three thousand magogs. If you are willing to bring them in dead, the amounts double." The newscaster raised her eyebrows and tilted her head. "Yes, I said dead and double. This is the first time since the last rule of Hitler that incentives have been given to turn on fellow citizens under the guise of what is best for the nation. Is history repeating itself or is this really for the betterment of society? We asked some citizens of Russia how they felt about this new law."

The first was a middle-aged, working-class man.

"It's about time. I got my mark and I have this neighbor who is like 'holier than thou' about it all. Now I look at him and I see money signs."

The second was a twenty-something woman with hardened eyes.

"Why shouldn't we be compensated? If we do the dirty work of turning in people we know, we had better get a new couch out of the deal."

Finally, a well-dressed businessman.

"We are at war. These people who don't want to conform are really our enemy. If they are too stupid to see the benefits we have to offer, then the world is better off with them dead."

The camera shifted back to the reporter.

"Well, you heard it here first. The country seems thrilled to be compensated for helping. I just hope Hitler can come up with the money to pay all these loyal citizens. We're going to go live now to Moscow where a gathering of elated citizens are demonstrating in support of this new law. This is Lana Boston reporting for NBC. Over to you, Mike."

Evan quickly scanned the scene. The picture had changed over to Red Square in Moscow. A large group had gathered and in the center of the group there was a scuffle. Several young men were holding another young man so that he couldn't run away. Evan leaned forward and rested on his elbows. The cameras tried to get a close-up of this man's face. Evan couldn't see a mark.

"This is Mike Morrison reporting from Red Square, Moscow. We are live in Moscow and a large group has gathered to celebrate the passage of the new law, the people are now calling the Freedom Act. I have with me, Gregor Gustav. Gregor, why are you calling this the Freedom Act?"

"Because now we have the freedom to free ourselves from the slavery of our enemy," he said with a heavy accent. "Before we had to wait for the police to find the nonmarkers, but now we can turn them in and earn magogs at the same time. These people have had enough time to mark themselves and their refusal is an outright rebellion to the peace of the world."

"So, who is this that your group has in custody?"

Gregor Gustav turned his head and called to his friends, "Bring him over here."

Then he turned back and answered the reporter's question.

"This is a guy I work with. For months now we have asked when he will take the mark and he says never. Well, it's legal now so . . . you're going to want to keep the camera rolling for this one."

Two of the men wrestled the young man to his knees. They forced him to bend at the waist and Gregor was given a sword from someone in the crowd. Evan straightened his back and stared, wide-eyed at the television, holding his breath. Gregor raised the sword above his head and the microphone picked up him yelling, "We live by the sword, you die by the sword." He brought the sword down on the back of the kneeling man's head. Obviously the sword had been prepared for such a blow, because the head of the martyr sliced right off and rolled a few feet in front of his kneeling body. The body slumped and the men on either side let go of his arms. Evan let out his breath and fell against the back of the couch. Gregor Gustav returned to the camera.

"I just earned enough for two months rent. I figure by the time this week is done, I'll be able to vacation in the south of France."

Mike Morrison turned to the camera, a bit pale from witnessing the beheading.

"And so begins the slaughter of the enemy. Will other countries follow suit? Only time will tell. This is Mike Morrison for NBC Nightly News."

The anchor returned and began coverage of the miracle of language that had spread across the world that day. Evan hit the mute and looked up at his mother who was standing next to the couch where he was sitting.

"What's becoming of this world? I remember when the terrorists did beheadings and it was considered barbaric. Now it's acceptable? I don't know if I want to live in a world that accepts beheadings."

That could be arranged, Evan thought to himself.

Evan's mom left the room to call her best friend. Evan got up from the couch, went to his bedroom and walked over to his desk.

"Was that awesome or what?" the demon in the idol asked him, as he sat down in front of his computer.

"For a moment it felt like I had a sword in my own hand."

"Maybe you should get one."

"I wouldn't know where to find one. Anyway, I spent all my money on my mark and I'm sure they're expensive."

"You know where your mom keeps her stash. Just borrow enough for the purchase. The day is coming that in just one or two slices, you will be able to pay her back with interest."

"Really? You think that will be allowed here in Shelton?"

"Can't you picture old Morty on his knees? You're standing over him. He's probably crying like a baby. One fell swoop—that irritation is gone forever, and you will get paid for it."

"Sounds like heaven."

"Careful."

"Sounds like earth?"

"That's what we're fighting for, right?"

Evan googled *swords* and found that they could be rather inexpensive. He had to find out how to sharpen it, though. What a bummer to slice someone's head and get the blade stuck on the spine or something. He would figure that out after he placed his order. The day wasn't turning out so bad after all.

This morning arrived and I could smell the coffee brewing from the kitchen. I slipped out of bed, grabbed my robe and quietly opened the door to my bedroom. It was just after six and no one was up—well, except for whoever it was that made the coffee. I tiptoed down the hall, past the bathroom, and headed for the front door. I reached for

the knob and just before I opened it, my dad snuck up behind me and whispered loudly, "What do you think you're doing?" I jumped so high I nearly hit my head on the ceiling.

"I want to see if our doorway is clear," I told him, after I gave him a playful shove. Together we opened the door and for the first time in three days the sunshine poured into the cave. I could feel the humidity of the July air flow through the doorway and I turned to my dad and hugged him.

What joy I felt to see the woods again. It meant that it was safe to go outside. It meant that the time of trouble was over. It meant that God hadn't forgotten about us. It really is an amazing time to be alive.

I often wonder what is happening to some of my friends from school. Did they take the mark? If they didn't, have they been arrested, or worse? What's really going on out there? Does Hitler really seem like the old Hitler? How much longer will God wait before He returns? What exactly will His appearing be like? Will we miss its magnificence because we're in a cave?

It's time for bed and I can hear Mom outside the door. She must be talking to the boys. I will sign off for the day. One final word—Thank You, Lord for loving me so!

Emma heard a knock on the door and a moment later, her mother stuck her head inside.

"I'm just making the rounds with hugs and kisses for anyone who wants one."

Emma's mom did that often, and all six girls usually got a hug.

"Mom, we've been discussing something that we're a bit worried about."

"What's that?" Lily asked as she bent over and kissed Emma on the cheek.

The girls were all in their bunks, tucked in, and ready for sleep. It was Monday night and after three days cooped up in the cave, they had spent most of the day at the Tabernacle with the youth, playing games and discussing the latest miracle. Emma found herself keeping one eye on the door, just in case another angel stopped by for a visit.

"Over the past couple of days every night before we go to sleep we have been reading Matthew twenty-four."

"Hmmm . . . extracurricular study?"

"The disciples ask Jesus what will be the sign of His return and He goes through this whole list of what will happen before He comes—all the bad things that are going on right now." Emma sat up and her mom came and stood by her.

"Right."

"So then, Jesus says right before He comes back that the sun will be darkened and the moon's light will go out and the stars will fall."

"Still right." Lily reached up and brushed an eyelash off of Emma's cheek.

"Then, when everything is black, it'll look like lightning flashing in the sky and Christ will come back with His angels. So, He will be this bright light that everyone will see. Right?"

"That's what it says. It even says that when the world sees it they will mourn, because they know it means judgment for them, but Luke tells us that when this happens, we should lift up our heads because our Redemption is coming for us."

"Okay. So here's the question." Emma looked around at the other girls. They were truly concerned about this and really needed an answer. "How are we going to see Jesus return—the lights go out and then this bright light of His glory—how are we going to see this if we are hiding in a cave?"

"We're afraid we might miss it all together, Mom," said Sarah, tears in her eyes.

Lily looked around the room. All six girls were either up on an elbow or sitting by now, anxiously anticipating her response. She sat down by Sarah and put her arm around her shoulder.

"Well, let me ask you a couple of questions first. What does Jesus tell the church to do when they see the signs of trouble?"

Leighsa called out, "Hide. Go to the mountains."

"And when does He tell them NOT to come out of hiding?"

"When people claim to be Christ but are really false teachers." This time it was Carrie Mason who answered.

"You're right, Carrie. Now, do you think that when Jesus returns, if we're not outside waving our arms, He might forget that we're here and leave without us?"

Emma smiled. "Of course not, Mom."

"Well then, if we walk by faith, believing God's Word, no matter . . . "

" . . . how we feel . . . " the girls all chimed in.

" . . . because God has promised a good result, right? So, going into hiding, we know He knows we're here. The angel told us that. So we need to trust what we know of God, His character, and believe that even if we are in a cave at the time, we will still be caught up to heaven with Him."

The girls quietly thought about her answer.

"Personally, however, I want to see it. So, I'm hoping that whoever is monitoring the radio at the time, tells us as soon as anything strange is reported and we can all run outside."

The girls wholeheartedly agreed.

"I'm so proud of you girls for looking at the Scripture yourselves and even coming up with questions. Get to sleep now. No more tears, Sarah." Lily leaned over and tucked in Sarah, kissing her on the cheek. "I'll see you all in the morning."

When Lily shut the door, Leighsa was the first to speak.

"It's going to be so rad! I can't imagine what the rest of the world is going to think, though."

"They'll probably be scared to death!" said Sarah.

"I just never dreamed it would be like this," said Emma. "We sit in these caves and we just wait. We don't know what is going on out there, but what choice do we have?"

"Well, I'm already running into a problem that could really cause trouble for me."

Emma looked over at Leighsa and said, "What?"

"I'm just about out of my candy apple red nail polish!" She smiled as she lay down and pulled the covers up to her chin. "Jesus had better come soon, or I can't be responsible for how I look!"

The girls giggled and Emma laid back down. She hoped it won't be too long, but in the meantime she had a distraction the other girls didn't have.

Adam.

"Now remember, kids, we can't stay late tonight," Mike Torey warned the youth. "At nine-thirty, each of you will have a parent from your cave here to take you back so keep an eye on the clock."

Adam was glad to be out of his cave, even if it was another karaoke night. The elders decided to allow the youth to hang out at the Tabernacle once a week, in an attempt to shake the doldrums because of being cooped up all day.

He grabbed Emma's hand and pulled her into a corner.

"A couple of us were talking," he began.

"Who?" Emma interrupted.

"Seth, Josh, Neil Cowlings, and Leighsa Torey. We can't take the boredom any longer. We've been locked up in the caves for long enough."

"Boredom? Last week wasn't exciting enough for you?"

"No, it was plenty exciting, but now we're back to the same old same old."

"We're limited for a reason, remember? This isn't a game. Our lives literally depend on us being hidden."

"Yeah, but listen to our reasoning. Do you remember that lake we found back when I first moved down here?"

"Yeah?"

"Well, God's proven that He will protect us on the mountain. We think that the lake is protected too."

"What are you talking about?"

"We want to take a little trip to the lake. Just for one day. We'll be careful, but that area is so hidden, no one will see us there. Wouldn't you love to go swimming? Throw a Frisbee around? Even just lie in the sun for a couple of hours?" Adam pleaded with his eyes.

"Of course, but we can't, Adam. It's too dangerous. A satellite could take a picture of us or something."

"I doubt we're that important that satellites are pointed at us. Come on, Emma, we just need a day away. Away from the little kids, away from the tension. Daylight would do us all good."

"It really doesn't matter if I agree or not, because our parents will never let us go!"

"Good grief, Emma. We're in high school. If we were in Shelton right now, we'd go all over the place without permission. Are you going to be a kid forever?"

Adam was starting to get irritated with her. He had made up his mind, whether or not she agreed to go.

"Listen, we're going on Thursday. It's a two-hour hike so we want to leave by nine. We'll be back by dinner. It's not that big a deal. I really want you to come, but not if you're going to worry all day. I just need the break. It's totally safe—would I put you in danger?"

"How're you getting out of Petra?" Emma seemed to be wavering.

"I'm just telling Mom that I'm going to spend time with Josh and vice versa. Technically, that's what we're doing. We're just doing it at the lake."

Adam sensed he had wedged the door open with his foot. "Just once, and we'll all feel like new." Emma squinted her eyes, still weighing her decision. "Please, Emma. Trust me."

"Oh, fine. But when we get nailed, you're taking the fall for me, right?"

"Sure. I can take it."

The two teenagers joined the rest of the youth group and from across the room, Adam gave Seth a thumbs up. Seth nodded and continued to search for a song to perform. Adam now had something to look forward to—two days later he would be swimming and chilling away from the cave.

Leighsa came running over and grabbed Emma by the arm and pulled her away. Adam watched the two girls madly chatting and he knew if anyone could take Emma's doubt away, it would be Leighsa. This was going to be a much deserved holiday and Emma needed it as much as any of them.

Two days and counting. It all made perfect sense to Adam. Why would God have provided such a beautiful lake and complete protection, unless they were free to use it? He was surprised no one else had thought of it first.

Emma didn't dare write about their plans in her journal. She didn't want any evidence of her disobedience put on paper. For two days she fussed in her mind about agreeing to go. By Wednesday night, she had decided to pass on the outing.

But then Thursday morning arrived and Leighsa had so easily received permission for the two of them to go to Adam's cave that she softened and again, agreed to go.

The two-hour hike seemed to take forever, and Emma was a bit grumpy and quiet while the other five goofed around and soaked up the freedom of being outside of the caves.

"Hey, Josh," Neil Cowlings hollered from way ahead of the rest of the kids.

"Yeah? Where are you?" Josh yelled back.

There wasn't a path to follow, but everyone was following Adam, because he claimed to remember how to get there.

"Up here," Neil called to the kids. "This would have been a great lookout tree It was super easy to climb."

The others looked up and saw Neil about thirty feet in the air, perched on a branch of a large oak tree. Another tree had fallen beside it and by climbing up the fallen tree, the lower branches were easily reached.

"Be careful up there," called Emma. "What if you would fall and break something? What'll we tell our parents then?"

"Oh, all right, Mom," Neil said as he worked his way back down to the ground. Once down, Neil jogged over to the group and elbowed Adam, who was continuing to lead the way. "I'm so glad you guys decided to bring Mom along."

Leighsa giggled and Emma recognized that laugh. She only used it when she was flirting. Emma shook her head and kept walking.

"I think I see the clearing." Adam pointed and Emma saw he was right.

The woods ended about a hundred yards ahead and she could see the light of the clearing. The five other kids broke into a run, but Emma continued to walk. She was feeling worse with each step and even the sound of the whooping and hollering was annoying her. But when she came into the clearing, the warmth of the sun and the sight of the boys running, shirts waving in their hands, and then jumping in the water changed her attitude. After all, they were already there and all her fussing hadn't changed anything. Emma ran to join the others.

Before long, Emma found herself sitting on a blanket, eating sandwiches in the sun, watching the clouds drift by—a wish come true. She decided Adam was right. This was a much-needed break.

She loved the feel of the warm sun on her face and the water was the perfect temperature for swimming. The kids were careful to lather up with sunscreen so they wouldn't have to explain a sudden case of sunburn to their mothers. And the boys swung on the weeping willow into the water until their arms ached with exhaustion.

"This is the life." Seth leaned back against the rock with a cookie in his hand. "No children, no moms telling me to study, and all the sunlight I could ever want!"

"Do you remember that swim party at Steve Meyer's house, Emma?" Leighsa was sitting next to Neil.

"Yes! That was hysterical! I felt so bad!" said Emma.

"Why?" asked Adam. "What happened?" He pointed at the bag of cookies sitting next to Emma and she grabbed it and gave it to him.

Leighsa explained. "The Meyer's had just moved into a new house and they invited the youth group over. We were all in middle school and still in that obnoxious stage." She leaned over and laughed, obviously remembering something but unable to share it, so Emma picked up the story.

"There was this guy who came—Mark something—and he was one of those pocket protector nerds. Well, he thought it was going to be a Bible study so he didn't bring a swimsuit. Mrs. Meyer felt so bad for him that she gave him one of Mr. Meyer's suits, which was way too big on him!"

"So he dives in the pool and he's so nervous about being in a big suit and swimming that he throws up! Right there in the deep end!" Leighsa explained. "All the girls start screaming and running out of the pool and he's just treading water with chunks all around him!"

"It was so nasty! But it was really funny too!"

"Whatever happened to Mark?" Adam asked around a mouthful of cookie.

Seth answered, "I don't think he ever came back."

The kids laughed and Adam looked at his watch.

"We'd better get going. We've got a good walk home." He stood and put his shirt on.

As they packed up for the hike home, Emma felt the pangs of guilt return. She looked at the others, seemingly guilt free and wondered why she couldn't be more carefree.

"Let's do this again next week!" Seth suggested on the walk home.

"It would give us something to look forward to and would make the caves much more bearable." Leighsa tossed a smile at Neil, who willingly received it.

"I thought this was a onetime thing?" asked Emma, clearly aware she was the only one worried about coming again.

"Well, this went so smoothly, I think we can confidently assume that we're protected on the mountain too," Adam said.

"We haven't gotten back yet, and we haven't had to face our parents, knowing we lied to them either." Emma stood firm.

"No offense, Mom, but if you're struggling with all this sun and water, go ahead and stay in the cave," Seth said. "Just don't rat us out. Next Thursday, I'm in."

"Me too," Leighsa chimed in.

"Make that three," Josh added.

"Four," Adam said.

"Definitely five," Neil called out.

All eyes turned to Emma. She was not happy Adam would put her in this position.

"We'll see," was the best she could come up with.

"That's better than a no." Adam smiled at her.

With that, the kids continued on their way. They were able to get back unseen and unsuspected. Adam kissed Emma goodbye at the door to Engedi.

"I know this was hard for you. Thanks for doing it for me. Sometimes I just feel like I'm going to crawl out of my skin if I don't get some fresh air."

"At least you noticed I did it for you," Emma said, still worried about keeping up the front with her parents.

"Oh, come on, you can't say it wasn't worth it. I think I saw you laugh once or twice."

Adam flashed her that smile she could never resist and she agreed. No one was hurt, everyone returned safely, and she wasn't a child anymore. She hoped she would eventually believe it if she said it to herself enough times.

twenty-seven

Adolph Hitler waited for everyone to take their places for the meeting. Normally he would make an entrance but today there was too much to discuss for pomp and circumstance. Each nation's leader was instructed to bring along their second in command. Now that interpreters were no longer needed, the meetings were shorter and quieter.

"It has been six months since I instituted the united world government."

Hitler was standing in his place at the head of the table, shoulders back, spine ramrod straight. He smoothed back his hair with his left hand. All eyes were on him. A few leaders nodded in agreement.

"In the past six months I have given incentives for your governments to enforce my marking system. But six months apparently is not enough time for you to accomplish a simple task."

He narrowed his eyes and scanned the room. No one moved but several looked down at their notes in front of them.

"No country is completely marked. Not one." Hitler struggled to keep his voice under control, but he didn't want to lose his temper too soon in the speech. He changed his tone and raised his right fist in the air.

"I have decided that it's time we let our citizens share in the wealth!"

The leaders of the FWP raised their heads in response to the change in his tone.

"I have a new initiative, based on a past, failed attempt to rid the world of Jews. Since I myself have failure in my past, I have chosen to revive a plan which, when implemented, I believe will be successful. In front of you are the specifics."

The leaders opened the folders. Inside lay Hitler's latest plan.

"Over four thousand years ago a brilliant leader devised a plan to rid his nation of an unwanted race. A race which threatened his own countrymen. He appealed to the greed of his people and offered them the wealth of their victims, if they would join him in his battle. On one day, they were instructed to kill any and every Jew they knew, and that Jew's wealth would be their own."

Hitler reached for a glass of water and took a drink.

"Unfortunately, his plan was thwarted because the Jews had infiltrated his very government and his king was in love with a Jew. But today, this plan will work. We will supply manpower through the local government to facilitate property and bank transfers. For six months we have prepared the people for this day. They know who the enemy is and now that it will directly benefit them, they will support this initiative."

Hitler spoke with confidence, though he could tell by the faces of those in the room they were not convinced.

It was Spain who broke the silence.

"This will never work. It will be mayhem. Our loyal citizens will turn on themselves to get to the nonmarked. Who would be safe?"

"Let them die, then," Szabo said. "That is a price worth paying. I do not think you are giving your citizens credit, though. There is an underlying anger against the enemy and our citizens are just waiting for the approval to act. Now we are giving them the opportunity they desire. They will be well aware of the risks and most will be willing to take them. Their newfound wealth will give them a sense of honor and loyalty to the FWP. That is how it will be promoted."

"What will we do with the bodies?" asked Nigeria.

"What are you doing with the bodies now?" Hitler responded. His point was clear. This issue should already have been addressed. "Dump them, bury them, or burn them. Tell your local governments to handle it."

"If you promote this right, we will know success," added Szabo. "Gone are the days of micromanagement. Let the people sort this out themselves. They desire it and the plunder will be their reward."

England joined the conversation. "But the government was instituted for order. This is a step in the wrong direction."

Japan agreed. "Mass executions done at the hands of angry mobs are barbaric! Can't we increase our military involvement and in an orderly manner"—

"Enough!" Hitler stood and swiped his arms across his body. "If your military had been successful, we wouldn't be having this meeting, would we? Do you not fear Satan? Do you not realize that I am not the force behind this edict? Can you not grasp this?" His voice boomed and echoed through the room.

Then the room fell silent.

Suddenly, the windows of the meeting room exploded into the room, as if a force outside had broken its way in. Those standing fell to their knees and hid their faces, as shards of glass sprayed the room. The shock of the explosion was overcome with the hot breeze that swirled in through the broken windows. Papers that had previously lay neatly stacked in front of each leader, now blew around the room like a massive ticker tape parade. The shrieks of surprise, pain, and confusion filled the room.

Hitler sat motionless in his seat. He watched the scene as if watching a movie, completely calm and unaffected by the confusion. He knew perfectly well what was happening. He looked to his left and saw that two of the leaders had sustained fatal wounds, as they were slumped forward in their chairs, large shards protruding from their necks. He thought it curious that no one moved to check on them, not even their second in command.

The wind continued to swirl around the circumference of the room, between the still-seated leaders and their cowering associates, until it looked as if the leaders were caught up in a whirlpool of paper, glass, and wind. Hitler was now amused at the display of power.

It was about time they realized who they were dealing with.

A stream of wind broke free from the swirl and snaked its way around the tables, as if examining the leaders and their injuries. It stopped in front of Hitler and for a brief moment, Hitler met eyes with Lucifer. He knew exactly what to do. He stood and tilted his head backwards and the stream of air flowed into his nostrils.

Immediately the swirl stopped and the paper and glass fell to the floor behind the seated, injured leaders. All eyes were on Hitler, whose body was lifted from his place at the table in a fully upright position. He rose fifteen feet in the air and slowly moved forward until he was directly in the middle of the room. Then his body was slowly lowered until he stood on his own two feet again.

His eyes glowed orange and it was clear to all he was no longer himself. He spoke and at the sound of his voice, demons appeared, surrounding the leaders in the place where the wind once swirled. There was a deep and raspy quality to his voice, clearly recognizable as the voice of Satan. Panic swept the room as the leaders realized they were surrounded.

"Your time is up. You are completely incapable of pleasing me. Your minds are filled with doubt—do you think I cannot see that? I have no use for weakness. From this moment, you are dead to me."

The low voice echoed in the large room.

With that, the demons each picked up a long shard of glass from the floor and thrust it between the shoulder blades of the FWP leaders until the demons' hands protruded through the leaders' chests. They dropped their bloody shards on the tables and then pulled their arms from the lifeless bodies. The dead leaders slumped over on the tables, joining their previously fallen comrades.

"Remove the bodies." Hitler's mouth. Lucifer's voice.

The demons, responding to Lucifer's command, threw the bodies out the broken windows. The bodies piled up on the sidewalk outside of the FWP national headquarters, barely missing the cache of reporters waiting for a statement outside of the Federation of World Powers Building. The vice presidents, now first in command, stood frozen, unable to move from the shock of watching their leaders murdered. Lucifer turned his attention to them.

"Welcome to leadership! Sit. Go ahead, don't be afraid—I have held your previous leadership responsible for your countries' inability to please me. You have a clean slate. Please, sit."

The new leaders of the FWP sat in the bloodstained chairs of their predecessors.

"Take a look at the blood on the tables in front of you."

Lucifer, in Hitler's body, walked over to the new Premiere of France. He picked up one of the bloody shards and handed it to him.

"As a matter of fact, take home the glass stake as a memento of this occasion."

He slowly walked around the inside of the square of tables, looking at the trembling world leaders, who could not make eye contact with him.

"You are now the leaders of your countries. Do not fail me. I want the followers of God dead. We do not have much time left. If you fail, you will be replaced. I can no longer wait. Get to work and prove to me you are far more creative and obedient than your friends lying on the sidewalk outside."

He circled back to Hitler's original place at the table, pulled out the chair and stood before the cowering leaders.

"Prove to me your worth or join your friends."

With that, Hitler exhaled and out came the breeze of Lucifer. A piercing laugh filled the room, followed by the cackles of the demons. It lasted just long enough for the wind to make one last lap around the room and then fly out the window. No one moved. When Hitler came to his senses, he found himself standing in front of his seat. He had a sense of what had happened, but the magnitude of what Lucifer had done to shake up the nations was just beginning to hit him. He purposefully chose not to act surprised or frightened. He would have Szabo tell him in detail what had happened but for now, he was in charge and would send out the leaders with a word of hope.

"Tell what has happened. Let the people see your fear of Lucifer. He has given you a second chance. If you succeed, you will be remembered as purveyors of peace—those who paid the unspeakable price for world unity. September twenty-first will be our Day of Destruction. That gives you seven days to work it out. You have the authority and the power, now go. Do what only you can do."

Slowly and shakily the new leaders of the FWP stood and exited the room. Hitler felt rather dizzy. He sat in his chair and Szabo offered him a glass of water. Hitler thought he saw disappointment on Szabo's face. Perhaps Szabo wished he had died with the others.

"Do you wish you were in my chair?" he asked Szabo.

"Not in a million years."

"Then wipe the disappointment off your face. I am not going anywhere."

"I will follow you to the death and you alone. Lucifer knows my loyalty. I am surprised you would think otherwise."

Hitler was satisfied with his response.

"I think Lucifer's actions here will move things along," Szabo continued. "His display of power, plus the plan for the Day of Destruction will greatly speed along our mission. The heart of man is lined with greed and desire. Promoted correctly, the twenty-first will be a wild success!"

Hitler put his hand to his pounding temple. "I have got to lie down. Wake me if anything newsworthy happens."

Hitler stood and headed towards the door, stopping at the broken windows. He looked outside and saw the reporters frantically gathering details. They were interviewing anyone who would talk, though not many of the new world leaders were stopping. The cameras wagged between the interviews and the bodies that were being carted away.

You think that is a big pile of bodies? Give it a week.

twenty-eight

"I called this meeting tonight because Herr Hitler has given us our marching orders."

The room cheered and Evan Stillman continued. The room was packed tonight. There had to be at least forty Shel-heads there. Evan stood by his chair, which was in front of five uneven rows of chairs in the meeting hall.

"We have waited patiently for our time and that time has finally come. Now that our government has agreed to adhere to the guidelines set forth by the FWP, we no longer have restraints on, but have the freedom to do the will of our savior! "

Another cheer, this one lasted longer. Evan raised a piece of paper over his head.

"In my hand is the Shelton listing of nonmarkers. Tonight we need to make sure that each nonmarker has a Shel-head assigned to them and that you are prepared to do what our savior has called us to do."

Again, cheering.

"I understand there is a financial blessing which comes from this task, but more important than the money is being the first town in all of America to be nonmarker free."

The cheer rose as the boys and men jumped to their feet, bodies slamming into each other in celebration. Evan's heart soared in anticipation and he knew he was far more prepared than anyone in the room. He was a true leader, and he would run this operation worthy of Hitler's approval.

"The city council is offering help with estate titles, but they require proof of death in order to make the transfer. And all they require is a head." Evan lifted his sword over his head and offered, "If anyone needs help, just give me a call."

The Shel-heads roared with laughter. Evan loved the energy he was feeling. This group alone could manage the list, but he was sure others in town would be greedy.

"We need to act swiftly, so that we can enjoy the fruit of our labors. So, who wants to go first? Is there someone who you are just dying to get your hands on?"

The laughter had died down and suddenly the room was unnaturally quiet. The Shel-heads looked around at each other and quietly sat. Evan was confused. What was wrong with these guys? This was their opportunity.

So, as a true leader, he stepped up and went first.

"I'll start then. I'm taking the Doughertys on Miller Street."

"Why them?" called a Shel-head to his right. "They're not worth anything if they live on Miller!"

"I don't need the money," Evan explained. "I'm going after a leader. This guy's been on my nerves for quite some time now. I'm thinking strategy here. If I take out an outspoken believer, maybe those on the fence will fall to our side. You all can fight over money, but there is a much bigger picture here. Hitler will never be securely in power until these people are gone. So, I'm going after one of their leaders."

Evan sat down and let his example sink in. Finally each Shel-head stood and took a name from the list. Three didn't, but they were only wannabes anyway. September twenty-first was going to weed out the look-alikes. The Shel-heads would be empowered by this raid and Evan was going to lead the way.

Evan's only concern was that old Morty would try to make a run for it. He would have to keep an eye on him. A close eye, and make sure he didn't disappear. Though Evan couldn't remember the ending of the first Morty's story, he knew the ending of the second. It was a good thing he ordered that sword months ago. He would have a lot to discuss with his idol when he got home.

As he locked up that night after everyone had gone, he wondered if he had been specifically chosen for this day. Did the others have talking idols or just him? No one had ever mentioned it, so maybe he was special. His mom always called him a born leader. Perhaps she was right.

The Day of Destruction threw a wrench in Rory's plans. In theory, having the man of the house take the mark put the man in the leadership position. He would be the one to provide for his family. Women who worked eventually found they needed the mark to be paid, but there were still all those stay-at-home wives who sat smugly in their seats at church, knowing their husbands had covered them. Now, that plan was out the window and, though Rory thought it was only fair for all the women to have to be marked, they had no choice in the matter. This was a problem because he had just calmed the people down about the men taking the mark and now they were all worked up about the women having to take it also.

As Rory drove home from work, he knew this topic was coming to a head with Donna. He was unable to protect her if she didn't take the mark, but she didn't see it that way. She was adamant that she wouldn't do it. She was mad at him for two weeks for taking the mark without telling her and didn't believe Rory's bind on earth/bind in heaven claim. They went round and round then until she cried and said he was going to burn in hell.

That didn't sit well with Rory.

Rory pulled into his driveway and looked at the clock on his dashboard. It was 4:17. He was home an hour early today. Much of his day was spent fielding church phone calls and he really didn't want to deal with Donna tonight. He would tell her he needed a nap before dinner, grab a Coke and the remote, and watch the Tigers on TV.

Technically, Donna had put him in a real bind. If she doesn't take the mark, and someone kills her, would that person get half of his estate? Half of his home? Half of his assets? Half of his savings? Half of her life insurance? In actuality, if Rory really wanted to protect his property he should be the one to …

He wouldn't actually let himself think it.

Rory walked in the back door and listened to see if he could hear the television on in the living room. He heard nothing. He walked through the kitchen. There was food in the Crock-Pot sitting on the counter, but no Donna. He entered the living room and heard a voice coming from the bedroom, but it wasn't Donna's. Rory recognized the voice and he froze in his steps.

His idol was talking.

Out loud.

To Donna.

He crept up to the door and saw Donna standing in front of his dresser. A basket of folded laundry was on the bed and a rolled up pair of socks were in her hand. That explains why she was in his sock drawer, he thought to himself. The manila folder, with Rory's picture of Hitler taped to the front, was lying on the floor. Donna must have dropped it.

By her physical stance, Rory could tell she was not doing well. She was breathing heavy and the hand with the sock was trembling. He strained to hear what was being said, without giving away his presence.

"Donna, I want you to pick me up and put me on the dresser."

Donna leaned over and picked up the folder. It opened slightly and she stood it on the dresser.

"Very good. You're not as stupid as Rory says you are."

Rory wished he hadn't told the idol about Donna.

"How . . . ? Where . . . ? What . . . ?"

Donna couldn't finish a thought, let alone a sentence. That should prove her intelligence.

"Listen, you think you're safe because he has a mark and can provide for you? Well, you're wrong. Dead wrong. You've put his life in danger because you won't take the mark. Don't you love him? I thought your marriage meant more to you than anything in the world. I guess I was wrong. Even Rory doubts your love. He told me just yesterday that he felt lonely in his marriage. Now why would he say that?"

Rory's lips started to curl into a smile at those words. He really was a friend. The idol was sticking up for Rory.

"Are . . . are you an idol?"

"Call it what you want, I'm only here to help. And lately, I'm your hubby's best friend. Does he talk to you anymore? He sure talks to me. He can't figure out why he's stuck his neck out for you. Why does he have to bear the weight of the mark? He thought marriage took two people and together they became one, fighting the world as one, facing any problem as one. He was wrong, I guess."

Oh, he's good, Rory thought.

"But why did Rory do this? Why did he build you?"

Still clueless, as usual.

"He knew that the mark alone wouldn't save his family. Now, he reaps the benefits that I have to offer. We talk every day. I give him advice and he's a good listener."

"Are you Hitler?"

"I speak for him."

"I can't believe this. Rory would never build an idol, especially one to Hitler. I mean, Hitler's the Antichrist. Rory knows that."

"Listen, Rory already took the number. He's mine now. There's no turning back and he knows it. Here's your dilemma. If you don't take the mark, he's got to kill you. The only chance he has of surviving is to get rid of all of the enemies. If even just one lives, our plan fails. So, either you take the mark and live with your hubby or he'll have to kill you. Simple as that."

Donna knocked the folder back into the drawer and pushed the socks over top. Rory could tell she was going to make a run for the door and he slid back into the bathroom and closed the door, so that it was only open a crack. He heard her slam the dresser drawer and run from the room. He watched her race through the living room and then heard her footsteps through the kitchen. As soon as the back door slammed, Rory stepped out of the bathroom. He heard the garage door open and her car back out of the driveway.

She must not have noticed my car, he thought to himself.

Rory wondered where she was going, but decided not to go after her. She needed some time to think. The idol was convincing and he spoke the truth. Whether or not Donna was smart enough to understand, that was another story.

Rory decided to head over to Flannery's. They'd have the game on and he could get a sandwich there. Plus there were no phones at Flannery's. Rory walked into the kitchen and lifted the lid on the crock-pot. He leaned over and took a deep sniff.

"And a sandwich it is," he said, walking out the back door to his car.

It was ten fifteen and Emma was sitting on the couch with Josh, Seth, and Leighsa, watching *The Bourne Identity*. She'd seen it about six times now, but it was a very exciting movie. Her mom had just slid in between her and the arm of the couch and handed her a hot chocolate. The caves were cool at night and the hot chocolate warmed her quickly.

Garrett tapped Lily on the shoulder and whispered, so as not to interrupt the movie, "I just got off the phone with Dan. They had their meeting and you'll never believe who is coming down now!"

Her dad wasn't a good whisperer and Josh pushed the pause button on the controls, which he held through the whole movie for some reason. Garrett looked up when he heard the volume mute and the four kids looked back at him.

"Who, Dad? Who's coming?" Emma spoke for all.

"I'm sorry. I didn't mean to interrupt your movie."

"Come on, Mr. Hamilton!" pleaded Seth. "Who's coming?"

"It's a long story, but it's worth the details!" Garrett sat in one of the chairs and leaned forward. Emma could tell this was going to be a good one.

"Well, it started about a month ago. Lily wrote a letter to the Dougherty's, pleading for them to come and join us. She said that their work was done in Shelton and it was time to come."

"So, it's the Dougherty's?" Leighsa interrupted.

"Just hold on. I'm getting there. So, in the last letter Dan sent us, he said the group was meeting tonight to decide what to do. He was going to read Lily's letter and out of the seven witnessers who stayed behind, he was going to see how many wanted to go. Now, with the Day of Destruction just two days away, it was time to decide. He asked me to call him tonight to find out what they decided. So I used Nate's phone and just called him."

"And they're all coming?" It was Lily now who interrupted.

"Hold on. There's a surprise. In the middle of their meeting tonight, Donna Appleton knocked on the door and came in crying, saying Rory had an idol in his dresser drawer who was threatening her."

"What?" said Josh. "Mr. Appleton made an idol? I thought the church up there just took marks but didn't make idols?"

"Apparently, that was not altogether true. Donna didn't know about it, but this talking idol terrified her and she ran out of the house. He must have been hiding it from her in his dresser. She wants to come down here and it ends up they are all coming."

"Oh, Garrett!" Lily had jumped to her feet and thrown her arms around Garrett's neck. "That's great news!" Emma saw the tears start to flow and she wasn't surprised. Her mom had been worried about them for months.

"When are they coming?" Emma asked.

"Donna went back to her house and grabbed some clothes. Thankfully, Rory wasn't there. They'll leave tomorrow."

"Mr. Appleton's going to flip when he finds out!" said Seth.

"Who knows what his mind-set is, but I do think Donna is right," said Garrett.

"It will be weird to have her down here, won't it, Mom?" asked Emma.

"I can't imagine what she's been through these past few months, but she knew exactly where to go, Emma. We will be kind and accepting of her, do you understand?" She had her mom tone on.

"Yes, Mom. She was never a very nice woman. You don't think she'll stay with us in our cave, do you?"

"Don't worry about that," Garrett said. "It'll all work out. Dan is coming a few hours behind the rest, but most should be here by sundown tomorrow night."

"Why can't he come with the others?" Emma asked.

"He's meeting a few men who aren't marked in the morning and he doesn't know how to reach them. He's sending Betsy ahead because she knows how to get here. She was here for the build out."

"Oh, I am so excited!" Lily said. "I have a lot to thank the Lord for tonight!"

"I'll get a hold of Mack in the morning and find out which caves have room. See you in the morning, kids. Shut off the lights when you go to bed."

Lily and Garrett left the living room and Josh hit the play button. Emma was happy that the Doughertys were on their way. They were like grandparents to her and she knew they weren't safe in Shelton. And they would have lots of stories to tell—new stories, from the outside.

Tomorrow would be an exciting day. She'd spend most of the day at the lake and then get home to see the Doughertys. She'll have to talk the rest into leaving a bit earlier from the lake, but it was for a good cause.

As Emma watched the end of the movie, she couldn't stop smiling.

At 11:47 p.m. Rory pulled into his drive. It had been an awful game. He should have left after the third inning, but coming home to Donna wasn't quite appealing enough for him to leave his hot wings and friends so he stayed until the end. The very end. By now she should be long gone to dreamland. They could talk in the morning.

He quietly closed the back door from the garage. He walked into the kitchen for a quick swig of orange juice and then it was on to bed. He stopped by the bathroom to brush his teeth and put on his pajamas that were hanging on the back hook of the bathroom door. Then he made his way over to the bed. In the dark, he could tell something was wrong. The laundry basket was still where Donna left it on the bed. He walked over to the light switch and flipped it on.

No Donna.

Rory walked through the house looking for her. At first he thought she might have fallen asleep in front of the television but she wasn't in the family room. He checked the guestroom. Maybe she was still upset about the idol and was making a statement. She wasn't there either.

He went back to the bedroom and opened the top drawer of his dresser. He pulled out his folder.

"Where is she?" he demanded.

"It took you long enough to ask. How many rooms did you look in before you decided to ask me?"

"Where is she?" Rory was raising his voice now.

"Well, you've really blown it, buddy. You had your chance and now she's gone. Packed her bags and left hours ago."

Rory ran to her dresser and pulled the drawers open. Each one was empty. He ran to the closet. Most of her clothes were gone, hangers and all.

"Arrgh!" Rory cried out in frustration. "Where would she go?"

"You tell me. She's your wife."

"You're the one who scared her. This is your fault." Rory sat down on the bed.

"You have been difficult to live with. Demanding. Ill-tempered. And you kept me a secret from her. Can you really blame her?"

"But where would she go? She has no family. I'm all she's got."

The idol remained silent for a while. Rory sat on the edge of the bed, racking his brain. After a moment, he threw the laundry basket, folded laundry and all, across the room. Then he turned out the light, pulled back the sheet, and climbed into the bed.

"That ungrateful wench. How could she leave me? I have given my life for her and how does she thank me? She runs away. She's not that clever. I'll make a few calls in the morning and I'll find her. And when I do, she'll pay."

"Atta boy! I knew you'd come to your senses."

"Oh, she'll pay all right. She'll pay with her life. If she's going to leave me, she may as well make me some money on the way out."

Rory Appleton fell asleep with revenge on his mind. He had been building up resentment for months now and Donna had pushed him over the edge. He didn't care what the congregation at Grace would think. He didn't care what anyone would think. No one else had lived in this house with that ungrateful, condescending, nitpicking woman. Only he had, and he had rights. Rory was going to make use of the rights afforded him by the government of the United States of America and the Federation of World Powers. He was going to do his part in ridding the world of at least one nonmarker. It was the least he could do.

twenty-nine

One day before the Day of Destruction. Evan had carefully stalked his prey and knew his routine. Every morning, Morty-guy would take a walk in the park near his house. He would talk to strangers, and it was guaranteed he would start a conversation with any non-marker he saw. It was like they had a bond.

Then he would head back home for lunch. After lunch, he would ride his bike to the grocery store or to the mall. Then home again for dinner. In the evenings, he would often have a bunch of people to his house. All nonmarkers of course.

It was one in the afternoon and like clockwork, Morty-guy pulled into the grocery store, but this time it wasn't on his bike, but in his car. Evan found this strangely alarming and he got out of his car so that he could see Morty better.

Dan Dougherty parked his car and got out. He walked across the parking lot to where two men were standing and the three of them started talking. Evan wished he could hear what they were saying, but he didn't want to draw attention to himself.

As the conversation continued, Evan walked over to Dan's car and looked in the backseat. There he saw the gas cans and the bag of clothes. His mind started to race. It seemed to him that old Morty was planning a trip. Why else would he have extra gas and clothes? It made all the sense in the world that he would run the day before the great Day of Destruction, because Morty would be on the list of victims.

Evan walked back over to his car and climbed inside. He kept his eye on the three men talking a few rows over and started thinking through his options. If Morty was leaving, in essence, the thorn in his side would be gone. He wouldn't have to deal with his constant babble and defiance of Hitler and the FWP. So, it really was good news that he was leaving.

There was a down side, however. That's the fact that Morty would still be alive. Hitler wants all followers of God dead. Period. If Evan let Morty go, then who would find him and kill him? What if old Morty was a great hider? What if he hid so well that after all non-markers were killed he somehow survived and that Jesus guy came back and because Morty was still alive, Jesus would take over the world? It could happen. No, Evan couldn't let old Morty just slip away. For the sake of the cause, he had to make sure Morty died.

Plus there was the sheer joy of using his sword and the government saying it was okay.

But that led to a problem. Morty wanted to leave today. Evan couldn't kill until tomorrow. Evan had to stall Morty and he had to do it quickly. He saw the three men shake hands, look at their watches and then the two get into their car. Morty watched the two men drive away and then headed to his own car.

Evan looked around the parking lot. No one was around. He started his car and backed out of his spot. Morty was almost to his car. Evan accelerated down the aisle and U-turned into Morty's aisle. He stopped his car directly behind Morty's car, just as Morty was opening his driver's door to climb inside. Evan jumped from his car, at the same time grabbing the bottle of cheap wine he had in the passenger's seat. In one swift movement he hit the old man on the back of his head with the bottle, shattering it with the force of his blow.

The old man fell to his knees, then splayed onto the asphalt. Evan looked around again and saw no one. He dragged the body to his car and shoved him into the backseat. Climbing into the driver's seat, Evan threw the car into drive and sped out of the parking lot. His adrenaline was flowing now and Evan looked in the backseat. The old man was lying there, blood dripping from the side of his head. Or maybe it was just the wine.

Evan headed home, putting the finishing touches on his plan to get rid of old Morty-guy. *What a rush.* His mom's car was gone, and that worked to his advantage. He pulled his car into the right side of the garage and shut the door. He got out of the car and walked to the middle of the garage. He reached over his head and pulled on the handle dangling from the garage door opener. The door was now disengaged.

Evan knew his mom well enough that when her garage door opener didn't work, she wouldn't bother to try to lift the door. She would probably have a heart attack if she did.

It was starting to cool down in North Carolina and the kids had decided they could only go one or two more times to the lake. The water had a chill to it, so swimming was not the primary activity, but the time away was still cherished by all. They didn't stay as long either, which eased Emma's conscience a bit. Emma knew she would be relieved once they stopped sneaking away, but there was a part of her that would miss it.

As they cleared the woods and saw the lake, Adam was the first to see a woman dressed in white sitting on the large rock they used as a diving board. He raised his hand to stop the kids. Emma froze behind Adam, unsure of what to do next. Adam looked back at the others. He put his finger to his lips and motioned with his head to go back towards the woods. Slowly and quietly they turned, when they heard the woman call out to them. Actually, she called out to Emma.

"Emma, is that you?"

Emma looked at Adam with panic in her eyes, asking him what she should do without ever saying a word.

"Emma . . . Emma Hamilton!"

She was waving her arms and Emma squinted her eyes, trying to recognize her face. But that didn't even make sense to her.

"He said you would be here. Don't be afraid." The woman stood, climbed off the rock, and headed towards the kids.

"What is she talking about?" Leighsa grabbed Emma's arm.

"I don't know," Emma whispered. "I've never seen her before in my life. What should I do?"

"It's gotta be an angel," Seth said. "Who else knows we're here?"

"The demons know," Adam said. "And have you ever heard of a woman angel? I don't think she's an angel."

The woman was motioning with her hand for them to come.

"Please, everyone, come join me. I am alone and I mean you no harm."

She stood open armed, as if that proved she was alone.

"There's more of us than there is of her, and she doesn't even have a purse or a bag with her, so unless she has a gun in that white gown, I think she's safe," Seth said, keeping his voice low.

"There's a bag on the rock behind her. And some things on that blanket. Do you see them?" asked Neil.

"It looks like food," said Leighsa.

The kids looked to their leader, Adam, to make a decision.

"Let's go, but stay close together and keep your eyes open."

Emma scanned the lake and the woods on the far side. She couldn't see anyone, but that didn't mean they weren't there. She thought back to her father telling her this morning that tomorrow was a worldwide Day of Destruction and it seemed too much of a co-incidence that this woman would show up today. She didn't like how this was feeling and she grabbed Adam's hand to feel safer.

As they got closer, Adam dropped Emma's hand and turned to her.

"Stay behind me and let me do the talking."

He stopped ten feet from the woman and the rest gathered be-hind him. The woman stood and was eye to eye with Adam, making her about five foot nine. She had shoulder-length blonde hair and she wasn't really in a gown. It was more like a sundress with a white jacket. She had beautiful blue eyes that seemed to sparkle when she smiled.

"Who are you?" Adam asked.

"My name is Melanie."

"Where did you come from?"

"I came from Mount Olive."

"Who told you we would be here?"

"Excuse me?"

"You said, 'He said you would be here.' Who told you that?"

"Jesus did."

Emma's heart started to race, not with excitement but with fear.

"In a dream?" asked Adam.

"No, in person." Melanie smiled.

"Now you've lost me. You've talked to Jesus. Face-to-face?"

"Yes, dear, face-to-face." Melanie had a sweet, soothing voice with a touch of a southern drawl. "I have wonderful news. He's back! He told me you would be here. So I came to ask you to come with me to see Him. He wants to see you."

"He wants to see us? Or Emma?"

"Well, all of you, of course! But He knew Emma would be here and told me to ask for her." She looked around Adam and met eyes with Emma. "You are Emma, aren't you?"

"Yes, ma'am," she answered, slowly.

"Oh, Emma, I have heard so much about you!" Melanie started to walk towards Emma as if she was going to hug her when Adam stepped in between them.

"That's far enough. Why should we believe you?"

"Please, come over to the rock and let's sit. Have you brought lunch because I have some with me?" She pointed back to the rock. "I have fresh fruit and cheese, deli sandwiches and homemade chocolate chunk cookies! Now, how can you say no to that?"

"I think we should try the food," Josh said, receiving a nod from Seth.

Emma was irritated at their trust based on chocolate. Melanie turned and confidently walked towards the rock. They cautiously followed her and saw the food lying on a blanket.

"How do we know this isn't poisoned?" questioned Adam.

"I'm hungry too. I'll eat with you. Here, pick any sandwich and I will eat whatever you choose!"

By that time the kids had sat and were practically drooling at the fresh food. They hadn't seen fresh fruit all summer, except for the wild raspberries they had picked in the woods. Adam picked up a sandwich and handed it to her. Melanie took a bite and wiped her mouth with a linen napkin. She smiled and motioned for the rest to eat. Adam was satisfied and took a sandwich himself. Emma cautiously followed suit.

"I can understand why you are so cautious. Really, I am not offended. How long have you been in hiding? Six months now? The Lord has been with you every moment and now He wants you to know that you don't have to hide anymore."

"But we know what to look for when He returns and it hasn't happened yet." Emma said, frowning.

Melanie turned her gaze on Emma and smiled.

"He said you were well studied. Well, Emma, how can I explain this? You were probably looking for all the lights to go out of the sky and then see Jesus return with a big flash, like lightning. Is that close?"

They all nodded.

"Well, sometimes the Scriptures give a clear picture of what will happen and other times it gives symbols of what will happen. It can be confusing. Even the greatest Bible scholars have difficulty deciphering what is symbolic and what is literal."

"So you're saying that when Jesus taught about the sun, moon, and stars falling from the sky, those were just symbols?" Emma asked, skeptically.

"Yes, He was talking about the darkness right before His return. Things have been very dark in the world. People's hearts have grown cold. They have turned from their Creator." Emma thought Melanie's face looked sad. "It has never been this dark before, but Jesus' arrival has changed all that. He came back last night and everything has changed. Do you get the local news in the caves?"

"Yeah, and the national news on the radio," said Adam. "We didn't hear about any of this."

"Of course, you wouldn't yet, especially on the national news. He hasn't made Himself known publicly yet. He is just going to places where He knows He has faithful followers and He will gather them and take them to Jerusalem with Him. There He will declare Himself King of Kings and Lord of Lords. Hallelujah!" Melanie raised her hands and face to the sky.

Emma was starting to breathe a little easier and she wasn't sure why. She decided to question Melanie further.

"Why didn't He just come to the caves? Why did He send you?"

"When Jesus puts on human form, He can't be everywhere at one time. There are several congregations in this area because it is so remote. I'll bet you didn't know that. I was actually hiding in a cave system on the other side of Mount Olive. He came to us and then sent me to find you."

"But why didn't you go to the caves? Why did you come here?"

"This is much closer for me and I have other believers who are going to your parents as we speak."

Adam stood. He reached for Emma's hand and pulled her to her feet.

"Then we should go back and be with our families!"

Melanie remained seated and took a bite of her cookie.

"Jesus is very anxious to see all of you. By the time you get back, they will probably all be gone to see Him already. Your parents don't know you are here, right?"

Emma felt her cheeks flush at that question.

"No," said Josh.

"He told me you have been swimming here every Thursday since July and that your parents don't know about it. Jesus knew they would think you were with other families and are planning to meet up with you in town. He sent me to bring you down to Him."

Emma thought back to her conversation with her mother with the girls. Up until now, everything had been literally fulfilled. It was hard to turn things symbolic.

"I don't know if we should believe you," she said. "The Scriptures say there will be people who claim Jesus was on earth, doing signs and wonders, but they were lying to bring people out of hiding. This just doesn't feel right."

"Oh, honey, you really are putting too much thought into it. You need to live by faith. I am telling you that if by faith you come with me, your faith will become sight, for you will see Jesus! How else would I know you were here? If I was lying and was trying to trap you, wouldn't I have come with the police or someone like that? But I am alone. I can return alone, but then you will return to empty caves, with no parents. You'll have to find your way down the mountain, hike into town and see if you can find your families. If you come with me, I will not only reunite you with Jesus, but also with your families."

Melanie stood.

"I am going to clean up our mess and let you decide what you are going to do. I need to get back and you need to make your decision. I can't force you—you have to come of your own free will. I am sure you will make the right decision."

The kids climbed off the rock and walked over to the edge of the lake, far enough that Melanie couldn't hear their discussion.

Emma started.

"I don't like this. It's not what we were taught to look for."

"How did she know we were here and that we've been swimming since July?" asked Seth.

"Yeah, and why did she come alone?" Neil asked.

"I don't know." Adam shrugged.

"She is so pretty and calm," Leighsa said. "I want to trust her."

"What about the rapture, guys?" Emma frowned again. "When Jesus returns, we're supposed to rise up and meet the Lord in the air. How can that be symbolic?"

"Well, there's the Scripture that talks about the faithful fighting with Jesus at Armageddon, right? Maybe He's taking us there to be part of His army," Seth said.

"No, the church is raptured and Armageddon is fought by angels or others," Emma said.

"What others? Hitler is trying to kill all Christians so that there is no one left here to fight for Jesus when He returns. If He is just going to rapture us, who will fight at Armageddon? We must be His army. When Armageddon is over, then we're raptured." Seth's expression was full of confidence.

"I wish I had my Bible," Emma said. "I'm so confused. We shouldn't even be here! We should be with our families. That's where we were safe."

Anger flashed in Adam's eyes.

"Emma, you've been safe all along. If we were seen by anyone, we would have been caught long before this. Do you remember the angel who visited us? And how about the demons in the woods? You believed those things. Just because this isn't how you pictured it in your head, doesn't mean it's not of God. Look at the facts. The more I think about it, the more it makes sense. By the time we got back to the caves, found the quads, got to the vehicle storage unit and tried to drive into Mount Olive, it would be way past sunset. We would be winging it. Maybe we should go with her. She seems trustworthy. Everything that has happened up until now has been so bizarre that this seems to fit. We're not going unless it's unanimous." He paused, looking right at Emma. "I say we go."

He took his gaze off Emma and looked around the group.

"Go," Leighsa said.

"Go," Neil said.

"Go," Seth said.

"Go," Josh said.

Once again, all eyes turned on Emma. Deep down she felt this was not right, but the thought that Jesus was in Mount Olive and she wasn't with Him made her heart want to burst. All she wanted to do was be with Him. That's why she was hiding in the mountains.

She had to walk by faith.

She made up her mind and cast the deciding vote.

"Go."

Nate and Sherrie were reading in their bedroom when Pam Johnson knocked on their door.

"Yes?" said Sherrie. "Come on in."

The door opened and Pam stuck her head inside.

"Garrett Hamilton is on the radio, asking to send Emma home early. Do you know what he's talking about?"

Sherrie sat up and furrowed her eyebrows.

"No, Adam's over at their place."

"I'll go and see what's up," Nate offered. He got off the bed and put his shoes on. "Is he still on the radio?" he asked Pam as they walked down the hall to the living room.

"Yeah, I told him I would get you."

Nate walked over to the ham radio unit and picked up the handset.

"Garrett, are you there? This is Nate."

"Hi, Nate. We need Emma to come home early. Lily's trying to get things set up for the Dougherty's arrival and the kids are decorating. We need Emma's help. Can she come home in the next hour or so?"

"Garrett, she's not here. Adam's over at your place today."

"No. Seth, Leighsa, Emma, and Josh said they would be over at your place."

Nate looked around the living room. There were several children there, but the teenagers were definitely not at Petra.

"They're not here, Garrett. Maybe they're at the Tabernacle."

Nate felt a touch on his shoulder and Sherrie was standing behind him with a questioning look on her face. There was a crackling sound on the radio and a voice other than Garrett's spoke.

"This is Tom Lehman. I'm at the Tabernacle, manning the radio, and there aren't any kids here."

"Adam's not at Engedi?" Sherrie asked.

"No."

Nate and Sherrie Reed stood in the living room at Petra. Nate put his hands on his hips and ran through options. It didn't make any sense. They couldn't have just disappeared. Where in the world could they be?

"They must be at another cave. They have lots of friends here. We just mixed up where they said they would be." Sherrie was trying to be positive.

"The Hamiltons mixed it up too? I don't like this," Nate said. "This doesn't feel right."

As they stood there, they heard Garrett Hamilton make a general request of all the caves.

"This is Garrett Hamilton. I am trying to track down my daughter, Emma, and a few other kids. Neil Cowlings, Leighsa and Josh Torey and Seth Mason. Does anyone out there know where they are?"

Nate and Sherrie waited for a response, but all they heard was static.

thirty

As the young people followed Melanie through the woods, Emma found it strange she wasn't more talkative. They walked along in silence and Emma kept trying to imagine what it was going to be like to see Jesus. But her mind kept wandering.

What's wrong with you? she asked herself a dozen times. *This is the moment you've been waiting for.* But it just didn't seem right. The others were quiet too, and Emma wondered what they were thinking. She was walking next to Adam, and he had a very neutral look on his face.

"What are you thinking about?"

He looked over at her and his eyes suddenly widened and he pulled Emma into an embrace and whispered in her ear, "Oh, Emma, I am so sorry!"

Emma tried to push away from him to figure out what was going on, but he wouldn't let go. Then she heard the sound of rifles loading and men yelling and running. She looked over Adam's shoulder and realized they were surrounded by men in dark navy uniforms with the letters S.W.A.T. in white on their backs. Their rifles were loaded and pointed directly at the group of young people.

"No! Adam, no," Emma cried. "This can't be happening."

She pulled away and looked for Melanie. She was standing with the men, facing the kids.

"What's going on here?" Josh yelled. "Melanie, you said you were taking . . . us . . . to see . . ." His voice fell off in a hoarse whisper as the realization hit.

Emma grabbed her heart, because it felt like it was about to shatter. The men rushed forward before a another cry or word was spoken by the youth and immediately separated them from each other.

Emma could hear Leighsa screaming and saw her kicking at one of the officers. Josh and Seth were fighting too, but Adam and Neil were walking with the men and not putting up a fight. A man grabbed Emma by the shoulder and she shrieked, more from fear than in pain.

Adam turned and called to Emma.

"I'm all right," she called back. She knew fighting would be a waste of energy, so she walked quietly with her officer.

"I'm going to take you to the Mount Olive police station. There we will ask you some questions. Do you understand what I just explained?"

Emma nodded. He walked Emma through the woods to a clearing, brought her to a car, and forcing her head down, pushed her into the backseat. He didn't put cuffs on her and she reached up and swiped the tears from her cheeks. The other backseat door opened and Leighsa was pushed in.

"Oh, Leighsa!" Emma cried and scooted over beside her best friend. Leighsa was crying too.

"What's going to happen to us, Emma?" she asked. "They're going to kill us, right? We don't have a mark. We're going to die!"

"I don't know, Leighsa." Emma grabbed Leighsa's hands and tried to calm her down. "Maybe they'll just question us and let us go."

Emma didn't even believe her own suggestion and Leighsa started to hyperventilate next to her. Emma pushed her head between her legs and rubbed her back, all the while saying, "Breathe, Leighsa, breathe."

Leighsa's breathing slowed and Emma glanced out the window of the car. She saw Adam and Seth in one vehicle and she assumed Neil and Josh were in the other. Her car started to move and Leighsa whimpered again.

"Just pray, Leighsa," Emma whispered to Leighsa. "Only God can save us now."

The squad car pulled away from the clearing and Emma looked through the window behind her. She would probably never see the woods again. And she would probably never see her parents again either.

She leaned back over to Leighsa and put her arm around her shoulder. Leighsa continued to sob and Emma whispered in her ear again.

"Whatever you do, Leighsa, promise me you won't take the mark."

Rory had called everyone he could think of and couldn't find Donna anywhere. By dinnertime on Wednesday, he had given up hope of an easy solution. He would have to wait. He was ready for her when she got home, though. She wouldn't stay away two nights. She'll be back tonight and tomorrow he would teach her a lesson.

A nagging thought ate away at Rory's conscience. Donna never took the mark. Did she think she was better than him? She wouldn't have left him to reunite with those nonmarkers. If she did, her life would be over tomorrow anyway. He wondered if she went to Dan and Betsy Dougherty for help. He walked over to the phone and looked up their number. He dialed the Dougherty residence and let the phone ring. No answer and no machine.

To rid himself of this idea, Rory decided to drive over to Doughertys to see for himself if she was there. When he pulled into the driveway, it was 5:37 p.m. They were probably having dinner. He went to the front door and knocked. As he stood waiting, he quickly came up with a lie for being there. He didn't want to embarrass himself any more than necessary. His wife hiding at the Doughertys was embarrassing enough.

No one answered so he walked around to the back. He peered in the back window and saw that the kitchen was empty. There was no dinner on the stovetop, the table wasn't set and there was no movement anywhere. He tried the door handle, but it was locked. He looked around the outside of the house and found a hose with a spray nozzle attached. He unscrewed the nozzle and went to the back door. He broke one of the windowpanes with the metal nozzle and cleared the glass enough for him to slide his hand through the window and unlock the door.

As Rory walked through Dan's house, he could tell something was different. It was quite cold, as if the heat had been turned down. He walked through the living room and down the hall towards the bedrooms. The first one looked like a guest room. The bed was unmade. He moved to the next room. It was the master bedroom. Again, an unmade bed.

For a moment, Rory thought about the Scripture that spoke of Christ's return. It said a man and a wife would be asleep in bed. Christ would return and one would be left and the other gone. He stared at the unmade bed in the master bedroom and wondered if he had missed the rapture. His stomach began to turn. Maybe taking the mark wasn't such a good idea.

He sat on the bed and put his head in his hands. That's why Donna is gone. She'd been raptured along with Dan and Betsy. Rory sat stunned and he glanced across the room. He noticed a partially open closet door. He walked over to it and opened it farther. The closet was empty. He checked the dresser drawers and they were empty as well.

It suddenly hit him. The rapture hadn't happened. *They've left town!* Rory started to laugh in relief. Still laughing at himself for being such a fool, he headed down the hallway for the guest room again. In the corner was a pile of clothes. They looked familiar and Rory walked over and picked up one of the shirts. It was Donna's pink button down shirt she always wore to movies. A cardigan sweater she often wore with it lay underneath the shirt. He rifled through the clothes and recognized other pieces.

Rory went back into the kitchen, still holding Donna's pink shirt. He sat at the table and tried to figure it out. Donna left his house, taking all her clothes. She came here, spent the night, packed half her clothes, and left with the Doughertys.

Then it came to him. They had left for North Carolina.

Forty minutes later Rory stood up from the table. He was sufficiently chilled by this time. The shock of reality had been too much for him. He had sacrificed his eternity for this woman and she left him. She left him alone.

Rory wasn't alone, though. He had his idol. He decided to go home and tell the idol everything and see what he suggested. Maybe he should go look for her. Or maybe he should just go for a drink. Either way, he had to get out of that house.

Across town, Dan laid on the floor of the garage of Evan's house. Evan sat in a lawn chair, his eyes adjusted to the dark, looking at the crumpled form of his prisoner. He had decided not to tie him up. Morty was an old man and Evan could handle him. He heard a moan and stood, walked over to the light switch and flipped it on. He watched as Morty covered his face with his hands and then noticed they were stained with blood. This seemed to alarm him and he tried to roll over and stand up, but winced in pain and stayed on the ground.

"So you decided to wake up, Morty?" Evan was enjoying this.

"I'm sorry, who"—

"Did I ask you to talk? My question was rhetorical! Even an old fool like you should understand that!"

Evan walked over to Morty and stood over him. When their eyes met, Evan didn't see fear or anger. This ticked him off and he began to circle around him.

"Don't look at me. You have no right to look at me. You are a filthy enemy of the Federation of World Powers. I have heard you preaching your gloom and doom all over town and I am sick of it."

"What's your name?" the old man asked.

Evan didn't want Morty to talk. He didn't want to converse with him. That would only make him more human and he wasn't human. He was the enemy.

"None of your business. You preached against Hitler. I heard you. You said he was a tool of Satan. And you were simply stating the obvious. Of course he is. That's not a big secret. You said your God would defeat Satan and all would be judged by His holiness. That's where your lies began."

"I've seen you around town too. You have quite a few friends." Morty shifted up onto his knees, which were obviously painful beneath him.

Evan could feel his blood pressure rising. He was losing control. In his mind, he could hear a voice, calming him down, instructing him what to do next. He grabbed the lawn chair he had been sitting in and pulled it over in front of Morty.

Tell him he deserves to die. He is the enemy.

"You deserve to die. You are the enemy and if a nation lets the enemy live within its borders it is doomed to fall. America will not fall to the enemy. The world will not fall. We will rise up and serve our true master, Lucifer the King."

"Son, you are the one who believes a lie. This plan of Hitler's will fail. I know because the Bible already has laid out the ending."

Evan looked in this man's eyes and still there was no fear. He looked tired and hurt, but he had an annoying calm about him.

Don't let him call you "son." He's not your father. He's a lying, angry enemy of Hitler.

"Don't throw the Bible at me! That book is for weak men who need the security blanket of someone telling them what to do!"

"And you're not just following Hitler's instructions?"

"Stop it! Stop talking!"

Evan leaped from his seat and went to the corner of the garage. Leaning against the wall was his sword. He grabbed it and walked back over to Morty, then stood in front of him. He wanted to give the old man time to compute what was coming next.

"I told my idol you were in the garage. He told me to bring him your head. That's exactly what I plan on doing. I will serve my master with this act of loyalty. At midnight tonight, all of Shelton will become a slaughterhouse for the unmarked, for believers, as you would say. But I will offer my sacrifice early, to show my honor to my King."

Evan unsheathed the sword. It made the perfect swooshing sound, just like he had practiced. Fear would be flowing through the old man's veins now. He raised the sword behind his head like a batter in the batting box. He had longed for this moment.

Morty was on his knees still, head bent over, almost like he was giving Evan a clean swipe. Evan was a little disturbed that old Morty didn't try to defend himself. He just sat there like a dumb fool. Dumb fools deserved to die.

Then Dan began to speak. Not to Evan. But to his God.

"You have prepared me for this time, Father. And now Your Spirit is upon me."

Evan paused, waiting to hear what else he would say.

What are you waiting for? Do it! Kill him!

Morty raised his head and his eyes locked onto something near the ceiling in the poorly lit garage. He looked at Evan and smiled, pointing to the ceiling.

"Can you seem him? He's right there! The Lord has sent an angel to take me home." His eyes returned to that spot on the ceiling and

Evan followed his gaze. There was nothing. The old man was hallucinating. "Oh, he's so beautiful! Look at his white robe!"

Dan reached his hands up in the air, like a toddler reaching for his father. His face was still peaceful, but his eyes were almost dancing with joy.

Enough of this. This man has lost it. Be done with him. Obey your master and offer this sacrifice. Now!

Evan wasn't going to play this game any longer. He had been gracious to even converse with the enemy and time had run out. Evan swung the sword with all his might. He sliced through the base of Dan's neck, from the left side straight through to the right side and out. The blade didn't catch on the bone, but seemed to cut clean through like a hot knife through butter.

Evan stood with the sword in his hands, as if waiting to see what would happen. The old man's head stayed perfectly still and in place. Then his eyes shifted from the ceiling and looked straight at Evan. They held the stare for almost ten seconds. There was that peace, a calm in those eyes that Evan found completely foreign.

This angered Evan beyond measure. The rage tore at his soul and Evan raised the sword for another swing. Before he could release, Dan's head tilted back and fell behind him, his body lurching forward onto the garage floor. Blood drained out onto the floor.

"Now that was cool."

Well done, faithful servant.

Evan stood over the dead body of Dan Dougherty. It wasn't going to bring in a big payday, but he would get a house out of it. He would move out of his mother's now and be on his own. And he had this old guy on the floor to thank for that.

Evan picked up an old towel on one of the shelves in the garage and wiped off his sword. He slid it back into it sheath and held it in his hands for a moment. It had worked better than he could have imagined. And it would be a shame to spend all that money for one swing.

Evan decided to take it out in the morning and see what he could find. It was going to be a great day.

The Reeds and the Cowlings joined the families at Engedi. When they entered the cave, Nate realized this was the first time he had entered and not heard kids or a movie. But the atmosphere was heavy and though he knew there were still children in the cave, they were nowhere to be seen. By now the kids would normally be back home and the lateness of the day was weighing on everyone.

As Sherrie and Nate pulled up chairs to the table, Lily was speaking.

"Where could they be? Let's logically think this through." Lily looked across the table at the other moms and dads.

"Okay," started Eva Torey. "For the past six weeks or so the kids have met on Thursdays at Petra for their day of video games and movies."

"And they've gone to the Tabernacle on those days too. I think to help prepare for youth group," added Lily.

"Wait a minute," said Sherrie said. "They haven't been at Petra. I thought they were here."

"And they haven't helped me at all for youth group," said Mike Torey.

Another lie, thought Nate. This really is bad.

"So, they've been gone every Thursday since the middle of July," said Lily. "I even asked Emma once if the group wanted to be here, but she said since four of them lived here, they wanted to be at Petra. What have they been doing?"

"All we know is that for the past two months, they have been going somewhere for most of the day and it hasn't been where they said they were." Marty Mason sounded angry as well as distraught.

"This just doesn't sound like any of these kids," said Paul Cowlings. "Neil absolutely loves being with all of them because they're really good kids. Could they have built a fort or something like that?"

"Then they would be home by now," answered Marty. "I doubt they'd keep that a secret. And I don't think any of them are that handy, anyway."

They all sat in silence for a couple of minutes as the seriousness of the situation settled on them. The kids had been lying and now they are missing. Eva ran down to the bedrooms to ask the children if any of them knew where the other kids were, but none of them knew any more than the parents. Apparently, they were even tight-lipped with the others.

Nate couldn't come up with any logical explanation, except the obvious one. Whatever they were doing, at least Adam didn't have a problem with lying. His own father had lived a lie and had gotten away with it. Nate thought of the example he'd been, and his heart sank.

Garrett finally broke the silence. "All we can do right now is wait. I'll call the Tabernacle and ask them to monitor local radio stations to hear if anything unusual has turned up in Mount Olive."

Garrett got up from the table and went to the radio.

"We should go look for them," said Mike. "I could check the vehicle storage unit and see if a van is missing."

"They wouldn't leave the mountain!" Sherrie said. "Adam knows that would be too dangerous. And where would they get gas? Where would they go? I can't believe this is happening."

Nate could hear the desperation in Sherrie's voice and he put his arm around her. Most of the other women were on the verge of tears and the men were at a loss for words, let alone good ideas.

Garrett returned and sat down again.

"They're going to let us know if they hear anything. In the meantime, it's not going to help for us to wander aimlessly around the mountain. It will be dark soon and that only hurts our cause."

"But what if someone's hurt?" Sherrie asked. "I know they've lied about where they are, but they're always home by now. Maybe we should go out and call for them!"

"If one of them is hurt," Marty said, "then the others could get help. I think something else must have gone wrong."

Garrett spoke again. "We have to wait. We need to pray."

"Yes, Garrett. Will you pray for us?" Lily took her husband's hand and lowered her eyes. The husbands grabbed the hands of their wives or put their arms around them and lowered their eyes too.

"Father, we know we serve a sovereign Master, who sees all things and is never surprised. Right now the gap between You and those of us at this table is huge. We're really in a bind, Lord. The only comfort we have right now is the fact that You are with the kids and know exactly what is going on with them. Our hearts are aching, Lord, because we feel so helpless. We ask Your protection on the kids and we ask You to bring them home safely. We don't know what else to do." Nate could hear Sherrie sniffling as well as a few others at the table as Garrett continued. "Open our eyes and show us, Lord. If they are hurt, bring help or give them wisdom. We're just at a loss and can only lean on You. Forgive our anxiousness, but we love those kids, Lord. We know You love them too. So we lay them in Your arms and again ask that You bring them home to us. Thank You for promising to be with us and giving us the Comforter. May we feel His presence at this time. We love You, Lord. Amen."

Nate wasn't used to being so helpless, but right now he was at a loss. They were all good kids. Why would they lie?

Stan Phillips, who had joined the group for prayer, stood.

"I'm on at the Tabernacle at midnight. I'll keep you posted if I hear anything. I'll be praying for you guys and the kids."

He turned and headed toward the front door. Nate heard the door shut.

"Lily, how about some dinner?" Garrett tried to change the subject. "Most of us haven't eaten yet."

"Where could they be, Garrett?" Lily didn't move.

"Let's eat. Could you whip up a batch of those double chocolate brownies too?"

"I can't believe you have an appetite!"

"It sounds good."

"Yeah," added Mike. "I could go for your brownies too."

Lily and the women headed into the kitchen. Nate knew no one had an appetite, but the women needed something to do to pass the time. The rest of the men sat in silence, waiting to hear something on the radio, or even better, the front door to open.

thirty-one

Emma sat on a bench along a wall in the police station. Leighsa was sitting next to her and was still crying softly. They hadn't seen the boys yet but Emma was pretty sure they were in the station somewhere. No one had officially talked to them and she figured the boys were being questioned first. The girls would be next.

It was late, and the police station was quiet. Emma squinted to focus her eyes, which were tired from crying. She could see a clock on the far wall. It was almost eleven thirty. Her parents would be sick with worry by now. How would they find out what happened to her? She felt the lump in her throat grow when she considered the next time she might see her parents would be in heaven.

Emma heard a bell go off and remembered it was the same sound she heard when she had entered the station. There must be a bell on the door when it opens, she thought to herself. She and Leighsa were sitting in the back but if she leaned forward, Emma could see the front desk.

It wasn't like anyone would help her, even if she could get someone's attention. She was a stranger in Mount Olive. And she was not marked. She looked at the clock again and realized that in thirty minutes, it was going to be legal for these police officers to shoot her, no questions asked. Not that she had any property for them to acquire, but she was a nonmarker.

So she had thirty minutes to live. Any time after that would be a gift.

Another bell. It seemed the station had traffic even at night. An officer came out of a back office and Emma glanced his way. As he shut the door behind him, she thought she saw Adam sitting in a chair. She sighed and watched the officer walk up to her and Leighsa. It must be their turn.

Emma heard someone clear their throat at the front of the station. The officer in front of her kneeled down to eye level with her and Leighsa. Another cough from up front.

"Hi, girls," said the female officer, in a very controlled, kind tone. "My name is Officer O'Brien and I am going to take you to an office in the back so that we can talk. Is that okay?"

Another cough from up front, this time it was louder.

Leighsa nodded as she stood.

Emma stood also and heard another cough. As they followed the officer toward a room farther back in the station, Emma glanced over her shoulder to see who was coughing.

A gray-haired woman, wearing a baseball cap, met her gaze. Standing next to the woman was a younger man also in a cap.

Emma halted mid step. There was something familiar about the woman. Then the woman touched her ear. Emma's heart skipped a beat as Officer O'Brien called to her. Could she have been imagining what she just saw? She blinked back her tears, thinking of the signal of love between her mother and her father.

"Let's go, Emma," the officer called again.

Emma started forward, but glanced back as often as she could to the woman in the ball cap. Just before she entered the interrogation room, Emma hesitated. The woman was watching her intently.

Tentatively, Emma reached up and pulled her ear.

The woman pulled on her ear again, then she turned with the man, and walked out the door of the station.

Once in the room, Emma saw Melanie sitting on top of a desk with a phone to her ear, two chairs in front of her, with Leighsa already sitting in one. Officer O'Brien motioned for Emma to sit in the empty chair and Emma obeyed. The officer left the room and closed the door behind her.

Melanie stood and turned her back on the girls, obviously involved in an important conversation.

"We did everything by the book, Sean. You don't have to worry about a thing."

Leighsa was staring at the floor, completely exhausted. Emma nudged her but she didn't look up.

Melanie continued. "They'll probably be extradited back to Michigan on Monday, if you really think that's necessary."

As Melanie continued to discuss the details of her arrest, Emma nudged Leighsa harder. This time she looked. Emma slowly mouthed to her, "I ... saw ... Betsy ... in ... the ... front ... of ... the ... station!"

Leighsa mouthed back, "Betsy Dougherty?"

Emma nodded.

"Here?"

She nodded again.

Melanie hung up her phone and turned around. She stood behind the desk.

"Girls, we need to talk."

"Why should we talk to you? You lied to us." Emma was surprised at her own anger.

"Well, you can talk to me, or you can be shipped to Michigan and talk to my superior. Either way, you're going to talk."

"Maybe we'll wait to talk to your superior." Emma was stalling, but she didn't know what else to do.

Melanie came from around the desk and sat on the front edge again, considerably closer than before. She leaned over and anger burned in her eyes.

"Don't play games with me, little girl. I have the power to extend your life and I have the authority to take your life. Up until now I've been kind. I let you girls ride together. I didn't let them cuff you. But my generosity is running out, so don't push your luck."

Emma clenched her jaw and decided to shut up. That's when Leighsa decided to ask a question.

"How did you know we would be at the lake? And how did you know all about Emma?"

"We have satellites, dear, and when you play in a clearing, you're easy to spot. But we don't have time for this. We need to get down to business. Those boys in the other room are pretty tough. They are refusing to lead us to your caves."

Emma smiled.

"Very commendable, but incredibly stupid. I'm tired of wasting my time with them, so I am here to cut a deal with you."

"What kind of deal?" Emma asked.

"If you take me to the caves, I will spare the lives of the boys in the other room. If you refuse, I will kill all of them. One at a time. In front of you."

Emma's eyes widened and she told herself this was just a bad cop routine. Melanie had probably threatened the boys with the same deal. While Leighsa began to cry again, Melanie stood up and walked around the desk. She picked up a piece of paper and a pen and walked back over to Emma and handed it to her.

"This is a map of your mountain. I have highlighted where your vehicle storage unit is located. I want you to mark where your homes are. I don't care about specifics, I just want a general location."

"I can't do this!" said Emma. "I can't tell where anything is on this map."

"Fine." Melanie turned around and pushed a button on the phone which was sitting on the desk. A voice responded.

"Yes?"

"Have Officer O'Brien bring in the boy named Adam."

Emma started to panic. Melanie walked around the desk and opened a drawer. She pulled a small gun out and shut the drawer. At the same time, the door opened and Adam was led into the room.

"What's going on?" he asked. His hands were cuffed behind his back and he had a cut underneath his right eye.

"She wants to know the location of the caves, Adam. I can't do it. They'll kill all of them."

The officer pushed Adam over to the desk and had him face Melanie. By now, she was standing, flipping open the barrel, and checking the bullets.

Adam looked over his shoulder and called out, "Don't tell them Emma! They're going to kill us all anyway!"

Melanie held the gun in her right arm and extended it, pointing it at Adam's chest.

"I'm going to ask you one more time, Emma. Where are the caves?"

Adam yelled again, "Don't say a word. It's going to be all right."

Emma froze. Leighsa's sobbing grew louder.

"Then you've made your choice. Sorry about this, Adam."

As Melanie cocked back the hammer, the lights in the room flashed for a moment. Emma closed her eyes, not wanting to watch Adam die, but the shot never came. The room began to shake and she quickly opened her eyes. The window behind Melanie shattered and Melanie covered her head to shield herself from the flying glass. The lights were flashing and the desk was shifting.

At once, Officer O'Brien fell to the ground and Emma looked down at her. She didn't see anything hit her, but it was as if she had been knocked unconscious. Melanie fell too and didn't move. Adam swung around and brought his hands in front of him. The cuffs had fallen off and his hands were free. Leighsa and Emma jumped up and ran into his open arms.

The room continued to shake and Emma could hear glass breaking through the closed door. Emma also thought she heard thunder and saw lightning outside the window in the back room.

"What's going on?" Leighsa yelled over the noise.

"Just wait," said Adam. "Hold on to me."

He steadied himself, his arms wrapped tightly around the girls. The shaking slowed down and then stopped. The lights flickered, and then shut off completely. The three kids stood in the dark, clinging to each other for dear life.

Finally Adam said, "I think we should leave."

As he spoke, the door flew open and a flashlight shone directly in their eyes.

"Are you three going to just stand there hugging each other, or do you want to leave?"

It was Josh, with Seth and Neil behind him. Josh led the way through the station. Officers lay on the floor unconscious. Maybe even dead, for all Emma knew. Through the broken windows in the front of the station, Emma could see streetlights flickering. Apparently they were damaged also.

"Careful of the glass," said Neil.

"Is everyone dead?" Leighsa sounded terrified.

"No, they're breathing," Adam said. "It's like they're asleep."

They got to the front door and though the door had been shattered, Josh carefully opened it and they all walked through. The rain had stopped and there wasn't a car on the road. A few of the lights continued to flicker. Down the center of the road was a huge gaping hole that ran the length of town. The sidewalk had buckled in several places and Emma could see large cracks in some of the buildings.

"An earthquake?" Seth breathed in awe.

"No kidding, Captain Obvious!" Josh said.

"Do you think it was the rapture?" asked Emma. "It's just about midnight. Maybe God decided not to allow the Day of Destruction and Jesus just came back."

"One little problem with that, Emma," said Adam.

"What?" she asked.

"We're still here. I know we're in trouble, but we're still His children. I doubt He overlooked us."

"Yeah, but ..." she began to protest.

"Think about it. My cuffs fell off and everyone just fell asleep. We walked right out of there and"—

"Look, guys!" Neil was pointing. "Headlights!"

Neil was right. There were headlights coming right at them, brights flashing on and off.

"Should we hide?" Leighsa wanted to know.

"No," Emma said. "It's got to be Betsy."

The car was getting closer.

"What are you talking about?" Adam asked.

"I saw Betsy Dougherty at the police station. She kept clearing her throat and coughing until I looked at her and she pulled her ear."

"She what?" Adam asked again.

"She pulled her ear. She was the one who taught my mom to do that. It was an unspoken way to say, 'I love you.' Mom does it all the time to dad and to us kids. That's how I knew it was Betsy!"

The car was close now and it was too late to run. They stood on the sidewalk as the car slowed to a stop on the other side of the crevasse. The window rolled down. "Get in, kids," he said. "I'm Kevin and I'm with Betsy Dougherty. She's just up the road with the rest of our group."

The kids climbed carefully through the crevasse and back up onto the road. Emma and Adam jumped in the front seat next to Kevin and the rest piled in the back of his white Taurus. Kevin pulled into a gas station and circled around.

"Are you guys all right?" he asked once they were on the road again.

"That was you with Betsy in the police station, wasn't it?" Emma asked.

"Yes. We stopped to get gas with our last few magogs and Betsy spotted you being brought into the station. It took us some time to figure out how to get in there and see if it was really you, but we asked directions and tried to act confused. When we finally got your attention, we'd just run out of questions. Hey, look, the crack in the road has gone."

Emma glanced out the window and saw that the road was whole again. Kevin eased back over into the right lane and continued on.

"Where did you go then?" Adam asked.

"We headed out of town and pulled over to try to figure out what to do. I guess I should ask you why you were in there in the first place?"

Emma started to cry again, this time from a combination of embarrassment over her sin and relief of being safe. Adam answered.

"We've been sneaking away to a little lake on the far side of the mountain. We figured we were safe, but we weren't. They spotted us with a satellite and basically set us up. They told us Jesus had returned and wanted to see us and we fell for it."

"You mean exactly how Jesus said people would lie?"

"Yeah, we were pretty stupid. How did you know to come back?"

"When the earthquake hit, it was like a lightbulb went on for me and I ran to the car and told the others to wait for me. There they are now." Kevin pointed up the road. "Do you see them on the side of the road up ahead?"

"Dude, how did you get magogs, do you mind me asking?" Seth asked from the backseat.

"A friend of mine traded some cash for magogs for me a few months ago," Kevin answered as he pulled up behind a large Winnebago. Emma saw Betsy standing outside with her hands on her hips. "Nobody will exchange anymore, so we had to make these last."

Kevin put the car in park and turned off his lights. Adam opened his door and stepped out, letting Emma free to run to Betsy. She ran straight into her arms and started crying.

"Oh, Betsy . . . I can't believe you're here," she cried.

"That makes two of us, dear." Betsy wrapped her arms around Emma. After a moment, Betsy pulled away. "We'd better get on the road, in case anyone comes after you kids. You come with me."

Emma got in the Winnebago with Betsy and Adam jumped back in front with Kevin. The two vehicles pulled back onto the road and began the two-hour drive to the mountain base. Betsy introduced Emma to the others in the camper and Emma recognized Mrs. Appleton sitting at the kitchen table. She immediately felt ashamed for her response to Mrs. Appleton's arrival.

Emma and Betsy sat in the back of the Winnebago and had a lot of catching up to do and in that two-hour span, Betsy heard exactly how the five teenagers ended up at the police station.

"Oh, Emma, I know you want to grow up, but this was such a foolish thing to do."

"I know, Betsy. I don't know which is worse, sitting in that station thinking about never seeing my parents again or sitting here thinking of my parents' faces when I confess everything."

"Sitting in the station is definitely worse. Your parents know how to forgive, but allow me to give you one piece of advice. Don't make excuses, just fess up and let them have their say."

Emma nodded solemnly. "I still can't believe God saved us. We deserved to be exactly where we were—awaiting a death sentence. We lied to our parents, ignored what we knew God's Word said, and did what felt right. Yet He still provided a way of escape. I feel so unworthy, so ashamed." Tears welled up again in Emma's eyes. She knew she had broken her parents' hearts as well as their trust, let alone disobeyed God.

"You know I was in the same boat you're in right now."

"You were? When?"

"Yes, I was. So was your mom, your dad, and even Pastor Gentings."

"I don't think any of you ever did anything like this."

"Emma, sin is sin. Turning away from God's instructions and living by your own desires is just what sin is—you've described exactly what we all have been saved from. None of us has deserved His gift of salvation and we were all sentenced to death."

"But Betsy, you're talking about an unbeliever accepting God's gift of salvation. I'm a believer and I still behaved this way."

"Well, you've heard the saying, 'nobody's perfect'? It's true. After salvation we still battle temptation and our flesh pulls us strongly towards sin. Now, I'm not saying what you did was justified. I'm saying it was to be expected when someone chooses to ignore God's instruction and follow his natural, fleshly tendencies." Betsy reached over and put her hand on Emma's. "There're many examples in Scripture of believers who fell into sin. David with Bathsheba, Abraham lying about Sarah, Jonah running away, even Peter denying Christ to save his own skin."

"So, you're telling me I'm in good company?"

"No, I'm telling you God is forgiving. Look at what He thinks of you. There's a town in shambles down the road because of you. That's how much He loves you. Your mom and dad will forgive you too. They love you more than life itself."

"I know they love me, and I know I'm just being selfish here, but do you think they will ever forgive Adam? I can't bear the thought of them hating him. What if they say I can't see him again?"

"He's definitely in the doghouse—I can guarantee that. But from what I hear, he's a good kid. Give your dad some time and let him cool down."

"Are you worried about Dan?"

"What?"

"Not to change the subject, but are you worried about Dan getting down here?"

"If I know Dan, he won't be traveling alone. If he is, he'll stop if he's tired, and there's a good chance he'll beat us to the caves. Have you ever driven with the man?"

Emma laughed for the first time since they met Melanie earlier that day. Emma threw her arms around Betsy and gave her a big hug. She had a way of making people feel better. Emma was not only grateful for her salvation that day, but she thanked the Lord for sending Betsy. He could have sent anyone, but He chose someone whom Emma thought she would have to wait until heaven to see again.

Once Dan arrives, we should have a party. Emma laid her head on Betsy's shoulder and closed her eyes. They would be at the base of the mountain soon and Emma was so tired she could hardly think straight. She was still talking to her heavenly Father about His grace when she fell into a deep sleep.

They were on their third pot of coffee when the radio cackled.

"Any one there? This is Kevin Portman from Shelton? Can anyone read me?"

Immediately Garrett looked at Lily, jumped up from the table, knocking over his chair, and ran towards to the radio. Nate looked at the clock and it read 2:07.

Mike Torey called out to Garrett. "Let them answer at the Tabernacle, Garrett!"

"Yeah, we read you, Kevin. Where are you guys? This is Stan Phillips."

"Hey Stan, are we glad to hear your voice."

"We? Who's with you?"

"There's a bunch of us, including Betsy Dougherty. But more importantly, we have six teenagers that belong to you."

Sherrie slumped in her chair and the tears began to flow. Nate knelt beside her and wrapped his arms around her. He whispered a prayer of thanksgiving.

"Where exactly are you?"

"We're at the vehicle storage unit. We came from Shelton this morning. Had some trouble getting down here but we've finally made it. Has Dan made it yet?"

"No, I don't think we've heard from him yet. Where did you find the kids?"

Nate squeezed Sherrie's hand and tried to quiet her so he could hear.

"It's a long story but we'll just say it was God who saved them, not us. We'll tell you all about it in the morning. We're going to stay the night down here and at daylight we'll start your way."

"Tell you what—we'll send some quads to get you here quicker. How many total are there?"

"Six teenagers, and six of us from Shelton."

"We'll see you in the morning. Welcome home! You've given us all something to rejoice about!"

"Thanks. Oh, one more thing. Is Garrett listening on the line?"

Nate looked at Garrett, as he ran to the radio. He grabbed the handset and pressed the side button.

"I'm here."

"I've got someone here who wants to say hi."

The whole room waited to hear Emma's voice.

"Hi, Daddy!"

"Are you all right, Emma?"

"I'm fine. I'm so sorry, Dad!"

"Emma, we're just thankful you're safe. We'll see you in the morning. I love you, Emma. And tell the rest of the kids their parents love them and will see them in the morning. Stan, put me on that list to go get them."

"You're on, Garrett. Tell Mike, Paul, and Nate they're on the list too. Over and out."

"Will do. Over and out."

"See you all in the morning."

The women could no longer hold in their sobs. The whole room filled with the sounds of thankful parents, clinging to each other and thanking the Lord. Nate held Sherrie in his arms until he felt her settle down. Then he let go and looked at Garrett.

"We're heading home. We'll see you in the morning over at the Tabernacle."

Garrett walked over and shook Nate's hand. "It's a relief, isn't it?" Nate nodded but the words wouldn't come. Garrett pulled him into a hug and the two men cried together. The tension from the day had melted away and it was time to sleep. Nate and Sherrie walked home through the dark woods, thanking and praising God for His mercy and grace. He would have to be up in just a few hours, but he really didn't mind. All he wanted now was to see his son and in a few hours he'd have his wish.

thirty-two

Emma woke to the rumble of quads. They obviously had left before sunrise, because the sun was just peeking through the base of the trees in the east. She sat up and looked out the window. It was not surprising that her father was leading the pack. But was he smiling? That was still to be determined.

Emma folded her blanket and went to the door. By the time she got down the steps to the ground, her father had parked his machine and was running towards her. She thought that was a good sign. Her fears melted away when she saw the look on his face and she ran into his open arms. He hugged her so tight and so long that she thought maybe that would be her punishment—asphyxiation!

When he finally let go, she saw tears streaming down his face and her heart broke again. His tears were her responsibility.

"How is Mom?"

"She'll be fine in a couple of hours."

"Can you ever forgive me?"

"Did it yesterday. But that doesn't mean I don't want to hear the story, and I mean the whole story."

"I'll gladly tell you everything, Dad. It'll be a relief to get it off my back."

Garrett looked over at the new residents and tossed a smile and a wave at Betsy. Emma saw Adam hugging his dad and behind them, she noticed Donna getting out of the Winnebago. Garrett saw her too.

"Is that Donna Appleton?" Garrett asked Emma.

"Yeah."

"Did you talk to her much?"

"Not really."

"Well, let's get going. There will be plenty of time to talk back at the cave."

The men had brought trailers and the bags of the people from Shelton were thrown in the back. Then the vehicles were parked in the garage. After hugging Garrett, Betsy asked about Dan and wondered if she should wait there for him.

"I think it would be better to get you back to the caves. It's safer there and you can get a hot shower and some breakfast. I'm sure he'll be here soon."

"Don't worry about him, Betsy," reassured Emma. "You know Dan. He always does what he says he'll do. He probably spent the night on the side of the road. He'll be here soon."

Betsy reluctantly agreed and climbed on a quad with Stan Phillips.

It took a little longer to get to the caves because the ground was soft from the rain the night before and the trailers kept getting stuck. As the quad neared Engedi, Emma could see her mother with Ben and Sarah standing outside the door, waving in the distance. When Garrett pulled up to her and shut off the engine, Emma could tell her mom had cried all night. She jumped off the quad and ran into her mother's arms.

"Mom!"

"Oh, Emma!"

That was all it took. The floodgates opened and they stood in the middle of the forest, locked in an embrace for what seemed like an eternity.

"Come on, you two. Are you forgetting someone?" Garrett was feeling left out.

"Group hug!" Emma called out. Soon, Garrett, Ben, and Sarah joined in. The Hamilton family was back together and Emma heard her father breathe a sigh of relief.

Lily reached out and drew Betsy into their family embrace.

"I don't know where you found her, but I have praised God all night that you did."

"The good Lord gives and the good Lord takes away. I'm just glad you were on the receiving end this time."

The group headed inside and Emma knew she would have a lot of explaining to do. All the kids and their families were gathering at Engedi to talk. Emma entered the cave, and was at once overwhelmed with emotion. As she stood, looking around the room, wiping her tears, Lily came and put her arm around her.

"No more tears, dear. You're safe now."

"I didn't know I could cry this much. I'm so sorry, Mom. I must have had you so worried!"

"I forgive you, Emma. Right now, I'm just grateful you're here. And what about Donna?"

Emma looked across the room and saw Mrs. Appleton sitting alone on the couch.

"She didn't talk much, Mom. I don't really know what's going on with her."

"I'll be right back."

Emma watched her mom walk across the room and throw her arms around a surprised Donna.

"I don't know how this happened, but I am so glad you're here," she heard her mother say.

Donna seemed to appreciate the hug. Emma saw her wiping tears from her eyes. Then Betsy came over to the two and grabbed Lily's arm.

"Now, what's a gal have to do to get some coffee around here?" Emma watched the three of them disappear into the kitchen and she was amazed at the kindness her mother was able to show Mrs. Appleton.

In no time flat, the moms quickly fed the hungry group and then the parents sat with the kids to hear their story. They explained how they started to go to the lake back in July, to get a break from being holed up with the younger kids. They didn't try to justify what they did, they just simply told the truth. They explained how Melanie had shown up, saying that Jesus was in Mount Olive and that their parents were already on their way to meet Him.

Emma and the others let Adam do most of the talking.

"I know it sounds ridiculous," Adam said. "We have been taught what Christ's return looks like and we know about the false claims to get people out of hiding. We were just so convinced we were protected at the lake that we readily believed her story. Apparently there is a satellite taking pictures of the mountains, because that's how they knew we were there."

"So when did you find out she was lying?" asked Nate.

"We followed her through the forest on the far side of the lake. We probably walked three miles. Before we knew it, we had walked into a trap. These agents came out of nowhere and surrounded us. Seth and Josh tried to fight."

"So did Leighsa," added Emma.

"But the rest of us just went with them," said Adam. "They were a lot more in number, a lot stronger and they had guns."

"That must have been horrible." Eva Torey put her arm around Leighsa.

Adam continued. "They put us in large vans and on the way to the Mount Olive police station they explained why they were taking us. They had explicit orders from the HS/DIU to apprehend the children of the cult members on the mountain."

When Nate heard the DIU mentioned, he groaned.

"How did you cut your eye, Adam?" asked Mike.

"They asked us where the caves were located and we refused to answer. That really ticked them off. They got a little rough, but it was more of a slap than anything. They had taken us boys to a back room and were threatening us pretty heavily when Emma heard someone clearing their throat from across the room."

"That's when I saw Betsy," Emma said, "and for a moment I had hope that we would be saved. Then they took us into a back room, and they wanted Leighsa and I to draw a map of the mountain. When we refused, they threatened to kill Adam and that's when the earthquake hit."

"Earthquake?" Lily frowned.

"Oh, it was a biggie!" said Seth. "Our handcuffs fell off, the windows at the station were blown in, and the officers were all unconscious when we walked out the front door. Then Mr. Portman pulled up in his car and we sped off! It was a miracle, Dad!"

Marty Mason put his arm around Seth.

"None of us deserve the grace the Lord has shown to us. I'm still struggling with you kids sneaking off and putting not only yourselves but all of us at risk. It was selfish and deceitful!"

"We completely agree, Mr. Mason," said Emma. "We all accept responsibility and ask your forgiveness. We are so ashamed of ourselves."

"Of course you're forgiven, Emma," continued Marty. "There's a greater lesson here. This story reminds me of the story of Abraham and Sarah fleeing to Egypt because of the famine. Not only did Abraham not trust that God would supply for him, but he lied about his wife. When he found himself in a terrible position, or rather Sarah was in the terrible position, God saved him. God plagued Pharaoh's house until Sarah was released. God knew Abraham was a man of faith, though sometimes his faith was weak. As he matured and saw the character of God, his faith grew. God knows we are faithful, though weak, and he still protected you and saved you. We need to see the character of God in this. He is faithful, gracious, and loving."

"Merciful, protecting, and forgiving," Lily added.

"Mighty, awesome, and all-knowing," Adam threw in.

"And don't forget powerful—that earthquake was incredible," Emma added.

After a time of thanksgiving and prayer the conversation turned to Donna. She shared what life had turned into for her and Rory. She told of Rory's personality change and when she found the idol in his dresser drawer, she realized why he was so different.

"The demon's influence on Rory was undeniable. He made a terrible mistake taking the mark. We argued about it, but he was going to do what he wanted. What breaks my heart is the fact that if he has an idol, I'll bet all the men in the church have one too. If they do, they are all under demonic influence."

"I don't know why this comes as such a surprise to us," said Garrett. "Revelation thirteen describes who the Antichrist was going to be and it also tells of talking idols that would identify believers. I just never thought of this kind of influence before, but if there is one in every home, it suddenly makes sense why this world is so upside down."

"Well," continued Donna, "it's a horrible thing and the women and children are in a terrible bind. I didn't know what to do or where to go, so I turned to Betsy and Dan. God bless them for opening their door to me."

"Speaking of Dan, where could he be?" Betsy said. "I'm getting worried that we haven't heard from him yet."

The conversation then went on to what Dan and Betsy, as well as what the other witnessers had been doing for the past couple of months while they were out of contact with the church. Stories of testimony opportunities warmed Emma's heart, and they shared how the antichristian environment was growing. Even within the church, there was such confusion that the church was rejecting the Scriptures and starting to come up with symbolic interpretations to try to explain what was happening. Bottom line, the church felt it had been abandoned by God and it was every man for himself. That's why men took the mark to provide for their families, because God obviously wasn't going to step up and do it. Bad decisions made at time of crisis.

After what seemed like hours of conversation, everyone needed a break. Several of the cave units had spare bedrooms, because only three of the four bedrooms had been initially filled. Everybody from Shelton was assigned to a cave and they were taken to them so they could get settled in.

As the room cleared, Adam motioned for Emma to stay behind.

"I didn't have a chance to talk with you last night, since we were in separate cars."

Emma looked quietly at Adam's tear-filled eyes.

"Emma, I need to ask your forgiveness. You would never have gone to the lake if I hadn't pressured you. To think I almost ..."

"I decided for myself—I knew it was wrong and I don't blame you for my decision."

"You're not listening, Emma. I wasn't being the friend God would have me be—I was selfish and I led you into making a sinful decision. I even bullied you into ignoring what you had been taught as truth, and we almost ended up dying. Listen, I want you to be able to trust me, and that starts with recognizing I caused this and asking your forgiveness."

Tears rolled down Adam's cheeks. The stress of the past twenty-four hours had taken its toll and Emma started to cry too. Adam pulled her towards him and whispered a prayer in her ear.

"Father, forgive me. How could I have done this?"

At a time when God's supernatural protection was becoming commonplace amongst the members of Grace, Emma stood in awe of His care and rested in His forgiveness. She looked into Adam's eyes and saw the same awe she felt. She had learned firsthand about His mercy and she would never be the same.

In light of the fact that the Day of Destruction was upon them, the elders had called for a meeting at the Tabernacle that night. The adults wanted to hear what the news was reporting and the youth wanted to hear what had happened to Emma and Adam and the others. As the day passed, there was still no sign of Dan Dougherty. This worried not only Betsy but Emma also.

She could tell that Betsy knew it was bad but was keeping up a strong front. Emma hoped his car had broken down or he was simply delayed, but she knew if he was still in Shelton he was a man with a target on his back. He had been so outspoken, that everybody would recognize him as a nonmarker. He wouldn't survive the day there. Betsy knew it. Emma knew it. Everyone knew it.

Rory awoke on the morning of the Day of Destruction. Half of the world had a head start and Rory flipped on the news to see exactly what was happening. Every news station was covering the mass slaughter of nonmarkers. It was an absolute frenzy in most countries.

Rory sat his idol on the kitchen table so he could see the news too. They had spent a lot of time that morning already deciding what to do that day.

"Maybe she got out of town and maybe she didn't," the idol said.

"She's gone. I know it. None of them are at Dougherty's and their clothes are gone too."

"Well, you had better be sure she's gone, because if she's walking around town, someone is going to steal your joy and whack her head off before you get the chance."

There was a lot of truth to that statement and Rory picked up the remote and turned up the volume on the television. The mayhem was incredible. These idols are working overtime, Rory thought to himself. But they're just doing their job. They are in as much trouble as mankind if Jesus comes back and finds faith on the earth.

NBC reported that the Day of Destruction was a wild success in the eyes of the Federation of World Powers and ultimately Hitler, and it was only half over. Governments were reporting numbers of murdered nonmarkers in the hundreds of thousands. The reporters claimed the governments weren't keeping up with the transfer paper work, yet the people didn't care. They killed for the good of the Federation. They killed for ultimate peace. They killed for Hitler.

And they killed because they hated God.

By ten o'clock in the morning in Michigan, due to the wild success around the world, the FWP had decided to extend its generous offer for six more days. One week total. Kill and seize. CNN did a report on how poor men were becoming rich overnight. As each minute ticked away, the FWP knew they were drawing closer to the ultimate victory. Every nonmarked Jew, Christian, or human killed. Dead. Gone.

Rory turned off the TV and decided it was time to see what was going on in town. He wanted to be sure Donna was no longer in town, so he started by making phone calls but no one was answering today. They must have other things on their mind. When all roads led to a dead end, he stopped calling and started wandering. He could hardly believe his eyes when he saw the heads on the street. The people of Shelton were out of their minds. They were cutting off heads and lining the streets with them.

As Rory walked along the street, he looked at the faces of the martyrs. Many were from his church. His old church. They had stopped meeting a few weeks ago. The Shel-heads had targeted the women without marks and many were on the curb already. Houses were burning and Shel-heads were drinking in the streets, but nobody was mourning. There was almost a feeling of victory in the air—anticipation of something great just around the bend. Rory simply felt numb. He wasn't in shock and he wasn't appalled. He was just numb.

Rory found Dan by accident. He thought he saw one of his employees but when he got closer, it wasn't who he thought it was. Next to him was Dan's head. Rory let out a chuckle.

Imagine that, he thought to himself, Donna went to this loser for protection and look where he ended up.

Then it occurred to him that Donna might be on the curb too. If Dan was there, Betsy and Donna were most likely there too. He started to panic, not because he feared her death, but he wanted to be the one to take her life. If she was already dead, the joy had been stolen from him!

Rory ran up and down the streets, checking the various heads for Donna. When his cell rang, he almost didn't answer it. When his voice mail didn't pick up, he flipped it open.

"Yeah?"

"Rory?"

He stopped dead in his tracks. He knew that voice. He'd known it for forty years.

"Donna? Is that you?"

"Rory, are you okay?"

"Where are you?"

"Rory, I'm safe, but I'm not coming home. I just thought you should know"—

"Where are you? I'll come right now and get you!"

"Rory, you can't come here. I just wanted to say goodbye."

"I know you stayed at Dougherty's. Are you with Betsy?"

"Goodbye, Rory."

Before she disconnected the call Rory said, "You know Dan is dead. I'm looking at his bug-infested head right now. By the looks of it, he's been dead for quite a while. Probably got nailed early in the day."

"Not Dan."

"Yes, Dan. Since when did you care about anyone but yourself?"

"I cared about you."

"If you cared, you wouldn't have left me."

Rory knew if he kept her on the line long enough, she'd blurt out where she was and he could go and get her.

"I found your idol, Rory. It talked to me. I suddenly realized why you had changed. You belong to him, now. You belong to Satan."

"Oh, it's easy for you to get all high and mighty on me, but I made this deal with Satan to save your neck. Sleep on that tonight. Where are you? Are you in North Carolina? Did you and Betsy run down there?"

There was no response.

"So, that's where you are. Well then, Donna, my love, I'm coming to get you."

"Don't, Rory. Don't come down here."

"But you can't live, my dear. None of you can."

"Rory, how can you say that? What has happened to you. You'll never find us. You don't even know where to look."

"Oh, dear, you have gravely mistaken my capacity to discover your secret. I know where the caves are and I will come for you. When I do, you'll wish you'd never left Shelton, because everyone will pay. Not just you. You have brought the wrath of Satan to the church of the mountains."

Donna flipped her phone shut just as Nate entered the living room. She had been placed in the extra bedroom at Petra and most everyone was off to bed by that time.

"Uh, Donna?" he said.

"Yes?"

"I don't know if you know this, but we're not supposed to have cell phones here. I don't even know how you got reception down here."

"I'm sorry. Here. I was just talking with Rory. I wanted him to know I was safe."

She handed the phone to him and he pressed the power button and turned it off. He would give it to Pete Johnson in the morning.

"What did Rory say?"

"Oh, he was horribly angry with me. Threatened to come down here and kill us all!"

"Wow, it's really gotten bad. He doesn't know the cave system, does he?"

"He knows in general where the mountain is, but he doesn't know the layout. He threatens a lot, but I doubt he'll really come. I think it was just an empty threat."

"I hope it was," he replied.

"He did give me some bad news, though."

"What was that?" Nate asked.

"I'm not really sure how to say this, but Dan Dougherty did not survive today."

"You mean he's dead?"

"Rory said he saw his head lying on the street."

"His head? How in the world?"

"Better question, how are we going to tell Betsy?"

Nate would spend another sleepless night, knowing the life-changing information which he would have to share in the morning.

Emma was sitting at breakfast, after an incredible night's sleep, when Pastor Gentings showed up at the front door. Betsy had slept on the couch at Engedi that night, simply because she wanted to be near Lily.

Emma watched Pastor go over to the couch and sit with Betsy. She began to cry and Emma knew it was about Dan. She didn't want to interrupt, but couldn't help walking over to Betsy and sitting at her feet.

"He had a heart for the lost and gave his life for them," Betsy cried. "My heart is aching and a bit empty, but it won't be long before I see him again, will it, Pastor?"

"Perhaps sooner than we realize," said Pastor.

Three days later a memorial service was held at the Tabernacle for Dan. Everyone attended and most everyone shared a memory. It was a precious time of recollections, and ended with heartfelt worship.

Emma sat on one of the benches and closed her eyes. It was less than a year ago the angel had visited them. He called them Philadelphia, and sitting in that service, Emma listened to Philadelphia testify to the character of their God and praise His goodness displayed through the life of Dan. That night, Emma poured her heart out in her journal.

Betsy was right. It won't be long before we join Dan. Things are so bad out there. I doubt Jesus will wait much longer. God the Father is a patient God, and His timing is perfect, but if He doesn't come soon, He won't find any faith left on the earth.

Dan taught me how to ride a bike. My dad had bought me a bicycle for my sixth birthday and I just couldn't get the hang of it. It had little pink training wheels and I constantly leaned to the right. Dan came over and watched Dad struggle for an hour before he marched out to the sidewalk, took me off the bike, removed the training wheels and told me to get back on. I was terrified, but he said,' Don't worry. I promise not to let you go until you're ready.' He ran alongside of me and soon I was riding and though I thought his hand was still in place, he was actually just running beside me to make me feel secure.

Dan showed God to me. He fleshed Him out for me. He told me that God would never let me go and would always be right there beside me. I miss him dearly already, but I know it will only be for a short while that we will be apart.

Since the trauma of the last week, I have rededicated myself to being a servant here in the caves, rather than a self-centered teenager.

Father, forgive my selfishness, and may I love and serve You like my dear friend, Dan Dougherty.

thirty-three

Life in Shelton found a new normal after the Week of Destruction. After the week of carnage was over, the heads were gathered and burned, along with the bodies in the center of town, right in front of the idol the town had erected. Rory had gone down to the town's center to watch the burning. The idol taunted and yelled with its constituents and then told them their work was not over: There were still nonmarkers among the townspeople. The mayor then offered one thousand magogs cash for every nonmarked body brought to the steps of the town hall. The people cheered, thrusting their fists in the air, then with bloodthirsty cries, went on the hunt. Rory didn't care about the money anymore. He only had one target in mind: the woman who ripped out his heart and trampled on it.

After the crowd dispersed, Rory stood before the large idol and vowed to find Donna. It would become his life's quest. For the next few months he spent day and night, fixated on the whereabouts of Donna and the church. He drove to North Carolina several times but didn't get much farther than Mount Olive. He knew the mountains were south of there, but the chain of mountains was too massive to explore. He knew the church members used ham radios, so on two of his trips he spent dozens of hours driving around, scanning stations to try to find their signal, all to no avail. He showed pictures of Donna, the elders, Pastor Gentings, and Mack Silver around town, to see if anyone recognized them.

On his sixth trip to Mount Olive, he stopped at a gas station for fuel. Behind the counter sat a weathered old man, in a blue coverall. There was a patch on his chest with "Ben" written in cursive.

"Good morning, Ben."

"Good morning, there, sir. How can I help you?"

Rory looked outside at the police station. There was some scaffolding around the north side of the building.

"They're doing some work on the police station?" Rory asked.

"Repair work. We had a bad earthquake here a couple of months ago."

"Really. Your road looks brand-new."

"Oh, it was a mess. You want to see some pictures? I'd never have believed it if I hadn't seen it myself. I've lived here in Mount Olive for seventy-one years and there's never been a single earthquake before that day."

The man pulled pictures from a drawer behind the counter and out of courtesy, Rory flipped through them. Then he pulled a picture out of his own pocket and handed it to the man.

"I've got a friend that lives around here, but I lost his address. You ever seen him?"

The man took the picture of Mack Silver and looked at it. He frowned and scratched his head.

"Yep. This guy used to come in once a month or so, but I haven't seen him in a long time."

"Well, in case you see him again, will you call me? Here's my name and number. Feel free to call me collect."

The old man took the paper and dropped it in the drawer with his pictures. Rory headed back to his car and left town. It was time to go back to Michigan. He doubted this guy would be any help anyway.

The greatest help he had was sitting at home on his dresser. He always had good input, good ideas.

The idol had advised him to move into a different house, one without so many memories of difficult times. So, two months ago he did as he was told. It advised him to burn anything that reminded him of Donna. So, he did. It advised him to stoke the fire with his Bible. That was a little tougher, but he never used it anymore and really didn't have a future with God, so he did. It advised him that loneliness could be alleviated with a girlfriend. So, he found three. But no matter how he tried to distract himself, Rory could not let go of his obsession to find Donna and the church. Then his revenge would come and it would be sweeter than ever.

Sean Aumonti had been right. When the Day of Destruction turned into a week, it generated months of work for him. But the church hiding in the mountains was never far from his mind. As time passed, that group became more valuable, like good wine and old cheese. Sean determined not to let that group slip through his fingers. Destruction of the group was vital to the mission of the FWP.

Sean contacted Melanie Westering and found she hadn't forgotten the church either. He suggested they drop a dirty bomb on the mountains, but she protested they deserved the payout for that group.

"They have embarrassed us," Melanie said when they spoke on the phone, "and we can't let them get away with it. I want to look in their eyes when their heads roll."

"After New Year's, my caseload will slow down. Maybe the two of us can put our heads together and come up with an infallible plan."

"I'd like that a lot, Agent Aumonti. But don't be disappointed if I find them before Christmas."

Sean laughed. Melanie was a lot tougher than most women he knew. When this was over, they should have dinner. Nothing was going to happen before Christmas. They would have to work another angle, but he was confident their moment would come.

The phone rang four times and the answering machine picked up. Three minutes later, it rang again. And again. And again.

Finally, rather irritated and not in a mood to talk to anyone, Rory got off his couch and walked into the kitchen. He picked up his phone.

"What?"

"Nice way to answer a phone. My name is Sean Aumonti and I work for Homeland Security in the DIU division. Am I speaking to Rory Appleton?"

"Yes. What do you want?"

"If I could have just a moment of your time. I think you and I have a similar quest in life and I wanted to see if you were interested in joining my team."

"What team? Are you fundraising, because I need every magog I can get my hands on."

"I'm not fundraising, but I am talking about getting your hands on a lot of magogs."

"You have my attention now, so, go ahead."

Rory sat at the table and poured himself a cup of coffee. He was running out of coffee, as well as food in general. He cursed Donna and then focused back on the caller.

"I have an agent, Melanie Westering, who lives in Mount Olive, North Carolina. You do know the place, right?"

Upon hearing Mount Olive, Rory's ears perked up.

"Yeah. What do you know about it?"

"I know there is a church that moved its members onto the mountains south of Mount Olive. I know they're hiding and they're all nonmarkers. I also know your wife is with them."

"You know a lot."

"I know you have been asking questions in Mount Olive, not only about your wife but about the leadership of the church. I also know you are marked. So I have deduced you are planning on finding the church and your wife and perhaps a big payoff in the process."

"You must be a mind reader."

Sarcasm oozed from his mouth. So far, Aumonti hadn't told him anything he didn't already know.

"Mr. Appleton, am I making a correct assumption?"

"Yeah, what of it?"

"I think with your knowledge of the people down there and our information, we can find them."

"What information do you have?"

"We have a file on the group. I had an agent in the congregation who moved down there with the church. Just before we raided the place, we lost contact with him and haven't heard from him since. He's either dead, converted, or a captive."

"He's not a captive. They're not violent or even suspicious people."

"In addition to that, we had six of their kids in our custody and lost them."

"Lost them? How?"

"Long story. Needless to say, we know the mountains. We've been to their garage where they store their cars. We just can't find the congregation. That's where we want you to step in. You know these people. Maybe if we put our minds together, we can figure this one out."

"You keep saying 'we.' You're talking about this Westering, right?"

"Yeah, she's my local. I want us to meet down in Mount Olive. Can you get away?"

"Not so fast, slick. I'm not meeting with anyone until I know how the cut works. Alone, I'm looking at three to four hundred thousand magogs in my pocket. I don't know if I can find them, but that's a real good reason to keep looking. Actually, that's about three hundred thousand good reasons to keep looking."

Rory smirked away from the phone. He could play the game as well as anyone, and he didn't want to seem eager for help, but this may be the break he needed.

"I have been authorized to offer you two hundred thousand plus an additional three hundred magogs per person killed. Children included. That could figure into another hundred thousand. Your odds of finding them are much better with me than racing against me."

"What's your cut?"

"Doesn't matter. I have a personal vendetta here, so price isn't the first thing on my mind," explained Sean.

"Where and when?"

"Today is Tuesday. Let's meet next Monday at noon at the café on Wells Street. You know the one?"

"Yeah, it has a killer meatloaf plate. And I mean killer."

"See you then."

"Hey—how will I know who you and Melanie are?"

"Don't worry, I already know what you look like. I'll find you."

Rory hung up the phone. His coffee was cold, but he didn't really care. He was finally going to get the revenge he dreamed about. As he poured the cold coffee into the sink, he realized his foolishness. Revenge would be sweet and reward would be the icing on the cake. Things may be tight now, but he was coming into some big money. Why be angry at a woman who is going to provide so much through her death?

He decided to go out for a Starbucks, compliments of Donna.

Emma woke up to the smell of coffee. The room was dark and Emma quietly slipped out of bed. She reached into Sarah's bunk to stroke her hair, but only felt the pillow. She felt around and found the bed empty.

Funny. Sarah never got up before her.

She left the bedroom and went down to the kitchen. The coffee was brewing but the kitchen was empty. Emma walked down to her parents' room and knocked on the door. Maybe she would climb into bed with her mom and snuggle a bit before breakfast. But Emma couldn't find her parents. They weren't in their room. She ran through the cave, looking in every bedroom but no one was there. The kitchen was empty and the living room was the same. No one was at Engedi.

Where could they all be? Emma racked her brain to try to remember. Was there a meeting at the Tabernacle today? Were we all invited to Petra for dinner? Or maybe she missed the rapture? That thought sent chills through her body. She decided to try the Tabernacle.

She grabbed her coat and ran to the door. A fresh snowfall was on the ground and she saw no footprints leading to or from the cave. Another indication of the rapture. How could she miss it?

She ran through the woods, her bare feet nearly freezing in the snow. No one was outside. Their outside time was limited so that didn't surprise her. As she neared the Tabernacle she could hear singing and her heart lightened. The rapture hadn't happened. She didn't miss it. She was just late for a meeting. She strained to hear what they were singing.

As she approached the entrance to the Tabernacle, she realized it wasn't singing she was hearing, but screaming. Awful, echoing screaming. Women and children.

What could be happening? She ran in through the door, fear tearing at her chest. When she entered the main room, what she saw made her heart stop. The room was filled with Nazi soldiers, all with swastika bands on their arms. They were beating people with the butts of their guns. Some had swords in their hands and they were slicing through the room with abandon.

She madly looked for Adam and her parents. Her father was struggling on the stage with two soldiers. She saw one of them take out a gun and point it at her father. She screamed as he pulled the trigger and her father's body fell to the ground.

Emma sat up in bed, drenched with sweat. She looked around. She was in her room, that much she knew. She swung her legs off the side of the bed and stood up. She reached into the bed above her, fearful of finding it empty, and touched Sarah's cheek.

It had all been a dream. And it wasn't the first one. Emma had been having some bad dreams lately. Dreams of the end. Not flying through the air and seeing Jesus dreams, but dreams of infiltrators and beheadings. Hearing the news of the worldwide phenomena of beheadings must have taken its toll on her. Most of her dreams ended with Adam or her dad being beheaded. It was unbearable.

When she woke, she would logically think through where she was, why she was safe, and why Adam would never be beheaded. No matter how logical she could be, her fears continued to hover in the back of her imagination. Strange noises made her jump. She decided she was getting cabin fever and tried not to feed her paranoia.

But she couldn't shake the feeling of danger. She had never felt it before in the caves. This was something new.

When Rory arrived at the diner, the two Homeland Security agents were already there They were seated and had ordered, making it clear that it was time to get down to business. Rory ordered the meatloaf just to make a point.

"We all know why we're here," started Sean. "We need to come up with a way to draw these people out of hiding." He laid a topographical map out on the table and pointed to two highlighted areas. "Here's where the mountains are." He pointed to the one on the north. "This is the one that has the garage on it. It's marked with that red dot."

Rory stared at the map.

"Anything? Any suggestions?"

The three of them just sat looking at the map. Finally Melanie spoke.

"Let's go over what we know for sure. There are three hundred to three hundred and fifty people on these mountains. They are living in caves. Do we know whether or not they are on both mountains or just one?"

Rory thought Melanie was pretty, for a blonde. He himself preferred brunettes, but he wouldn't hold that against her.

"I know they built out the first mountain before the move," he said, "and were planning of exploring options on the second mountain once they moved."

Melanie took a sip from her diet soda. "What else do we know? They don't leave, they don't move around, or at least we haven't spotted movement yet. We have tracers on their vehicles, but they haven't moved since we marked them. We haven't detected any phone signals and no longer have the tracer on Reed's phone."

"Nate Reed?" asked Rory.

"Yes."

"How do you know him?"

"He is one of us," said Sean. "But as I told you on the phone, we lost contact with him months ago."

Rory remembered when Nate switched from one of his followers to one of theirs. It hadn't made much sense to him. He and Nate often had coffee together and talked about the church. After a meeting at Dan's house, though, everything changed. Nate wouldn't return his calls and then Rory found out Nate had moved with his family. Now it all made sense. He was ordered to go and for appearances, he had to separate from Rory.

"Figures. Do you know about the radios? They have a ham radio system on the mountain to communicate between caves. I don't know how much they use them, but I know they have them."

"Are they on all the time?" Sean asked.

He shrugged. "How would I know?"

Obviously ignoring Rory's sarcasm, Sean continued in an enthusiastic tone. "If we can get a powerful enough receiver, camp out at the base of the mountain until we pick up their conversations . . . we may just find them."

Rory sat back with a smug smile, pleased he had been the one to give Sean the information that might crack this case. It was a good thing they called him. This was turning out to be a good relationship.

As Melanie and Sean began plotting their new plan, Rory excused himself and headed to the restroom. Once locked in a stall, he reached into the inside pocket of his jacket, pulled out the manila folder, and unfolded it. It was the idol's idea to come along. "Don't trust anyone," it had said. "These people will cut your throat as soon as you're no longer valuable to them. I'd better come along to help you."

In the bathroom, Rory stood facing the toilet and he set the idol on the back of the tank.

"You doing okay?" Rory asked.

"I figured out how we're going to pull this off."

"How?"

"Listen to this."

Rory leaned closer to the folder.

"Betsy, it's me, Dan. I'm alive! I know Rory said I was dead, but he's just a drunken fool. I'm at the base of the mountain and I want to come up. Can you send someone down to get me?"

The idol's voice was a dead mark for Dan's. Same inflections, same raspy intonations. Rory stared in astonishment.

"Dan, is that you?"

"No, you idiot!" Its voice had returned to normal. "But impersonation is only one of my many talents."

Rory smiled, folded the idol back into his jacket pocket, and went back to the dining room and sat down in the booth.

"I've figured it out," he announced.

"Let's hear it," Sean said. Rory thought he heard a touch of doubt in his voice, but he didn't let it bother him.

The food had arrived and Rory reached for the ketchup.

"When my wife came down, she came with a woman named Betsy Dougherty. She and her husband were self-proclaimed witnessers for the end of the world."

"Dan Dougherty, right?" asked Sean. "Nate had given me his name on our last phone call."

"Yeah. Well, last minute they decided to come down here. They were going to be martyrs for Jesus in Shelton, but they must have chickened out."

Rory poured the ketchup onto his plate and set it back on the table. He cut himself a large piece of meatloaf, dipped it in the ketchup and put it in his mouth. As he chewed, he loved the fact that two agents were hanging on his every word.

"For some reason her husband stayed behind and was going to follow later. I saw his head during the Week of Destruction, and I'll be the first to say he got everything he asked for. When I spoke with Donna, shortly after she arrived to tell me she was here, I told her Dan was dead. I knew it would hurt her."

"Nice story. The plan?" Melanie seemed to be a bit impatient. She was all business and Rory liked that.

"So here's what we do. We set up your receiver and we find their channel. We can monitor it as long as you want but when you're ready, we'll let my idol take over."

"What?" Sean gave him a confused look.

Another smug smile as he chewed. Then he said, "I've got this idol that can mimic Dan's voice." Rory saw the wheels turn in Sean's head. He leaned forward, his elbows on the table. "We'll have him say he wasn't dead but that it took him months of traveling underground to get here. Have him ask to send someone to get him from the bottom of the mountain. Then"—

"Then," Sean broke in enthusiastically, "the satellites can target those who come out to get Dan." He leaned forward. "We'll have people on the mountain before the call is made, and they can hone in as soon as we find movement. We'll bring in quads, take out the first person who comes out of hiding before they can radio back a warning. This is perfect." Sean pulled his eyes from Rory and addressed Melanie. "I think it will work."

Rory took another bite of meatloaf. He was pretty proud of himself. Here these two government agents had spent months racking their brains for a plan and in just an hour Rory had provided the answer. So, he had come down here several times. That was all in the past. Technically they all needed each other, but Rory was the key to their success and it felt good to be needed.

The next two hours were spent over at the Mount Olive Police Department in a back room, going over the specifics until a proposal was drawn up. Sean explained he had pushed the ticket on this group already, but with Rory's counsel, the HS/DIU readily passed the proposal. The date was set and the receiver was put in place. Once they located the channel, it would be a go.

Sean shook Rory's hand.

Rory walked out of the police station. In his mind, he heard his idol speaking. He liked this form of conversation because it was so secretive.

Watch your back, Rory. I don't trust this guy. I don't care what he promises you, he can just wipe you out when he wipes the church out. Don't get too comfortable.

The idol's words bothered Rory. Killing Donna wasn't necessarily worth the price of his own life, but then again, he wouldn't miss this opportunity for the world. He would have to stay alert. He may look like an old man, but there was still a lot of fight in him. One thing he'd learned over the past year is that you can't trust anyone. Not your wife, not your church, and not your neighbors. The government wasn't any different.

Tonight, there would be no more meatloaf. He was opting for steak. Filet mignon. The best he could find. Thanks to Donna and the others, he would soon be a rich man.

thirty-four

*T*he days are getting longer, it seems. I wonder if it's because I don't see Adam as much as I want or if it is because I long to be with Jesus. It's probably a combination of both. The two can't possibly compare, yet the Lord made me with the ability to love and I love Adam. I love him with all my heart! What a strange turn of events. I sit in a cave, waiting for my Savior to come and get me, and while I wait, He gives me an opportunity to love like I have never loved before. I don't regret that it came at this time. I thank God He gave me this friendship, this love! It has helped the time go faster. Up until now. Now it's slowing.

I hate sleeping. My dreams only make my life worse. Why am I so frightened in my dreams, when while I am awake I fear nothing? I know the character of God—I know He is good. Yet when I sleep I can't find Him and I fear He has left me. I watch my loved ones die and I can't understand that I will see them again soon, like the peace Betsy had. In my dreams I think I will never see them again and I awake weeping.

Enough about bad dreams. I have great daydreams! I know the rapture is getting closer by the minute and my imagination soars when I think of it! My heart races and I struggle to describe my feeling. It's more than excitement. It's more than exhilaration. It's . . . What words could possibly describe such an eve—

"Emma, we're going to be late!"

Sarah was standing in the door of the bedroom.

"We have to get over to the Tabernacle. It's worship night. What is wrong with you? You're usually standing at the door waiting for darkness to come. Have you broken up with lover boy?"

Emma sighed and closed her journal. "I just lost track of time." She tucked it back under her mattress with her coveted pen.

"Come on, let's go!" Sarah's impatience was growing.

The girls ran down the hall just as Ben, Lily, and Garrett reached the front door. Darkness had fallen and it was time to go. When they opened the door, Adam was standing in front of them.

"Hi, I . . . um . . . got out a few minutes early and thought I'd walk with you to the Tabernacle."

"You mean walk with Emma!" Sarah giggled.

They made their way over to the meeting. It was a beautiful May evening. The air held just a hint of a chill. The sky was lit by a full moon and the stars seemed close enough to touch.

All the families had gathered for their night of praise. Mack Silver sat in the back at the sound booth along with Mr. Phillips. Emma heard him tell her dad that Mack was handling the sound tonight and he would keep the headphones on to monitor the radio. The service began and the congregation lifted their voices in song.

As they sang, Emma noticed that Mr. Torey was suddenly distracted as he played the guitar and led the singing. His face looked confused and he glanced over to Garrett and nodded towards the back of the room. Emma's heart jumped and she turned to see if another angel had arrived. But all she saw was Mr. Phillips standing in the back with his headphones on, waving his arms. The music stopped.

Mr. Torey called to the back of the room.

"Is there a problem, Stan?"

"I've got someone coming through on the radio. It's fuzzy but I think the voice sounds familiar."

Garrett got up from his seat and headed to the sound booth.

Stan pulled the cord to the headset out of the ham radio box and the static filled the Tabernacle. After some crackling, they all heard a voice.

"Hello, anybody? Is anybody there?"

It was still fuzzy and Stan twisted a few knobs.

"Hello, anybody?"

Emma immediately recognized Dan's voice. She scanned the room for Betsy, who was already running towards the sound booth.

"Dan? Dan is that you? It's me, Garrett."

The congregation stirred but remained mostly quiet so that they could hear the conversation.

"Garrett, old buddy. Is it good to hear your voice."

"Where are you? We were told you were dead."

"Let me guess. Rory Appleton."

Ben and Sarah chuckled at that comment and Emma flashed a dirty look at them. Mrs. Appleton was sitting just a few rows away.

"Yeah, when he found out Donna was here, he said you were dead. He said he had seen your head set out on the street on the Day of Destruction. What happened to you?"

"I got hung up and almost lost my head, but a family hid me. I've been working my way down here for months, using an underground system of homes that will hide nonmarkers. I'm here where you've stored the vans now and I want to see my wife."

Emma saw Betsy wiping her tears as she stood by Garrett.

"Well, praise the Lord, Dan! You are another miracle for us to add to our list."

Garrett handed the handset to Betsy and she raised it to her mouth. Emma heard the sniffling of the women in the congregation and she strained to hear what Betsy would say.

"Dan?"

"Betsy? Is that you?"

"Oh, Dan! Can it really be true?"

"It's really me and I need someone to come down here and get me."

"They'll come right now, dear. It'll take some time to get to you. Are you hurt?"

"No, no, I'm fine. I'm just anxious to get to a safe place and to see you. Got any chocolate chip cookies up there?"

The whole Tabernacle laughed with that comment, knowing Dan's fondness for Betsy's cookies. They were so loud, Emma missed Betsy's response.

Emma saw her dad talking with Mack and Mr. Reed. He patted them on their backs as they turned and headed out the door of the Tabernacle. She figured they were going to get Dan. Betsy had handed the handset back to Stan and walked over to her dad. They hugged and Lily joined them.

Mike Torey tapped the mike, then said, "Another miracle, wouldn't you say? We have a lot to be thankful for today."

A few of the youth yelled out "Ni-ke" from the back of the room.

"Let's split up into groups of three and four and thank the Lord for Dan's safety."

As Mike softly chorded on his guitar, the congregation started to pray. Adam turned to Emma and asked if she wanted to go first. She held her finger up as if to say, one moment. Adam looked at her and she smiled.

"I love that sound."

She listened again and the low murmur of Philadelphia talking with their Provider was like sweet music to her ears.

Rory picked up his idol and put it inside his coat pocket. The Homeland Security technician sitting in front of the radio looked up at him.

"Quite impressive. It seems they fell for it."

"It's like leading a lamb to the slaughter."

Now started the waiting game. Rory was given free rein to walk around and monitor the operation. He deserved to be treated with respect. After all, none of this would have happened without him.

You mean without me.

Rory conceded and decided to find Sean. He wanted to know how soon they would be leaving for the caves.

"The infrared picked up movement about an hour ago. It looks like all the movement is headed for the same location."

Sean stood over the technician manning the satellite screen.

"That's consistent with our conversation with them. They're all together."

The technician pointed to two green dots moving on the screen.

"Now we have two images moving away from the location."

"That would be the congregants who are coming to supposedly get Dan. We have an assault team not far from that spot. Tell them to take them out as soon as they get close. No questions asked."

"I've got the coordinates of this meeting place, sir."

"Get them to the squad commanders. Let them know I am coming in by helicopter. Once everyone is in place we will proceed on my command."

Betsy sat in the sound booth, stunned, unable to move.

"It just seems too good to be true. His voice sounded good, didn't it?"

"Yes, it did," answered Lily. "I think any sound coming from him would sound good!"

"How long ago did they leave?"

"Only fifteen minutes."

"I should have gone with them."

"Oh, Betsy, it's a hard ride in the daylight. At night, it's nearly impossible. Let them bring him to us. The Lord brought him this far, He'll get him the rest of the way."

Nate was riding on his quad, singing in his heart the last song he had heard.

Restore my soul, refresh my heart, renew my life in every part . . .

He was following Mack and in the dark he could see his taillights easily. Every once in a while his quad would bounce on the uneven ground and his headlights would flash on Mack's back.

. . . Reveal to me what sin remains and lead me to the cross again . . .

Dodging the trees, Nate sped up as he saw Mack pick up the speed. They had been riding for about twenty minutes and at this pace they would make it to the vehicle storage unit in under two hours.

. . . At the cross, I'll find the way to live the life Your hand has made . . .

The trees sped by and Nate's lights caught the back of Mack's shirt. There was a wet stain on his back and Nate thought it was strange that he would be sweating. It was actually rather chilly out.

Suddenly Mack's quad slammed into a tree, and Nate watched as his friend fell to the ground and rolled on his side. Nate stepped on the brakes and added the pressure of the hand brakes. He lurched forward and steered the quad over to where Mack was lying.

A sharp pain ripped through Nate's chest and in shock, he looked down at his own shirt. His quad came to a stop and in the dark, he couldn't see much but he felt a cool sensation flow to his arms and legs. He put his hand on his chest and felt a warm flow of blood pumping from his heart into his hand.

. . . So find me there, Lord, and help me stay . . .

He suddenly realized what had happened and he fell off the quad to the ground. He was struggling to breathe. Every breath felt like he was underwater and he coughed to clear his lungs.

. . . In true surrender . . .

Liquid flowed from his mouth and he rolled over on his side to avoid choking on his own blood. Lying on his side, however, brought such unbearable pain that an involuntary scream came from his lips. Rolling back over, once again Nate felt his lungs filling with blood and the breathing became nearly impossible. He coughed again and his chest heaved with shooting pain. He couldn't feel his arms or legs, just a searing, burning sensation that flowed with every fluttering beat of his heart.

Then slowly the pain started to fade. Nate laid on the ground looking through the forest trees at the sky. The moon was full and clear, but his eyes started to blur.

He tried to call out to Mack but no sound came. He could hear men's voices and footsteps coming near. Then a man was standing over him, a flashlight in his face. He couldn't close his eyes to stop the blinding light, but strangely it didn't hurt them.

. . . With You, my Savior . . .

Then his eyes came into focus and Nate realized he wasn't on earth any longer.

Emma and Adam had finished praying and were quietly chatting. Most of the congregation was done and she could see Mr. Torey was patiently waiting for everyone to finish up. Lily and Garrett had rejoined their children and they were still praying when shouts ripped through the Tabernacle.

Emma jumped from the surprise and looked towards the back of the room. Pouring into the room were men in uniforms holding guns, obviously ready to use them. Emma recognized the uniforms and her heart leapt into her throat.

They kept coming, dozens, perhaps more. They quickly surrounded the congregation, circling the perimeter of the room, with even more taking their positions along the center aisle.

Emma froze. There was no escaping this time. The officers rushed the stage and grabbed Mr. Torey and pushed him onto the front bench. Emma heard Leighsa scream. Emma felt helpless.

The officers shoved their guns into the chests of those who attempted to move. Soon, the congregation sat still, afraid to move, almost afraid to breathe.

Adam reached for her hand and squeezed tightly. Soft sounds crying carried toward them. From the back, a man and a woman made their way to the stage. Emma recognized the blonde immediately. Melanie. The woman who tricked them once before. As the woman passed Emma in the aisle, she turned her head, and winked.

Emma looked around the congregation, heard the crying, saw the cruel and angry faces of the officers . . . and something nagged at the edges of her mind.

Then it hit her. The dream!

She turned her head towards Adam and whispered, "This is it."

"What?" he whispered back.

"This is it—the appearing!"

Adam obviously couldn't understand her because he said softly, "They're already here."

Emma shook her head and said, "Just wait!" Hope filled her heart. In her dreams she couldn't grasp the character of God, but awake she saw the big picture. Rapture or not, she would be with Jesus in just a few minutes.

Sean walked onto the stage and stood in front of the microphone.

"Well, well, well. You people were hard to find!" His voice echoed in the cave. He looked around at the rough, hewn benches and the makeshift stage. "Nice place you have here. My name is Sean Aumonti and I work for Homeland Security." He looked through the crowd and his eyes rested on Sherrie. "And you must be Sherrie Reed. I've seen your picture. Haven't heard from your husband lately. Do you know where he is?"

Sherrie didn't respond. Emma wished she had been sitting with her and Adam, so that she could put her arm around her. She looked so alone.

"Well enough of the small talk. If your husband was here, I would remind him of back when we set up the first raid on this mountain? He never showed and I got egg on my face. Then there was the time my agents had your son and his friends in custody."

Emma cringed.

"Somehow they got away," he said. He took his focus off Sherrie and scanned the room. "You people have embarrassed me and my department for over a year now. Well, tonight it ends."

Still no one moved. Sean paced across the stage, holding the mike in his hand.

"I don't know how much news you people have gotten in here, but things have changed in the real world. There aren't many of you left. One by one, we are ridding the world of the enemy and you, my friends, are a very big catch."

The congregation began to stir uneasily and Emma knew what was coming next. She was confident, not in what Sean would do, but in what God would do.

"But here's the deal. I don't have to bring you back. I don't have to book you and I don't have to even take your picture. All I need is your heads. Your heads are cash money, my friends, and there's only one easy way to get them. So, if I could have the following women come up front."

Sean reached into the pocket of his pants and pulled out a list. One by one the names of the elder's wives and pastor's wives were read. When Lily's name was read, Garrett jumped to his feet. Emma shot a look down the aisle at her dad and saw the butt of a gun hit him in the stomach. He fell to the floor and Lily kneeled down at his side. She put her hand on his shoulder just as an agent grabbed her by the wrist and pulled her to her feet.

Emma shrieked and tried to stand, but Adam held her down. Then she heard her mother say, "It's all right, Garrett. I'll meet you in heaven."

Lily and Eva Torey made their way up the aisle together, but no other woman moved. There were seven names read and Emma could tell Sean was not a patient man.

"Oh, come on now. Did you think I wouldn't be able to find you on my own? I have a secret weapon." Then in a game show host voice, he said, "Rory Appleton, come on down."

Emma heard Donna gasp just a few rows ahead as Rory walked down the center aisle. Emma couldn't believe her eyes. Here was a man who chose not to come and hide. He knew the Scriptures and he refused to obey. He of all people should have recognized what was about to happen when Hitler revealed himself and demanded the worship of the world. But instead, he took the mark, created an idol, and was now aligning with the enemy to identify women for them to kill.

Rory easily picked out the women on the list and the officers forced them to go forward. Emma watched as other men were pushed into their seats if they resisted and each woman pleaded with their husbands not to fight. By now, Garrett had returned to his seat and was holding his stomach. Emma saw sheer terror in his eyes and her heart broke for him. She wanted to move over to him and comfort him, but any movement brought down the wrath of the officers.

Emma looked at her mom on stage and their eyes met. In Emma's worst nightmare it was never her mother who was killed. Now she would be a witness to her mother's murder, just before her own.

The women stood in a row and Lily was the closest to Sean. He walked over to her, then looked out at the congregation.

"Logic would say kill the men first, but then they wouldn't suffer quite enough. They would die and miss out on the experience of watching their wives and children die."

Sean turned to Lily, and Emma saw her father wipe the tears from his eyes. She felt that lump forming in her throat again, but held on to the hope that Jesus would save the day. He had in the past, and could full well do it again. But no matter what His plan was, Emma was ready to be with Him.

"Now, as much as I would like to have a chat with you, we're just going to get this over with. Don't take it personally. We have a long evening ahead of us."

He put a hand on Lily's shoulder and forced her to kneel, her head bowed forward. Emma heard her mother cry, most likely out of fear and not pain. Cries from the congregation began to rise, but to her side a hoarse "Ni-ke!" was heard. It was weak at first but it grew. Her dad was calling out Philadelphia's battle cry. Emma looked at her mother. Kneeling before her executioner, she raised her head, reached up with her right hand and pulled on her ear.

Garrett's voice cracked with emotion and Adam stepped into his place.

"Ni-ke! Ni-ke!"

He yelled it with all his strength. Emma joined in and soon the whole youth group was chanting. She heard one of the officers call out to Sean, asking if they should quiet the kids.

"Let them chant," he said. "It will be their last words."

Sean put his right hand out, leaving his left hand on Lily's head, and one of the officers ran forward and handed him an unsheathed sword. Emma stared in disbelief. Was she really going to see this happen? He raised the sword above his head.

Garrett cried out from the bottom of his soul.

"Maranatha, Lord Jesus! Come quickly!"

The room started to rumble. Emma watched Sean Aumonti lose his balance and lurch forward, missing her mother by inches. Lily, free from his grip, jumped up and looked at the ceiling. The lights were shaking and pieces of rock were starting to fall. In a flash, her dad was on stage. He grabbed her mother's hand and pulled her off the platform. The officers were too preoccupied with the falling stone to notice.

The room continued to rock and sway. Emma jumped to her feet and stared at the ceiling. A dozen large holes broke through, each twenty feet in diameter—almost as if tunnels had just been bored through the rock. The sky outside was now visible and the first thing they noticed were shooting stars. No, not shooting, falling stars.

From the far right a voice cried out. "Look at the moon!"

The openings had grown wider now, and Emma could see the moon. It was as red as blood and was quickly turning black. The room continued to shake but the people cried out in joy, the young people cheering, "Ni-ke," and the adults shouting, "Maranatha!"

Emma turned to Adam. He was still sitting and there was a look of awe on his face.

"I told you," she cried above the noise. "I tried to tell you He was coming!"

She looked up again and the sky was black. Completely black. Another earthquake hit, more vigorous than before. The cave lost all electricity. The congregation stood in total darkness and complete silence. In the distance, a pinpoint of light could be seen in the sky. It was growing quickly.

Emma felt an arm around her waist and, thinking it was Adam, she turned. But it was not Adam who was by her side. It was a being with a beautiful face, glowing in the dark that Emma alone could see. She wasn't afraid. The face was sweetly familiar. Then she smiled. This was the angel who brought the message to the Tabernacle a year ago. His wings thrust together and they were airborne.

"I remember you," she said quietly.

"You have an appointment with the Master."

He looked at her with kind, tender eyes. The air was cool on her face, but the angels arm was warm and strong. Below her, the cave was disappearing. The forest was shrinking and the world was fading. Emma took a deep breath and let the clean air flow through her lungs.

She looked up in the direction they were flying. It was as if they were going directly towards that light in the sky. The only Light in the sky. Emma was so focused on the Light that she couldn't look at anything else. She didn't look for her dad. She didn't try to find her mother. She didn't even wonder about Adam. She was amazed at how quickly they gained altitude, how small the earth seemed and how warm the air felt. She knew very little time had passed. Maybe only the twinkling of an eye.

Pure joy. If she had her diary, she would only write two words. *Pure joy.*

Rory stood in the middle of the ruins that had once been a Tabernacle. He put his hands to his face. If he kept his eyes shut, perhaps they would still be there when he opened them. Slowly he opened his eyes. Other than the agents, the room was empty.

One moment they were all here. The next they vanished into thin air. He had met eyes with Donna during the earthquake. Rory had seen her raise her hand to her mouth, and she was gone. There was not a trace left of her. Nothing.

Fear gripped his heart. The faithful were caught up by God and now His judgment would come. That was what the Scriptures said. He looked up into the heavens. Still complete darkness, but for one glowing light. It was more of an aura or . . . he couldn't describe it, but looking at it dropped him to his knees. It was the most awesome and terrifying light he had ever seen.

His heart ached and his head pounded. What was this he was feeling? It was anger mixed with fear. Rory was no longer playing a charade. He knew Who that Light was and there was no escaping His judgment. He raised his hands and cried out for mercy on deaf ears. He fell on his face, sobbing.

Then a response came. It wasn't the voice of his idol. That was finally silent. No, this voice was powerful and frightening. And the words tore through Rory's soul.

You took the mark. You made your choice. Now face my wrath.

thirty-five

The Light continued to draw near. Adolph Hitler stood on his balcony, eyes raised towards the light. His knees became weak and he leaned over the railing's edge and vomited. He knew that Light. That Light was coming for him.

At that moment, Hitler knew in his heart the battle was over. He had seen his enemy before and now that He had come to earth, Hitler knew he did not stand a chance. Oh, he would fight. He would lead, but he would never win. He knew it and there was no stopping it.

The Light was now taking on form. Four legs of a horse appeared first. Sitting on the horse was a man in a white robe, stained with blood.

Hitler knew the Light had a job to do. He had been here before but this time it would be different. His blood spoke volumes. It spoke of His plan. Like himself, when the Light came the first time, He was misunderstood. Unlike himself, however, His second coming would be clear and successful.

He wasn't a victim.

He never was.

He was and always will be the Victor.